ONE HELLUVA SOLDIER

[signature]

PHIL KLINE

One Helluva Soldier / Phil Kline

One Helluva Soldier

copyright©Phil Kline 2015

ISBN-13: 978-151799105
ISBN–10: 1518799108

No part of this book may be reproduced in any form, or by any means, including electronic, without written permission from the author, except for brief excerpts for the purpose of reviews.

PRINTED IN THE U.S.A.

1

June 21, 1950

Under an overcast Texas sky, Luisa Martin gave George a hug, squeezing two-month old Mario between them. "How can they take you from your wife and son?" she said through tears. "Is how they treat families in United States?"

"Luisa, don't you understand? It's my fault. What I did was wrong."

"But Mario and I pay. Is not fair what they do."

Lieutenant Martin picked up his barracks bag, then leaned down and kissed Mario on the forehead before kissing the tears from Luisa's cheeks. "I love you," he whispered, then turned and walked to a taxi waiting to take him to the train station. Halfway into the cab, he climbed out and ran back to his wife and son.

Luisa met him with her free arm out. She laughed as tears flowed. "You don't go?"

He held her face in his hands and kissed her, then kissed her again and again. Their tears mixed and wet their faces. He broke away and hurried back to the cab.

Two days later, leaving his family still haunted George as he walked with Melvin Austin through Seattle drizzle, to board a four-engine C-54 cargo plane. Mel had to duck his head in order to enter the hatch of the converted DC-6.

Inside, they sat forward of forty enlisted men lined up on two long, temporary bench seats. Their gear was tied to hooks on the floor in front of them. With engines revved to a high pitch, the plane shuddered as it bounced down the runway. After liftoff, the ride became smoother.

George peered through a tiny window to watch his country fade beneath the haze. When the plane leveled off, and the noise tapered down, he glanced at the double row of men. *Just kids,* he thought. *Right out of basic, I'd reckon.*

Mel shouted through cupped hands, "Hey, where you guys from?"

A young private near the back shouted, "Fort Benning. Basic training, Sir."

Mel turned to face him. "Infantry, huh? Japan's a great station. You should enjoy your tour."

The private nodded.

George said to Mel, "I envy you guys going to Japan. I never even heard of Okinawa till Officers Candidate School."

"I don't remember them mentioning Okinawa at OCS."

"The instructors didn't, but some of the guys from the platoon were talking, hoping to get stationed there rather than Japan."

"Why would anyone want to go to Okinawa?"

"Lee and Perry said they didn't want to end up as clerks on occupation duty in Tokyo."

"Hah. Those two would rather see combat than have it cushy. Not me. I want a desk job and a cute secretary."

"Tall as you are, you'd never see more than the top of her head."

"You don't understand," Mel winked. "I want a full service secretary."

George peered through the window again, trying to see the ocean, but his view was blotted out by the reflection of Mel eyeing him. George turned to him again. "What?"

One Helluva Soldier / Phil Kline

"You always been tough?"

"What you talking about now?"

"Your fight with that professional boxer."

George glanced down at the ocean and laughed.

"What's so funny?" Mel asked.

"You remind me of Pa. He always wanted a tough son."

"Are you saying you fought Hayes to please your dad?"

"No. He wanted me to be like his friends' kids. I liked school. Most of the others dropped out to work on the farm. Pop didn't even think I was tough enough to become a man, much less a soldier."

"What did he think of you fighting Hayes?"

George shook his head. "I never told him."

Mel stared at George. "Did you join the army to please your dad?"

No. I did it out of respect for a guy I worked for who served in World War II. What about you?"

"I've wanted to be a soldier since I was a kid." He elbowed George. "That's why I'm infantry instead of artillery.".

George elbowed him back. "Watch out, man. Remember, I'm tough."

*

After a refueling stop at Shemya Air Base, on the tip of the Aleutian Chain, George lay awake. He was awake for most of the ten hour flight across the Pacific. He was still not even drowsy when he stepped off the plane at Haneda Airport in Tokyo the morning of 24 June, 1950.

2

Mel rode away in a staff-car. George buckled himself into a jump seat behind the pilot of a B-26 bomber headed for Okinawa. On the approach to Kadena Air Base, he peered out through the canopy at sunken freighters scattered about the Naha Harbor. He wondered why they were still there five years after the end of World War II.

On the rough ride to the 65th Antiaircraft Artillery Battalion at Kawasaki, the Jeep created a rooster tail of yellow dust that matched the color of George's hair. The contrast between the bright green vegetation across the landscape and the drab gray huts of the villages reminded him of the sweet and sour of the last few months. On one hand was the thrill of having a son while on the other was the disgrace of standing before a Disciplinary Board of Officers.

The Jeep stopped in front of a green and white Quonset tied down by cables buried in concrete. George brushed the dust from his khakis, pulled his barracks bag out of the vehicle, and entered battalion headquarters.

A steel spring banged the screen door shut behind him as he approached a sign with S-1 written on it and a finger pointing to the right. He walked through an open door at the end of the room to face the personnel officer, a captain, behind an old oak desk. George saluted.

"Sir, Lieutenant George Martin reporting for duty."

The S-1 avoided eye contact. He saluted by touching his brow with two fingers as he tossed two letter size sheets of paper at George. "You're being placed on temporary duty as a forward observer with the 29th Infantry Regiment. You're to report to them immediately. Here are your orders." He finally glanced up at George. "A vehicle will be here soon to take you."

Minutes later, George threw his barracks bag into the back of a three-quarter-ton truck and climbed in. As it sped along a road made of crushed coral, he recalled the S-1's attitude and wondered if everyone on Okinawa has been notified of his indiscretion at China Night Cafe.

When the truck stopped at a cement block building housing 29th Infantry Headquarters, he jumped out and again brushed the dust from his khakis.

Inside, he located the duty officer, a pudgy captain in sweat-soaked fatigues. George set his bag down and handed the captain a copy of his orders. "Sir, Lieutenant George Martin reporting for duty with the 29th."

"You sound like a Texan, but you don't look like a cowboy."

"Michigan, Sir."

After a grunt of acknowledgement, the officer said, "I'm Captain Scarf, S-3. You'll be reporting to me for duty assignments. I expect you to conform to the high standards of conduct that we require of our own people. Someone's waiting in supply to assign you a billet. Go there again Monday and draw supplies you'll need for your job." He waved toward the door.

George walked out, thinking, h*e read my file, too.* At an outer office desk, he asked a private where to find Supply.

"Two buildings down, Sir." The clerk pointed to the right. "S-4's not in today, but somebody's there to take care of you."

"Do you have a roster of the regimental officers?"

The clerk pulled a paper from a desk drawer. "Yes, Sir. Brand new."

One Helluva Soldier / Phil Kline

George accepted the roster and scanned through the names. "Dennis Nixon," he said, aloud, reading. "Walter Perry, Reed Rayford, Tommy Trexler...oh, and John Hayes in Tank Company."

"Those are the new officers, Sir. Right out of Officers Candidate School."

"Me, too. We graduated together. OCS Class 9-A."

"You're the new forward observer, aren't you?"

George nodded. "That's right."

"I sure wouldn't want to be an FO. That's the worst job in the army."

George laughed for the first time since arriving on Okinawa. "Only when there's a war going on," he said, grabbing up his bag and starting toward the door. He stopped and turned around. "I have a question. How come those wrecked ships are still in the harbor five years after the war?"

"They're not from the war, Sir. They're from Typhoon Gloria, this spring."

"Thanks for your help."

George walked to the supply building and picked up a key to room seven of bachelor officer's quarters. "Now, if you'll tell me where the BOQ is," he said to the corporal on duty, "I'll get some rest. It's been a long day."

"Down the company street you'll see a typhoon-proof concrete building that looks like a cheap motel. Number seven's at the end."

3

George wrinkled his nose at the smell of stale cigarette smoke as he looked around in his new home. It was furnished with what appeared to be homemade furniture, heavy and ugly. He put his clothes in dresser drawers, made the bed with linens that lay on a chair then located a shower at the end of the hall. After bathing, he climbed in bed, pulled his mosquito net into place, and was asleep in minutes.

A pounding on the door woke George. He looked at his watch: 0935 hours.

"War!" someone shouted through the door. "Intelligence briefing at G-2, in a half-hour."

George sat up. "With who?" No answer. The messenger had left.

Twenty minutes later, George walked into a headquarters briefing room full of officers, all talking about that morning's invasion of South Korea. Four of them were the infantry lieutenants who had graduated with him from Class 9-A. After shaking hands with most of them, he spotted John Hayes and smiled.

John punched George on the shoulder. "What in hell you doing here?"

"FO with the 29th."

"Jesus."

Their conversation was cut short when Major Garfield, Regimental S-2, entered the room.

One Helluva Soldier / Phil Kline

"Good morning, gentlemen," the general said. "Be seated." After the clatter from folding chairs subsided, he faced the officers. "I assume you've all heard about the invasion of South Korea by Communist North Korea this morning, and wondered how it will affect you. At the Island Intelligence Briefing an hour ago, Division G-2 said, and I quote, 'The view of the majority of the Joint Chiefs of Staff in Washington will probably be that the defense of South Korea is not a high enough priority to merit the use of American military forces'."

Some officers nodded while others shook their head. George did nothing to indicate what he thought of the Joint Chiefs' views.

Major Garfield scanned the group. "I personally believe President Truman will want to put a halt to this attempt at communist expansion. I believe American forces will be committed, and I also believe the 29th will be one of the first units sent to help the ROK defend their country. And we'll do so still at half strength."

A captain raised his hand. "What's ROK stand for, Sir?"

"Republic of Korea, the South Korean army. By the way, you'll hear a lot, too, about the NKPA, North Korean People's Army." He looked around, but didn't get any other questions. "That's it. I'll keep you posted."

Walt Perry grabbed George by the arm. "Don't leave. I'll introduce you to some people you may be directing fire for. I'll be right back."

Walt reminded George of someone he'd seen fighting in the bullring in Juarez—not the matador, but the bull. Walt returned, accompanied by two first lieutenants and a captain.

"George Martin, our new FO," Walt said to the new men. "He was in my OCS class. You'll like him. He's a fighter who doesn't know the meaning of quit."

George shook hands with them. "I look forward to working with you gentlemen. I hope I can live up to Walt's introduction."

The captain put his fists up in the pose of a boxer. "You a boxer?"

"No, Sir. Just one stint, as a sparring partner."

The captain nodded. "I'm not going to try you out. We have a professional boxer in the battalion that you can fight." With that, the three officers turned and left.

Walt nodded toward the departing captain. "You know who he's talking about?"

George nodded. "Hayes."

Walt pointed at a building with row of picture windows, above a hill to the south. "He, Trexler, Nixon, and I are meeting at the Officers Club at 2000 hours. You'll join us, won't you?"

"I'll be there."

*

In lingering daylight, George walked up the long line of steps, toward the windows that reflected scattered clouds hovering over the Pacific. In the club dining room, his four OCS buddies sat at a round table while couples struggled to dance the *Mambo Jambo*. No one at the grads' table paid attention to the dancers or the Filipino band; their attention was focused on Walt.

George pulled up a chair as Walt said, "Our job's cut out for us. American combat training has deteriorated to a miserable point. We just completed a year of the best combat training in the world, so we're combat- ready, but look at our men. They're barracks trained, all spit and polish. They have no idea how to stay alive in a war, much less become an effective fighting force." Walt waved toward the others sitting around the table.

"If we serve in Korea, we're going to be the backbone of our country's troops."

George leaned toward Tommy Trexler. "If soldiers could vote to choose their commander, they'd elect Walt."

Tommy's reply was louder than George expected. "Commander's a good job for him. My job's to do whatever my country expects of me."

Walt smiled.

Tall, thin, Dennis Nixon leaned on the table and pointed a thumb at Tommy. "He looks like he should be in the Boy Scouts instead of the infantry, but you don't know that little shit like I do. I served with him at Benning, MPs in Sin City, across the Bama line. We dealt with problem guys, most of them drinking, and I'll tell you the truth, Trexler's not afraid of anything or anybody. He might be just a curly-headed kid, but he's tough."

Walt turned to Tommy. "If you managed to keep Denny happy, you must be a good soldier. I'll take you on my flank any time."

Dennis gazed at Walt. "But I don't know if you'd want Martin there."

Only John Hayes indicated he'd heard the remark. He leaned toward Dennis and shook a fist at him. "Shut up."

Dennis seemed not to notice. His glance took in the others. "You guys know where Korea is?"

They all nodded.

"Ha. Bet you all looked it up today. Three hundred and fifteen miles from the northern tip of the island. If America gets into it, we'll be the first to go. The occupation army in Japan's not ready. They got their training in the bars."

"So what's different here?" Walt asked. "I'm probably the only guy in the platoon who can make it up the hill to the club without calling for a taxi. How old are you, Dennis?"

"Twenty."

"What about you, Tommy?"

"Twenty."

"And you, George?"

"Twenty-one."

Walt nodded. "The American army is being led by children." He laughed, picked up his beer, and took a swig.

"Okay, old man," George said, "what are you? Twenty-three?"

"Twenty-four, and I can outrun you, soldier. But Dutch was the old man of the class. I think he was twenty-five in OCS."

John asked Walt, "Where is the old fart?"

Dennis answered before Walt had a chance. "He's in the 13th Field Artillery, in Fukuoka."

"What kind of guns they have?"

"They had 105-mm howitzers."

John flipped a hand at Dennis. "Hell, I got bigger stuff than that on my tanks."

George stood, leaned over the table and pointed directly at John. "But he'll be firing in Korea when your tanks are still sitting in sheds waiting for spare parts."

"Not if Patton was here."

George grinned. "Don't rightly know if I've ever heard of him."

John shook his fist at George, but he was grinning.

Walt said, "I saw Dutch last month. Sure, he has six howitzers, but five of them have been condemned as unsafe to fire. Their breech blocks have been painted pink."

Dennis piped up. "That's Defense Secretary Johnson's doing. You're right, Walt. If we go to Korea, we're in trouble." He looked around at the others. "None of you seem to be worried. It's like you accept going into combat as a normal day's work."

"It is our normal day's work," Walt said.

Tommy shrugged. "We're in the army, aren't we?"

One Helluva Soldier / Phil Kline

John said, "If I had a choice, I'd rather not, but it's okay."
George nodded.
John looked at his watch. "It's getting late. I don't know about you goddamn ground pounders, but armored has to get up in the morning." He stood amidst jeers, saluted them, and punched George on the shoulder before he swaggered to the door.
George stood and waved goodbye to John. As the others followed suit, bidding each other goodnight, Dennis tapped George on the arm. "May I talk to you, Martin?"
"Sure."
They walked out onto a deck that overlooked the North Pacific. Dennis faced the ocean. "Excuse the remark I made about you. I was kidding. I accept you as one of us."
"Accepting me is not being one of you," George said tightly.
Dennis stared at George for a moment. "Anyway, we're all in this together," he said, then turned and walked down the steps leading to the BOQ.
George leaned on the railing and listened to breakers crash on the beach. *He says we're in it together, but walks alone to our BOQ.*
Back in his quarters, George sat at his desk. He picked up a photo he had taken of Luisa and Mario on Skyline Drive, above El Paso. He propped it up next to the lamp then wrote to Luisa. When he finished that letter, he wrote one to his mom, telling her what he also said to Luisa, that he'd probably go to Korea. He didn't tell them he'd be a forward observer, in case someone told them the FO was the one soldier the enemy most wanted to kill. When he'd finished the second letter, he turned out the light, laid his head on the pillow and thought about his situation.
Being an FO in combat may be what I need. I can find out how much of a man I really am.

One Helluva Soldier / Phil Kline

4

Next morning George went to S-4 to draw supplies and was issued, among other items, a World War II radio that didn't work. Figuring the problem was a dead battery, he picked through a box of batteries until he found one that gave the radio life. He located two more live batteries for spares, but wondered how long they would function.

That afternoon, he was listening to Armed Forces Radio when the announcement came: *"An ROK commander ordered the demolition of bridges across the Han River to slow the fast-moving NKPA. As a result, over a thousand soldiers and civilians were dumped into the river, and 40,000 of the ROK's troops were trapped on the north side."*

*

George attended a G-2 intelligence briefing early next morning. Without any preliminary pleasantries, Major Garfield said, "You are going to hear first what every other American soldier in the world will soon hear or read. Last night General MacArthur's Supreme Headquarters in Tokyo issued the following press release: *General MacArthur and his staff paid a visit to the front in Korea today. He stood on a hill overlooking the Han Valley and witnessed the retreat from the capital city of Seoul by both military and civilians. The general sent a message to the Joint Chiefs of Staff in Washington D.C. stating that the*

One Helluva Soldier / Phil Kline

ROK will not be able to stop the invaders. 'Without the aid of American ground forces, South Korea will be lost to Communist expansion'."

Dennis said, "Hot dog. We're going on a cruise to Death Valley."

Major Garfield shot him a disapproving glance. "There's more. Here's General Bentley to tell you the latest."

Everybody stood as the portly general strutted in.

Reed Rayford leaned toward George. "He's called Flashbulb Bob because his army issue glasses reflect the flash when his picture's taken for the island newspaper, which is almost every issue."

George smelled alcohol on Reed's breath.

General Bentley gave the men a chin-forward Mussolini look. "At ease." He glanced around, coughed. A silly little fake cough. "President Truman has ordered the use of U.S. air and sea forces to support the ROK. He has given General MacArthur permission to use one regimental combat team to help stem the unprovoked invasion of South Korea by the armies of Kim Il Sung, Communist puppet leader of North Korea. In addition, he's given General MacArthur permission to use, and I quote, 'Other troops under your command if the RCT isn't enough.' The 29th is going to war."

The general struck his Mussolini pose again with his head held high so flashbulbs wouldn't reflect off his specs. After his photographer took pictures, he marched back through the door he had used for his entrance.

Captain Scarf motioned for George to remain after the officers were dismissed. He crossed his arms as he addressed George. "The regimental combat team headed for Korea has requested four junior officers to bring them up to strength. Orders have yet to be cut by Far East Command, assigning you and the three others to Task Force Smith. Eight hundred of you

One Helluva Soldier / Phil Kline

against 100,000 of them. I suggest you make out a will. Also, while you're waiting for FECOM to cut orders, you might write to your boyfriends and tell them goodbye."

"Captain, you obviously have read my 2-0-1 file, which states I stood before a Board of Officers. They didn't determine I was homosexual, just that I drank beer with four of them." He crossed his arms, imitating Scarf. "Captain, I'm an open-minded kind of guy. I'd even have a beer with you."

Scarf scowled and walked out of the building.

One Helluva Soldier / Phil Kline

5

On July first, Armed Forces News broadcast that the regimental combat team commanded by Lieutenant Colonel Charles B. Smith had sailed from Japan to Pusan, Korea. The announcer read intelligence dispatches from FECOM G-2 indicating that Task Force Smith had been understaffed and supplied with obsolete equipment but brought to strength by adding soldiers serving on occupation duty in Japan. Two days later, George received orders to observe artillery for Charlie Company of Task Force Smith.

The four lieutenants met at Kadena Air Base and boarded a C-47 transport headed for Korea. Sitting across from them, George rode in silence and listened to their conversation. They didn't seem to have qualms about going into combat. He wondered how he'd react under fire. *Do I have the balls to do the job?*

The roar of the engines made it difficult to understand all of the three lieutenants' words, but George caught enough to know they were talking about how their girlfriends walked. It reminded him of a story his dad had told, about how soldiers in Laredo used to sit on a bench on the American side of the Mexican border, watching girls walk around the town square.

George's nervousness faded when he recalled the first time he had watched girls promenade in Mexico.

Two years earlier, after he finished basic training at Fort Bliss, Texas, George rode a train from Juarez to Torreon, where he boarded a bus that smelled like chickens and rode like a hay wagon as it bounced to Durango.

The air was sweet in Durango. Flowers surrounded a fountain at the center of the city square and lined the front of La Victoria, a white stucco hotel with black wrought-iron balconies that made it look like a Mexican hotel should look.

He ambled through the open door to a front desk on the edge of an interior patio lined with flowers. The aroma reminded him of his mom's garden in front of his home in Michigan. He approached the desk clerk. "Do you have a single room?"

"*Si, senor,* have room."

"How much?"

"*Cuanto? Ocho pesos.*" The man held up one finger. "One, *oro.*"

"*Oro?*"

"*Oro es Americano.*"

"One dollar, one night?"

"*Si, senor.*"

George gave the clerk three bills and held up three fingers. "*Tres noches.*"

The clerk took the dollars and gave George a key large enough to be a key to the city.

George climbed iron steps to a second floor lined with eight-foot-tall doors, befitting a castle. The four-poster bed, dresser, and chairs carried on the castle theme. He opened French doors and stepped onto a balcony overlooking the square.

The perfume of flowers drifted up. A bronze man, twice as tall as the people walking the square below, stood on a granite pedestal in the middle of a fountain.

An hour later, George ate enchiladas and beans in an ancient 12x12 stucco dining room, then sat on a bench in front of the hotel and listened to a man, a woman, and two children play marimbas. He drank a Rum Collins and watched girls walk around the square, looking straight ahead but sneaking occasional glances at boys who lined the benches.

His gaze locked onto a pretty girl in a flowered skirt and peasant blouse who walked alone. One long braid crossed over her right shoulder and down the front of her blouse. She looked straight ahead without glancing at a boy who said, "*Ay*, Luisa." The second time she circled by, George spied an almost imperceptible glance his way. He had no idea what got into him. Perhaps it was the rum. He sprang off the bench and joined her.

They walked side-by-side, not looking at each other, not speaking, not smiling, and not acknowledging that they were walking close to each other. After five times around, she stopped where a street intersected the square across from La Victoria. She glanced at him with no change of expression and gave a slight nod. She turned to go down the street, and as she did, her hand brushed his and caused a tingling sensation throughout his body.

He called out, "Is your name Luisa?" But she was gone.

He stared at an empty street then looked around as if she would reappear from another direction. She didn't.

He walked to his room, lay on his bed in the dark, and listened to the marimbas.

The music stopped, leaving only the conversations of people below and the voice of a vendor hawking his wares. Soon the sound of a mariachi band replaced the near-quiet. George walked onto the dark balcony and listened to music float through the night air. The circling girls and watching boys were replaced by couples coming from streets that met at the square.

Those, who chanced to look up toward a balcony on the second floor of La Victoria, may have seen a *gringo* talking to a statue. "*Senor* Bronze Man, Luisa is so beautiful. Tell me, will I see her again?"

The bronze man was silent.

One Helluva Soldier / Phil Kline

*

The following night, George was sitting on a bench in front of the hotel when Luisa walked by. He smiled, but she didn't look at him. He watched as she walked around the square again and didn't acknowledge him, but the third time, she stopped, folded her arms, and stared at him. He bounced up and hurried to her. In his excitement, he forgot how to ask, How do you do in Spanish. He was embarrassed. Then it came to him. "*Como esta usted?*"

She smiled. "*Bien.*"

As they strolled, her hand brushed against his. It happened four times during the hour they walked together. The next night they strolled again. He waited for her hand to touch his. When it happened, he held it, and they walked hand in hand.

He pointed to himself. "George Martin."

She pointed to herself. "Luisa Josifina Elazio Hernandez." She laughed when he tried to pronounce it. She had as much trouble saying his name, but he didn't laugh.

Nine months and several bumpy rides to Durango later, George and Luisa stood before a *padre* in an ancient cathedral. George didn't understand much of the ceremony, but when it was over, he was sure he was a married man.

*

George's daydream came to a halt when he felt the lurch of the landing gear being lowered at Taejon. A captain, wearing a hooded poncho, met the four lieutenants after they dropped down from the hatch. They stood under the wing, sheltered from the rain.

"Yesterday," the captain said, "the Regimental Combat Team was trucked into position north of here. Their job is to get the North Koreans to turn around and go back home. Of course that won't happen. So your job is to slow them down and stay alive until we get enough men here to fight a war. Which one of you is Martin?"

George raised his hand.

The captain pointed to a three-quarter-ton truck parked off the edge of the runway. "That truck will take you to Charlie Company. They're already in defensive position. Get rid of that bag and put what you'll need in your pack."

Rain drummed on the canvas top of the truck as it left with George in the back, transferring clothing and other necessities from his barracks bag to his pack. When he finished, he strapped his pack on his back and then tried to call the RCT's fire direction center, but all that came from the radio was static. The truck stopped.

"This is as far as we go," the driver yelled.

George jumped out, and his boots went splat in the mud. He told the driver. "Take my barracks bag back to the airport. Have them ship it to the 29th Infantry on Okinawa."

"Sure, I'll just do that. I may even put it on a plane myself." The driver pointed to a hill a half-mile from the road. "C Company's on this side of that hill."

George pulled his poncho around his neck and slogged through mud, toward C Company's headquarters at the base of the hill, as the truck turned around and sped away.

The C company commander, an unsmiling captain, gestured toward the top of the hill. "You'll be with Lieutenant Lee in the lead platoon. He's up there. Good luck."

George climbed the hill between shrubs, occasionally slipping in the mud. He hoped Lieutenant Lee, the captain mentioned, was Henry Lee from his OCS class.

When he reached the back side of the hill, George's mind was drawn away from his own problems. Forty sad-faced GIs stood watching muddy run-off pour into their foxholes. A soaking wet, crusty-looking GI, in his forties, made his way to George and saluted with a cupped hand.

George returned the salute. "Lieutenant Martin, Forward Observer. I'm to report to Lieutenant Lee."

The GI swung a hand back and forth. "He's somewhere out there, trying to find the other platoons and, I hope, some food. I'm Sergeant Duma, 1st Platoon Sergeant."

"Don't you have radio contact with them?"

"The batteries are dead."

"I have a couple extra you can have. What about the field phone?"

"Lieutenant, this isn't a training exercise. It's a war."

"The men have K-Rations, don't they?"

"They don't have K-Rations or any other kind of rations. There is no food."

Duma motioned for George to follow him. When they had walked to the side of the hill away from the men, Duma pointed back toward them. "I don't want the men to hear any more bad news. They're a bunch of kids who don't know anything about combat, and they've been sent here to stop an army. Most of them haven't even fired their pieces. Why are we here, Lieutenant? Why are we fighting in this godforsaken country, anyway?"

George shook his head. "I don't know any better than you, Sergeant." He pulled two batteries out of his pack and handed them to Duma. "I wish I had some food for your men."

"Me, too. But thanks for the batteries, Sir."

Henry Lee charged up the hill, a half-drowned, six-foot-five Alan Ladd look-alike who didn't have the smiling face George was used to seeing. Henry's helmet was tucked under his left arm, and a carbine slung over his right shoulder. He gaped at George.

"Martin? Is that you?"

George took off his helmet and shook Henry's hand. "I reckon I do look different."

Duma stepped up. "What did you find out, Lieutenant?"

"The 2nd Platoon's a mile to our right, and Weapons Platoon's on our left, by the road. We have no heavy artillery or air support, but Intelligence says the North Koreans don't have armor, so I guess we're safe."

"Good thing. Weapons Platoon has 2.36-inch rocket launchers."

"They won't stop a tank," George said. "Why don't you have 3.5's?"

Duma shrugged. "Who knows? Maybe supply just never got around to issuing them." He turned toward Henry. "What did you find out about food?"

Henry shook his head. "There isn't any."

George glanced at the men slumped in the rain. "This is not how I envisioned war. I always pictured going in gung-ho, attacking the enemy in sunshine, with a full belly under my belt."

"I know what you mean," Henry said. "It was a shock to me, too. Still is. Look, I have to get acquainted with my men. We'll talk later." He turned to Duma. "Let's see if there's anything we can do to help them make it through the night."

Henry and Duma sloshed toward the platoon.

George found a spot on the crest of the hill from which he could see the front. He fumbled with the radio, trying to contact Fire Direction Center. The radio worked, but he received no answer.

A rumble came from the north. He looked down the road but saw nothing. The rumble got louder. Goose bumps covered George's arms and legs. He recognized the clanging and squealing of tank tracks. Again, he tried to contact Fire Direction Center, without luck. He felt useless as he watched a dozen Russian T-34 tanks cruise around a bend in the road. He knew they'd either shoot hell out of the platoon or pass by and surround it. They could easily wipe out the two hundred men that made up Charlie Company.

Henry returned, running toward George. "Get us some fucking artillery!"

George spread his arms and shook his head. "I can't reach FDC. I thought you said they didn't have tanks."

"Intelligence said that, not me." As soon as he spoke an explosion rocked the hill and mud rained on them. Henry ran to his men, who made splashes as they jumped into their foxholes.

George lay flat as rounds began to burst around him. When the firing ceased, he crawled behind a log on the front slope and watched six men from Weapons Platoon fire a 75mm recoilless and a rocket launcher at the tanks from the edge of a ditch at the base of the hill. The rounds just bounced off, and the tanks opened up with machine guns. The force of multiple 50 caliber rounds blasted the men off their knees and into the water-filled ditch.

George raised his carbine. "You bastards." He fired a magazine of 30 caliber rounds that bounced off a tank. He reached to his belt for another magazine, but then realized the idiocy of rifle against tank. He dived to the ground as the tanks raked the hill with machine gun fire.

After the T-34s roared past the hill, the men crawled out of their water-logged foxholes. None were wounded, but they dragged around like zombies. Duma walked among them.

"You've seen the worst of what can happen, and you made it." The men's expressions didn't change. Duma walked over to George. "We have orders to withdraw but we have to get past those tanks." He turned toward the men. "Down the hill, men, we're going back to our lines. Follow me. Lieutenant Lee will cover the rear."

One Helluva Soldier / Phil Kline

George went ahead of Henry, carrying the radio and his pack. He followed the men, running and sliding down the hill, and along a path between rice paddies. He felt useless and angry, with no ability to fire artillery and no command authority.

From in the distance, a burp-gun fired a burst at the platoon. Three men went down and didn't move. Another, who looked to be in his teens, lay in the muck, holding his hands on his stomach. "Help me," he pleaded. Others didn't even look as they ran past him. George stopped to help him.

"Keep going!" Henry yelled. "We can't endanger the others for one guy."

George felt guilty, but started running again.

Henry stopped and looked at the wounded man, then hurried after the rest of his platoon.

Two men, one of them a corporal, walked to the side of a hill between two trees. They tossed their rifles and helmets down, and sat as if taking a break. Henry stopped, but said, "Keep going."

All but two of the men kept running. "What are you doing?" Henry yelled at the two. "Get back with the platoon." He grabbed a corporal by the shoulder. "You guys, get out of here. You'll be killed." The corporal pulled away from Henry's grasp.

Small arms fire popped through the trees. Henry gave an arm signal to move on. The two men didn't move as Henry and George ran to catch up with the other men who were running like a mob.

At the top of the hill Duma spied a platoon of NKPA down below. He yelled, "Hit the ground." His men settled down during a fire-fight with them, but soon they ran out of ammo.

Duma directed them to a ravine where they camouflaged themselves with brush. The enemy never saw them and passed on by.

One Helluva Soldier / Phil Kline

*

Early in the morning, the platoon survivors entered what appeared to be a deserted village. An ancient- looking woman, accompanied by an old man with a long white beard, came out of a hut and walked toward Henry. She held a bucket of fish out to him and motioned as if she were shaking a pan, then pointed at the men.

Henry gestured as if he were eating. She nodded. He placed guards and thirty minutes later, twenty hungry Americans sat along the side of the road, feasting to the sound of rifle and cannon fire. George didn't like fish or turnips, but wolfed them down.

Henry shook one of the old man's hands with both of his then kissed the woman on her cheek. He gave her a five dollar bill, and she bowed. The man pointed to a path that led up the hill, between the pines. Duma led the men up with Henry and George following.

Rounds hit the dirt near the ridge line, followed by the faraway sound of a 30 caliber machine gun being fired. A commotion took place toward the front. When someone yelled "Lieutenant!", Henry and George rushed forward. Duma lay on his side across the path, but didn't appear to be wounded. Henry pulled on his shoulder to turn him on his back. When he did, George saw one side of the sergeant's face had been blown away.

Henry hung his head, closed his eyes, and choked out the word, "Duma." Then he opened them and eased off one of Duma's dog tags. His tears flowed as he lifted his dead sergeant and carried him to the shade of a pine tree where a branch had been shot off. He knelt and held Duma's right hand. "Goodbye, Sergeant."

One Helluva Soldier / Phil Kline

   He raised himself to a standing position and walked toward the men. Sporadic rifle fire again came from the distance. Henry's legs crumpled and he fell to the ground. Everybody else hit the ditch next to the path.

6

George and Corporal Anderson half lifted and half pulled Henry into the ditch. George searched for wounds, but all he saw was a puncture in the right hip. He sighed when he saw Henry's chest move up and down.

"Thank God, you're all right," George whispered. Henry didn't respond.

Anderson called for two men. "Give us a hand with the lieutenant, but watch out for that sniper." The two helped carry Henry over a rise, and George checked him over. "Where'd he get hit?" Anderson said. "I don't see a wound."

George touched a red blotch on Henry's hip. "This is all I found, but he's in shock."

He helped Anderson make a stretcher from two M-1's and a shelter half then assigned four men to carry their two-hundred-twenty pound leader along the steep terrain. An hour later, Anderson dropped back to where George walked beside Henry. He pointed at a trail fifty yards below, where an old Korean led a ragged looking donkey pulling a cart.

George raised his arm and called, "Stop the men." He ran down the hill, jumping over rocks and bushes, and grabbed the Korean by the shoulder. He handed the man a dollar bill and pointed at the donkey, then toward the path above.

The old man nodded and led his donkey up the hill, still pulling the cart. George pushed until they reached where Henry lay. Four men lifted Henry onto the cart then the thirty survivors continued along the path, with Anderson in the lead. The Korean followed, leading his donkey and the cart, with Henry curled up in it.

The hills became steeper, and the path narrower. The men unhooked the cart and lifted Henry across the donkey's back, but the animal started bucking, so they pulled him off.

George handed his helmet and carbine to one of the men, grabbed the donkey's rein and straddled him. The donkey circled up and down the path, bucking all the way, but George stayed on, holding the rein with one hand and waving the other in the air, as if riding in a rodeo at the State Fair. When the donkey settled down, George hopped off.

A tall private walked up to George. "Lieutenant, ya'll did that as well as anybody in Texas could'a done." He extended his hand.

George grabbed the hand and shook it. "I'm from Michigan, and I did it better'n anyone in Texas coulda' done."

Three men put Henry on the donkey, with his head on one side and his feet on the other, almost touching the ground. The Korean held the donkey's rein and walked the path. Henry lifted his head and looked to the front.

"Welcome back," George said.

Henry kept his head up and strained to talk. "I can't move my leg. It hurts all the way down to my ankle."

George laid a hand on Henry's. "We'll get you to a medic... I'm sorry about Duma. Did you know him before you came to Korea?"

"No." His breath was labored; talking was difficult. "I've ...only known him a week... but I... really respected him."

"Okay, rest now. We'll get you to a medic."

When they reached a medic tent behind friendly lines, George gave the man his last dollar bill. The old man bowed and led the donkey in the direction from which they had come.

One Helluva Soldier / Phil Kline

George walked beside Henry, as he was carried by stretcher to a MASH unit. He watched while two bleary-eyed surgeons, assisted by a frazzled blonde nurse, sewed up Henry's wound.

One of the doctors turned to George. "He took a bullet that hit his hipbone and traveled down his leg. We sewed him up, but he has to go to the States to get the bullet and bone chips out. He's awake now, so if you want to talk to him, you have a few minutes."

George walked to where Henry lay on a stretcher. "How you feeling?"

Henry pointed at the nurse. "Isn't she beautiful?" He used his index finger to jab into the air. "What pisses me off is Intelligence giving us that shit about them not having any tanks."

"You're feeling better."

"Yeah, and I'll be back so we can do it again when we're giving instead of taking."

"One of the surgeons said you're headed to the States."

"He doesn't make the decision."

George shook his head. "You want to come back here?"

"Yeah. I don't like getting pushed around."

"You're married, aren't you, Lee?"

"Sure, you know that."

"You've done your part. Go back to your wife and raise a family."

Henry struggled to sit up. "Look, I'll spend time with her and have kids when the war's over. Bobbi knew who I was when she married me, and she knows how I feel. I don't expect you to understand. You're just a farm kid who got caught up in a war."

"You think so, huh? Let me tell you something: I'd rather be here than on a farm."

Two medics walked up. "Sorry, Lieutenant," one said. "We have to take him now."

George and Henry shook hands, and the medics hauled Henry away.

George left the MASH to locate 21st Regimental Headquarters. When he found it, he discovered the headquarters staff people were about the only ones left; the rest had been either killed or captured. A surviving captain in personnel interviewed George. "You come from the Twenty-ninth Infantry?"

"Yes, Sir."

The captain shuffled papers, read from one, and looked up. "They're due to debark in the next couple of days. You can submit a request in personnel to be transferred back to them."

George thought about it. "I don't think that'll work. The S-3 has a bug up his ass about me. He'll veto it."

A lieutenant motioned for George to come to where he stood. "The 8th Army Headquarters has arrived in Korea. They're located north of Pusan. Go there. Find some underling in personnel and tell him you were on temporary duty with the 21st, and you're supposed to go back to the 29th. They're so disorganized he'll probably cut the orders and be happy he did something right. Then go to the Pusan docks and wait for them."

Two days later, George reported to 8th Army Headquarters, approached a junior officer in G-1, and said to him. "I was assigned to the 29th Infantry, but was put on TDY with the 21st. Now I'm to be transferred back."

He walked away with orders that transferred him to 3d Battalion, 29th Infantry Regiment; orders that Captain Scarf couldn't countermand. He was told the battalion was due to debark in Pusan the next day.

George located an empty 6x6 headed for Pusan just as the rain came, blown by strong winds,. Three men occupied the canvas covered cab, but George was invited to ride in back. He climbed on, pulled down a bench seat, and sat with his poncho wrapped around him as the truck moved out. The rain, driven by a howling wind, still found its way under his poncho.

Huts along the road were being blown apart, and pieces of them flew through the air. George moved to the truck bed and lay under the seat.

Near the edge of a village, the truck slowed down. George raised up and looked ahead. Fleeing Koreans crowded the road, headed in the same direction as the truck.

The truck swerved back and forth on a road covered with water. Women, carrying children on their backs, moved aside and raised their arms, begging for a ride. The truck moved on, but soon the driver pulled off the road. A rope holding the canvas top, pulled from its grommet, then another. George wedged himself under the seat. With a *whoomp*, the canvas flew into the night.

The truck bed collected water, so George leaned up against the back of the cab seats. He was surprised when a hand reached back and handed him a K-ration. He looked at the description: MEAT AND BEANS; the same meal he and Luisa ate when they vacationed at Lewis and Clark Park.

He ate the cold meat and beans, stale crackers, and tropical chocolate, then crawled to a cooped up position under the seat. He had been cooped up before.

*

Five years earlier, George had been taken to Grandma Kate's rickety house in the middle of a field of weeds, five miles west of Potterville. His mom cried as she drove the pickup down the rutted road to the house. Chickens flew out of the front door followed by Grandma swinging a broom at them.

One Helluva Soldier / Phil Kline

"Take your stuff upstairs," she hollered at George.

He watched his mom drive back to his dad who had said, "I don't want no pris living in my house." So, George climbed the narrow stairs, just inside the door, carrying his suitcase full of clothes, and was cooped up in a room that was to be his home for the next two years.

One Helluva Soldier / Phil Kline

7

Dawn brought a milder wind and lighter rain. The road was still muddy, but no longer covered with water. The truck started moving and, within an hour, pulled into the Port of Pusan.

George hopped off and walked into a long, low building to get dry. He found he had entered a mess hall. A sergeant walked up to him. "You look like you could use some scrambled eggs and bacon. They're leftovers from breakfast. You can have all you want."

George ate six eggs plus bacon and toast, but as he drank coffee, he knew he had eaten too much on an empty stomach. He left the mess hall and, minutes later, lost his breakfast while walking toward the docks through mud that reeked of sewage.

When he reached the gate to the docks, he asked the lieutenant on duty. "How do I get to where the 29th Infantry's unloading?"

"They won't unload here. The water's too rough to dock. What's your problem?"

"I'm supposed to meet them."

The lieutenant pointed to his left. "They're scheduled to unload on a sheltered beach south of here, close enough to walk. Go north for six blocks and you'll see a sign pointing to Chinhae Bay. Take that road three miles, then south along the river another two."

The rain stopped. George took off his wet fatigues and walked.

One Helluva Soldier / Phil Kline

He arrived at Chinhae Bay in time to see four LSTs lower their ramps. He put on his still damp clothes and watched the 3d Battalion disembark. The men shuffled down the ramps, into shallow water, like condemned men walking their last mile. Walt Perry worked with his men, getting them unloaded and in formation.

The rain started again as the battalion marched away from the beach. George walked at the rear, encouraging stragglers to pick up the pace and look forward to a dry place ahead. No men dropped out during the seven-mile trek.

On the outskirts of Pusan, they arrived at a schoolhouse that stunk of sweat and piss, and didn't have enough room for all of the men inside. Many pitched tents in the pouring rain.

After the men were situated, Walt Perry found George outside, leaning against a post on a dry, less smelly portion of the porch.

"I haven't been ignoring you on purpose," he said. "I was just too busy. I'm glad you were here to save men from quitting. I don't believe we lost any of them on the march."

"I may have saved some to die here."

Walt sat and removed his boots. "And some to live. Many of these men are recruits who came from clerical jobs in Japan. They never envisioned anything like what's happened to them these last few days. Some didn't know if they'd make it here or even if living was worthwhile. For two days, they wallowed on an LST that had been used to haul fish, sick from the smell and forty degree rolls." He pushed his feet next to one post and leaned against another. "Damn this feels good."

"Do you know about Henry's situation?" George asked.

"I heard he's headed to Tokyo General."

"The medic said they were going to ship him to the States."

Walt looked up from rubbing his feet. "You know Henry. They offered to transfer him to the States after he's repaired, but he wants to go back into action. They may send him home, but he's adamant about coming back. He's lucky that Bobbi'll understand. What's Luisa think about you being here?"

George stared into the dark. "I don't know. I haven't got any mail so far. I wonder if we'll get any here."

"One battalion of the Twenty-ninth is still on Oki. They'll make sure we get our mail."

George turned toward Walt. "Luisa took it hard just to see me leave, so I reckon she'll be upset if she finds out I'm in combat. She's alone in a strange country with a two month old kid."

"Tough, but I'm sure she'll make it. By the way, I've requested that you travel with my platoon. You can bring me up to date on the situation here."

The two sat against their posts for a half-hour while George told Walt about his experiences with Henry's platoon. Walt shook his head. "Both Intelligence and Public Information said Task Force Smith was holding its own."

George's face wrinkled in a frown "Don't believe it. The 24th is here now, and they're getting their ass kicked, too. We don't have the men, the equipment, or the ammo. We're trading lives for time... By the way, where's Trexler?" He pointed toward Chinhae Bay. "I didn't see him on the beach."

"He's still on Oki. Scarf says he's too immature to command."

"Scarf's full of shit. From what I hear, Tommie's a good soldier, more grown up than I am. What about Hayes? Is he here?"

Walt shrugged. "Tank Company was to follow later."

Yelling erupted inside the schoolhouse. Walt stood. "I'd better get it quieted down inside so they can get some sleep. We're supposed to be in Chinju in the morning."

One Helluva Soldier / Phil Kline

*

At dawn, the rain stopped. The men marched for two hours on muddy roads in muggy heat then were crammed into boxcars, which accentuated the heat and the heavy odor of sweat. They traveled between pine-covered hills, interrupted by valleys of rice paddies and bamboo thickets.

On arrival at Chinju, George received a message from a runner, directing him to report to 3rd Battalion Headquarters.

Battalion S-2 asked George to accompany him and Walt on a twilight Jeep patrol to gather intelligence about the NKPA in the vicinity of the village of Hadong. He was seemingly unconcerned about probing deep into enemy territory in an unarmed vehicle.

Walt approached the Jeep and came to an abrupt halt when he saw George in the back seat. "What are you doing here?"

George laughed as Walt climbed on. "I know the territory. I hiked it."

As they approached Hadong, young Koreans dressed in typical white clothing, all with cueball haircuts, waved from the side of the road. George shuddered. He leaned toward the S-2 in the front seat. "Those guys are NKPA."

The S-2, a tall, skinny second lieutenant, jerked his head toward the Koreans. "They didn't kill us. They must want bigger game."

The Jeep continued to patrol between the hills. Walt pointed to the glow of cigarettes in the woods and glanced at George.

George nodded. "Somebody'll have to deal with them, too."

After the patrol made it back to their lines without being shot at, George joined the S-2 where he made his report to the operations officer about the young Koreans dressed in white, in the villages, and others smoking in the woods. "It's a trap waiting to be sprung," the S-2 said.

One Helluva Soldier / Phil Kline

The S-3, a major, sat on his empty ammo box and listened politely, then shook his head. "You Intelligence guys have overactive imaginations."

George stepped around the S-2 and up to the major. "I've been with Task Force Smith and have seen that before. Those guys were NKPA."

The major said, "We'll see," and waved goodbye.

*

George marched alongside Walt as Love Company climbed a wooded hill east of Hadong. They searched the woods but saw no sign of the NKPA. "Your company's going to be attacked," George said, "and the odds against you will be overwhelming."

"You may be right, but we have orders, in line with an 8th Army directive, to slow the NKPA down until United Nations forces get organized."

Walt set a mobile defense on the crest of his hill position to protect it from all sides, while George contacted Fire Direction Center. He fired on a lone bush on the side of a bald hill to establish a checkpoint from which he could adjust artillery. Then they waited.

Captain Eddy, commander of Weapons Company, an older man, ran huffing up the hill to where Walt and George lay prone on the forward slope. "Help me. My company's under attack." Burp-gun rounds went thud as they tore through cloth and flesh. The captain spun around and fell to the ground.

North Koreans charged up the hill on the west side of the position. "Over here," Walt hollered, and twenty of his men joined him. They lay flat and tossed grenades down the slope, then fired their rifles, driving their attackers down the hill. "They're headed for cover in the woods," Walt yelled.

One Helluva Soldier / Phil Kline

George was surprised how calm he was when he ordered artillery. "Fire mission. Enemy troops in woods. From Checkpoint A, left one hundred, drop five zero, fire for effect."

A barrage of thirty-six rounds passed overhead, *roar, roar, roar,* sounding like a freight train crossing a bad section of track, followed by high explosive shells bursting in the trees, huge firecrackers that sprayed the North Koreans with steel fragments.

The platoon was attacked from different sides for two hours. Each time, Walt led his men against attacks he didn't know were coming until the enemy was almost on top of them.

They maintained their position against the assaults, but Battalion ordered a withdrawal.

Walt led the men back down the hill and across a rice paddy. George ordered a fire mission on the hill the platoon left and ran after the platoon seconds before the first rounds burst on the summit.

Rifle and machine gun fire hit Love Company men as they raced along the levees or sloshed through the water. Some were killed. Others lay in the paddy, drowning, or bleeding to death.

George looked with frustration at American planes circling above, unable to help because the ground-to-air radios didn't work. He lost his footing and fell in the muck. He lay there for a moment and heard rifle fire coming from the hill they had vacated. He picked up the mike. "Fire mission--"

He released the button and heard the message, "Firing battery surrounded and has march ordered." Love Company was on its own.

George stood and zigzagged through the paddy as rifle fire hit the water near him. He came to a river that blocked the retreat. The bank was littered with rifles, ammo belts, boots, and helmets. Men waded into the fast, rain-swollen river. Some had even discarded their uniforms. Walt ran back and forth, encouraging the men to keep their equipment, with little success.

George watched helplessly as some men were swept away by the current, while others lay still after being hit by rifle fire. Walt was one of the last to leave, taking strong strokes as he swam with his helmet and carbine intact.

George waded into the muddy water and started to dog paddle, the only stroke he knew. He zigzagged toward the middle of the river. Rounds splashed around him. With a twenty-pound radio on his back, he was sure he couldn't make it, but he kept the radio and ditched his helmet. He held his breath and swam as fast as he could. He felt the jolt when a round hit the radio.

He knew the splashes made a good target, but continued kicking and tried to unstrap the radio at the same time. The buckle didn't budge. He lifted his head. Air filled his lungs as he breathed in gasps. Two more rounds slammed into the radio.

Holding his breath, and trying to float with his face down, he got nowhere except downstream. He knew he'd have to chance splashing water. Paddling without kicking his feet, he made no headway, so he kicked.

He raised his head, took a breath of air, and opened his eyes. He was halfway across the river. He straightened his legs but couldn't reach bottom. He paddled until he was beat. When he had to rest, he stood and felt stones under his boots. He knew he would be home free if he could get to the woods without being shot. Keeping a low profile, he waded to the bank and dashed between the trees.

He pulled the radio loose, threw it down, and ran through the woods along the river without seeing any North Koreans. He spied a clearing through the trees and snaked along until he came to a road. Looking south he saw survivors from the platoon climbing onto a truck a hundred yards away. He ran

One Helluva Soldier / Phil Kline

down the edge of the road yelling and waving his arms as the last man climbed on. His shoulders drooped as he watched the truck leave.

8

Hugging the woods on the side of the road as he hiked toward Chinju, George heard Asian voices close by. He slid down into a man-made ditch that supplied water for a rice paddy. The voices came closer. He lay on his back between reeds with his face above the surface. He felt his heart beating in rhythm with the pounding of feet as a column of North Koreans marched along the edge of the ditch, within five yards of where he lay.

After ten minutes that seemed like an hour, they were gone. He waited to make sure there wasn't a rear guard, then slowly raised his head from the water and peered around. He neither saw nor heard anyone. He crawled to the top of the ditch and looked. He was alone.

A half hour later, George again heard sounds indicating that a group of marching men were approaching. There was no ditch in which to hide and no logs to get behind. He sneaked into the woods next to the road and found a thicket of a prickly plant. He wormed his way into it.

A hundred or so young Koreans, with short-cropped hair, and wearing the white clothing of peasants, marched by in military formation. After they passed, George continued his trek to Chinju in the dark, careful to see without being seen, and to hear without being heard. He hid once more from a company of the enemy before making it to Chinju.

One Helluva Soldier / Phil Kline

Arriving in Chinju at dawn, he found the remnants of Love Company in formation, forty survivors, most without boots or equipment. Walt was addressing them.

"Our other two companies also lost most of their officers and men. We'll join them and form one platoon to be attached to A Company of the 27th Regiment." He pounded a fist into his open hand. "We'll be issued new weapons and gear, but you must keep them for us to function as a fighting unit. That's the only way to stay alive. Too many of our men died because they quit."

Looking as if he'd swam an ocean of mud, George stopped at the edge of Walt's formation, and Walt walked over to where he stood. "I hesitate to interrupt your formation," George said, "but I have to know where I can locate headquarters of the 27th."

Walt shook both of George's hands at once. "That's all right. I want the men to think about what I just said."

After Walt gave him the directions he wanted, George left to locate Major Bane, operations officer for the two battalions of the 27th.

*

Major Bane was standing in the G-3 tent talking to a built-like-a-bulldog sergeant and a skinny little private who, if he were a girl, would be called frail by the guys.

When George walked in, Bane stopped talking and grabbed George's hand, pumping it like he was jacking up a dump truck. "Last word I had," he said, "was that you drowned trying to save a piece of shit radio."

George laughed.

"Welcome back to the living; made it in time to take over as FO for our 1st Battalion." Bane nodded toward the enlisted men. "Sergeant Patrick and Private Tisdale are part of your team. You join Baker Company tomorrow on the line west of Taegu, fifty miles north of here." Indicating a field radio on his desk, he added, "Sergeant, it doesn't look like you'll have a problem carrying one of these twenty pound radios."

"No, Sir."

"Ever operate one?"

"It's been a while, Sir."

"Tisdale, how old are you?"

Tisdale's lips quivered. "Eighteen, Sir."

"Expect you never worked with a forward observer."

"No, Sir."

"Ever shoot a carbine?"

"No, Sir, but I can learn."

Major Bane pointed at Patrick and George. "You'll have to. Your job's to protect these two." He turned to George. "Take the rest of the afternoon to get cleaned up, eat, and prep them. Had a pretty good introduction to this kind of war, haven't you?"

"Yes, Sir."

"By now, you know to get batteries that work. A Jeep will be at the motor pool at 0600 hours to take you to B Company's position. I suspect you know to take plenty of repellant." He shook George's hand again. "Good luck."

Outside the tent, George introduced himself to his two men, then said, "Let's go to supply right now. Sergeant, draw a radio and make sure you get batteries that work. It's yours. Don't let it out of your sight. Tisdale, bring your M-1 and your ammo. We'll swap it for a carbine and the right ammo. Pick up two 5-gallon water cans and fill them. Each of you get six grenades. Oh, and get enough mosquito repellent to last two weeks."

The FO team drew equipment from the supply tent while George picked up two sets of clothing in addition to his gear. He laid them on the ground before taking a shower under a bag hanging from three poles. He donned his new clothes before he met the two men at the rear of the supply truck.

"We start our training in a half-hour," he said. "Meet me here with what you're taking with you and we'll do inventory. We may be on the hill for one hour or maybe a week."

"Yes, Sir," Tisdale said.

Patrick didn't say anything.

George walked into the G-3 tent. Through the tent wall he heard Tisdale say, "Why do we wear two sets of clothes, Sergeant?"

"It's easier than carrying them."

Then he heard a voice he didn't recognize. "You going on the hill, Sarge?"

"Yeah."

"Who's your FO?"

Patrick's voice: "Lieutenant Martin."

"The blond kid with the gold bars I saw you talking to?"

George and the major stood still and listened as Patrick answered, "Shut up."

"What's the matter? I hear that if you can't find a woman, the next best thing's a cute boy." Then the unidentified voice yelled, "Hey, guys, Patrick's going to be living on the hill with Blondie."

"Didn't I tell you to shut up?"

After a strained, "Just kidding, Sergeant," it was quiet.

Major Bane glanced at George to see how he was taking it, but Martin's expression was neutral. Both George and the Major chuckled when Tisdale said, "That guy was five inches taller than you, Sarge, and you lifted him right off the ground."

"Remember that."

*

One Helluva Soldier / Phil Kline

Late in the afternoon, George motioned for Patrick and Tisdale to lean on the front bumper and put their gear on the ground in front of them. He turned on the radio. It worked. He checked their carbines to make sure they operated. They did. He checked what they were carrying: canteens, knives, ammo, and what was in their packs.

He opened the 5-gallon cans and smelled the contents, then nodded. "Most of the time we'll be on our own with no protection other than what we provide for ourselves. In a way, we're expendable. If we work together, we can kill more enemy than the Infantry can. Their job's to slow down the North Koreans, and if our men retreat, we may be left all alone in front of the lines. You know what that means?"

Patrick nodded. "It means we direct fire on our own position, then run like hell."

"That's it. It's imperative that we work together as one." George saw the statement didn't bring a reaction from either of the men. He increased the volume of his voice. "If we function as a team, we may be alive a week from now."

The two men nodded.

George made sure the radio was turned off as he ran a practice fire mission. "Fire mission. Enemy platoon. From checkpoint A, right three-hundred, add two-hundred. Sergeant Patrick, repeat the words to me and into the mike. Left one-hundred, add five-zero. Fire for effect."

Patrick repeated the words into the mike.

George said, "Cease fire. End of mission."

Patrick repeated the commands.

They ran another imaginary fire mission. After he was satisfied with Patrick's use of the radio and fire commands, George ran Tisdale through the same procedures. When finished, he said. "We have to be able to do each other's job in case one of us can't function. Any questions?"

Tisdale raised a hand. "I'd like to learn about the carbine, Sir."

"I'll show you," Patrick said.

George turned to leave. "See you at zero six hundred hours at the motor pool."

He didn't eat breakfast. He didn't want anyone to see him if he threw it up. On the way to the motor pool, he stood straight and tried to walk with confidence even though his insides were churning.

Patrick stood by the truck next to his equipment. He walked up to George. "Lieutenant Martin, I've been assigned to be your radioman, and I will obey the order. But I request that, as soon as possible, you find someone else who can work better with you."

"What do you mean 'work better with me', Sergeant Patrick?"

"I just feel that you can get someone better suited to work with you."

"Quit beating around the bush."

"Ahh, Lieutenant--"

"Sergeant, when I'm forced to serve with someone who may be responsible for whether I live or die, I'm apprehensive, so I understand your feelings. Now, I want you to understand mine. We're going to be engaged in the most dangerous job in this here war, and we're going to depend on each other to stay alive. I don't care what you think about me, and I don't care what I think about you, we have a job to do together."

They stood in silence until Tisdale arrived, then tossed their gear into the Jeep.

The morning was so quiet, George was sure his crew would hear his stomach churning. After an uneventful ride, they left the Jeep and climbed a hill a quarter-mile away.

One Helluva Soldier / Phil Kline

Company B was digging in a defensive position in the midst of shrubs that resembled stunted oaks. George met the company commander, Captain Yost, a man with a muscular physique and a friendly way.

George set up on top of a hill, far above the stench of night soil. He sniffed air that contained the fragrance of pine. He surveyed the panoramic view of rice paddies surrounded by pine-covered hills beneath a picture postcard blue sky. *What a great place to have a picnic with Luisa and Mario,* he thought.

He set a checkpoint by firing high explosive shells into the grove of pine trees that nestled next to a gentle curve in the road. After the rounds shredded the pines, he gave Fire Direction Center corrections to his position in case he had to leave in a hurry.

An hour later, after he and his team had dug foxholes, someone behind him said, "Hello." He turned and saw the lead platoon leader, a short, stocky, lieutenant with the deep tan of a lifeguard.

The lieutenant knelt next to George and pointed down an extension of the road past the trees he had set as a checkpoint. In the distance, George saw movement he couldn't identify. He picked up his binoculars and recognized a column of T-34s headed toward the platoon position.

George stepped back to where Patrick had the radio, and yelled, "Fire mission. Enemy tanks. From checkpoint, add three-hundred."

Patrick relayed the command to FDC. Two rounds came in and hit the road forward of the lead tank.

Patrick relayed the order to FDC. Within seconds, high explosive rounds fell among the tanks. The tanks continued down the road.

The lieutenant slammed his fist on the ground and sprung upright. "Damn it. You can't knock out tanks with one-o-fives.

One Helluva Soldier / Phil Kline

We need tanks. We need air support." His carbine dropped, his helmet flew off in a gusher of blood, and he crumpled to the ground.

George picked up the dropped carbine and crawled to the slope. The hair on his arms and neck stood up when he saw a squad of North Koreans creeping up the hill, with more following.

They pointed rifles at him. He ducked. Rounds cracked as they passed over his head. He rolled three grenades down the hill, then stuck the carbine over his head and fired four automatic bursts to the front.

Crawling back toward Patrick, he spied Baker's lead platoon retreating down the hill. He grabbed the mike. "Martin to FDC. Enemy coming up our hill. We're leaving. Fire on my position."

He handed the mike to Patrick. The prickly feeling in his arms and neck was gone.

He motioned for his team to follow him along the back side of the hill. Halfway down, rifle fire hit the shrubbery around them and, soon, incoming artillery exploded on the hill behind them. They ran in the open toward a rice paddy.

George looked ahead and saw bullet splashes around the forty men of the lead platoon. Some of the men fell and didn't get up again. He waved to his two men. "Don't run straight. Zigzag!"

Past the paddy, they ran between stunted trees and up a hill. "We'll set up here," George said. When he saw tanks covered with infantry coming up the road alongside the paddy, he kneeled and called out, "Fire mission." He didn't hear Patrick relay the message to FDC. "Didn't you hear me? Fire mission… Where's the radio?"

"I couldn't run with all that weight. I tossed it."

"Where?"

"At the bottom of the hill."

"You damned fool!" George jumped up and ran down the slope. He spied the radio lying in a patch of weeds. He picked it up and ran back up the hill where he met Tisdale coming the other way. Shots came from their flank. Bullets thudded into the dirt around them.

Tisdale knelt and raised his carbine. "I'll cover you." He shot rapid-fire in the direction from which the rounds came.

George ran up the hill with the radio. On the way he passed Patrick going down. He heard the two men firing their carbines as he called a fire mission to hit the foot soldiers riding on the tanks.

Patrick trudged up the hill, supporting a limping Tisdale with one arm, and carrying two carbines with the other. "We ran them off," Patrick said. "I'll go back and make sure."

"No. Get Tisdale out of here, straight south. I'll take the radio. We're alone and the Koreans know it."

Patrick looked at him as if to say something.

"Get out of here," George shouted.

Patrick hustled down the back of the hill, half-carrying Tisdale.

George crouched down with the radio and watched the rounds come in, long and off to the right. He called in corrections and fired for effect.

Rifle fire came from the hill they had vacated. Tanks fired cannons and machine guns at a hill to the south. George grabbed the radio and raced toward where his men had gone. As he sped down the hill, he radioed FDC, "Tanks headed toward the battery position."

He followed his crew around the hill the tanks were pulverizing and caught up with them on the other side. Patrick had put a shirtsleeve tourniquet on Tisdale's leg. George carried the radio, the carbines, and Patrick's pack. Patrick hauled Tisdale in a fireman's carry.

Half a mile later, they reached the howitzer battery. It was pulling out. They hurled Tisdale into the back of a truck and jumped onto the bed, as the truck moved away.

*

At regimental headquarters, George located Major Bane. While reporting his failure to stop the T-34s, he had an attack of diarrhea and ran to a slit-trench, making it there just in time. He returned to Bane and apologized.

Bane laughed. "Get used to it. Common before a hairy experience or after it's over. Called a panic shit."

George made his report, found out where Baker Company was located, and got a ride. Then he found Patrick and discovered him waiting outside of G-3, carrying the radio, the two carbines, and his gear.

Patrick cleared his throat. "Lieutenant Martin, I apologize for my actions back there. I want you to know it won't happen again. And if you'll still have me, I'd be proud to remain as a permanent member of your FO team. You're one helluva soldier, Sir."

George gazed at Patrick for a moment. "Thank you, Sergeant. Baker's going on the attack, and we're going with them right now. How's Tisdale?"

"He's okay, Sir. An ambulance took him."

Baker's men rode in trucks down the gravel road toward the village of Anui with its huts made of mud and grass. Patrick carried the radio and rode in the lead Jeep with George and Captain Yost. Climbing higher, they looked toward rugged hills of hardwoods that hugged the road on both sides, but saw no signs of life.

One Helluva Soldier / Phil Kline

The Jeep crawled up the narrow winding road in second gear, with the engine growling. Yost cupped his hands around his mouth. "Our assignment's to engage the North Koreans and hold them back until reinforcements can be brought in. Nobody knows where they are, so I'm not sure where we'll make contact."

As if on cue, they glanced toward the woods beyond the spotty green cover that partially hid brown dirt on both sides of the road. The hills appeared to be deserted.

The caravan wound its way through the town of Anui to the cheers and applause of Koreans dressed in typical white garb.

Yost looked back at George. "We may have it easy today. Even the locals are out."

George pointed back toward Anui and yelled, "I don't think those guys are locals. They're too young and too neat."

Yost shrugged. "We made it by them so I guess we're okay. And we have to finish our mission."

One Helluva Soldier / Phil Kline

9

Company B trucks followed Yost's Jeep by fifty yards. As the first truck came around a bend, the engine gave off a fireball. The truck, its engine compartment smoking, blocked the road. Rifle fire came from bamboo thickets to the east and from the rear. Some of Baker's men were killed while sitting in the backs of stalled trucks. Others slumped over to die later. Those who were able, dived into a ditch alongside the road and fired on an enemy they couldn't see.

Yost jumped out of the Jeep and yelled over the din, "Follow me!"

George, Patrick, and the Jeep driver ran hunched over and followed him into the woods on the east side of the road. Bullets thumped tree trunks around them.

George slowed down to contact Fire Direction Center. FDC answered, "We have no artillery in the Anui area." Another dozen or so Baker Company men joined him, and they all raced up a hill to the east where they caught up with Yost.

Yost radioed battalion. "Send help. We've been ambushed."

The reply: "We can't. The reserve company's under fire."

The band of Americans moved in a crouched position through the woods, firing their rifles in an arc into the underbrush. Bullets zipped through the shrubs next to George. The driver went down. George and others gave running fire as they wound their way to the far side of the hill. They won a quick fire fight with Koreans dressed in white. After the fight,

One Helluva Soldier / Phil Kline

George pulled on the collar of a dead one, revealing a military uniform underneath.

An hour later, the survivors arrived south of Anui where D Company had been in reserve. D was gone. George turned to talk to Patrick, but he wasn't there. He called to Yost, "Patrick's missing. I'm going to see if I can find him."

"These hills belong to the gooks," Yost yelled.

George ran to the north. A quarter of a mile around the west side of the hill, he saw movement on the ridge to the right. He went to his knees and raised his carbine. In the dim light, he saw five men, looking much like a band of boy scouts following their leader. As they came closer, George raised his carbine and aimed at the leader.

"Patrick?"

"Is that you, Lieutenant?"

"Yes. Down here. Where've you been?"

Patrick approached George. "I went to the back of the column to see if anyone was following us. I was about to catch up with the rest of you when I saw these guys down below. They're from Baker, but had no idea where to go."

By the time they rejoined Yost's group, except for an occasional shot, firing no longer came from the direction of the ambush. George estimated the number of survivors at eighteen. One hundred and thirty-two men had either been killed or captured, and all of the company vehicles destroyed or lost.

After the band of survivors joined the other companies at Masan, the battalion received replacements and new equipment. Five Sherman tanks, commanded by John Hayes, joined them. George, Dennis Nixon, and Reed Rayford were visiting with John when a runner from Battalion brought a message: "Third Battalion is ordered to retake Chinju."

Minutes later, two squads of Nixon's men rode on the outside of John's five Shermans, leading an attack, which wound up a narrow road toward the mountain ridge. They were followed by two trucks carrying the rest of the men from Nixon's platoon, with George and Patrick in the cab of the lead truck. Next in line was Rayford's platoon in four more trucks.

The tanks passed through a cut and down the other side of the hill where a sheer cliff rose on the left, and a deep gorge dropped on the right. As the lead Sherman approached the bottom of the hill, a track flew off in a blast of light, leaving it disabled in the middle of the road. Tanks and trucks that followed couldn't pass and had no room to turn around. Machine gun and rifle fire came at them from across the gorge.

George and Patrick jumped out of the truck and climbed through bushes toward the crest of a hill above the road as the stalled American tanks fired cannons and machine guns at attackers hidden in the hills.

Some men followed the two officers, but many crawled into the ditch. Enemy fire ruptured a truck's gas tank, and gasoline poured into the ditch. Tracer bullets from a machine gun ignited the gas and fire traveled down the ditch at high speed.

Men on fire sprang out of the ditch and ran down the road. Others danced frantic gyrations, trying to beat out the flames. George was horrified to see soldiers roll down the hill, catching brush on fire as they went by. He and Patrick helped beat out the flames on men, who made it to the top of the hill, but the fire left them beet-red and charred.

Reed's trucks had stopped behind Dennis', and his platoon joined the fight, enabling trapped men to run back to them. Many were wounded. Some had their clothes burned off. Some had their skin burned black.

Reed's men led the wounded and burned men up a mountain path. George and his group of men joined them. They were involved in a fire-fight with the NKPA for an hour and could do little for the burned men.

One Helluva Soldier / Phil Kline

Later, George tended to a badly burned soldier in his teens. George took off his own top shirt and wrapped it around the youngster as they followed the crest of the hill south.

George said, "I don't want to touch your skin. You'll have to make it on your own, but I'll stay with you."

The kid walked, but cried out in pain with every step.

They climbed over the ridge and located a truck with other wounded on it. George left him there and returned to the top of the hill.

He tried to get artillery fire with no success. He lay and listened to the firing of cannons and machine guns from Sherman tanks. After the firing stopped at dark, he couldn't locate Sergeant Patrick, so he stole back toward the American lines, arriving minutes after Hayes.

"We were doing fine," Hayes said, "shot into the hills, until some of the bastards came down from behind and crawled on top of us, firing into every crack they could find. Shot my loader in the eye, but he kept on loading with his eye hanging out. We fired at our own tanks. Made a hell of a racket, but killed most of the fuckers, and the rest of them scattered. We picked them off with machine guns. After dark, we disabled the tanks and hauled ass."

Walt and Reed joined the two friends just as Hayes was leaving. Walt wiped tears from his eyes when he spoke to George and to a sullen Reed Rayford. "The 1st Battalion's been so badly decimated that the colors of the 29th are being returned to Okinawa. I'm going to King of the 35th. Nixon and Rayford have been attached to Love Company."

One Helluva Soldier / Phil Kline

10

George was assigned as a 35th Regiment FO to travel with King Company, which was ordered to occupy the flat top of a hill overlooking the Bowling Alley, so-called because of the many tanks and trucks that rolled down a road flanked by ditches.

That evening, George, Yost, and Walt sat on a log near the mess truck, wearing undershirts. Steam rose from everything wet or green. Sweat dripped in a stream from their chins onto their roast pork, boiled potatoes, and corn. After eating, George patted his stomach and yelled to the mess sergeant, "You're a better cook than my mother, but don't tell her I said so."

The sergeant saluted. "Thank you, Sir. Notice I picked a warm day to serve a hot meal."

Walt rose and grabbed a half-empty pitcher of water to wash his mess kit. "It was a fine meal, Sergeant." After washing his kit, Walt turned to the other two officers. "See you later. I have to meet the guys in my platoon."

As George washed his kit, he said, "Captain Yost, that really was the best meal I've had since I left home, and this is the first decent break I've had in weeks."

"Yeah. For a change the food's good and the air's fresh." Yost took a deep breath and lit a cigarette, then sat on the remains of an old rock wall. "Call me Dan. As long as we're bound to live and die together, we can skip the formalities."

George hooked his mess kit to his belt and sat next to Yost. "You expect to die here?"

"Not really. It's a lot better than before. You learn how to survive. Men who've made it through a taste of combat, have a better chance now."

"Yep. A few weeks ago, I was a recruit. Now I'm a seasoned veteran."

Yost watched a smoke ring come from his cigarette. "Another thing. The men aren't as likely to surrender now they know the North Koreans execute prisoners."

George leaned forward and looked over at Yost, realizing more story was to follow.

"You didn't know? When you went back to find Patrick, I looked down the hill and saw four guys on the edge of the road. No rifles or helmets, and they had their hands in the air. The North Koreans had them lie face down on the road, then shot them full of holes. Now, every man in the battalion knows. There are few secrets in combat." He gave George a sidewise glance. "How you doing with Patrick?"

"Fine. And I got a replacement for Tisdale; a tough guy named Murphy."

"You're okay, Martin. Patrick told me how you straightened him out."

"He told you about tossing the radio?"

"I didn't know about that. I'm talking about how you set him straight."

George looked up in the air, then at Yost. "He's a good man. Twice I thought I'd lost him, but each time he was helping other guys make it."

"By the way," Yost said, "when I talked to him, he said you're one helluva soldier."

For a moment the only sound was the kitchen truck pulling out.

One Helluva Soldier / Phil Kline

George ran a hand through his hair. "This stuff was the butt of a lot of the kidding I took as a child, and it still is, occasionally."

Yost pointed at George's hair. "I'll tell you what. Take good care of it. If you get killed, I'll cut it off and glue it to my head."

George laughed. "Then you'll have to take the crap that goes with it."

Yost took a puff from his cigarette. "Why'd you join the army?"

"That was a quick change of subject."

"I expect you could have taken over the farm instead of being here."

"I wouldn't have been able to answer that two weeks ago, but I've thought about it a lot this last week." George stood and walked to the front of the hill to look north, then turned to face Yost. "For two years, I stayed with my grandmother and worked for a farmer named Dave MacMillan. One day we were working on equipment. Snow was whipping across the field, so we took a break behind a shed to have a cup of coffee from his thermos. He said, 'I wish I'd had hot coffee like this during the Battle of the Bulge.' I just looked at him. 'Yep,' he said, 'everybody knew the war was about over, and then the Germans made a drive at us. Surrounded us. No food and little ammunition. It was snowy and cold, with the wind whistling across the snow. The weather was so bad our planes couldn't airdrop supplies. The German commander demanded our surrender. General McNulty sent back the message: Nuts."

Yost smiled. "I remember reading about that."

George pointed at the horizon. "I knew the reason the general could say, 'nuts' to the Germans was because he had soldiers like Dave. That night I pictured fighting alongside him. It seemed more exciting than farming. Next day I asked him why he didn't stay in the army. He said, 'I wouldn't want to be in the army again, but I wouldn't take a million dollars for the experience I had while I was in.' I thought that was a strange thing to say and told him so.

"'The army made a man out of me,' he said. 'I was about your age when I joined, and I thought I knew everything about everything. I learned that I didn't know nothing. The army taught me responsibility. I learned that I wasn't alone. The most important thing I learned was how to be part of a team with other guys and how to earn their respect'."

Yost nodded. "An important lesson."

"Yes, but I kind of forgot what he said until I was in Austin, Texas; no job and only forty dollars in my pocket, standing on a street corner, wondering what to do with my life. A bus stopped in front of me and the door opened. The driver's uniform reminded me of Dave. He jiggled the door and said, 'You getting on?' I asked if he went by the Army Recruiting Station.

"He said, 'Yeah. Get in. I don't have all day.' Within an hour, I was in the army. I guess I joined to earn the respect Dave talked about. How's that for a long answer to a short question?"

"Well," Yost said. "you've earned my respect. You're an important part of my team, and I'm sure you have the respect of every man here who knows you. If your friend, Dave, could see you in action, he'd be proud of you."

"Thank you, Dan."

Yost offered his hand. "Patrick was right. You're one helluva soldier."

George shook his hand. "Thanks. I feel the same about you."

Yost walked to where his other officers sat, leaving George thinking about how he had made the right decision that day in Austin.

One Helluva Soldier / Phil Kline

*

The night was quiet and George slept well. No rain and nobody shot at him. As the sun peeked over the hills, he slid out of his sleeping bag to the rattle of pans, indicating another warm meal was on the way. He had not yet gotten to his feet when a shell hit on the hill.

The impact knocked him a couple of feet to the side. Even with his nose bleeding, he smelled burnt powder. Even though blood ran from his right ear, over the ringing, he heard soldiers scurrying to their foxholes. He crawled to his, dropped in, and picked up his field glasses to look across the front. He didn't see any enemy activity.

The mess truck spun its wheels on its way to safety, and the area got quiet except for an occasional explosion in the distance.

Boom! A round dropped near his position. The sky rained bowling ball sized clumps of sod. George put his arms over his head for protection.

Patrick crawled over to him. "You okay, Lieutenant?"

"I'm fine. See anything out there?"

"No, Sir. I've been looking, but don't see nothing. Probably a mortar."

Soon multiple rounds dropped on the position and mud rained down.

Patrick picked up his glasses and looked to the front. "Damn."

"What?"

"A thousand gooks coming out of the woods."

George verified the sighting and said, "Notify Captain Yost." He called a mission, using variable time fuses. When two rounds burst in front of the North Koreans, he yelled, "Repeat range. Fire for effect."

One Helluva Soldier / Phil Kline

King infantrymen ran past George and fired rifles from the crest. Mortar rounds pounded King Company's position. Through flying dirt and smoke, George watched the VT rounds burst over the Koreans, spraying them with steel. Many went down, but the rest kept coming, giving running fire at K Company men.

Walt and his men double-timed to the front of the hill. Weapons Platoon fired mortars and recoilless rifles into the advancing troops. The Koreans suffered heavy casualties, but continued the attack.

Patrick tapped George on the shoulder and pointed to the sky. "Look."

George saw what appeared to be a private pilot flying over the war zone, a Cesura Bird Dog spotter plane. Then a roar came from the east as three Marine FLU Corsairs swept over the advancing troops and dropped canisters that flip-flopped down.

George forgot about his fire mission as he watched the base of the hill burst into waves of flaming jellied-gasoline. Screams filled the air. He felt the heat as if sitting in front of a fireplace.

NKPA soldiers screamed and dove into the rice paddy. Three more Corsairs flew low and dropped napalm into the paddy, spreading the fire like oil on water. Most of the King Company men quit firing and watched.

The Corsairs returned, their six 50-caliber machine guns leaving a trail of smoke behind inverted gull wings. Then the Bird Dog and the Corsairs left as quickly as they had arrived.

Quiet reigned except for screams in the distance.

Another sound erupted. King Company men stood and cheered, but quit when a Sergeant ran up and said, "Captain Yost is dead."

George walked to the side of the hill and cried. Minutes later his mind was diverted from grief when Walt gave his first order as a company commander. "Counterattack."

One Helluva Soldier / Phil Kline

Walt ran down the hill with three platoons of men following him. George, Patrick, and Murphy joined them.

They came across hundreds of blackened, burned, and still burning North Koreans. George gasped for breath at the stench of burnt gasoline and scorched flesh. He told himself they weren't people but only an enemy. It didn't help; he still got sick to his stomach.

He followed King Company men who ran toward the hills where the enemy attack had started. They encountered no resistance, but halfway up a hill George heard the radioman call to Walt, "Regiment says to fall back. We're ahead of everybody else."

They retreated.

The rains came, and fire from North Korean artillery pounded the men into the night. George didn't get much sleep. He was tired the next morning, but the daylight hours were quiet. He had no targets. The men talked and joked as they ate another hot noon meal, then sweated during a blistering day of rest and relaxation.

That evening, George sat next to his foxhole, thinking how combat had begun to seem like a regular job. It was almost as if killing people before they killed you was a normal way to make a living. His thoughts were interrupted when Patrick approached.

"Something's going on in the village in front of us." Patrick said. "The lead platoon heard noises down there."

Asian voices pierced the quiet at the front of the hill. Rifle fire followed, too close to the platoon to call a fire mission. King Company men ran to the front slope and fired into the dim light. The NKPA bounded into the position with bayonets fixed.

The King Company men didn't have their bayonets on. Order was given to retreat. George and Patrick followed King down the hill with the NKPA close behind. Near the base of the hill, the company set up in the ditch, on the other side of a road, and fired at the enemy. Many went down, but others kept advancing.

King retreated up the next hill and met portions of Love Company coming to assist them. George and his crew joined the two companies in a defensive position. The NKPA was left in the open between the hills, and withdrew under fire. The rest of the night was quiet.

In the morning, George was called to Regimental G-3. When he arrived with his firing team, Major Bane walked from behind a wooden crate that served as a desk. "Taking you off the line a few days, Martin. Understand you were wounded."

"Just a bloody nose from a mortar round."

Bane pointed at Patrick, then at Murphy. "You could both use a couple days rest too. I've arranged for each of you to have a three day pass."

Murphy's head bobbed up and down. Patrick looked at him with a wrinkled brow.

Bane walked back to his makeshift desk. "Lieutenant Martin, there's a cripple waiting for you at the mess tent."

One Helluva Soldier / Phil Kline

11

Dutch Nelson sat on a folding chair, his long legs spread apart and an empty coffee cup dangling from one finger. A black cane, with a brass handle, leaned against his leg. A cook, next to him, stood and saluted Dutch when George walked into the tent. "Nice talking to you, Sir," the cook said, and walked to the kitchen truck.

Dutch turned his attention to George. "Where you been?"

"Here at Regiment, with a few side trips."

Dutch held up his cup. "Watch those side trips. They'll get you."

"Haven't got me yet." George grabbed the cup, filled it with coffee from a dented aluminum pitcher then poured some into his own canteen cup. He gave Dutch the cup of coffee and pointed at the cane. "What's that for?"

"Uh, for show mostly."

"What's the part other than mostly?"

"God, I don't need a wife with you around."

George grabbed the cane. "May I?"

"Sure."

George hobbled around on the cane then handed it to Dutch. "Well?"

"Shrapnel."

George crossed his arms and stared at Dutch.

"All right. All right," Dutch relented. "I'll give you my favorite war story. You know how a bunch of our recruits don't know their ass from a hole in the ground? Of course, I can't blame them too much, there's a lot of senior officers the same way. They don't know shit. Some idiot colonel from Regiment sent us to the top of a hill, near Taejon, to get three tanks a patrol had spotted."

"You know better than that. You can't get tanks with howitzers. And you don't put them on top of a hill."

"Sure, I know that. Everybody knows that." Dutch waved his arms as if he were fighting a fly buzzing around his face. "He told me to do it, so I did it. There was only room for one piece. We towed it up with a three-quarter ton and wiggled it in place by hand. Here's our plan. First we fire an anti-tank round, then another anti-tank round. We follow with white phosphorus and then we pull out. A great plan. The only problem is, it won't work.

"The tankers saw us pull the damned thing up the hill. All of a sudden *kaboom*." Dutch raised his arms. "The howitzer flew seven feet up in the air and bounced down again. I flew backwards." He waved his arms about. "Wow, I'm hurt. I can't breathe. I'm dying. You know the shit that goes through your mind. Sergeant Butler crawled over to me. He picked up half a bayonet. 'Jesus Christ, you're lucky, Lieutenant. The shrapnel cut your bayonet in two. Saved your leg. All you got was fragments.' He helped me down the hill to a medic."

Dutch gestured wildly as he talked. "The medic's taking fragments from my leg. He throws them in a metal tray, *clang, clang, clang*. He scrubs the wounds, pours iodine on them, gives me a shot, and bandages up my leg. I don't feel a thing. He says to Butler, 'You head back to your outfit. He's not going back into action.' They leaned me against a wall. I sat there in a daze." Dutch tilted his head back with his mouth open wide.

"But you went back, right?"

Dutch lowered his head. "Oh, yeah. The medic brought me a pair of crutches and a pistol. .I said, 'What's the pistol for?' He said, 'We're going to get out of here.' I asked him, 'How you going to do that? We're surrounded.' He said, 'I know, but we got a steam engine and a boxcar hooked to it. We're going to load our wounded on it and ride out of here. You want to be evacuated, don't you'?"

Dutch took a long drink of coffee. "Sounded good. I thought about it for a moment. I wasn't hurt that bad. I told him I had to get back to my battery. He said, 'Suit yourself.' I could hear the sound of my battery firing, so I grabbed the crutches and headed off in that direction. I found it just in time to pull out with them."

George leaned toward Dutch. "You said you were surrounded."

"Yeah. We pulled the guns right through downtown Taejon. The town was on fire. Telephone poles down across the road. We had to winch some of them out of the way. Dead MPs lying around. An old sergeant sat behind one of the poles with two dozen bullet holes in him. Big pile of blood. Hundreds of shell casings around him. He'd kept firing at the bastards till they finally got him."

Dutch stopped talking and wiped his eyes with his sleeve. He closed his eyes and took a deep breath, then let it out.

"Right through the center of town we went. Came to a crossroads. A bird colonel stopped us. 'Don't go down that road you're headed down. There's a bunch of tanks waiting for you. Go down that other way.' And he pointed. Then he went back to the door of a building where there were a couple of guys with bazookas. I'm sure one of them was General Dean."

"Dean's missing in action. You knew that."

"I heard that. I guess I was one of the last to see him. Fighting T-34s, him and his staff. They saved my ass. We went the other way. Just like a class B movie. Gooks in the buildings shooting at us. We're shooting back at them. Gooks throwing

One Helluva Soldier / Phil Kline

grenades at us. We're throwing grenades at them. Lost a howitzer and two trucks and a bunch of men. Went down the road for another two miles. Gooks shooting at us all the way. We finally got out. It was a bad day. First men I lost in combat." He closed his eyes, and shook his head. "It was a bad day."

"They let you stay with the battery on crutches?"

"I was the only officer left." He pointed at George. "How you doing?"

"Still alive."

"Still alive's a good sign."

"It hasn't been too bad. A lot of people have it worse."

"You're tough," Dutch said. "Even in OCS you were tough. Like fighting a professional boxer. I've wondered about that ever since. Sometimes I lie awake at night wondering about that. Sometimes when I'm surrounded and being shot at, I wonder about that. Why'd you do that?"

"Why'd I do what?"

Dutch swung a fist at George. "When we had boxing at Fort Riley, why'd you volunteer to fight Hayes? You knew he was a professional. And why volunteer to be his sparring partner?"

George laughed. "Hayes asked me why I volunteered to fight him. Of course, he used more flowery language."

Dutch nodded. "He does that well."

"I told him because he needed a partner. I remember his exact words. 'I won't be your partner. I'll be your fucking opponent'."

"Anyway, I told him, I know. He said, 'Then why'd you raise your fucking hand?' He pointed a finger toward the windows, where a bunch of candidates were watching us talk between the barracks. 'See those guys?' he said to me. 'Some of them will cheer when I beat the shit out of you.' I told him I was used to it.

"He laughed, then he laughed again and shook a finger at me. 'I think you just outsmarted everybody in this whole fucking company,' he said. 'You got guts out the ass. Tell you what I'm going to do. You see, I'm a little queer myself, not the same as you, but a lot of people steer around me.' He clenched his fists as if to hit me and pounded the air in front of his face. 'I need a sparring partner to get ready for the post championship matches. You may get banged around a little, but guys don't beat up their sparring partners.' He said then he pointed a finger toward the men in the windows. 'Not only will those guys see you stand up to me in the ring, but later, when they find out you're my sparring partner, I guarantee you'll never have to worry about taking shit from any of them.'

"We went to the main post gym that night and climbed into the ring. I was apprehensive, but he just had me try to hit him while he evaded my punches. We talked for a while and then he gave me a lesson in boxing. I learned a lot. We eventually got down to serious sparring. I got hit some, but he never hurt me."

"You did well," Dutch said. "I don't mean in sparring. In front of the company. Real early when he knocked you down, the candidates cheered. But when you got up swinging, they cheered just as loud. How many times he knock you down?"

"I don't remember. A few."

Dutch jabbed a finger at George. "But you always got back up."

"Wouldn't you?"

"Yeah, I guess so. Anybody ever make fun of you after that?"

"Not the guys."

"Who?"

"Remember Captain Hinch?"

Dutch doubled up his fists and put his arms up as if to show off his muscle. "Sure. The instructor who lifted weights. Walked like a gorilla."

"That's the guy. He was hoping to see John beat hell out of me."

"You ever have any trouble with him?"

"Not really. After I got my gold bar at graduation, I passed by him on the way back to my place in the ranks. He said, 'I'll make sure you get what you deserve'."

Dutch held his cup up, took a sip, and breathed out audibly. "Did he ever do anything?"

"Naw, and he probably won't. There are thousands of officers in the artillery. I doubt if I ever see him again."

"Hayes lost his post championship match, didn't he?"

"In the semi-finals. He was out in the sleet all day on a tactical exercise. That night when he got in the ring to fight, he was still cold. But enough about me. You still CO?"

"Nope. We got a new captain, so I'm the exec again. I've been FO a couple of times, but I wouldn't choose it for a career."

"How come they use the exec as an FO?"

"FOs were killed. Look, I've got to get back." Dutch picked up his cane. "I wanted to see you and give you the latest. I wish I'd had a chance to see Perry. Last time he stopped to see me, he told me what happened to Lee."

George dumped the rest of his coffee. "Lee's like you. He's coming back, too."

Dutch leaned back. "Hey, what do you think about Trexler?"

"What about him?"

"He's in Korea."

"Last I knew, he was still on Oki. They said he couldn't make it in combat."

"Martin, nobody thought I could either, but I do okay. Anyway, he's here. He bugged personnel till they shipped his ass to Korea. Funny because the captain who kept him on Oki, I think his name was Scarf, well, when Trexler got off the boat at Pusan, there was Scarf on the dock."

"Like me, he looks like a kid, but he's tough."

Dutch nodded. "I believe that. Lots of guys didn't think he'd make it through OCS. I can see him now, wearing his hat right square in the center of his head like a Tenderfoot Boy Scout and giving commands with his voice changing."

"You never know about people. They surprise you, and themselves too."

Dutch cocked his head. "You're talking about you, aren't you?"

"Probably. And about you."

"You're a good man, my friend." Dutch stood and extended his hand.

"Thanks. You, too." They shook hands and saluted each other.

After he turned away, Dutch stopped and hobbled back. He leaned on his cane.

"What's the matter?" George asked.

Dutch looked up in the air and seemed to be searching for words. "Something happened yesterday. I don't know if I should tell you. It scared me as much as anything since I got off the boat. I should tell somebody, so I don't carry it around alone."

"Go ahead."

"We were surrounded again. That's happened more times than I can count. But we always made it back to our lines. We've lost men, and we've lost equipment, but we always had a place to go. Yesterday I looked off to the east. It scared hell out of me." He rubbed sweat from his brow. "It scares me now."

One Helluva Soldier / Phil Kline

Dutch shook a finger at the end of the tent. "There was the ocean. We got no place to go. For two months, we've been backing up. There's no more room. Nobody talks about it. The commanders don't. The men don't. The politicians don't. I'm not predicting doom, but we don't have no place to go from here. Do you know what it means if we get pushed back one more time? Just one more time? Goddamn fucking suicide."

12

George pulled off the clothes he had worn for a week, took a cold shower, and climbed into his sleeping bag, wearing only his underwear. The next morning he put on clean fatigues over better smelling underwear. He ate ham and eggs for breakfast, then caught a ride in a three-quarter ton mail truck.

When he arrived on the outskirts of Pusan, he was surprised to see the city as calm as if it were thousands of miles from a battle zone. He felt like a tourist as he strolled through a quiet part of town full of mud huts with straw roofs that resembled uncombed hair. In the main section of town both the calm and the huts became history. Piles of crates, stacks of 5-gallon gas cans, boxes of food, clothing, ammunition, and a multitude of other items lined the sidewalks in front of concrete buildings.

George backed up against the mountain of supplies and watched thousands of soldiers march toward the front, stirring up clouds of dust. After they passed, another large group came: U.S. Marines.

Dusty MPs, wearing .45 caliber automatics on their hips and carbines over their shoulders, scrutinized him. He wondered why until he realized he and the MPs were the only Americans in sight, other than marching troops.

Adding to what seemed like Dante's Inferno, a hellish clanging from down by the docks grew louder and louder. Soon, tanks and personnel carriers rumbled toward him. The marines gave way, joining George and the MPs, all of them pushing up

One Helluva Soldier / Phil Kline

against the mountains of supplies as tanks bore down on them, creating even dustier dust that reduced visibility to a few feet.

George was pushed up against a little shop that exuded an aroma more potent than the dust. He turned and, through a dusty glass door, saw a Korean with a wrinkled face.

George turned and walked into a tea room that had photographs of families on the walls. The aroma from a counter of baked goods in the middle of the room swept him back to the time he and Luisa visited a bakery in Portland. He changed from happy tourist to lonely soldier.

He sat at a 2x2 table near the window and watched the caravan that resembled a modern mule train traveling through Death Valley. The little man with the wrinkled face came to the table and bowed.

"Tea and cake," George said.

The man nodded and left. Within three minutes, he returned with a crispy white cake on a little plate, and green tea in a cup.

George raised the teacup to his lips and sipped. He felt grit in his mouth. He moistened his handkerchief with tea and wiped grit from his lips, then enjoyed tea and cake in a world apart from the one outside. He jerked his head toward the window when, from the corner of his eye, he saw a tall soldier walk by. "Ross Sitler," he exclaimed under his breath, and jumped up.

George ran outside. When he caught up with the man, he was embarrassed to see it wasn't Ross. "Excuse me," George muttered. "I thought you were somebody else," an apology probably not heard over the noise of equipment going by.

When he returned to the tea room, his mind raced back to Fort Riley, to Ross Sitler, one of the unlikely candidates in Class 9-A. Tall and gangly, with a voice that cracked when he got excited, Ross became an infantry officer. Some of the guys questioned whether a clown in uniform could get respect from men in combat.

One Helluva Soldier / Phil Kline

George finished his tea and cake, and ordered a second serving of both. He looked at the baked goods in the counter and his shoulders sagged with loneliness for Luisa. He recalled the day the two of them had taken a bus from the Lewis and Clark State Park to a bakery in Portland. They didn't tell anyone the sweet rolls they enjoyed were the first food they'd eaten in five days that didn't come from an olive-drab K-Ration box.

George left half of his second cake uneaten, paid the bill, and walked away from the sweet smell, into dust that hung heavy in the air.

He crossed a dozen railroad tracks before arriving at the docks where hundreds of Koreans worked, unloading cargo from fishing boats and troop landing ships, without benefit of forklifts or other heavy equipment. He watched for half an hour then strolled along the ocean front. The further he got from the docks, the stronger the odors of mud flats and sewage.

Walking back into town, George entered a section that seemed oblivious to an enemy bent on destroying it, an enemy that had advanced to within forty miles. The place reminded him of Juarez, Mexico, except the vendors here in Pusan dealt exclusively in black market goods.

Down a side street the scenery changed to rows of wooden houses with straw roofs. They were the size of a two-car garage. As he passed one where two young children stood in the doorway, he became conscious of an odor more obnoxious than the ever-present stench of sewage. He walked, holding his breath as long as he could, but when he breathed again, the odor was still there. He was about to turn back when his preoccupation with the smell disappeared.

A shapely, miniature, teenage girl, in a short black skirt and white silk blouse, came out of a hut and walked next to him. In record time, she had his fly unzipped and her hand inside his shorts. He was a bit shocked, but his penis appreciated what she

One Helluva Soldier / Phil Kline

was doing. For a while he let her continue her exploration, but soon he removed her hand and looked down at her smiling face. "Young lady, you're hustling the wrong man." He zipped up his pants. She stopped in the middle of the street and, with her hands on her hips, stuck out her tongue.

Once the girl was out of sight, the foul odor again became apparent. He decided against braving it and walked down a side street, toward the edge of town. With each block, the stench faded, the houses became smaller and the streets narrower, until it looked like every other Korean village he had seen. Only the children were different.

They were dressed in the same shapeless gray pants and jackets he was accustomed to seeing, and they spoke the same words he didn't understand, but they laughed more, and there was no look of fear in their eyes.

George heard American music. He turned down another side street, and walked between tiny mud huts, until he came to a wooden house with a sign over the door: RESTAURANT. A loudspeaker blasted the voice of Tony Bennett singing *Rags To Riches*.

Inside, he was met by a generously endowed young woman wearing a gossamer white blouse and no bra. She wrapped tiny arms around him and did a belly-rubbing dance with him. "My name Kye Hun. Can call me Kye. What your name, pretty boy?"

"George."

As he danced robot style, he looked around at walls that appeared to be the New York City skyline. They were painted dark and light blue, white, red. American flags decorated a border around the ceiling. Little black tables, and straight-back wooden chairs, lined a dance floor. The aroma of hamburgers and French fries reminded George of an American curb service restaurant, but there were no customers.

One Helluva Soldier / Phil Kline

Dancing with Kye resembled a belly massage. When his arousal became obvious, Kye looked up at him and smiled. He shook his head and stepped away from her. "You have food here?"

"Got chicken; got great steak and fries." She moved her body against his again. "You sure pretty boy."

"You have steak and fries here?"

"Sure, pretty boy. I got everything." She wrapped her arms around his butt, pulled him closer, and rubbed against him. "I can tell you want some."

He pushed her away. "I want two orders of steak and fries."

Kye put her arms back around him, snuggled close, and gazed up at George. "I have good loving, 'specially for you."

He pulled away. "I bet, but steak and fries will do. You have coffee?"

"I have coffee, I have American beer, I have Canada Club whiskey. I have what you want." She reached down and caressed the bulge in his pants.

He shoved her hand away. "You have a telephone here?"

The sultry voice disappeared. "Sorry. Phones not work."

He moved away from Kye and sat at a table. "A cup of coffee and two orders of steak and fries will be fine."

"Yes, Sir." She stuck her chin up and marched through a door behind the bar.

Fifteen minutes later, Kye brought George a platter filled with two steaks and French fries. Without another glance at her, he ate the steaks, almost all the fries, and drank his cup of coffee. After a long sigh, he stood, paid for the meal, and left the restaurant… and the girl in the gossamer blouse who had everything.

*

One Helluva Soldier / Phil Kline

George checked with a Negro transportation company and found a 6x6, going north. He sat next to a driver who dwarfed him, and said. "How long have you been in Korea?"

The driver glanced down at George. "Too long. A month."

George held his nose. "I want to ask about a rotten smell here."

Wrapping his arms around the steering wheel, the man laughed so hard the seat jiggled. "Did you smell it near a Korean house?"

"Yes. It almost made me sick."

The driver slowed to show papers to a guard at the compound gate then turned to face George. "Hey, Man. Don't knock it till you taste it."

George wrinkled up his face. "They eat that stuff?"

"Yes, sir. That's *kimchi*."

"You eat it?"

"Sure. It's slimy and it stinks, but it's not bad tasting."

George leaned back and stared at the driver. "What is it?"

"They take cabbage, radishes, garlic, and spices, and boil 'em. Then they put it in a big crock, and I think they bury it for a week or two, till it gets slimy and stinky."

"I don't think they should ever dig it back up."

"Try it."

"I'd rather go back into combat."

The sound of the diesel took over from conversation during the half-hour drive through hill country north of Pusan.

The driver parked by the side of the road on the edge of a village. "I turn here, but I'll wait until you get a ride north." Minutes later, another 6x6 came along. George flagged it down and was happy to find it was headed right past his battalion. He thanked the driver who ate *kimchi*, and climbed into the 6x6 cab.

One Helluva Soldier / Phil Kline

The night was quiet when George arrived at the battalion. He crawled into his sleeping bag and slept with both hands across his belly as if to protect his two steaks and fries, happy he hadn't ordered *kimchi*. He knew he could sleep as long as he wanted, so it irritated him when a runner woke him at 0800 hours to hand him a note: Call Major Bane at Regimental G-3.

George crawled out of his sleeping bag, used a slit-trench with a toilet seat, and went to the orderly room to call Bane.

"Hate to do this to you," Bane said, "but we need you. Get ready to go on the hill."

"What happened?"

"We used two new second lieutenants to replace you. They were killed by snipers."

"What about Patrick and Murphy?"

"They got Murphy, too. Patrick's okay. He's in the area."

"How'd they get Murphy? He was on pass."

"He volunteered to go on the hill with one of the new FOs... Patrick's found a replacement who's ready to go."

"Thank you, Sir." George was putting the phone away when he realized the major was still talking. He lifted the phone back to his ear. "Lieutenant Perry was wounded yesterday. Sniper shot him in the calf. Hobbled to the medic tent, so I guess he's okay. On the way to Japan. New CO is Harry Jones, little guy with freckles, from Texas, I think."

George walked to the mess tent. Breakfast was over, so he was surprised when a cook asked what he wanted to eat. Five minutes later, the cook set scrambled eggs and bacon in front of him. "Sorry about your buddies," he said.

After the cook returned to the kitchen truck, George picked up a strip of bacon but stopped his hand halfway to his mouth when he wondered who the cook was talking about. *The only buddy of mine he knows is Walt.* Then it dawned on him the cook was talking about the replacements who had been killed when they took his place on the hill. It struck him that he didn't even know their names. *Murphy and those two guys died in my place, while I was playing tourist.* He put the bacon back on his tray and dumped his breakfast in the garbage can.

He filled his canteen cup with coffee and walked to the edge of the area to sip it while looking over the peaceful hills of Korea, hills that fostered instant and violent death.

He stared at clouds reflecting the morning sun, and wondered why he felt he should have died rather than the others. He tossed his coffee out, threw the canteen cup on the ground, and stomped on it until all that remained was a flat piece of aluminum. He picked it up and sailed it as far down the hill as he could, then sat on a rock in silence.

The supply sergeant didn't ask questions when George requisitioned a new canteen cup. He probably understood how an FO could lose things on the hill. From supply, George went to the battery orderly tent and asked for Sergeant Patrick.

Minutes later, Patrick walked in with a young private. "This is Private Gomez," he said. "He's new in the battery and didn't have a job assigned. I think he'll be good. He does everything I ask and accepts training well."

George's irritation at losing Murphy still showed in his voice when he spoke to Gomez. "Did you volunteer for this job?"

"Yes, Sir. It sounds more exciting than being on a gun crew."

"Is that what you're looking for? Excitement?"

Gomez shook his head. "No, Sir. I should have said I'll have more control over what I do here than I would in a gun section."

"Do you know how long we'll be up there on the front line?"

"Yes, Sir. Until we get killed or they call us in."

George leaned forward and stared at Gomez. "Doesn't that bother you?"

"Yes, Sir; it's scary."

"Glad to have you with us. Be ready to go in a half-hour."

"Yes, Sir."

George walked to his area, donned another set of fatigues, and picked up his toiletries, field glasses, M-1, ammo, and grenades. Within a half hour, the three were in a Jeep headed to King Company's position on a partially wooded hill overlooking the Naktong, a peaceful river running through the calm countryside north of Masan. They couldn't see much of the river from their position, just a line of trees that signified water.

After checking in with Lieutenant Jones, George dug his foxhole then ambled to where Jones stood on the back side of the hill, talking to a private.

"Coffee, Martin?" Jones asked.

"Sounds good, if it's black."

Jones set his cup on a rock and said to the private, "Get the lieutenant a cup of black coffee, will you?"

When the private brought George coffee in a metal cup, Jones picked up his, and they walked to the front where they could see the Naktong basin.

George looked toward the river. "I should keep our FO position here so I can see this beautiful scene for the duration."

"If you'd been here yesterday you'd have seen a parade."

George sipped his coffee and looked at Jones over the cup.

Jones took a long drink. "Yesterday General Walker came through here, just a-roaring up the hill, standing, and holding onto a bar above the windshield of his shiny Jeep. He and his staff were gone almost as soon as they got here. Quite a show."

"What was his purpose?"

"I suppose to let the troops know he's a regular feller and right there with them."

George glanced sideways at Jones. "You from Texas?"

"No way. Atlanta. I can't tell where you're from 'cept the Midwest."

"Michigan."

"How come the hillbilly accent?"

"Look up hillbilly in the dictionary. It means a backwoods person. By the way, did you hear General Walker's latest order?"

"Don't think so. What was it?"

"No more retreating. We're to stand, live or die, right here."

Jones nodded. "I didn't hear that, but it had to come sooner or later."

They sipped their coffee then Jones set his cup on a rock next to his foot. "I'm sorry about Captain Yost. I understand you two were close."

George gazed toward the front. "I only knew him for a month. Strange, the affection you can develop for someone so quickly in combat. He was a great soldier, a great soldier."

"I heard that." Jones pointed toward the front. "That there river is now the dividing line between North and South Korea. We're supposed to keep this little corner of the world all to ourselves and not let anybody else join us here."

"Except Marines."

Jones jerked his head toward George. "Yes. When I was in Pusan yesterday, I watched American troops coming this way. They wore Marine uniforms."

"That's good to hear. How many?"

"Maybe two thousand. They had Pershing tanks."

"Great. That's what we need, protection from T-34s."

George picked up his field glasses to check the hills on the other side of the river. "We're getting there."

"See anything?"

"Nothing and nobody."

One Helluva Soldier / Phil Kline

Jones picked up his cup off the rock and tossed the coffee out. "That worries me."

George put his glasses down. "Why do you say that?"

"Those guys always got something going on. They never let it get this quiet."

"What do you think it means?"

"They're going to try and run us over in the morning."

One Helluva Soldier / Phil Kline

13

After a quiet day, artillery and mortar rounds began to pummel the company position, throwing chunks of dirt at the mess truck. The explosions blotted out other sounds, and the acrid odor of burnt powder overpowered the aroma of stew and biscuits. Without a word, the four company officers and George jumped up from the makeshift table, leaving their evening meal behind. Mess personnel covered the food on the chow line and jumped into foxholes.

Patrick and Gomez were in their foxholes at the crest of the hill when George got there. He dropped into his and looked forward, under an overcast sky, but saw no activity. He heard explosions, and flashes lit up the low hanging clouds above Love Company's position. What resembled heat lightening, flashed in the distance. Soon mortar and artillery rounds racked all sides of the hill.

Jones crawled to George's foxhole. "It's safer here than in the company mess."

George shook his head. "I don't see anything out there."

"You're gonna. I got word they're hitting us along the front from Taegu to south of Masan, looking for a weak spot."

George looked toward the river. "They still have to cross the Naktong."

"Yeah. I'm sending a patrol there. I'll let you know what they find."

"How are your men doing?"

One Helluva Soldier / Phil Kline

"Not too bad. Lost a couple, and a few got concussions."

As soon as those words left Jones's mouth, a mortar round hit the other side of him and blew him over the top of George's foxhole.

The air was heavy with the odor of burnt powder. Dirt rained down. George climbed out of his hole and crawled to where Jones lay face down. He didn't see any wounds. He turned Jones over and saw his eyes were wide open.

Jones shuddered. "That son-of-a-bitch," he growled.

"I thought you were dead."

Jones shook his head like a dog shaking off water. "I thought I was, too. Last time I'll visit you." Jones crawled away. "That son-of-a-bitch."

George yelled to Patrick standing next to where Jones landed. "You guys okay?"

"Just hit with dirt," Patrick said.

The barrage ended. George searched the front but saw nothing in the fading light. "Damn, I wish we had star shells."

One of the platoon leaders approached George. He pointed to the front. "Something's going on down there. Our patrol said people are in the river, but nobody's crossing."

George called on the radio, "Fire mission. Enemy troops in river. From checkpoint, left one hundred, add three hundred." As soon as the rounds hit that side of the river, he yelled, "Add five zero. Fire for effect."

A barrage of 155mm rounds roared in. Afterward, George added the platoon leader's observations to his report to FDC then yelled to Patrick. "Take over. I'm going to S-2."

He trotted down the hill, found the S-2 tent, and told Lieutenant Porter what the patrol reported and about his fire mission.

Porter called a runner. "Get Lieutenant Rayford here double-time."

One Helluva Soldier / Phil Kline

Minutes later, Reed Rayford strolled in. He sat in front of Porter, lit a cigarette, and propped his combat boots on the corner of Porter's field desk.

"Rayford, I want you to do something."

"What?"

"I want you to take your goddamn feet off my desk."

"That's not a desk. It's more like an egg crate."

Porter jabbed a finger at Reed. "Off."

Reed scraped dried mud from his boots onto the desk then moved them to the ground. "Why am I here? Another shitty job of collecting intelligence for you, I bet."

Porter flipped the mud off his desk with the back of his hand. "I want you to lead a patrol down to the river."

"Why? What's going on?"

"That's what I want you to find out. Martin says something's happening there."

Reed pointed his thumb at himself. "How come it's always me?"

"They call the guys you use for patrols the suicide squad, that's why. It so happens that you, and that group of misfits who run with you, do a better job of intelligence gathering than anyone else. Is that what you want to hear?"

Reed picked a piece of mud off the top boot from his crossed legs and placed it on the desk. "They're not misfits. They just think it's boring to get killed the regular way."

Porter flipped the piece of mud to the ground. "Go. Now. The captain needs to know so he can make some decisions."

"Hah." Reed stood, turned, and walked out. As he reached the tent fly, he lifted his left leg and farted. Porter shook his head and waved a hand back and forth in front of his face.

George hid a snicker. He left and walked toward the position where Patrick lay looking at the river through binoculars.

Patrick glanced up. "They're building rafts in the middle of the river."

Fifteen minutes later, Reed returned from the patrol and compared notes with George at the FO position.

"Come to S-2 with me," Reed said.

They walked to Porter's tent, and sat in the same chairs they occupied earlier, but this time Reed kept his feet on the ground. "Martin and I have the information," he said to Porter.

Porter crossed his arms and stared at Reed. "What's going on?"

"They're building bridges under the water, an old Russian trick."

Porter picked up a field phone and rang for Captain Scarf. Four minutes later, Scarf entered the tent. "What's this about?"

Porter pointed at Reed. "He says the gooks are building low-water bridges by laying logs in the river."

"He's crazy. They'd float away."

"I don't know how they keep them there, but they do."

"If they can walk out that far, why would they need a bridge?"

Porter walked around his egg crate. "Maybe they're going to run tanks across on them."

"Were you there?"

"No, but Rayford was."

Scarf glared at Reed. "Go back to your company, Rayford."

Reed ceremoniously lifted his left leg as he walked out.

Scarf pointed at George. "Why's he here?"

"He notified us first and then confirmed Rayford's report."

Scarf shook his head without looking at George. "I should have guessed." He waved his arm in a get-out-of-here gesture.

George tried to fart but couldn't, so he just walked out.

The information gained about the bridges was not relayed to anyone that night. The next morning, the reason for the activity became common knowledge when Regiment notified all their units that eight T-34 tanks, followed by at least one battalion of enemy troops, had crossed the river and were going around the hills where the 35th was dug in.

The North Korea People's Army had crossed the last line of defense of the Pusan Perimeter.

The 35th consolidated their position to defend all sides. George fired 155mm shells on the river, but lost the use of his battery when it was called on to hit targets someone considered to be of more importance. He was irritated that he hadn't dulled the attack by firing more artillery the night before.

Additional troops crossed the river during daylight hours, attacked King Company, and drove them down the back side of the hill.

Halfway down, Jones stopped, raised his rifle in the air, and yelled, "Fix bayonets. Follow me and give 'em the rebel yell." He ran up the hill yelling, "Hi, hi, hi." His men yelled and followed him, and the FO team joined them.

The North Koreans retreated down the side they had come up, with King Company men shooting at them. King's men fired their rifles into the air, and cheered before going back to their foxholes to defend against a counterattack. There was none.

King Company was relieved from the line and sent into reserve. George and his crew were relieved from the hill, too.

When he reached the reserve area, George was handed a letter from his mom, and four from Luisa who wrote of her love for him and how she missed him. She said their baby, Mario, was crawling and that he was beautiful. She asked when George would come home. On the last page of one letter, she wrote: *I married you to live normal life. I am cold without you. Come back so we can have normal life.*

George wrote back that afternoon: *I will love you forever, and before long, I should be with you to keep you warm. They*

One Helluva Soldier / Phil Kline

say the war will be over by Christmas. I hope so, then I'll stay with you forever, and we'll all lead normal lives.
Yo te amo ati,
George

    That evening, George leaned against a tree, as he might on a Sunday in the park, and relived memories of the time in Oregon when they frolicked in the moonlight at Sandy River, walked in the rain, and lived on meat and beans from five year old K-Rations.

    Tears rushed to his eyes and rolled down his cheeks. His mind jumped to the bayonet charge, and how he liked having been an infantryman for the day. *Not as dangerous as being a Forward Observer, but definitely more exciting.* He shook his head in disbelief at the thought.

    That night, from his sleeping bag, George looked up at the stars and thought about Luisa's letter. He realized that, for the past two months of combat, his sex drive had been dismantled except for brief moments with the two prostitutes in Pusan, but Luisa's probably wasn't. He was frustrated, not being able to see her or curl up against her. He came to the conclusion that, although he couldn't be there to love her, the feeling he had from being loved was ever-present.

    His thoughts switched to his need to be a soldier. He figured his personal life had to take a back seat to keeping Americans alive. Even staying alive himself was not a number one priority. Duty was first. He thought of the day he had run toward the enemy, to retrieve the radio Patrick had thrown away. *It never entered my mind not to do so. During the bayonet charge, I had no thoughts except that I was doing what I was supposed to do, and I was excited about it. Perhaps I'm strange, but I really am one hell of a soldier.*

One Helluva Soldier / Phil Kline

14

For three weeks George fought in the Battle of Pusan Perimeter with the Americans backed into a little corner of South Korea. Often, when not fighting for his life, he thought of Luisa and Mario. He wrote to her every couple of days, when he had a lull, and she wrote to him, sometimes in broken English and occasionally in Spanish. He found a military Spanish-English dictionary to help him understand her letters, but keeping a dialog going by mail was difficult. Letter delivery took a week, at best.

For the same three weeks, he had no opportunity to take a shower but washed using his helmet as a sink or, when possible, by skinny-dipping in a stream. Near the middle of September, his clothes were soiled enough to stand by themselves. He laughed. *If I take them off, they may walk by themselves and take over my job.* He developed an itch on his stomach and a circle of bumps that resembled insect bites.

A medic inspected the bumps. "Ringworm. Bathe more often."

On 14 September, just before midnight, a platoon leader who reminded George of a carnival's tallest man in the world, came to the FO position and looked down at him. "Something's going on at the base of the hill that sounds like pots and pans being rattled," the tall man said.

George and Patrick followed the lieutenant part way down the hill. They listened and agreed it sounded like pots and pans being rattled. George picked up the microphone and called a fire mission. After the mission was complete, he gave FDC his report.

"What did you hit?" the operator asked.

"I don't know what I hit. I fired at a noise and it stopped."

"I have to keep a record of the results of every fire mission. I have to know what you hit."

"I told you, I don't know."

A different voice came over the air. "Lieutenant Martin, this is Major Bell. We are low on ammunition and are particular about what we fire on. We must complete a report on every fire mission. What did you shoot at, and what did you hit?"

George paused then remembered what Al Brister, another Class 9-A FO, said when he got the same type of request for information. He repeated Al's words as well as he remembered them. "I shot at an old lady feeding a dog from a dish. I broke the dish, hit the old lady in the leg, and killed the dog."

A harsh voice came back. "Report to me at 0800 hours tomorrow."

"Yes, Sir. You gonna fire me? Gonna give me a lousy job?"

George didn't get an answer. He released Patrick to return to his position, and walked up the hill with the lieutenant. "Thanks," George said. "You done good."

"You're welcome. Oh, by the way, I came over with a lieutenant who looked like a kid."

"More than we do?"

"He said he knew you."

George's face shone. "Trexler."

"I think so. Anyway, yesterday he took two 30 caliber rounds. They went in his side and out his back."

"Is he still alive?"

"He was when they took him away. He already had a

shrapnel wound next to his eye when he led his platoon on a counterattack. They attained their objective, but the other platoons didn't, so the CO called for them to vacate. As I heard it, he told his sergeant to take the platoon down the hill while he stayed to give covering-fire. After the platoon left, a North Korean poked his head out of a hole and shot him with a burp-gun. He shot the Korean and killed him."

"How'd he get down the hill?"

"He walked."

"He walked?"

"Even then, he wanted to stay."

"Sounds like Trexler."

"He lost a lot of blood. You know, where a bullet goes in the puncture's small, but when it comes out, it makes a hole the size of a golf ball."

"God, I hope he makes it. He's just a kid."

The lieutenant pointed to George, then himself. "Like us."

"But we're still alive."

"Yeah, but someday we're going to have to cross the river, and we'll be sitting ducks, with no place to hide."

15

Early in the morning, 15 September 1950, Lieutenant Jones was called to the phone during a meeting of his officers and platoon sergeants. George watched Jones' lips spread into a smile. He watched his head bob up and down, like a toy dog in the rear window of a car.

Jones stuck the phone back in the carrier, raised his fist in the air, and shouted, "Yahoo. General MacArthur has completed an amphibious assault at Inchon, west of Seoul. Every unit in the perimeter has orders to attack tomorrow. The 8th Army Headquarters expects all resistance to end. We kick off at dawn tomorrow and head north."

A second lieutenant raised his hand. "How do we get across the river?"

"Who cares? We'll swim if we have to."

A tough looking old sergeant raised a hand as if he were in school. "From my experience in Europe, every time we got to a river, the engineers had boats waiting for us."

Jones pointed at the sergeant. "He's right. All we have to worry about are the two miles to get to the river."

*

At 0500 hours, George fired missions at suspected NKPA concentrations. Then he, Patrick, and Gomez advanced along a levee between rice paddies, with Jones and the 3rd Platoon leader. The company men followed in single file. George wished he could change clothes after a mortar round plopped to his right and soaked him with raw sewage.

The men crouched down to continue advancing. A round hit near the middle of the company, knocking three men down, then another round came in, then four more, sending another dozen men down into the nasty water of the paddy. Six of them never got back up.

Jones signaled the platoons to spread out. They did so, but heavy mortar fire still took its toll. Artillery joined in with deadly accuracy, and more men were knocked into the water.

George called to Patrick, "Get us some artillery."

Patrick talked to FDC then yelled to George over the din of exploding rounds, "They say they have more important missions."

"Get us some air," Jones yelled.

George spread his arms in a gesture of frustration. "I tried. Can't get any."

"We need help." Jones turned to his men. "Retreat. Pick up wounded on the way back."

They sloshed back through the paddies looking for wounded. The mortars kept firing.

Jones yelled, "Double-time back to the hills."

The sun beat down on them. More men were hit. George and his crew wandered the paddy looking for wounded. They found only six men alive.

The next day the company continued their advance to the river. As they crossed the paddies, Marine F4U Corsairs arrived and dropped napalm on the hill to their front. When he got to the hill with the lead platoon, George saw dozens of North Korean soldiers lying along the slope, charred black. Others wore uniforms untouched by fire, but with faces contorted from breathing in flaming gasoline. Survivors scurried toward the river with Corsairs strafing them. They didn't resemble real people but more like doll cut-outs in a booth at the fair, flipping over when someone scored a hit.

George felt neither elation nor sorrow. *I've become hardened to war and to killing people.*

As he crossed the flood plain beyond the hill, he watched enemy soldiers swim across the river without clothes or weapons. K Company men picked them off the way poachers shoot swimming ducks. Again he felt no emotion.

Jones approached him. "I'm going to take a squad and search for wounded from the first and second platoons. I'd like you to lead another squad to see who you can find from third platoon."

George walked through a paddy, his boots giving off sucking, splashing noises as he and eight men searched for bodies wearing American uniforms. He waded to a soldier lying face down in a circle of red water. When he turned the body over, he stared into open eyes of the lieutenant who had told him about Trexler. He groaned then yelled into cupped hands, "Help!"

Two men from the squad came and took the body to dry ground. They were so matter of fact, it seemed to George they didn't care that the dead body had been a live person only hours before. He sat in water up to his chest and wiped away tears.

Smelling of human feces, he walked between more dead, dripping water from his uniform, which had taken on a red tint from bloody water. He saw one of the platoon sergeants straining to hold his face above red water. The sergeant tried to talk, but sound didn't come.

George crawled around to hold the man's head out of the water. The sergeant resembled an animal that didn't understand why it was hurting. George called a nearby squad leader to help, and together they lifted the sergeant and carried him to solid ground with his intestines hanging out.

One Helluva Soldier / Phil Kline

"He was in the infected water," George said to the two medics who placed the sergeant on a stretcher. One of them poured liquid over the intestines and shoved them into the stomach cavity before they carried him away.

George walked further into the rice paddy without finding any other men. He was about to quit when he heard moaning coming from behind a fallen pine. He rushed through the water, onto dry land.

A young private lay pinned beneath the tree, but didn't seem to have a battle wound. It looked like the tree had broken his collar bone or his shoulder when it fell on him, and one leg was bent at a wrong angle.

George couldn't lift the tree alone. He called for help.

Two men came then George and one of the men lifted the tree while the other slid the private from under it. The kid's screams pierced the quiet. The two men left but promised to send a medic, while George sat next to wounded soldier and held his hand.

The screams stopped, and the young man raised his head. His voice was weak. "Am I going to be able to walk?"

"You will but not today. Lie still and we'll get you fixed up. How old are you?"

George barely heard the answer. "Sixteen."

The medics carried the youngster away with no display of emotion. George watched then felt the pressure of diarrhea. He ran into the paddy and relieved himself. As he did, he watched medics work. He envied them for being able to do so without shouldering the emotional load of the men they helped.

*

That evening, a mess truck pulled into the company's new position to serve a meal. George looked at the roast beef, oven-browned potatoes, and apple pie, but decided he wasn't hungry.

One Helluva Soldier / Phil Kline

Instead of eating, he filled his helmet with water from a tank truck and took a bath. The river was quiet.

Afterward, feeling certain there would be no attack, he took his combat boots off before climbing into his sleeping bag.

George was awakened by someone he hadn't seen before.

"Sir, I'm Sergeant Prentice," the man said. "I took over for Sergeant Munn. He was killed yesterday. Minutes ago, we spotted activity in the village across the river between our flank and Love Company. It looks like a staging area for some kind of operation. Can you check it out?"

"I'll take a look." George picked up his binoculars and observed North Korean soldiers going in and out of houses in the village. He grabbed the radio mike. "Fire mission. Enemy staging area in a village across the river."

A voice came back from FDC. "We can't fire into a village."

"They're using it as a staging area."

"Sorry, Lieutenant. Ww're no longer allowed to shoot into villages on orders from Far East Command."

"Let me talk to your officer in charge."

After a moment of silence: "This is Major Bolton."

"I called a fire mission on a concentration of North Koreans in a village across the river, and the operator told me we can't fire on them."

"That's right, Lieutenant. It's stupid, but Washington says some of our allies were upset by us shooting up villages, so FECOM says we can't do it."

George waved toward Prentice. "Give that information to Lieutenant Jones." Then he spoke into the mike. "I never heard anything so stupid. We're going to be crossing the river, and they'll pick us off in the water."

"I understand, Lieutenant. Nothing we can do about it. Didn't you get that message? Same time you got the beer order."

"The what?"

"You didn't get that either? Check with your radio operator and see what he's doing with messages."

"Roger. Wilco." He looked around for Patrick, but didn't see him. He picked up the mike again. "What's a beer order?"

"Actually it's a no beer order. No beer even when we're back for a rest."

"You're kidding."

"Some church groups feel it's sinful to issue alcohol to men who aren't twenty-one."

"You're kidding me."

"Just wait until next time you're off the hill. I hear you're just twenty."

"Well, I'm twenty-one."

"Happy birthday, Lieutenant. Out."

George hooked up the mike, stood, and kicked the radio over. He walked to the eastern side of the hill and looked in the direction of a distant Washington D.C. "You idiots. You goddamn idiots." He looked up at the sky. "Excuse me. I didn't mean to use your name in vain." He looked east again. "You fucking idiots."

George heard the company radioman relay a regimental message to Jones. "The west side of the river has been vacated. We're to cross when ready."

Within an hour, George and his crew walked down the hill, with Jones at the head of K Company. Trucks were unloading wooden assault boats.

"I'm glad to see those," Jones said. "I would have caught--"

A mortar round hit in the water, near the trucks then another and another. The soldiers finished unloading boats, left them lying on the bank, and drove up a road between the hills. Jones ran toward the riverbank, waving to his men. "Get those boats in the water."

One Helluva Soldier / Phil Kline

The K Company men hugged the ground as they pulled the boats to the river. George, Patrick, and Gomez were kneeling, waiting to get in a boat, when the company radioman yelled, "Battalion says it's a trap. Pull back."

Jones waved his men away from the boats and the exploding mortar rounds. After the company retreated, and the mortar barrage quit, Jones called his platoon leaders together.

"Crossing is postponed until dark," he said. "Take advantage of the quiet and give your men a rest."

George had no problem sleeping when the only sounds of battle were distant explosions. He had a warm dinner with the company and was shooting the bull with K Company men when the first sergeant stopped by to check their gear. He approached George. "Lieutenant Jones requests you ride with him."

*

At dusk the company assembled in the woods on the front side of a hill overlooking the Naktong. The night was quiet, and there didn't appear to be activity on the other side of the river.

George, his two men, Jones, and ten others climbed into a boat that sported large cracks but didn't leak. Two men pushed the boat into the current and hopped in. After that, the only sounds George heard were the whisper of the boat breaking water and a grunting from one of the men polling it into the river.

Quiet spread over the water until they were a third of the way across. With a quarter of a mile to go, the *pop-pop* of small arms, and *rat-tat-tat* of machine guns came from the other side. Splashes indicated the enemy knew the Americans were in boats.

One Helluva Soldier / Phil Kline

George watched the flashes of weapons and wished he was on dry land. He whispered a fire mission to Patrick, who used a low voice to call an artillery barrage on gun flashes.

Soon, King company's 60mm mortars went *whoomp*, and rounds from their machine guns made cracking sounds as they passed over the boats.

Nearly across the river, George was thrown down, and to the back of the boat, until he came to rest on the bottom. Water gushed over him, and everything went dark. His mind didn't work well.

Gomez's voice: "Lieutenant's been hit."

Voice unknown. "Where?"

"I can't tell."

Someone else had been hit, and the boat was taking water. Jones splashed into the water. "Follow me."

The infantry evacuated.

Patrick tapped Gomez on the shoulder. "I have to go. Wrap your shirt around the lieutenant. Get him on another boat and back across the river right now, and keep that shirt tight on his wound. He got hit by something big. Find a medic."

Patrick slid out of the boat and grabbed the side. "Goodbye, Lieutenant. If you come back, bring me a bottle of scotch. I prefer Chivas." Then he was gone.

Gomez yelled in whispers, "We need a ride. Lieutenant needs a medic. Take it easy; the other two're dead, but the lieutenant's alive. Careful."

Two men lifted George and carried him to another boat, then poled it into the current. Someone said, "Sit him up so he won't bleed to death."

As the boat slipped through the water, Gomez struggled to get George into a sitting position, then sat behind him and propped him up. At the same time, he compressed his shirt over the wound.

One Helluva Soldier / Phil Kline

Near the shore, one of the men called out, "We have a wounded man who needs a medic."

"We got to get to the other side," someone shouted from the shore.

Gomez shouted back, "Nobody's going anywhere in this goddamn boat till you get a medic for my Lieutenant. There's two dead men here, too."

"Okay, okay. Stevens, find a medic for that asshole. Meyers and Eckert, get those dead soldiers out of there."

Someone said, "Help me. He's unconscious." Two men lifted George onto the mud flat.

"Where's the medic?" Gomez shouted. He lifted George up to a sitting position then sat behind him, holding the compress on his shoulder. "We'll get you to safety. You'll be all right."

Two men came and put George on a stretcher, then carried him to an ambulance. "I'm going with him," Gomez said.

"There's no room for you."

An hour after being hit, George sensed a bright light through his closed eyes. *I'm in Heaven, and it smells like Listerine.*

He lay on an operating table in a MASH with the type of wound many soldiers envied, one that meant no more Korea. The surgeon stopped the bleeding from a severed artery, but didn't sew up the wound. Someone gave him plasma and pain medicine, put a compress on the shoulder, and immobilized it.

George went into his dream state to the sound of a loud whirring noise, accompanied by a whirlwind.

Then all sound ended.

16

George lay dozing in a bed on the seventh floor of Tokyo General Hospital. A cast covered his right shoulder. He became alert when, through white curtain dividers, he heard a familiar voice say, "Can he leave the hospital?"

A medic pulled the curtain from around the bed and said, "As long as it's not overnight... Lieutenant Martin, there's a Lieutenant Lee here to see you."

Next to the medic, who was holding his nose, stood Henry Lee wearing dirty fatigues and carrying a carbine.

George smiled. "Henry, what are you doing here?"

Henry walked to the foot of the bed. "You sound great. I thought you'd be weak."

"I'm in the artillery. We're all like this. What are you doing here?"

"I came all the way over here just to see you, ground-gripper."

George pointed at Henry with his left hand. "How come you're dressed like you're headed into combat?"

"Excuse me," Henry said, as he laid the carbine on the foot of George's bed. "Technically, I am. I'm an L-19 observer. We were flying to Taegu, and it was socked in, so the pilot headed over here." Henry shook his head. "Strange. Korea seems to be at the end of the world, but in reality, it's only an hour from civilization."

One Helluva Soldier / Phil Kline

George sat up and grimaced, as he pointed his right hand toward a steel chair next to the bed. "Had to go back to war, didn't you?"

Henry sat in the chair. "Oh, this feels good."

"How's the hip?"

"Surgeon said I should get an easier job. How's your shoulder?"

"Fine. Just scraped the clavicle and cut a couple arteries. They tried something new—put the arteries back together. Do you know if Trexler's here?"

Henry nodded. "Yeah, but no visitors."

"What do you hear from the other guys?"

"Saw Hayes, saw Dutch. Hayes was shot twice, but he's okay. And I saw Sitler. Hear about him?"

"No. I thought I saw him in Pusan, but it wasn't him."

Henry slid the carbine aside and got up to sit on the edge of the bed. "He got the Distinguished Service Cross. Went after a couple of wounded who were lying on a hill his platoon had vacated. Some gooks with a mortar played the game of hit the running soldier, but Sitler kept going. Carried one man to safety with rounds chasing him, then went back and brought another out. They finally dropped him when he was on his way to help still another of his men. Two guys went to get him. He waved them off, said, 'Get that guy first.' They did, then came back and brought Ross out. Broken back. He'll never walk again."

"He had command of Audie Murphy's old platoon, didn't he?"

Henry nodded then stared at the window next to George's bed. "Fassett, Hopkins, Kamps, Watson, Wilkerson, all dead."

George shook his head in slow motion. "I saw Hayes."

Henry chuckled. "Quite a guy—thinks he's Patton. You remember Captain Hinch?"

George felt as if his heart skipped a beat.

"I saw him," Henry said. "He's with the Forty-seventh Field. Keeps himself in really good shape. Hey, let's head to the Embassy Club for a drink."

"What did you say?"

Henry stood. "Let's go to the British Embassy Club and have a drink." He sat on the bed again. "I just remembered I have a problem. I was in the Officers Club a while ago, and they threw me out. They may not want me at the Embassy, either."

George had begun to get out of bed, but stopped with his legs hanging over the edge.

Henry patted the carbine. "They didn't like this thing. And I haven't changed clothes for a week."

"I never would've guessed."

"Remember, I'm still in combat. There was a dance going on. Everyone was decked out pretty-like, and they looked at me as if to say, 'What do you think you're doing here dressed like that?' Good thing they didn't know I had live grenades in my pockets."

"Where are the grenades now?"

Henry stood and patted his pants pockets. "Right here."

"You have live grenades with you?"

"What do you expect me to do? Check them at the front desk? Anyway, they're all right as long as people can't see them."

"Take those clothes off and wear something of mine."

Henry laughed. "Hell, man, I'm six inches taller than you. I'd look like a clown."

"You want a drink?"

"Yeah."

George pointed to a dresser. "Second drawer, Emmett."

Henry took off his shirt and pants. The pants hit the floor with a thud and a grenade rolled out, dragging a blue bandanna with it. Henry picked up the bandanna and wrapped it around his neck. He assumed an heroic pose. "How do you like it?"

"Where'd you get that?"

"Sears."

"How do you order from Sears when you're in combat?"

Henry removed the scarf and pulled a pair of George's pants from the drawer. "We were in reserve."

After Henry got into the pants, George slid to the edge of the bed. "You look better now. I still detect an odor, but I can stand you."

Henry set three grenades on the floor.

George glanced down at them. "Hide 'em."

Henry poked his grenades in his dirty pants pockets and slid the pants under the bed. He removed the magazine, checked to make sure there was no round in the chamber then stuck the carbine and magazine under the covers. He turned toward George. "Something I have to ask you."

"Yeah?"

"When I got shot, it was the worst thing I ever felt in my life. What about you?"

"I didn't feel anything."

Henry peered at George with his eyes half-closed. "Fuck you, Martin."

George hobbled, and Henry limped down the hall. On the elevator they joined an older man and two women dressed as if they should be in a chorus line. The wounded men said nothing until the man and two women got off at the second floor.

George stared at the elevator door after it closed. "That was Bob Hope, wasn't it?"

"Yes, it was."

"Why didn't you say something to him?"

"Like what?"

George followed Henry out of the elevator at the ground floor. "I don't know. Anything."

"Why didn't you?"

"I didn't want him to know I hobnob with a clown."

Henry shook his head. "That was funny. Nobody said anything."

The two friends walked through the cool night air, down a dark street, and around a corner to the British Embassy Club where they were led to a table by a young woman who smiled a Japanese smile and spoke with a British accent.

When their waitress came, Henry said, "I'll have an ale."

George nodded. "The same."

"You drink?"

"Yes, Dad."

"Oh. That's right. Happy birthday."

When he got his ale, Henry closed his eyes, sniffed the brew, and set it down. "Let's drink to our comrades who didn't make it." They held their glasses high. "To our fallen comrades." After the toast Henry was quiet for a moment then said, "What do you think about Trexler?"

"I think he's a great soldier. Why?"

Henry took a drink. "He didn't go to Korea with the Twenty-ninth. The S-3 said he couldn't make it as a combat leader, and here he is inspiring us."

"I think we all feel the same about him."

Henry nodded. "You're kind of inspiring, too. I'm an FO, but I'm safe in the air. It's nothing compared to doing it on the ground like you do."

"Thank you." George took a drink, set the glass down, and stared at Henry.

"What?" Henry said.

"You know I stood before a Board of Officers at Bliss."

"I heard that."

George glanced at the ceiling, then back at Henry. "I may as well tell you about it. Somebody in the group should know what happened. It really was fairly innocent. I was fixing up an apartment in El Paso, getting it ready for Luisa to join me. I was tired and went to a Chinese place, China Night Café, it was called. I just wanted some Chinese food. Four enlisted men were drinking beer and having a good time. I thought it would be fun to join them."

"Did you?"

George shook his head. "No. But a month later I went back, and they were there again. I drank with them and got home late. Luisa wasn't happy. Caused our first argument."

"How'd that get you in front of a board?"

"Criminal Investigation Division had the men staked out, trying to get enough evidence to bust them out of the army for being homosexual."

"Were they?"

"I'm sure they were."

"But all you did was sit with them."

"Yes."

"Does Luisa know about that?"

George closed his eyes and nodded. "She knows everything about me."

"Does she know you're in the hospital?"

"I haven't heard from her since I've been here. She doesn't have a phone, so I can't call. I've written, but as you know, it takes two weeks to get an answer."

"You've moved around so much, it's a miracle she's kept up with you at all. By the way, how'd you end up with Task Force Smith in the first place?"

George picked up his glass and held it as he spoke. "Captain Scarf, the same guy who refused to send Trexler to Korea, sent me there to get rid of me, probably after seeing the record of the Board of Officers in my 2-0-1 file."

Henry glanced at George, then at his glass. He slid his fingers up and down on it, wiping off condensation. He looked up at George again. "I realize it's none of my business, but back in the room when I mentioned Captain Hinch, you turned white."

"I didn't know it was obvious."

"I knew Hinch didn't like you in OCS. He was vocal about it."

George took a long drink. "He threatened to follow me and get me someday."

"He hasn't caused you any problems, has he?"

"No, and I expect he's forgotten I even exist."

Henry met George's eyes squarely. "I feel honored just knowing you, and I'm sure just about everyone else who comes in contact with you feels the same way. Don't let that one asshole get to you."

"I've dealt with Hinches all my life, kids in school, the principal, even my father."

"Your father?"

"Yeah. He never came right out and said anything to me, but it was there. The last time I saw him I was sixteen. I came home with a black eye. I'd had a fight with some kid who called me a cotton-headed fairy. Dad couldn't deal with hearing his son was queer. He and Mom argued. He wanted me gone, and she said, 'No.' They compromised. I was sent to live with my Grandma Kate. I stayed there, five miles from home, until I joined the army."

"You joined to get away?"

"Actually, no. I worked as a hired hand for a World War II veteran while at Grandma's. He told me he earned respect in the army by being part of a team, and respect's what I wanted."

Henry raised a hand toward their waitress. "Another round, please." He turned back to George. "Excuse me. So you joined."

"Not right then. A couple months later I turned eighteen and Grandma kicked me out of her house. She didn't tell me to go. She left a birthday card outside my door with thirty dollars in it and a suitcase next to it."

Henry shook his head.

"It was time. I went to Austin, Texas and got a job as a busboy. My meals were free and I earned money."

"What prompted you to join?"

"The guy who hired me wanted me to be more than just a busboy. I left without taking my pay. No job; no money; Army, here I come."

"You did the right thing. The Army needs officers of your caliber. Walt always used a phrase for people he respected: 'I'd have you on my flank anytime'. That's the way I feel about you."

Henry reached out and shook George's hand. They emptied their glasses in silence. Henry paid the tab, and they left the club.

Outside the hospital front door, George stopped. "I know I'm different, but somebody once told me we're all different one way or another."

Henry walked around in front of George and glared at him. "What makes you so different that you didn't feel anything when you got hit?"

George laughed so hard he thought his shoulder might hemorrhage.

Henry shrugged, grunted, and they marched inside.

As soon as they entered George's room, Henry pulled his carbine and magazine from under the bed covers. "I have to go. Pilot's probably wondering where I am."

One Helluva Soldier / Phil Kline

He whistled the Field Artillery song as he removed the clothes he wore, then grabbed his own, clutching the pockets so the grenades didn't drop out. He held up George's khakis. "What'll I do with these?"

George waved his good left hand. "Burn 'em."

Henry laid them on the foot of the bed, then grabbed George's left hand. He didn't shake it, but just held it for a moment. "Adios." He hobbled toward the door, then turned and waved once more before leaving the room.

George tossed the clothes Henry had worn into a far corner. He brushed the dirt out of his bed, undressed, climbed in, and nodded off before his head reached the pillow. His last thoughts before sleep were: *He doesn't just accept me. He looks up to me.*

17

Early the next morning, George pulled a cord and, within three minutes, a tall, thin nurse appeared at the door. He winked at her.

"Hi, beautiful."

She peered at him through half-closed eyes. "Okay, what do you want?"

"My brother Tommy. He's in the hospital, and they say he's not to have visitors. Can I sneak in his room and see him? I won't wake him if he's asleep. If he's awake, I want to whisper to him that I'm taking my nurse to dinner at the Embassy Club."

"What room's he in?"

"That's what I want to know."

"What time?"

"What's best for you? By the way, he uses an assumed name. Trexler."

She pointed at the door. "Nineteen hundred hours, I'll be at the front door of nurses' quarters. You know where that is?"

"I will by then."

George's backless hospital gown waved in the breeze as he closed the door to Tommy Trexler's room.

Tommy resembled a mummy, lying in a high bed with bandages wrapped around much of his body. He turned his eyes toward George. "Good evening. I'd have gone to see you, but they won't let me out."

George walked toward the bed. "How you doing?"

"Sore."

George inspected Tommy's bandages and said, "I hear you took two rounds right through you."

"That's what they say."

"So, what's the prognosis?"

"Nothing permanent. Does Luisa know you're hospitalized?"

"I've written, but haven't heard back yet, so I don't know."

"Takes a while, doesn't it?"

"To tell you the truth, I wasn't in a hurry to let her know I was wounded. She was unhappy enough just with me being in Korea."

"I can understand that."

George moved his head back and forth slowly. "The problem is that Luisa's a Mexican living in a strange country and has Mario to take care of." He moved a chair next to the bed and sat down. "Living in America was exciting to her until I left. She doesn't understand why I have to fight a war in Korea. She wants me home. Mom, too. Neither of them think I should be here."

"Ha. Same with me except I get it from the army." Tommy shook a finger. Unfit to be an officer because I look fifteen, that's what Scarf said. And I had pretty much the same problem with my father. When I was accepted for OCS, he said, 'You shouldn't be in the Army, much less as an officer'."

"Maybe we're related. My dad was happy to see me leave home, but you have an advantage over me."

"How's that?"

George lowered his voice. "Once when I came home with bruises and a black eye in the seventh grade, Mom went to see the principal. I was in the next room when she talked to him, but I heard everything through the door. He said, 'The problem as I see it is not who's picking on your son, Mrs. Martin. It's more about who made the initial contact in those fights. In every case, your son hit the other boys first. They were just defending themselves.'

"Mom told him they called me a fairy. I remember the principal's exact words. 'If George were a normal child, there'd be no name-calling, so I don't see how you can blame them'."

Tommy shook his head. "Nice guy."

George looked at his watch. "I have to do a favor for the nurse who got me in here to see you." He pulled the chair away from the bed and walked to the door. "I'll be back again."

When George entered his room, he met a man in white coming out. "I see you've been gallivanting around," the man said. "I dropped off some mail for you from somebody named Martin. Went to Korea and back by slow boat. There's seven letters. I threw them on the bed. Need anything else?"

"Not a thing."

"By the way, I'm Mike, your private attendant." He walked toward the door, stopped and looked back. "If you need me, just pull the cord. I'm on the other end of it."

"Thanks, Mike."

George watched until Mike was headed down the hall then crawled into bed. Two of the envelopes were addressed in his mom's neat handwriting, four in Luisa's, and the other was in the scrawl of Joe Martin.

With his left hand, George picked up the letter from his father. He stared at it as if it were an advertisement for Carter's Little Liver Pills, then threw it back on the bed. He started to pick up the two from his mother, but let them lie and picked up the four from Luisa.

He moved his hand up and down as if he were weighing them, then one after the other, held them against the bed and ran his thumb under the flaps.

One Helluva Soldier / Phil Kline

The first letter was four weeks old but still smelled like her. She wrote how lonely she was without him and how she wished he would come home. The next two said about the same. She still didn't know he had been wounded when she wrote the last one.

I have not received a letter from you for a week. I am worried. I am lonely. I married you to have a normal life. All I have now is letters. Life without you is not normal. Life with no friends is not normal. I cannot live like this. I will leave El Paso, but I do not wish to go to Mexico. I have a cousin who was a good friend when I was growing up. She lives in Seattle, Washington. She came to see me and Mario. She asked me to live with her. I think I will go there. Mario and I need somebody to help us live life until you come back. I love you.
Luisa

George read the letter again, about the misery he had caused his wife. He picked up the letter and read it once more, then held it at his side, thinking about the good friend in Seattle. *She'll be with someone she can relate to.*

He dropped the letter on the bedside table and picked up one of his mother's. Like others she had written, it told whom she had seen lately, that she hadn't heard from his friends, and ended, "*I love you.*"

He set it on the table, then opened and read her other one. It looked like a reprint of the first one except the date was different, and some of the words were different. He set it on the table with the others and picked up the letter from his dad.

The corn is in. We had a good year with two ears on almost every stalk. I will be harvesting as soon as we have a few more days of dry weather. I have been reading what is going on in Korea and am proud of our fighting men there.
Joe Martin

One Helluva Soldier / Phil Kline

George rose to a sitting position by using his left arm. His shoulder hurt. He eased back down to read the letter once more, and his shoulder hurt again. He saw his father in the words, none of which had anything to do with him. He thought it was nice that his father had written, but the letter never mentioned the word son.

He reached for the cord, and pulled it. Within two minutes, Mike came in. "Yes, Lieutenant. What can I do for you?"

"I want to write a couple of letters."

"And you don't have a pen or stationery." Mike turned away. "I'll be right back." He walked out of the room. Within minutes, he returned with official hospital stationery, a Reynolds ballpoint pen, and a food tray. He cranked George's bed into a sitting position, put the tray upside down across his lap, and laid the pen and paper on it. "Anything else, Sir?"

George nodded. "How do I tell my mother I was shot in the shoulder, I'm in Tokyo General Hospital, and when I get well, I may be going back to Korea and hope I can make it through the war without being shot again?"

Mike shrugged, shook his head and walked out.

George picked up the letters and fanned them out. He tossed his parents' letters toward the night stand, and they ended up on the floor. He read Luisa's fourth letter again and picked up the pen to write to her, but ended up tossing the pen and the paper to the table. He lay back, thinking, *If they send me home, that will solve the problem. If they ship me back to Korea, that will make it worse for my family. I have no choice in the matter. I'll just have to wait until the Army makes a decision.*

Faint voices and soft music outside the door reminded him of the night in Durango, when he first saw Luisa wearing the flowered skirt and peasant blouse. For no reason he could think of, he suddenly remembered his promise to take the nurse to dinner. It was 1850 hours.

One Helluva Soldier / Phil Kline

He dressed, combed his hair, and almost made it to nurses' quarters on time.

During dinner she asked about his brother, so he told her how Tommy had gotten his wound. After dinner he took her to her quarters and thanked her for locating his sibling.

She smiled. "He may resemble someone else in the family, but certainly not you."

*

The next morning George awoke to the sound of his own laughter. The dream had been a good one.

Mike and another man dressed in white, stood next to the bed. "Where've you been?" Mike asked.

"Mexico."

"Stay here for a while. Doctor wants to talk to you." Mike pointed at the other man. "This is Major Davis. He did your surgery."

The doctor waved. "How do you feel, young man?"

"Okay, I guess, Sir."

Doctor Davis raised George's hand to take his pulse. "Need pain medication?"

"No."

"Are you trying to act tough?"

"No. It just doesn't bother me."

After taking George's pulse, the doctor said, "You're lucky. Whatever hit you went through without damaging bone or nerves. You'll be on your way home within a week."

No emotion showed in George's voice. "I want to go back to Korea."

The doctor raised his brows. "Aren't you married?"

George looked at Mike. Mike was staring toward the ceiling. George turned his head back toward the doctor. "No, Sir."

One Helluva Soldier / Phil Kline

"All right. We'll set you up for therapy as soon as you're ready. It'll mean you'll be around for a few weeks before you're released for combat duty. Good luck, Son." Then he walked out.

The doctor had called him son.

George lay awake for a long time that night, wondering how he would tell Luisa he couldn't turn his back on his country, or away from the men who might depend on him to return to their families someday.

And he thought again how the doctor had called him son.

18

After a bumpy flight across the Sea of Japan, George stepped off the C-119 Flying Boxcar at Taegu and got a whiff of Korea's distinctive odors, *kimchi* and feces. He pulled up the collar of his field jacket to protect his neck from the October wind and headed toward a row of wooden buildings.

Three men stood at the tailgate of a three-quarter ton truck parked on the edge of the tarmac. One of them was John Hayes.

George cupped his hands around his mouth. "Hayes!"

John trotted over. "Martin, you son-of-a-bitch." He struck a boxer pose, punched George in the left shoulder, grabbed his right hand, and pumped as if he expected water from a well. "I thought you'd be stateside by now."

George didn't let on that the pumping hurt. "I like it here."

John pointed to the mess hall. "Eat yet?"

"No."

"Goddamn it, let's do it." On the way John scrutinized George up and down. "You look great. Hospital food's good for the body."

"You should know."

"Shit, man, I've been there twice. Fukuoka. You were in Tokyo with the other guys, right?"

"Yep."

"Living high on the hog."

One Helluva Soldier / Phil Kline

The aroma of chicken being fried overpowered the *kimchi* and feces odor as they stood in the chow line. George saw that John's left arm didn't hang straight.
"What's with the arm?" George asked.
"It works."
"They going to fix it?"
"It works." As if to offer proof, John swung the arm that had an unusual bend at the elbow.
George shook his head. "Going back to your old outfit?"
"Hell, yes. You?"
"Hell, yes."
John moved ahead in the line and looked back at George. "Watch your language. You're startin' to swear like a fuckin' sailor." He punched George's left shoulder again. "You get downtown Tokyo?"
"Sure did."
"Get any of that slanted pussy?" He turned his head away and put his hands in front of him as if to push those words away. "Excuse me. Sometimes I talk without thinking. Most of the time I talk without thinking."
"That's okay. I know you're that kind of a guy."
John laughed. "I'm not that kind of guy. You are." His smile disappeared. "Damn, there I go again. I apologize. I know you're married, and I know you have a son, still I go shooting my mouth off without any idea of what's going to come out of it. Luisa, right?"
"Yes."
"What's she think of you coming back to Korea?"
"I wrote and told her before I left the hospital, but she doesn't know I made the decision. I don't see any reason to tell her until I get home. It's tough enough on her as it is."
They picked up trays that were almost too hot to hold, and filled them with servings of fried chicken, scalloped potatoes,

green beans, a biscuit, and a slab of Neapolitan ice cream, which they ate before it had a chance to melt.

Before he had eaten half his meal, John put on a serious face. "You see Dutch in Tokyo?"

"He didn't get wounded again, did he?"

"No. He was in Fukuoka on R and R for a couple of days. I thought maybe he'd gone from there to Tokyo to see you guys."

"What's with him?"

John held his knife in his right hand and his fork in his left, his arms resting on the edge of the table. "He had to get away from it, so he went back to Fukuoka where he was stationed before Korea. You know, to get his head back on straight."

"From what?"

"You heard about the time he got fixed up by the medic in Taejon, didn't you?"

"Yeah. When he got shrapnel in his leg."

John sighed. "After the breakout, he went back through Taejon and saw the medic tent where he got fixed up. They were still there, the medic and the wounded." John stopped talking momentarily. "The bastards had tied the medic's hands behind his back and shot him in the head. They poured gasoline on the wounded and burned them alive." He bowed his head. "You know, I've been shot twice. I've killed men from two feet away while I looked them in the eyes. I've had friends killed that were so close I could reach out and touch them. I took that stuff, but I have a difficult time with what those bastards did at that aid station."

For a while the two of them ate in silence then John looked across the table into George's eyes. "Something else. I haven't told this to anybody. You're the only one, and I doubt if I'll ever tell it again, but I've got to say it once. I have to."

George quit eating and listened as John talked in a monotone, his lips barely moving. "After the breakout we were

One Helluva Soldier / Phil Kline

haulin' ass. The gooks were on the run, and we were trying to catch them. We were about to get into a tank battle, so the infantry, riding on us, got off and headed to the top of a ridge. We outnumbered the gooks, and after we took care of them, we drove up the ridge to pick up the men. I was in the lead tank. The men were looking at something in a series of trenches. They motioned for us to get out of the tanks."

John closed his eyes and then opened them. "We walked along the trenches. We counted them. Eighty-six Americans and over three hundred ROK buried up to their waists. The lucky ones had been shot in the head. Most of them had been beaten to death. Can you imagine how they felt watching it happen to others, knowing their turn was coming?"

John closed his eyes again and put his head down on the table. Tears rolled down his cheeks. He sat up, pushed his tray away, wiped his eyes with a fist, and shook his head.

George picked up their trays. "Let's take a walk." He dumped the uneaten food in a GI can, and they walked out of the mess in silence.

John pulled out a khaki-colored handkerchief, wiped his eyes, and stuck it in his shirt pocket. A bit later, he pulled it out and wiped them again. "Where you go from here?" he asked, when he could trust his voice again.

"Twenty-seventh Regiment, somewhere south of Pyongyang."

"Going into the capital, huh? I may end up there, too. I wonder how much defense the fuckers will put up to save face."

"Not much I hope. I don't look forward to street fighting. If you end up fighting there, maybe this time you'll be my partner."

John stopped walking and looked at George. "What in the hell are you talking about?"

One Helluva Soldier / Phil Kline

"When we talked before the matches at OCS, you said I wasn't your partner, I was your opponent."

"I probably said, 'My fucking opponent'."

"Actually, I was more of a partner. You never beat me up." George shifted his weight from one foot to the other. "Question: What makes you think I'm queer?"

John crossed his arms. "Goddamn it, don't you know?"

"No. I've lived in this body all my life, and I've never analyzed how I look. I grew up on a farm and never was around any that I know of. I have nobody to compare myself with."

"You're not kidding, are you?"

"No."

"I haven't led a protected life, so I pretty much know a queer when I see one. It's easy when they get together because of the shit they tell each other."

"I know that."

"It has a lot to do with their looks, the way they talk, the way they carry themselves." He pointed at George. "You don't walk or talk like one. You're military. I don't know. Goddamn it, you just look like one. I'll tell you something though, when you talk, you use air from your mouth rather than from your lungs. I don't know how to explain it."

"I do what?"

"Say, 'Hey, Joe'."

"Hey, Joe," George said, a shade higher than a whisper.

"Now say it louder."

George did so.

"Now, it's less sing-song, but it still comes from your mouth. Say the same thing again except in a deep voice using air from way down in your lungs."

George looked around and didn't see anybody he knew. He gave a deep, "Hey, Joe."

One Helluva Soldier / Phil Kline

John made an okay sign with his thumb and a finger. "Now, I don't say you're supposed to talk that way. I just want you to see the difference. I don't know the answer to your question. Sometimes regular people, or whatever you call them, imitate you guys. Excuse me for saying so, but if those fuckers can imitate you, you can imitate them."

"You're talking about normal people versus queers, right?"

"Yeah, I guess. You may not be queer, Martin. But you have to admit you're not normal either. And remember, I'm not normal myself."

"I hate to make you feel bad, John, but you're about as queer as I am."

John stuck out his chin. "I think you're full of shit, too."

"You may be right, but thanks. I appreciate your advice." George balled both hands into fists. "If I can ever do something for you, like beat somebody up, let me know."

As they approached a convoy of 6-bys, John said, "I'll keep that in mind. In the meantime, take care of yourself."

"You, too. Keep your head down."

They shook hands and saluted each other. John walked down the line of trucks, toward the front. He looked over his shoulder and came back to where George stood. Pointing at George, he said, "I've always been proud of myself for having a queer as a friend. You've blown that away. Thanks for nothin." He poked George on the shoulder again and said, "See ya."

*

A light rain started as George hurried to the freight-loading platforms. Trucks were moving out only minutes after they were loaded. He hustled around, checking drivers to find one going to the southern outskirts of the North Korean capital. He checked seven drivers who said no before he came to a tractor with the diesel engine knocking and three GIs in the cab. Behind it, on a lowboy trailer, a canvas tarp was pulled tight over boxes that covered the bed to a depth of only two feet.

He shaded his eyes from the rain and looked up at the driver who had red hair over his head and most of his lower face. "I need a ride," George said. "Where you headed?"

"Where you want to go, Lieutenant?"

"Chunghwa."

The driver pulled a wrinkled map from the visor and looked at it. "South of Pyongyang?"

George nodded. "That's it."

The driver looked at the corporal on his right. The corporal nodded. "Fine with me, Red."

Red nodded to George. "Git on. We're headin' out."

The rain started to come down in torrents. In record time, George yanked a sweater out of his backpack, took off his jacket, pulled on the sweater, and donned his jacket again. He untied a rope on the bed of the lowboy, pushed his duffle bag under the tarp, and climbed in after it. He yelled from underneath the tarp, "All set." The bed lurched, the boxes jiggled, and the truck moved.

George leaned against some boxes, but soon the back of his head got wet where it rubbed on the tarp. That's when he saw writing on the boxes: DANGER AMMUNITION 105 MM.

*

The truck stopped and George awoke. Red was walking to the back of the lowboy with a flashlight. Snowflakes floated through the beam of light as he lifted the tarp and pulled out six cans. Then he carried them, two at a time, to pour fuel into the tanks.

George sensed a drop in the temperature and donned his soft cap. Two thoughts came to him when the truck started

One Helluva Soldier / Phil Kline

moving: *I'm hungry,* and *I'm sitting on a load of fuel and munitions in a war zone.* He went back to sleep.

It was still dark when the truck started bouncing as if traveling on a road of medium-size boulders. George peered into the darkness while holding onto the tarp. He looked to the front. From the dim glow of the cat-eye headlights, he saw six inches of snow and more coming down to hide the sorry excuse for a road.

At dawn, the truck came to a halt. George looked out in the dim light. Men along both sides of the road were pointing rifles at his bed of fuel and explosives.

One Helluva Soldier / Phil Kline

19

One of the soldiers standing to the right of the truck, shined a flashlight into the cab. The corporal rolled down his window and shaded his eyes.

"What outfit is this?" The soldier moved his light so it didn't shine into the corporal's eyes.

"52nd Field. Who are you looking for?"

"We have a lieutenant in back who's looking for his outfit, 3d Battalion of the 27th Infantry."

"Drop him off. We'll take him there."

George threw his bag into the snow and climbed down. He noticed a sergeant was standing beside, but somewhat back from, the soldier.

"Thanks," the corporal said. "That'll make it easier for us."

"Where are you headed?" the soldier with the flashlight asked.

"The 24th Division, supply."

Coming closer, the soldier's flashlight shined on his own collar. He wore the silver bars of a captain. "What are you carrying?"

"Ammunition, Sir."

"What kind?"

"105, Captain."

"We're artillery for the 24th," the captain said. "We'll unload it for you."

The corporal shook his head. "Can't do that, Captain."

One Helluva Soldier / Phil Kline

The sergeant stepped closer to the captain. He put his hand on his M-1, patting it above the trigger housing.

The captain pushed the flat of his hand toward the sergeant then spoke to the corporal in the cab. "We can unload it for you," he repeated.

The corporal looked back and saw several boxes of ammo were already on the ground. He also saw the sergeant had both hands on his rifle. The corporal had second thoughts. "Sounds fair to me, Captain. If you can serve us breakfast, we'll be headed south within the hour."

The captain turned to the men pulling boxes off the truck. "Hold it. Let him pull the truck over to the ammo pit."

Within a half hour, the flatbed was bare except for enough diesel for the truck to make it back to Taegu. George, and the three men who had come with it, were Captain Allen's guests. They sat at a folding table, wolfing down bacon and eggs.

Captain Allen looked across the table at George. "What outfit did you say you're with?"

George took a sip of coffee from a tin mug. "13th Field."

Allen leaned over and touched George's shirt collar. "I thought you said you were infantry. Where are your cannons?"

"Underneath. I'm FO for the 27th."

"So?"

George touched his jacket collar. "A friend of mine was walking a ridge with his company. He had his brass on when a bullet hit two inches from his foot. A sniper had picked him out of the bunch because he was the only one wearing shiny insignias."

The captain nodded. "That's nice to know."

"Something else I know that you don't."

"What's that?"

George pointed at the ammo pit. "That ammo you unloaded belongs to the 13th."

"How do you know that?"

"That's why I'm on the truck, to guard it from people like you."

Allen tapped a finger on the table. "So, what are you going to do about it?"

George drank the last of his coffee. "Nothing. When a truck from the 13th comes to pick me up, we'll only take half of it. I'll tell the CO that's all we got."

The three men, who had been sitting in front of the truck, looked at George, then at each other.

Captain Allen glanced at Red then back at George. He tapped his finger on the table again. "I can live with that. I'll call the 13th and tell them to come pick you up. That's the least they can do as long as we're giving them half of our ammo."

The four guests finished their breakfast and walked to the truck. The corporal put his hand out to shake George's. "Thank you, Sir. Now I don't have no explaining to do when I get back to supply."

George climbed onto the running board. "Thank you for the ride." He shook hands with each of them, leaning way over to grab Red's freckled hand. As soon as he jumped off, the truck pulled out of the woods and headed south.

A 13th Field 6-x-6 came into the area, and the men from the 52nd loaded half of the 105 mm rounds onto the bed. George said his goodbyes and climbed into the cab. Ten miles and a bunch of bad roads later, the truck arrived at a gun position a quarter-mile behind a cliff a hundred feet high. George located the executive officer, Lieutenant Calahan, in the mess tent.

"I have a gift for you," he said. "Follow me."

Calahan stood still. "Who are you?"

"Follow me."

They walked to the 6-by, and George pointed to the ammo. "Do you need it?"

One Helluva Soldier / Phil Kline

"We sure do."

"Courtesy of Second Lieutenant George E. Martin, FO, 3rd Battalion. I need a ride."

Calahan shook George's hand. "I've heard about you."

"Don't believe a word of it."

Calahan left and soon came back with a captain. "Captain Gordon, our new CO."

The captain returned George's salute. "So, you're Martin. Glad to meet you. What's this about a gift?"

Calahan pointed to the ammo. "We went to pick him up at the 52nd's position, and they loaded this on our truck."

"Good. We were expecting it."

George shook his head. "Not this load."

"I won't ask." The captain waved toward his tent. "Come in. Now I have a gift for you."

They entered a heated squad tent that smelled of kerosene in woods that smelled of pines.

Gordon reached over the top of a field desk and pulled an item out of a drawer. He turned up George's right collar, removed the gold bar, and pinned a shiny silver one on. "Congratulations, First Lieutenant Martin."

George returned the salute. "Thank you, Sir. Thank you."

"First Lieutenant Martin, will you be my guest for lunch?"

George nodded. "I'd like to clean up a mite first, and I want to pick up my mail."

"I'll get your mail while you clean up. There's a water bag out back. After you get washed up, I'll tell you about your new assignment, and I have another surprise for you."

George started to ask for more details, but changed his mind. He picked up his bag and walked out of the tent.

Tarps sheltered a canvas bag hanging from a tree limb. An icicle dangled from a spigot at the bottom of the bag. George decided he didn't need a shower. He took off his clothes, changed underwear, and put his clothes back on. He broke the icicle off the spigot and washed his face and hands. After a rub with a thin towel, he tied it to his pack.

In the tent, Gordon met him with a handshake. "You've been awarded the Silver Star."

"For what?"

"A commendation letter goes with it; something about using it to direct fire on your own position. Here." Gordon handed George a letter and a little box with a silver star hanging from a ribbon.

"Who submitted it?"

"I have no idea. And there's something else; Calahan checked the mail. This is what he found." He handed George one letter from his mother and five from Luisa.

George opened the first of Luisa's letters. "Excuse me," he said. "I move around so much, I have a tough time getting mail."

He read all his letters while eating beef stew. Gordon and Calahan ate theirs in silence.

"Be glad you got those," Gordon said when George finished reading. "The army's more interested in war than in letters."

George laid his mail next to his tray. "It doesn't sound that way to me. I haven't heard a fire mission since I arrived."

"We're getting set to go into Pyongyang tomorrow. We're not sure what surprises they'll have waiting for us, so we're getting super-ready for the big push. We've been waiting for supply lines to catch up with us."

"I got here just in time, didn't I?"

Gordon nodded. "We needed the ammo. By the way, your replacements have done well. Perhaps that's why you're being sent to 2nd Division."

George touched his ear. "Did I hear right? I'm being transferred to the 2nd?"

"That's it. I'll make sure your mail is forwarded."

"Which battalion?"

"47th Field."

George closed his eyes and shook his head. He looked away from the two officers and mouthed, "Shit."

"What's the matter?" Gordon asked.

George opened his eyes only to slits. "I was thinking of something I thought I'd forgotten."

"Something I can help you with?"

"No. Do Patrick and Gomez go with me?"

"Of course."

"When do we have to report?"

"When you get there, I guess. Nobody knew you were coming today."

"Good. I want to see Lieutenant Jones at King before I go. Do you know where they're located?"

Gordon pointed toward the side of the tent. "Sure do. You can use my Jeep."

After eating a light lunch, George climbed into the Jeep and headed for King Company. Wind whipped the dry snow under a cold overcast sky, but he didn't pay much attention to the weather or the rough road that wound around the hills.

When he arrived at his destination, he re-read Luisa's letters that reflected the deterioration of her attitude, then he looked up at the sky, wondering if Hinch was still with the 47th.

Jones didn't wait for George to climb out of the Jeep. He walked to it and turned up George's collar, exposing the new silver bar. Then he turned up his own and shook it. It held captain's bars. They shook hands and said, "Congratulations," almost in unison.

Jones waved toward a tent. "It's a lot warmer inside." He led George to a table on the back side of the tent and filled two tin cups with coffee from an olive drab, two-gallon, vacuum jug. "Tell me some lies."

George sat on a folding chair and looked around. "You have it nice."

"Actually, it is the best part of the war."

"I understand. I hear you've been running cross-country."

"As fast as we can. It feels good to kick ass."

"Not over yet though, is it?"

Jones shook his head. "It's a long haul to the Yalu."

"It'll be interesting to look across the river and see China."

"And hope we don't see the Chinese Army."

"You think they'll come in?"

Jones rested his chin on his hand. "The brass doesn't seem to think so. I hope not. Guys are already talking about going home. What about you?"

"What do I think about the Chinese, or am I ready to go home?"

"Both."

George cocked his head and thought a moment. "I don't know about the Chinese. What I've seen since I got back is soldiers acting like the war's over, and that's dangerous. Going home? I'm ready as soon as it's over. Luisa's uptight about me being gone."

Jones clapped his hands together. "You're right about us acting like it's over. We have to get ready to go back to war tomorrow. I don't think the North Koreans will give up their capital without a fight. How's your shoulder?"

"Fine." George patted his right shoulder. "They fixed it up like new. I'm raring to go, but I won't be with you. I've been assigned to 2nd Division."

Jones leaned forward. "I wondered why the Jeep stayed. Why didn't you tell me?"

"I have a hard time saying that I'm leaving you guys."

One Helluva Soldier / Phil Kline

Jones's shoulders sagged. "We're going to miss you."

George stood. "I'm sure I'll see you again."

They shook hands again, and George returned to the frozen Jeep. As he drove off, he looked back at Jones standing next to the road, until pines blocked his view.

Patrick and Gomez, with their gear, were waiting for him at the 13th headquarters tent. They saluted. George returned it then shook their hands like he would with old friends at a reunion.

Patrick nodded toward a three-quarter-ton truck. "That's ours."

"I'll be ready as soon as I tell the CO goodbye. Oh, Sergeant Patrick, this came with your name on it." He handed Patrick a wrinkled paper bag, then watched as Patrick spread open the top and looked inside.

A smile swept across Patrick's face when he read the name *Chivas Regal* on top of a silver box. He snapped his heels together and saluted George. "Thank you, Sir. I thought you were unconscious."

"My subconscious was in working order. I owe my life to you and your friend. Also, it's in honor of your promotion. Give Private First Class Gomez a congratulatory drink, too."

"Thanks for the *Chivas* and for the recommendation, Sir."

"And I thank you, too, Sir," Gomez added.

Five minutes later, the three of them climbed in, and the truck moved onto a bumpy road. A light snow fell as they pulled into an artillery position, next to a stream flowing down from a flat-topped hill.

Gomez sat up straight and sniffed. "I smell chicken."

As soon as the truck stopped, George jumped out. "Wait here. I have something to do." He located the S-3 tent and walked in. Hinch sat behind a field desk.

"Hello, Captain Hinch," George said, and his lips automatically formed the word asshole.

"I can read lips, Martin."

"Then read this. I have two hungry men. Can they get something to eat?"

Hinch walked out to the truck and directed Patrick and Gomez to follow him. The two grabbed their mess gear, jumped out of the truck, and went with him to a mess tent, where he authorized them to eat.

Hitch poured himself a cup of coffee and walked to a table under a lean-to tent. He sat across from George with his elbows on the table and his hands wrapped around the cup. "Been in Korea quite a while, haven't you, Martin?"

George displayed no emotion. "2300 hours, the first day of July."

"Task Force Smith. Wounded on the Naktong. Right?"

"Nineteen September."

"I understand you requested to return to Korea."

"Yes, Sir."

"But you're married."

"That I am."

Hinch nodded slowly.

George stared at him. *He's making a decision.*

Hinch maintained a poker face. "You've been transferred to the 17th Regiment. I warned them you were coming."

George stood. "My record means nothing to you. You're so pigheaded nothing can change your mind."

"Is that so?"

"Yes. I've faced prejudice from bigots like you before."

Hinch glared at George. "I can have you court martialed for saying that."

"Go ahead. Then tell the 17th they don't need artillery."

Hinch thrust a hand toward the open end of the tent. "Get your ass out of here."

"What about my crew?"

Hinch jerked a thumb toward the open tent fly. "Out."

As George walked out, he thought he heard Hinch say, "Tell Luisa hello for me."

The snow had stopped falling, but the temperature was below freezing when the Jeep carrying him, Patrick, and Gomez, arrived at the wooden floored regimental headquarters tent at 1900 hours. The tent was packed with officers being addressed by a skinny bird colonel. George asked a captain sitting in the back row where he could find the S-1.

The captain pointed to the end of the row. "Major Miller. The tall guy with the long nose."

George walked behind the row of officers, to Major Miller. "I'm Lieutenant Martin reporting in from 47th Field."

"You have a crew?"

"Yes, Sir"

Miller waved for George to follow him. "See the little guy with blond hair near the back of the tent? The one sitting like he's at attention. Tell him to put you and your men in the infantry for the next few days. You'll learn what it's like to be a soldier."

George felt like calling Major Miller an asshole, but figured having already called a captain one was enough for the day. He turned his back on Miller and headed to the back row of the tent, to talk to the little guy who was supposed to teach him what it was like to be a soldier.

One Helluva Soldier / Phil Kline

20

George wound his way around to where the blond captain sat. "I'm George Martin on temporary duty from 47th Field. I'm a forward observer, but I'm to tell you to turn me and my crew into infantrymen so we learn what it's like to be a soldier."

Two lieutenants, sitting near the captain, smiled. The captain stood without smiling. "You must have met our esteemed S-1."

George kept his expression serious. "He didn't tell me who you are."

"Bob Starr, Baker Company. Stick around to hear what else Colonel Norton says then we'll head to my command post where I'll give you and your crew intensive infantry training before we have the company briefing."

Starr led the FO crew to his CP, which was a three-quarter ton truck. "You'll have to wait for an assignment. We're getting ready to go into Pyongyang, and there's no FO job open. That's why Major Miller said to put you in the infantry." He pointed toward Patrick. "You and the private will be riflemen with 2nd Platoon."

Patrick touched his stripes. "Beg pardon, Sir. I'm a sergeant."

"I know. And I'm a captain." Starr touched the sleeve of a thirtyish soldier with a pot belly. "This is Sergeant Bradley, your platoon sergeant."

Bradley led his two recruits away.

Starr escorted George to a hill where he met the 1st Platoon leader, Second Lieutenant Herb Michaels, who walked like a cowboy. The tip of a Confederate flag hung from his pants pocket. Starr said to George, "You outrank Michaels, but he's in charge."

"I understand, Sir."

Starr touched his brow with two fingers, in a half salute. "Briefing in a half hour for officers and NCOs, at my tent."

Michaels glared at George. "Take care of your stuff," he said, "and be back in half an hour." Then he walked away.

Starr scowled at Michaels, and George wondered if either of them ever smiled.

*

George was part of a group standing near the entrance of the tent when Starr joined them. Inside, Starr held up an acetate-covered Japanese map of the northern half of Korea, overlaid in English.

Pointing to the southwest corner of the map, he said, "Pyongyang is the largest city in North Korea, with over two million people, established before the birth of Christ, and it's probably heavily defended. We won't have tanks in our portion of the attack, and we have no idea what resistance the North Koreans will put up to defend their capital." He pointed out the company's present position and made platoon assignments. "The mess is open. Get something to eat and an early sleep. We go at zero-six-hundred."

George had SOS and black coffee for dinner. He put up his shelter and crawled under it, feeling squeamish about maybe being killed while street fighting on a dimly lit avenue in North Korea. *I wonder which would be worse, being killed or having nobody here to grieve for me.*

*

Someone touched George's shoulder. "Time to get up."

One Helluva Soldier / Phil Kline

George opened his eyes to see stars barely visible through high cirrus clouds. After getting to his knees, he reached into his helmet, lifted out the ice, splashed water on his face, and wiped it first with a hand and then a sleeve. For breakfast he drank coffee, but didn't eat the cold bread fried in egg batter.

The hint of light from the east, diffused by the clouds, reminded George of a spring morning in Michigan.

He found Michaels. "Tell me what my job is and what you expect of me," George said.

"I'll tell you when I need you," Michaels replied. "We leave in ten minutes." Then he walked away.

George walked alongside the platoon ten paces behind Michaels and Sergeant Bradley, down a steep slope to a flood plain, then to a river with ice along its banks. George watched men of Company A on their right as they stripped. They held their weapons and clothes over their heads before wading into the current.

Michaels directed his men toward a steel cantilever bridge that spanned the river to the left of where 1st Platoon was to cross. George ran ahead to Michaels. "Stop. Let's talk."

Michaels glanced at him, but kept the platoon moving.

"Stop them now," George yelled.

Michaels halted the platoon and stood with his hands on his hips.

George pointed at the bridge. "Don't use it. They left it for a reason."

Michaels glared at him. "All right. Now get back to your position." He turned to the men. "Off with your clothes. We ford." He began unbuttoning his field jacket.

Some of the men undressed in slow motion. Sergeant Bradley hollered, "Off with them. The quicker you do, the quicker it'll be done with." He undressed.

A few of the men grumbled, but followed his lead.

One Helluva Soldier / Phil Kline

George shivered as he stripped. He was about to step in the water when two men passed him, running into the icy river with their clothes held over their heads. They slipped on ice and fell, dropping their clothes in the water. Nobody else ran into the river, they walked carefully, even gingerly.

Most of the men had passed the ice, and were in the current, when a Jeep started across the bridge. An explosion lit up the river. George and the men watched as the Jeep was hurled into the air. It hit a bridge beam, flipped end-over-end, and crashed to the deck. The forms of four men hung suspended in the air before two fell to the deck, and the other two splashed into the water below.

Sergeant Bradley pulled himself through water to where the two men floated. He yanked off their dog tags, and rejoined the platoon.

George walked up the other bank, dried himself with his field jacket then waited until the last of the men were dressed. Most wrapped their arms close around their chests and hunched their shoulders as they marched.

In the morning light, George walked a few paces behind Michaels. George took a last look at the bridge, grateful and relieved that he had spoken up.

Michaels signaled George to join him. "Our mission is to advance up this road. It winds between the hills south of Pyongyang. Somewhere along the way we can expect to be challenged by gooks. You take the first two squads up the road." He pointed north. "I'll be in the trees with the other two on 2nd Platoon's flank." He motioned to the right.

George trotted to the front of his two squads and relayed Michaels' order. "We'll be in the open so keep a lookout for snipers. We'll march double-time a while to warm up."

He trotted again with his men for a half-mile, along the edge of the road then slowed down. A mile down the road, the unmistakable drone of alien motors caused the hair on the back of his neck to stand on end. He ordered his squads into the edge of the woods, on the right side of the road, and dropped down into the ditch. "Hold your fire until I give the order."

Three gray stake trucks came around a bend in the road and lumbered toward them. When the lead truck was within fifty yards, George yelled, "Fire!" at the top of his lungs. The men fired rifles and a light machine gun at the trucks and at the North Korean soldiers who jumped out of them.

A short time later, George yelled, "Cease fire. Stay where you are. There may be others."

George crept toward the trucks. A dozen of the enemy lay on the road, and six in the trucks. None appeared to be alive. He called his men forward, one of whom limped from a wound in the thigh. A squad leader looked into the back of the first truck and hollered, "Lieutenant! Big mortars and ammo."

George nodded. "We should drive these trucks back to our lines. Contact Lieutenant Michaels on your radio to see if he agrees."

"Yes, Sir." The corporal left in double-time. Minutes later, he came back with the answer: Michaels agreed.

The six North Koreans were thrown from the trucks, to the side of the road, and the three vehicles headed to the river, one carrying the wounded man.

Five minutes later, the radioman ran up to George. "The rest of the regiment hasn't encountered any enemy. Our squads are to return to the river to be trucked forward."

George shook his head. *It would have been nice to ride the trucks back or stay here and wait for them, but Starr said Michaels was in charge.* He called to the men, "We're going back to the river. We'll ride from there."

He led the column of men down the road in single file as enemy artillery roared overhead. Then artillery made the same sound going the other way. By the time the squads got close to the river, enemy mortars had joined in.

One of the squad leaders walked up next to George. "Sir, we're heading into a barrage."

George glanced at him. "We'll go toward it, but not into it."

The firing stopped before they got to the river. The men climbed onto the North Korean trucks, which weren't damaged, and headed north, past the dead they had left alongside the road.

Four miles down the road, they ran into sporadic rifle fire from a distance, possibly from Americans firing at the North Korean trucks. The spent rounds just bounced off, so nobody was wounded.

The men jumped off and climbed through wooded hills to join a thousand soldiers who resembled extras in a war movie.

One of George's men reported a camouflaged T-34 poised in a thicket at the base of a hill. George called for weapons platoon and watched a 3.5 rocket launcher team run through open ground. They fired a round that traveled in an arc toward the tank. The round missed. The T-34's turret swiveled around toward the team.

George felt his heart pound as he watched. It seemed like it took hours for the ammo man to creep up, put another round in, connect the wire, tap the trigger man, and duck. A rocket *whooshed* off and hit the tank broadside. After a sharp explosion, one crewman scurried out of the hatch to be shot by men who had watched the action.

George turned to a squad leader. "Remind me to recommend medals for that bazooka team."

With Michaels in the lead, and George following, the platoon raced to the crest of a hill that had been pounded by artillery. The few remaining North Koreans were severely wounded or dead. A long line of American tanks and trucks moved north on a road below. Military ambulances raced toward the rear.

The platoon established a defensive position on top of the next hill from which they could see down the main road leading into Pyongyang.

That night, after the evening meal, a squad leader from the 1st Squad walked up to George. "You told me to remind you to recommend medals for the bazooka team."

"Thanks."

"Lieutenant, what's a bazooka?"

"That's the nickname for a rocket launcher. It fires an armor-piercing shaped-charge"

"I know that, Sir, but what's a bazooka?"

"Corporal, years ago there was a comedian named Bob Burns, the Arkansas Traveler. Back then, hillbillies made their own musical instruments to form a washboard band. One was a gut-bucket, a washtub that had a mop standing up on it with a clothesline stretched from the top of the mop to the tub. That was their bass fiddle. Somebody else would rub a clothespin against a washboard to keep time. Burns took a stovepipe, put a small extension on it to blow through, like a tuba, and he called it a bazooka. The rocket launcher looks like the bazooka and makes a sound like it when the rocket goes off. *Whoom.*"

"Oh."

21

The next morning the company rode through Pyongyang, encountering no resistance. The city was in American hands.

Baker Company had an uneventful tour as they rode mile after mile of narrow dirt streets lined with mud huts. The North Korean capital was a village of two million people in rags who watched as if they didn't know who the Americans were or why they were there. Most were old men, women, and children, with a smattering of dogs and pigs mixed in.

George shook his head over and over at the contrast between those who resembled people from the middle-ages, and the well-clothed, well-fed NKPA, armed with Soviet high-tech weapons.

A heavy snow was falling by the time the trucks reached the northern outskirts of the city. Starr set up camp in a school yard between two hills. George turned in the names of the bazooka team to the first sergeant then put up his shelter.

No sounds of fighting were heard, but the noise from traffic on the road out front reminded George of a holiday weekend in the States.

It was no holiday for the American soldiers, most of whom hadn't been issued winter clothing. Like George, the majority wore two pair of pants, two shirts, and a light field jacket. The temperature was below freezing, and falling.

Baker Weapons Platoon men set up so they could fire in any direction from their hill position, while George and his crew dug foxholes next to the forward platoon. In the failing light, he heard complaints that the men hadn't eaten since breakfast. One of the men said, "The first sergeant says regiment thinks it's too late to get a mess truck here."

Michaels came to where George sat, his sleeping bag wrapped around his shoulders. "Captain Starr wants to see you. Get over to his CP right now."

George hurried to Starr's command post, a foxhole on top of the hill. Patrick and Gomez were there.

Starr spoke so softly the team members leaned forward to hear. "The rest of the division doesn't know you even exist. You are the only personnel qualified to do an important job that must be carried out with the utmost secrecy." He looked around as if to make sure nobody else could hear what he had to say. "The men haven't eaten all day, and regiment decreed it's too late to serve dinner. I saw a kitchen truck in a convoy, and I believe it's not far ahead. Find it. If you get caught, I'll swear you stole my three-quarter-ton."

George glanced at his two men and said "Let's go."

Patrick drove and Gomez rode in back. Three miles down the road, George spied tracks leading into what resembled a roadside park. He tapped Patrick's arm. "Pull in."

Patrick turned off the cat eyes and eased into the area. At the end of a row of vehicles, an unguarded mess truck stood out like a North Korean soldier at an American Legion convention. A 6-x-6, carrying wooden boxes, was parked next to it.

Gomez climbed into the back of the 6-by and grabbed a box. He had just whispered, "Hot dogs, four cans, fifteen in one," when a truck geared down to turn into the area. Gomez set the box on the truck bed and dropped down next to it. George and Patrick hit the dirt, burying their heads beneath their arms.

After the truck passed, Gomez handed down two boxes, one of hot dogs, and another labeled *Raw Potatoes, 4 cans, 15 in 1.*

One Helluva Soldier / Phil Kline

"Six boxes of each should do," George whispered. Minutes later, the hot dogs and potatoes were a hundred yards down the road and picking up speed.

That night the men of Baker Company ate cold dogs and potatoes for dinner, while those in other companies went hungry.

*

George had just fallen asleep when the sound of gunfire woke him. It lasted only a few minutes but began again when the company was attacked by what he estimated to be battalion strength.

They were repulsed by Baker riflemen and machine-gunners who had the advantage of a hilltop and pre-set fields of fire. George heard that the enemy who had been killed in front of the position wore uniforms different from the NKPA.

*

As daylight filtered through the trees, Michaels led a six-man patrol down the hill. They returned twenty minutes later, carrying two wounded Asians wearing quilted uniforms but no indication of rank. One appeared to be in his teens.

Michaels called for a medic to tend their wounds and sent a runner for Starr.

Starr brought with him an Asian-American who questioned the soldiers. He said, "They claim to be part of a Chinese volunteer force here to protect their North Korean cousins from American aggression. The young one thanked us for not killing him."

The two Chinese were put on a three-quarter-ton to be hauled to Battalion S-2.

Starr met with his officers and told them of the interrogation, then contacted the S-2. "We sent you two Chinese who say they're part of a large force of volunteers. Our patrol said the dead in front of the position wore the same kind of uniform as those two... You figure it out."

The FO crew joined 1st Platoon for a breakfast of pancakes and sausage then George decided to check his mail. He was told he had none.

"You're still assigned to the 47th, aren't you?" the mail clerk asked. "Maybe they're holding it for you. I'll check."

While George was at battalion, the S-3 collared him. "Captain Starr requests that you and your men be assigned as the FO team to travel with Baker Company." An hour later, they loaded onto a three-quarter-ton truck headed north, happy to be a team again.

For two hours Baker Company advanced without opposition. They stopped at a dried-up rice paddy where they unloaded and carried their gear past other outfits camped there.

The mail clerk located George. "The 47th has no mail for you, Lieutenant, but when they get some, they'll forward it."

Later, George was giving his coordinates to FDC when he heard Henry Lee's voice from the road. "Captain Starr."

Starr yelled, "Lieutenant Lee," and told a platoon leader, "Take over." Then he darted over to where Lee stood. They hugged, slapped each other on the back, and talked. All the while Lee laughed, but Starr didn't even smile.

George finished his transmission and trotted toward them. "Captain Starr, Lieutenant Lee."

They waved him over and, for a few minutes, the three of them talked, standing in a circle, with their arms over each other's shoulders.

George poked Henry on the arm. "What are you doing here? I thought you were still doing the L-19 bit."

"I'm on a three-day pass. The Army Air Corps is great duty."

One Helluva Soldier / Phil Kline

For twenty minutes, the three friends talked then George excused himself to help his crew set up an observation post.

Starr came to the observation post at 1830 hours. After telling George how he knew Henry Lee, he lowered his voice. "Lee said his men smelled beer as they came through Pyongyang. He wanted me to go with him to investigate, but I'm busy. You want to try?"

George thought for a moment. "Sure."

"There may be snipers."

Henry drove the Jeep, pulling a trailer that had sixteen 5-gallon water cans, and George rode shotgun through the dark streets of Pyongyang. At an intersection, near where men said they had smelled the brew, the two lieutenants saw their first sign of life. An MP sat on the porch of a hut with three Korean children, all four chewing gum. The MP approached the Jeep.

Henry held the windshield and stood. "Where's the brewery?"

The MP pointed down a dark road. "Over there somewhere, but nobody can get in. They have it under guard."

Henry put the Jeep in gear and headed in that direction.

The MP yelled after them, "Good luck. And bring me a beer."

They pulled up to a fenced-in brick building that had two smokestacks and a bunch of pipes sticking through the roof. It exuded the sweet smell of malted brew.

Two MPs, one tall and the other short, stood at the front gate, armed with carbines plus .45 caliber automatics on their hips. Henry stopped in front of the shorter MP and leaned out of the Jeep to talk to him at eye level. "What do we have to do to get in this place?"

"Nobody gets in without Lieutenant Henslee's permission."

Henry glanced at George and back at the MP. "And where do I find this Lieutenant Henslee?"

"I can call him, but it won't do you any good."

"Just tell him Lieutenants Lee and Martin want to say hello."

The taller MP towered a full foot over his counterpart. He cranked the phone. Seconds later, he said, "Sir, Lieutenants Lee and Martin want to tell you hello." A strange look came over his face. He glanced at the two officers. "He said to let you in." Then he looked at his buddy as if to seek his advice.

Henry pointed a hand toward the taller MP. "You going to do it?"

It was the smaller fellow who opened the gate. "Go to the green door on the right side of the first building."

Henry drove to the door. Waiting there was Allan Henslee, from Class 9-A, sporting a wide smile.

"Good to see you guys. What are you doing here? Oh, forget I said that. A dumb question."

The two got out of the Jeep and pumped Allan's hands. When he finally pulled loose, he said, "Come in. I'll buy you a beer."

Henry and George followed him and, for the first time, George recognized a limp in Henry's gait.

They entered a room the size of a double bed, crammed full with an oak desk, an oak swivel chair, and two metal cabinets. "I smell beer," Henry said.

"Really?" Allan picked up a set of keys from the top desk drawer and walked down a dimly lit hall that smelled like beer. He unlocked a door at the far end and flipped on a light.

They stepped down into a cement-block room containing four large copper kettles with stainless steel pipes leading in and out of them. The floor was covered with six inches of amber liquid.

Henry closed his eyes. "Ahh... what's that wonderful smell?"

"Is there anything in the vats?" George asked.

Allan nodded. "A couple are almost full."

Henry faced Allan. "We brought 5-gallon cans just in case we ran into anything in the city we could put in them."

Allan walked along a row of sacks on the floor, and his friends followed. The path ran out of bags, and they stepped down, into beer that came over the tops of their boots.

George pulled up his pant legs. "I'll never wash my socks again."

They walked to a vat on the right, and Allan pointed toward double doors. "Pull the jeep up to the right of the building, next to those doors. They'll be open when you get there."

George walked through the beer and out of the room. When he returned with the Jeep, and entered the double doors, his two friends were drinking beer.

Allan handed a full mug to George. "It's good to see you. The only one of our guys I've seen is Kamps, and that was a while ago."

Henry bowed his head. "He's dead. I heard he took a mortar round in his foxhole."

Allan stepped two feet away from Henry then turned toward him. "Who else?"

"Fassett, Burrows, Watson, Wilkerson, Hopkins."

He looked back at Henry. "All infantry."

Henry nodded. "Where the action is."

"I agree. I'm safe here, but I don't like it... I'd better get you guys loaded and lock up. You're not supposed to be here."

Twenty minutes later, Henry and George were on the road with two mugs of warm beer in their bellies and eighty gallons in cans, cooling down in the November chill.

When they arrived at the intersection where the MP had given them directions, the MP came running toward them with a canteen cup. "I saw you coming, but had to get my cup."

George climbed out and filled it.

One Helluva Soldier / Phil Kline

"Can I get a canteen full, in case I run into a friend?" the military policeman asked.

"Sure." George poured the canteen full. Then he and Henry waved goodbye to a smiling MP and headed north through deserted streets.

Henry wrapped his arms around the top of the steering wheel as he drove. "We've traveled a long way to get where we are, liberating beer from a brewery in a city we hadn't even heard of when we were in OCS."

"Life here's no stranger to me than OCS was," George said. "That was all new to me, too. I wasn't used to that stuff."

"What stuff?"

"First day, zero-five-thirty hours, a madman charged into the barracks, blowing his whistle and bellowing, 'Out of the sack. Fomation in the company street in ten minutes'."

"Hobbs."

"I was standing in the street with two hundred other guys, when this shrimp comes strutting through the ranks, yelling, 'Ma name's Sergeant Hobbs, an' you better git used to me 'cause ah'll be with you till you wash out or become second lieutenants, which from what ah see, won't be many.' I wasn't used to that kind of talk. I was just a Michigan farm boy."

Henry said, "He did rant and rave somewhat, didn't he?"

"He stood right in front of me and yelled at the top of his lungs. Almost blew me over. 'Attention. Yore drill manual, Twenty-two Dash Fav says, head held back, stomach in, chest out, heels together, with feet pointed out at a thirty degree angle, and the butt of yore piece even with the tip of yore rat toe. Before the day is out, y'all git yore drill manual out an' study it till you larns how to stan at attention lak a soldier'."

"You know that verbatim," Henry said.

"He drilled it into the 2nd Platoon."

"We learned the same stuff in the 1st."

One Helluva Soldier / Phil Kline

"I was so happy to hear Hobbs call my name at graduation," George said. "I was as proud as I've ever been when Colonel Hollingsworth pinned that gold bar on my collar."

"You left right away with Hayes, as I remember."

"As soon as I could. Luisa was having our baby, and I wanted to be there. I tried to leave right away, but I had to find my hat. I should have watched where I threw it or grabbed somebody else's. I finally made it out of the madhouse in time for Hayes to give me a ride to Kansas City, where I caught a bus to Mexico. I didn't make it in time. Mario arrived two hours before I did."

When Henry drove into Baker's bivouac area, most of the men were hanging around the mess truck. It seemed they knew dessert was coming.

George yanked the tarp off the cans with a flourish. "Give me a hand with these." A bunch of hands reached in to take out cans. "Hold it," he said. "We get eight and the others go with Lieutenant Lee. Take ours to the mess tent. They'll dish it out."

The two friends had another beer as they talked, then Henry drove off with the rest of the booty. As they partied, the officers and men of Baker Company toasted Lieutenants Martin and Lee. The beer was still warm, and it was flat, but most of the men claimed it was the best-tasting brew they'd ever had.

For two hours they seemed to forget about the war; they ignored how poorly they were prepared for the cold, and acted like high school kids instead of soldiers.

George thought about the bond he and Henry shared, a bond impossible to gain by normal people in normal occupations, a bond so deep, those who had not served in combat would find it difficult to understand. *Henry would be willing to die for me, and I expect I'd do the same for him.*

One Helluva Soldier / Phil Kline

22

George and Starr rode at the head of the company, on a gravel road that wound between pine-covered mountains, in North Korea. They were bundled up in the face of a November wind, which shoved ten degree blasts across two feet of snow and through the open sides of the Jeep.

Starr looked at George in the back seat. "If they held a popularity contest in the company today, you'd win. All I could hope for would be second place."

"It's just the memory of warm, flat beer."

"I don't remember it being warm or flat."

George shivered. He pulled the collar of his field jacket tighter around his neck. "I don't remember what warm feels like."

"If you see a drive-in, let me know, and I'll buy you a cup of hot coffee."

George shook his head. "I'm full of coffee. I think I'll start drinking hot water... You know, I feel like I'm unemployed. Do you realize I haven't fired a mission in four days?"

Starr pointed at the frigid terrain. "Who would you shoot at?"

"Is the war really over, or will the Chinese spring a trap on us when we get to the Yalu?"

"We may know soon. The brass thinks it's safe enough for Bob Hope to do a USO show tonight." He glanced at George. "Personally, I believe it's a big mistake."

One Helluva Soldier / Phil Kline

George tightened his collar again. "He'd better have his woolies on." He nudged Starr with his elbow. "Why aren't you cold?"

"I'm numb, but I'm going to see Hope. He's a real hero. He performed for more troops than any other two entertainers during World War Two."

"Did you know Lee and I rode an elevator with him at Tokyo General?"

"No, I didn't."

"We were so startled we never even said hello. I wish I'd had him autograph my cast." George sank deeper into his jacket. "I wish I had a cast over my entire body."

Starr pointed to where a stage was being built at the base of a foothill. "Get his autograph tonight before the Chinese kill him."

George stared at the stage. *A stage flooded with light, and a couple thousand troops sitting in the open will make a perfect target.*

*

That night, George watched Hope from the back, but spent much of his time searching for snipers in the hills. Halfway through the show, he reasoned that if the enemy was within ten miles, they'd have heard the cheers for the entertainer and his chorus girls, and would have already done their deed. He enjoyed the rest of the performance.

*

Two weeks later, George and Starr huddled in front of a fire in a temporary bunker. "I'm worried," George said. "I haven't received a letter from Luisa for a month. The last time I heard from her, she was moving to Seattle, but I don't know her address."

One Helluva Soldier / Phil Kline

"Do you get mail from anyone else?"

"From my folks."

"They don't have her address either?"

"No. I checked with the Red Cross, but they haven't answered."

"Of course."

"Then Army Finance Office should know where she is. Let's check with them when we get to Regimental Headquarters."

"Good idea."

*

George sat on the front edge of a hill bordering a dried-up rice paddy, two ridge lines from the Yalu River, one of a thousand soldiers watching Gregory Peck and Jennifer Jones on a wide screen. As he'd done during the Bob Hope show, George spent more time looking at the hills than at *Duel in the Sun*.

He wore two sets of fatigues, a sweater, and a field jacket but still shivered in the below-zero weather. Snow began to fall. George could no longer see the screen, so he left and climbed into his sleeping bag, still wearing two sets of clothing.

During the night a hand grabbed his shoulder. "Wake up. We have to get out of here. We're surrounded."

George squirmed out of his sleeping bag and pulled on his boots, sweater, and jacket with grenades attached. It was snowing hard now, having added six inches of new snow to the two feet already on the ground that muffled the sounds of others preparing to leave.

He stuffed his sleeping bag into his pack, then left to wake Patrick and Gomez. "We're surrounded," he told them. "Bring what you need."

He left them, packed his shelterhalf, snapped on his ammo belt, picked up his carbine, and headed back to them. "They're bound to be sticking to the roads. Our best chance for survival is to move up to the ridge to the east."

As they started up the mountain, Sergeant Hill and sixteen others from the regiment joined them, some without rifles, ammo, helmets, or even warm clothing.

While trudging through snow up to their knees, George and the others heard an Asian voice. The men crouched and were silent. The voice was not loud, but soon there were many voices, and they came closer. Some of the men covered the backs of their heads with their hands. A column of Chinese, going south on the ridge above, took five minutes to pass. When the sounds died down, George led his men in the same direction as the Chinese, but down from the ridge.

Shots came from behind, and two Americans fell forward into the snow. The rest stumbled downhill in the darkness.

George and a corporal slipped off to the side and knelt behind logs piled high with snow. Four men in quilted coats ran down the hill, following the Americans' tracks. George's automatic carbine burst made a harsh sound in the cold, and the four fell. Seeing no one else, George and the corporal followed the path made by the rest of the men. Thirty yards down the hill, George stopped near a snow-covered mound of earth that resembled an igloo.

"Tell Sergeant Hill to get in a defensive position," he said to the corporal. "I'll see if anyone's following us." He circled back to the mound, crouched behind it, and listened.

He was about to stand when he heard a crunching of snow and saw two forms coming toward him. He couldn't tell if they were American or Chinese. He froze in position. One spoke Chinese. George swung around and shot them both, then dropped down in the snow and crawled to them. They weren't breathing. He looked around, but saw no other movement.

One Helluva Soldier / Phil Kline

He joined the rest of the men who were kneeling back-to-back in a perimeter defense, steam from their breath forming little clouds.

The sound of rifle fire came from below. The group moved further up the mountain, but stopped when they heard shouts in an Asian tongue and rifle fire on the ridge. They crouched down until it was quiet, then stumbled down the slope, through deep snow, to a ravine.

Sergeant Hill coaxed them to sit close together near a frozen stream and to be quiet. Two men lit cigarettes. "Stuff them," Hill whispered, "Chinese can smell."

Ten minutes later, they left the ravine. A half-mile further down the mountain, they came to a level spot between the trees and, in failing light, George pointed to a 155mm howitzer battery facing north.

Snowflakes fluttered down in front of a stand of pines and painted a peaceful scene, suggesting what an artillery Christmas card might look like. No guards were apparent. He stopped the men and crept toward a squad tent. He crouched down and yelled, "We're Americans."

"Then come on in."

George walked through multiple tracks in the snow and pulled the tent fly aside. He inhaled the aroma of fresh coffee then froze in place.

By lantern light he saw an M-1 pointed at him from the front and a Thompson submachine-gun from the side. A lanky lieutenant lowered the M-1. "Who are you and what are you doing here?"

"Get out of here," George yelled. "The hills are full of Chinese."

"Not here. We hold the ridges on both sides."

A man, holding the Tommy gun in one hand and a cup in the other, approached George. Bareheaded, with no sign of rank, he wore bandoleers of .45 caliber ammo across his chest, Pancho Villa style. He set the gun and the cup down, grabbed George, and swung him around as if doing a square dance. "Join the festivities. The girls will be here soon."

George pulled away.

The man stopped his dance and reached for a pint of bourbon whiskey sitting on the floor. "Coffee Royale. Have a cup. I don't like to drink alone."

George jabbed his thumb toward the tent fly. "Get out of here. The Chinese have us surrounded."

The lieutenant leaned his M-1 against an ammo box. "You sure? S-2 says that's baloney."

"Your S-2's full of shit. They own the ridges above us."

The dancer tossed the rest of his Coffee Royale down his throat and grabbed his helmet. "Thanks. We didn't get a warning at Anui, and a lot of men died. Get moving, Burt."

Rounds popped through the canvas. The dancer blew out the lamp. "See you later," he said, grabbing his Tommy gun. He pulled his helmet on, and ran past George.

George followed him out of the tent. The dancer ran up the hill, to the west, as Burt ran out of the tent shouting, "March order. Leave the tents and unnecessary gear, and get those guns hooked up right now."

George joined his men who were already in a defensive line, facing the woods.

Rifle fire came from the north and two of George's men were wounded, both in the arm. The gun crews fired to the north where they heard bugles and yelling. Small-arms fire came from the east. Three of the artillery men, and two more of the men who had joined George, went down. Shots were heard in the west, where the dancer had gone. The gunners had finished loading the trucks and hooking up howitzers when a bullet hit a howitzer tube, causing it to ring like a bell.

One Helluva Soldier / Phil Kline

The lieutenant yelled, "Don't worry about them. We're leaving."

The last of the howitzers were hitched, and the wounded shoved onto trucks, then Sergeant Hill and his men climbed on.

A 6x6 was already moving, its engine whining in low gear, when George grabbed the tailgate and jumped on. The driver speed-shifted and the truck jerked forward, toward the road, without lights, taking sporadic fire until they were a half mile away from the position.

Fifteen miles down the road, the trucks came upon an assembly area on a flat spot where the snow was only a foot deep. Numerous campfires sent their warm glow to light up a ring of trees beyond an area of flat ground. Some men stood absorbing the direct heat of the fires while others lay on bare ground or against trees. The aroma of burning logs added to the illusion of an outing in the park. There weren't even any posted guards.

Ambulances and Jeeps, with red crosses painted on their sides, were parked between the trees. George dropped off two of the seriously wounded near a fire and escorted the walking wounded to an ambulance. Medics returned with him to assist those who needed help.

The 155mm battery vacated the area as George walked toward Patrick and Gomez propped against a tree. "Who were those guys in that battery back there?" Patrick asked George.

"I have no idea. I never saw them before and if I ever see them again, it'll be too soon."

"Same with me." Patrick looked at other men leaning against trees and lying on the ground. "I don't see anybody I recognize."

"Let's find some Baker people."

The two of them walked through the area, but found no Baker personnel. When they returned, they joined Gomez, still propped against a tree, near a fire. Patrick took off his helmet, raised his head, and blew a kiss into the branches above. "I don't know which of you has the guardian angel, but I appreciate you letting me use her."

Within minutes, Gomez was sleeping quietly and Patrick was snoring. George felt someone shake his shoulder as he lay awake. A voice said, "Martin." George sat up and recognized the man standing over him. It was Henry Lee.

George jumped up and they hugged. "What are you doing here?" he asked Henry. "Aren't you still flying?"

Henry laughed. "Remember how I said it was so safe flying above the war? Well, one of those North Koreans didn't know that and he shot us down."

George checked Henry out. "You don't look like you've been shot down."

"We just lost engine power. The pilot coasted to a road behind our lines. The only trouble was that the Chinese were behind our lines, too, and we had to run like hell. We headed down the ridge line and almost got run over by a 6-by heading south. They picked us up and brought us here. What are you doing here?"

"I was asleep when the Chinese came. We fought our way back."

A white-haired sergeant ran up and interrupted the conversation. "Lieutenant, Sergeant Bradley was wounded. He's back there."

George looked around. "Where?"

"Where the movie was. We need to go get him."

George waved the sergeant away. "That's miles behind the lines."

"I think we can do it. The Chinese were up all night."

"They're not all asleep. No. Too big a risk."

One Helluva Soldier / Phil Kline

Henry poked George's shoulder. "Where's your sense of adventure? Let's go get him."

George stared at Henry as if he'd lost his mind.

"Come on. Let's go." Henry turned to the sergeant who was now crying. "You got a Jeep or three-quarter ton?"

The sergeant wiped his eyes. "The medics do."

"What are we waiting for?" George said then walked to a medic standing next to a Jeep. "Can we borrow your Jeep? We left a wounded man back there."

The medic surprised George by saying, "Let's go," and hopping into the driver's seat. George and Henry climbed in the back, and the sergeant sat in front. Moments later, they were speeding north on a narrow road with three inches of fresh snow covering the hard-packed old.

Four miles further they approached a wooden bridge over a frozen stream. Two engineers were setting charges. Henry yelled, "We'll be back in twenty minutes. Don't blow it." The engineers glanced at the Jeep and returned to setting charges.

The Jeep continued on, weaved between the hills with the engine disrupting the quiet of the countryside. The driver didn't slow down until they neared the spot where the screen still stood, like a gigantic square ghost on the rice paddy. Two American soldiers jumped from behind bushes and ran toward the Jeep. Another hobbled after them.

The sergeant ran toward them. "Have you seen Bradley?"

"He's under a blanket back there. He can't walk."

The sergeant pointed in the direction from which the two had come. "Grab him and let's get out of here before we wake up the whole Chinese Army."

The two left at a run and shuffled back, carrying Bradley. They climbed into the back seat then George helped the medic lift Bradley and the wounded man to lie across the two men's laps.

One Helluva Soldier / Phil Kline

George sat on the white-haired sergeant's lap in front and yelled at Henry, "This was your idea. Find a place and hop on."

Two bullets clanged into the side of the Jeep.

"Move out," Henry yelled. He ran with a limp and threw himself across the hood as the Jeep started to move. It swerved down the side of the hill, onto the road, with the tips of Henry's boots dragging. He grabbed the windshield and pulled his body higher on the hood. The right rear tire was hit and blew. Two rounds banged into the undercarriage as the Jeep careened down the road.

The rifle fire died out, leaving only the sounds of the whining engine and the flopping of a shredded tire. George squinted from the air blowing in his face as he peered over Henry to where they had to cross the stream. The medic didn't slow the Jeep to see if the bridge was intact. Fifty yards after they sped across, the end of the span was signaled by an explosion.

They vacated the vehicle like clowns pouring out of a small car at the circus. Bradley was lifted off and onto a stretcher at the rendezvous point. The medic drove his battered Jeep beneath the trees then walked the other wounded man to the aid station.

George gave directions to the two who weren't hurt so they could hitch a ride to the rear. He was walking toward the fire with Henry when he heard Bradley say, "Lieutenant, thanks for coming after me."

George walked back to the stretcher and placed his hand on Bradley's. "Thank Lieutenant Lee. He's the one who got me to go when the sergeant decided it was the thing to do. And we couldn't have done it without the medic's help. I just went along for the ride."

"Can you find them so I can thank them?"

One Helluva Soldier / Phil Kline

"You have to catch an ambulance and get out of here. Here's Lieutenant Lee. You can thank him personally, and I'll thank the sergeant and the medic for you."

While Henry knelt to talk to Bradley, George left. He located the medic and the white-haired sergeant at the aid station.

The medic had a strange look on his face. The sergeant was shaking a finger at him and giving him a tongue lashing in front of the other medics and the wounded.

"You medics are all alike. That was the worst ride I've had in my life. You were doing at least fifty with a flat tire on a shitty little dirt path with the lieutenant lying across the hood. You couldn't possibly see where you were going. Don't you ever ask me to ride with you again."

All was quiet until laughter sprang from the witnesses, the sergeant, and the medic.

A Jeep came for Henry. Trucks arrived to pick up George and the men, and they all left the area. When they arrived at Baker's position, First Sergeant Donaldson hurried to George. "Lieutenant, may I have a word with you?" He pointed to a knoll on the edge of the position.

Donaldson bit his lower lip. "Captain Starr's missing in action."

George closed his eyes and shook his head.

"He may be all right," Donaldson said. "People are still straggling in."

George clasped his hands in front of him, and lowered his head.

Donaldson spoke so quietly, George barely heard him. "I hated giving you bad news as soon as you got here, but I wanted you to know before you reported in to the new company commander."

George looked up. "Michaels?"

"Yes, Sir."

"Thanks. Where is he?"

"Operating out of Captain Starr's three-quarter-ton. I'll get your mail and bring it over there in a few minutes."

When George arrived at the three-quarter ton, Michaels was standing by the tailgate with his hands on his hips. "How'd you get back here?" he asked.

George told him about the trip along the ridge, to the firing battery.

"Why didn't you fire artillery at the Chinese?" Michaels wanted to know.

George stepped back and stared at the man. "It wasn't my artillery, and even if it was, I had no idea where the Chinese were, relative to our men."

"They were on the ridges."

"So were our men."

"Bullshit."

George glared at Michaels. "Twenty other men from the division joined us. The hills had to be full of Americans."

"You were with that battery when they pulled out. Why didn't you and your artillery friends direct fire on the Chinks with their guns?"

"And lose them? They'd never fire for you or anybody else again."

"You artillery guys don't have rifles?"

George pointed at Michaels. "Why are you giving me this shit? What's your problem?"

Michaels poked himself in the chest. "I'm commanding this company, and I don't want you here."

George shouted, "You're too unstable to be a CO."

Michaels shook a fist. "You goddamned fairy, I'm—"

In a flash, George pulled his right arm back and gave Michaels a cross to the jaw. Michaels twisted around and fell to his knees. A grin spread across his face as he wiped at a trickle of blood that dripped from his mouth. "You're gonna pay for that, sucker."

George took a boxer's stance. "As long as I'm paying for it, I may as well finish you off. Get up, asshole."

Michaels remained on his knees.

George drew his fist back to hit him, but decided against it. As he turned to walk away, he saw Sergeant Donaldson and a dozen enlisted men watching. He realized he had committed a General Court Martial offense, striking a commanding officer in front of his men, during wartime. It was an offense punishable by death.

Donaldson walked up to him and, without saying a word, handed him four letters he had written to Luisa, returned with the notation MOVED. NO FORWARD.

23

Colonel Norton, 1st Battalion Commander, thin as a half-starved prisoner of war, sat at a field desk with his arms folded. "Tell me what happened."

Michaels stood at attention in front of the colonel and spoke with a slur through his fat lip. "We had an argument." He followed with a fairly accurate account of what led up to him being struck, but omitted the fact that he had called George a fairy.

The colonel turned to George. "Give me your side of the story."

Knowing that being called a fairy was no defense for what he had done, George said, "That's about what happened, Sir."

"Nothing to say in your behalf, Martin?"

"No, Sir."

The colonel turned and stared at the flap of the tent as if words of wisdom were written there. He turned back and faced the two officers. "This has been a tough situation for everyone." He glared at Michaels. "You've been burdened with the loss of your commanding officer and many of your comrades. I don't expect you to just walk in and replace Captain Starr. That would be tough for anybody to do."

He shook a finger at Michaels. "But, I'll tell you one thing right now, you have a lot to learn about commanding, and you'd better learn it in a hurry. This is not your personal company.

One Helluva Soldier / Phil Kline

You have been given temporary control of a U.S. Army unit full of men who need a leader. Do you understand that?"

"Yes, Sir."

"And the next time I ask you a question, Lieutenant Michaels, I want the truth."

"I told you the truth, Sir."

He waved a hand at Michaels. "Don't give me that shit. You gave me an edited version so you'd look like the victim. Just how dumb do you think I am? Now, you go back to your company and think about what I've said."

"Yes, Sir." Michaels snapped his heels together, saluted, and left.

The colonel pointed at George. "And you, Sir, are an enigma. You came to us with high recommendations from your previous commands. You have a personal problem that's chased you around, but it looked like you were about to get it solved. Some of what I told Michaels goes for you too. I didn't ask for your 'That's about what happened' shit. I'm not going to be the only one in this battalion who doesn't know what's going on. You blew it, Martin. I'm placing you on temporary duty with Battalion S-2 until a transfer comes through. You'd better get your shit together and learn to control your temper."

The words were music to George, trading a court martial for an ass chewing and a transfer. "What about my crew, Sir?"

"They stay here."

"I understand, Sir." He left the colonel's tent with his head bowed, but soon sensed the message his posture was sending. He straightened up to look like a new West Point graduate before he entered the S-2 tent.

The S-2, a short Captain Mall, stood behind his desk, in a heated tent. George wondered how he managed to get in the army, being that short, until he heard him speak; he sounded like a bass singing lead in a barbershop quartet. "Colonel Norton called me this morning and said you'd be my assistant."

George thought about that. Only two hours had passed since he'd popped Michaels. "I'm happy to be here," he said, "I've always wanted to learn more about what Intelligence does."

Mall pointed at himself, and then at George, as he spoke. "I want to learn from you. Much of the information we're getting is sent down from the top, which is backwards from the way it's supposed to be. That's why 2nd Division's in trouble now." He looked at George as if he expected an answer.

George unbuttoned his field jacket and took it off. "I agree, Captain."

"Call me Gary." He came around his desk and pointed to a folding chair. "Have a seat." He sat on a chair facing George. "You have as much knowledge about what's happening in this war as any officer in the division. You knew the Chinese had come in."

"Yes."

"How long have you known?"

"A couple of weeks."

"Tell me about it."

"According to Captain Starr, you knew about it."

"Tell me what you know."

"After Pyongyang, we encountered heavy resistance, so Captain Starr sent a patrol out to find out why. They brought back two wounded Chinese who said many Chinese volunteers were here to help their North Korean cousins cope with American aggression. Starr said he notified you and said you told him you'd take the information to Division."

"I did, but Division said it was pure propaganda. They assured me the Chinese weren't coming in, regardless of the many confirmations of their involvement. Information of their entry into the war was ignored by General MacArthur. His intelligence chief sent garbage info down when he should have been collecting information from those who knew, and he's still doing it."

"Even after the last few days?"

Mall nodded. "Yes. A major Chinese force encircled 2nd Division, but FECOM says it was an isolated incident. We have orders to attack along the entire front, putting thousands of American lives at risk. We have no idea what we're up against. That's where you come in.

"You've been on and ahead of the front lines as much as anybody in 8th Army. You've been with the infantry on the attack. You've even led them on the attack. You know your way around, and you know how to stay alive."

"Tell me what you want me to do."

"I want you to find out what's out there, or maybe who's out there."

"The guys on the line can tell you that."

Mall shook his head. "Most of our troops are replacements. They don't have your experience. They have a hard time just staying alive. And they don't have the freedom you have to go where you want and do what you want."

"You want a one-man intelligence patrol."

"That's it. You'll be a lone ranger."

George pulled at the collar of his shirt. "When?"

"We cross the Ch'ongch'on at dawn, with armor and infantry. I want you to operate incognito. Report to S-3, 1st Battalion, 9th Infantry. He'll assign you to one of their companies as a Public Information Officer Observer. Don't expect them to like you. PIOs take the garbage they get from the brass, perfume it up, and spread it out for the press."

"Another question."

"Yes."

"Was this all decided by you and Colonel Norton before I got into it with Michaels?"

"Yes."

"Was Michaels part of this decision?"

"No. He just moved it ahead when he called you a fairy."

George pulled at the collar of his shirt again. "I'm ready." He didn't tell Mall he was also ready to get out of his hot tent.

Mall stood. "I'll buy you lunch now. It may be the best you'll get for a while."

They donned jackets and walked into the cold where the mess truck was shutting down, and got Salisbury steak, corn, and a slice of French bread.

George pointed to a folding table near the truck. "Eat outside?"

Mall walked to the table. "I know what you mean. I could use a little fresh air, too. Not too much, but a little." He sat on a folding chair. "Just like downtown, now that the war's almost over."

After they ate, George went to tell Patrick and Gomez goodbye and was irritated when he found they had already been sent to another battalion. He located the 1st Battalion S-3 tent and faced one of the few army officers he disliked.

Scarf scowled at him from behind a field desk. "You again. I read Mall's note about the hand-picked, experienced, combination forward observer-infantry lieutenant hero who was to be my assistant, and I was hoping against hope that there were two George Martins in Korea, and I'd get the other one. Sit down."

"I'd just as soon stand."

"Fast getaway, huh?" Scarf seemed interested and said, "I hear you were an assistant platoon leader with infantry on the attack."

"For a few days."

One Helluva Soldier / Phil Kline

"I thought your kind were all cowards."

"Captain, you have no idea what kind of person I am."

"Lieutenant, I've read about your stateside activities in your 2-0-1 file, and I'm also a pretty good judge of character or the lack of it. I've been told you're to be put on the line, so I'm assigning you as assistant platoon leader, 3rd Platoon, C Company, under Lieutenant Monroe. They'll be in reserve."

"Captain Scarf, I was told my job's to be an observer on the front line, not in reserve."

"Lieutenant Martin, my job's S-3 of 1st Battalion, and I determine what your job is and who's in reserve."

"If that's all, Sir, I'd like to report in to my platoon, Sir."

"Dismissed."

George walked to the tent fly then stopped. He thought about using Rayford's method of showing disrespect by lifting his leg, but decided Scarf wasn't worth the effort.

Outside, he stopped a corporal walking by. "Tell me where I can find C Company."

The corporal pointed. "Other side of that there hill."

George walked past the hill and went directed to a burly Negro lieutenant in his thirties, who stood looking toward the front.

The lieutenant turned toward George, but didn't smile. "I'm Lieutenant Monroe." He waved his arm. "Come with me." He led George around the platoon position in silence, ending up where they had started. "That's our position. You're free to do what you want. If you need me for anything, I'll try to help you, but don't interfere with my job."

"Look, I've been assigned to be your assistant. Tell me what you want me to do."

Monroe folded his arms and glared at George. "I understand you're a PIO assigned to my platoon by Captain Scarf. So I expect you're here to determine whether President Truman did the right thing when he integrated the army. Is that pretty close?"

"No, Sir. I'm your assistant platoon leader. I've had five months of combat, almost all with front-line infantry. Use me any way you want, to help you and your men in the attack."

Monroe motioned for George to follow him. "Come tell me what's going on."

Standing next to Monroe, in front of a Jeep, George said, "I'm to be your assistant platoon leader in the attack. It's just that, occasionally, I'll need to take side trips to gather intelligence. When the platoon's in combat, I have only one job and that's to fight with you and your men."

Monroe gave George his first smile. "Roger. Sorry I was short with you."

They shook hands.

*

That night, George shivered in below zero temperature. As the sun peeked over the hills, silence was broken by the clanging of tank tracks then came the roar of armored personnel carriers and trucks moving to the front. Machine-gun and rifle fire in the distance, and the sharp *boom boom* of high velocity guns, added to the din. Having no communication with the attacking Americans, George didn't know what was happening.

Soon, remnants of the regiment straggled back past Charlie's position. George slung his M-1 over his shoulder and ran to a ledge overlooking the road where he saw an American convoy speeding south, toward Kunu-ri. The back of his neck tingled when the sound of bugles and whistles pierced the air, to the north.

One Helluva Soldier / Phil Kline

He ran back to the platoon just before an avalanche of short men in gray quilted uniforms rushed down the hill, toward Charlie Company's position.

Evidently, the Chinese didn't realize C Company was still in a defensive mode. Automatic weapons mowed them down as they came down the hill. That halted the attack.

More vehicles speeding south indicated a general American withdrawal. Charlie Company was ordered to pull back. George led two of the squads along the side of a hill, next to the road. He heard heavy firing to the south.

They were surrounded.

A truck, heading south, stopped to pick them up even as it received small-arms fire from a ridge to the east.

Fortunately, nobody was hit.

The truck careened down the winding road until, at Five Mile Pass, they approached a line of trucks stalled by a tank on fire. George and the men jumped into a ditch to return fire onto a tree-covered hill, at an enemy they couldn't see.

George yelled to the men with him to join in covering fire as they dropped back to the other side of the trucks. Then they ran down to a frozen stream and hiked south, along the bank, where they were attacked by a company-size force. They took cover and fired back. During the fire-fight, they ran out of ammunition.

After the Americans stopped firing, Chinese soldiers advanced across the stream, with rifles pointed at the dozen men who were left. The Americans threw down their weapons and raised their hands over their heads.

A soldier, with no visible sign of rank, pointed a rifle at George's face. The soldier waved the muzzle of his rifle toward the south. "Go down stream. When you arrive your headquarters, say, Chinese Volunteers good to you and let you go. Say, we not kill you. We let you go to families and not make war on innocent people of Korea."

George motioned for the men to follow him in the direction the Chinese leader had indicated. With Chinese rifles pointed at him, George looked straight ahead and held his head high. Some of the men followed his lead with heads up, while others covered their heads with their arms, as if that would fend off bullets.

Thirty minutes later, the Americans arrived at 1st Battalion Headquarters. George pointed to a sergeant in the group. "Take these men to supply to get weapons and ammo." He walked to the S-3 tent and found Captain Scarf tinkering with a radio.

Scarf looked up. "What are you doing here?"

"There's a general withdrawal through the pass. The Chinese are on both sides of the pass, all the way to Kunu-ri. Our group ran out of ammo, and we surrendered. They let us go."

"What are you trying to pull?"

"Captain Scarf, get your head out of your—"

Firing came from the perimeter, and rounds popped through the tent. Scarf and George dropped to the dirt floor.

Scarf pointed to a rifle rack. "Grab one and let's get out of here."

George pulled down a carbine and four magazines. Scarf slid his colt .45 off the desk, and they crawled toward a ditch in back of the tent.

When they reached the edge of the ditch, what looked to be a tin can, with a handle sticking out one end and smoke coming from the other, landed between them.

Scarf kicked George in the hip, propelling him down into the ditch. As he tumbled toward the bottom, he heard an explosion. The acrid smell from the concussion grenade drifted down to him. Rifle and automatic fire came from above. Soon, the shooting diminished then ended.

George crawled to the top of the ditch and peered over the lip. He saw a circle where the snow was gone. Scarf lay in the middle with one foot blown off, most of his pants torn away, and blood oozing from his groin.

As George crawled toward Scarf, from the corner of his eye, George detected movement at the side of the tent. He slid back into the ditch and slipped a magazine into the carbine, then snaked back near the top. A Chinese soldier crawled up next to Scarf and started going through his pockets. George fired a burst to the soldier's midsection, and the Chinaman rolled over.

Working his way north, around a bend in the ditch, George saw two more Chinese creeping toward their comrade. He fired a dozen rounds into them. Blood spurted from their upper bodies, and they lay still.

He waited, but no others appeared. He listened to the sounds of automatic weapons and explosions that came from above. When the firing died down, he crawled up and checked the three Chinese to make sure they were dead then wormed his way toward Scarf, who lay in the same position as before and wasn't breathing. A brilliant light flashed and George felt like someone had kicked him in the head.

When he gained consciousness, he opened his eyes but couldn't see. He lay still, with his head to one side, his legs folded behind his body. Blood trickling down his cheek was warm against his skin. Hearing yelling in Chinese, he stayed motionless.

After five minutes of silence, he wiped his eyes with his sleeve. Light shined through. He had vision, but everything was blurred. He grabbed a handful of snow and wiped it on his eyes, restoring much of his sight.

One Helluva Soldier / Phil Kline

Blood dribbled into his right eye, and his head ached. Putting his hand to his forehead, he felt a two-inch gash where the skin was gone. He pulled out his handkerchief and pressed it against his forehead.

His carbine was nowhere in sight. The only noise was rifle and automatic fire in the distance. George crawled to the edge of the ditch, where Captain Scarf lay, and felt his arm. It was cold. He felt Scarf's chest. There was no heartbeat.

George lay flat, listening, until he was sure the area was deserted, then he slipped to the rear of the tent. He peered in. It was vacant.

He crawled in, stood, and tiptoed to the front. Cracking the fly open, he looked out. Satisfied he was alone, he searched around and spied a first-aid kit. He found a stainless steel mirror to check the gash on his forehead. He pulled the handkerchief from his forehead, looked at the wound and pressed a bandage on. At the edge of the mirror he saw a reflection of movement.

One Helluva Soldier / Phil Kline

24

George dropped to the floor, rolled over, and reached for his .45. It was gone. He closed his eyes. Hearing no shot, he turned his head toward the tent fly, expecting to see a flash of light, or at least see who would end his life. What he saw was the barrel of a rifle pointed at his face, along with two eyes and a nose visible beneath an American helmet. A voice said, "You're lucky. If I'd'a been a Chinaman, you'd'a been dead now."

It was the sergeant who had stumbled into Battalion Headquarters with him an hour earlier. He held a Chinese rifle. "We're 'bout even, Lieutenant," he said, stepping inside. "I'm lucky you didn't shoot me when I stuck my head in here."

"I would've, but I lost my .45. I should'a been more careful."

George stood and wiped his brow, flinching when his hand touched his wound. "You scared hell out of me."

"Sorry 'bout that, but I didn't know who was in here."

"No headquarters people. Do you know where they are?"

"They're gone. Vehicles are here. Chinks shot'em up—put holes in the engines and tires."

George reached again for the first aid kit. The sergeant stepped up and pulled out a bandage with tape attached. "I'll do it for you," he said.

After his wound was bandaged, George thanked him and walked to the weapons rack to grab the remaining carbine. He slung it over his shoulder and stuffed his pockets with six magazines. "What's your name and where were you during the shooting?"

"Name's Pick. You're Martin, ain't you?"

George nodded, looked both ways through the tent fly then stepped outside. Pick followed.

"We were trying to find supply when we heard shots," Pick said. "We didn't have no weapons, so we slipped down in a ditch on the edge of the woods." He pointed to his left. "When the shooting died down, I figured it was safe to come out."

"Where are the men now?"

"Looking for weapons, ammo, and warm clothing." He pointed at George's forehead. "What happened?"

"A bullet grazed me."

"Do you have any idea where we are?"

"Near where we were this morning. Not far from Kunu-ri. We have to get out of here."

"I agree."

George glanced down the street. "I wonder why they're not scavenging."

"Probably pressing their advantage."

"I think you're right. It means they're hanging close to the roads."

Pick pointed up a hill, to the west. "Yeah. We ought'a be heading back to the ridges."

"All right, Sergeant, after the men are armed look for wounded. Have them collect dog tags from the dead and take any warm clothing they can use. Find the mess truck, get a bunch of food together and we'll move out. See you back here in ten minutes. There's something I have to do."

"Got you."

George perused the area as he walked to where Scarf lay. He turned the dead captain over and worked the .45 out of stiff fingers. He pulled a dog tag from around Scarf's neck and a wallet out of his jacket pocket. Then he stood, put the wallet and dog tag in his own shirt pocket, and bent over to unhook an ammo belt from the lifeless form. He hooked the belt around his waist, stepped back, and saluted. "Thank you, Captain. Thank you for my life."

He walked into the tent, gathered all the papers he felt were sensitive, and carried them to a row of five trucks that appeared to be in good condition except for a burned out one at the end of the line. He tossed the papers on the seat of the first truck, then went back to the tent and searched for K-rations. He didn't find any—no surprise; headquarters people ate real food. He located two more carbine magazines and crammed them under his ammo belt.

In the back of the first truck, he found two 5-gallon cans of gasoline. He grabbed one, opened a door at the front, and poured gas on the papers in the seat. He had just pulled a box of matches out of his pocket, with the intention of burning the papers, when Pick came up from behind him.

"Lieutenant, there's no wounded. We took M-1s and ammo from some dead guys and pulled sweaters and jackets off them." Pick shook his head. "I never did that before, I felt like a buzzard. A couple of the men couldn't do it."

"What about food?"

"Ain't none. The burned-out truck's the mess truck. Crew's still in it."

George pulled a match from the box. Pick grabbed his hand and the match. "You smell like gas. You pour and I'll light."

George handed him the matches and left to douse gasoline on the seat of the second truck. Afterward, he heard a *whoosh* and felt heat from the first one. He poured gas into each truck while Pick lit balls of paper and threw them into the cabs from a distance.

One Helluva Soldier / Phil Kline

After finishing the torch job, they walked to where eleven men were warming themselves from a truck fire the way they would in front of a fireplace, toasting one side and then the other. A short guy, wearing a winter jacket way too big for him, called to Pick, "Hey, Sarge, why didn't you save one for us?"

"The engines were shot up."

The band of thirteen left the heat of the burning trucks, with Pick and George at the front of the column. George pushed brush aside to form a path for Pick and the men, as they tramped up a mountain, on the southeast side of Five Mile Pass.

"Three times today I've been lucky," George said. "Lucky the bullet just grazed me, lucky the Chink thought I was dead, and lucky it was you instead of them who found me screwing around in the tent."

Pick looked around at the hills. "I hope you're lucky enough to get us out of here."

"If we work together, we'll make it."

They climbed in silence for an hour, in a steady dry snow, without seeing or hearing any Chinese. When they came to a ravine with a frozen stream at the bottom, George said to Pick, "It's a good time to stop for the day. We can pack ourselves tight in the gully and stay warm."

Pick nodded and turned to the men. "Anybody got rations?"

The short man with the big jacket raised a hand. "I got two K's."

"Thanks, Runt." Pick pointed to the ravine and whispered. "Get close together in the gully, get a bite of Runt's K's, and be quiet. And no smoking. Put snow in your canteen and let it thaw inside your jacket. Who'll stand watch the first two hours?"

One Helluva Soldier / Phil Kline

Two men raised their hands, and Pick stationed them on the sides of the ravine, while the rest of the men climbed down to where Runt was doling out his K-Rations.

One of the men tapped a corporal on the shoulder. "What's a gully?"

"It's a mass grave. Be quiet and eat your last meal."

Huddled like a herd of musk ox under attack, the men ate their miniscule amount of food. Pick and George stationed themselves at opposite sides. "Jesus, who farted?" someone said.

"No talking," Pick whispered, "If you hear somebody snore, wake him up."

*

Pick woke George as sunshine lit up the tops of the trees. "We should be going." He pointed to tracks in the snow. "They'll know we've been here."

George stood and brushed off new-fallen white flakes before he led the men through snow up to their knees. The only sound was the crunch of boots on snow until there came a rumbling from down the hill. George halted the march and Pick chose a corporal to lead a two-man patrol to investigate. The corporal appeared to be beat and gave Pick a *do I have to go?* look.

George stepped up. "I'll go. I've heard that noise before."

Halfway down the mountain, looking through the trees, George saw the cause he'd expected: boots on road. Four columns of Chinese, dressed in quilted uniforms and fur caps, were double-timing to the south. They took five minutes to pass. The private on patrol with George grumbled, "We'll never be home by Christmas like General MacArthur said."

George jabbed the guy on the shoulder and whispered, "*Shhhh.*"

One Helluva Soldier / Phil Kline

After returning to the group, George gathered the men close to tell them what he had seen. He looked at Pick and pointed toward the south. Some of the men started talking about the patrol's discovery. Pick walked toward them and whispered, "No talking." Then he waved his arm for them to follow, and started walking.

The men went along in silence. George brought up the rear.

Low clouds rolled in, and the day warmed up before a heavy, wet, snow began to fall. An hour later, after they had traveled less than a mile over inclines as steep as Kentucky hill country, Pick held up a hand. He inspected tracks in the snow that came from below and turned south. He went back to where George stood.

"Squad size I'd guess, and they're fresh," Pick said. "We can't keep going this way."

George pointed up the hill. Pick started the climb, but the going was slow. The slope was steep, and the men sometimes stumbled on objects that lay under the blanket of snow. As they moved in a southeasterly direction, along the side of the hill, the snow kept falling. By dusk, the cover was so deep it came up to Pick's crotch as he led the way.

They stopped when they found a resting place on a level shrub-covered shelf. They assumed huddle positions, looking like a bunch of old men because of the frost on their new mustaches.

As sunlight faded, a golden glow, from down the hill, cast a dim light on the snow high up in the pines. George pointed it out to Pick. "Let's send out a patrol."

Runt volunteered. The man next to him, a head taller, said, "I'd better go, too, in case he gets stuck in a snow drift."

Runt made an obscene gesture with his left hand and right forearm. They trudged down the hill with their M-1s at port arms.

One Helluva Soldier / Phil Kline

On their return to the huddle camp, Runt reported directly to Pick. "Hundreds of Chinese sitting in groups around fires, having dinner. Halfway, maybe quarter-mile, down."

George looked at Pick. "They've left the road. That probably means we're getting close to our lines."

Pick nodded. "Could mean they'll be sending patrols out."

George walked back to where the men huddled together. "I realize you're hungry and tired," he whispered, "but it's dangerous here. If we keep moving, I reckon we can make it to our lines tonight." He waved to continue, and the men followed him.

The quiet was broken by the sound of metal tapping metal. One of two of the men who ran toward the noise yelled, "We're Americans."

From ahead, someone shouted, "Put down your weapons and come this way with your hands over your heads, or you'll be dead Americans."

One of the two men shouted "We're home" loud enough to wake up the dead, and maybe the Chinese.

Pick led the group through the woods, past the rifles of perimeter guards, to where a mess truck was serving breakfast to a line of soldiers. The two C Company men were standing near the head of the chow line, a sergeant waving a spatula at them. "This is L Company food for L Company men."

One of the two men stared at the food as if trying to hypnotize pancakes into flying to his open mouth. The sergeant shook the spatula at him. "Find your own mess."

Pick stepped up. "It was over run."

The mess sergeant gazed at Pick. "When's the last time you guys ate?"

"Day before yesterday."

The sergeant jerked his thumb at the head of the line. A minute later, the C Company men were in line. Two indicated they didn't have mess gear. The mess sergeant walked toward the truck but stopped when a perimeter guard ran into the position and yelled, "Gooks."

Men scattered as rifle fire banged into the truck. L Company men zigzagged to both edges of the clearing, and C Company men ran to the north. The mess personnel grabbed their weapons and ran to the south.

Chinese came from the east and west, charging into L's readied defense, firing their weapons as they bounced through the line of trees around the position. The Americans cut them down as soon as they came into view, and the attack was halted.

An American officer, who looked strange wearing sunglasses, appeared from the rear and ran toward the men on the east side of the position. He jumped over two of them and into the woods. "Follow me," he shouted.

Another led his men to the west side.

George ordered the men with him to follow, and they charged into the woods on the lieutenant's flank. George ran a hundred yards, jumping over four Chinese lying motionless in the snow. After finding no live ones, and hearing no noises, he and his men returned. The L Company men were already back at their position, one of them carrying a beat-up bugle.

A man, wearing a sleeveless khaki underwear top, told the mess personnel to start serving. He approached George. "I believe that was only a patrol that thought they'd catch us flatfooted. Who are you and what are you doing here?"

"George Martin with Charlie Company. Took us two days to make it. We got here just ahead of the Chinese."

The man extended his hand. "Captain Ernie West, Love CO." While they were shaking hands, a corporal ran up to them. "Captain, we didn't lose any men. Three have flesh wounds, but Sergeant Barnes was hit in the back; I think he's in bad shape."

One Helluva Soldier / Phil Kline

"Excuse me, Martin." West followed the corporal toward the rear of the position.

Five minutes later, George heard a three-quarter-ton head out of the area. He turned to Pick. "I'll be returning to my regiment soon. If I ever need a new commo sergeant, I'll call for you."

"Thank you, but my dad was an infantry first sergeant. He'd flip over in his grave if I joined the artillery. He always said anything other than infantry's a service unit."

"I'll remember that, and if you ever decide to get out of your combat branch to join a service unit, let me know. I'll take you with me next time I direct fire from a hill in front of the infantry."

Pick laughed, saluted George, and walked away.

West returned. "Mess is up and running again. Like to eat?"

"Yes, Sir."

"You don't mind waiting till the end of the line, do you?"

"That's fine."

"Good. Come to my tent for some coffee."

In the warm tent, George leaned back in a wooden folding chair. "This feels good."

"I bet." West poured coffee from a porcelain mug and handed the cup to George. "What's the bandage for?"

"A bullet creased it."

"When?"

George took a sip of the coffee, closed his eyes, and rolled the coffee around in his mouth. "Two days ago."

"I'll have my medic look at it." West stood and walked out.

He returned with a medic who peeled off the bandage, then said, "It'll heal faster if you leave the bandage off and let it dry out."

One Helluva Soldier / Phil Kline

A moment later, Sergeant Pick stuck his head inside the tent. "Lieutenant Martin, we can't find Runt. We're going to look for him."

George set his coffee down, grabbed his carbine, and followed Pick. He and three men went to the east while Pick went to the west with four others. The only men George found were dead Chinese. He heard the thumping of boots and turned to find Pick running toward him without his jacket. "We found him, Lieutenant. He was hit in the stomach. Looks bad. We wrapped him up, and two guys carried him to the company position."

Pick and George found the medic tent where Runt lay face down on a cot. The medic poured a liquid onto a bleeding wound in Runt's back then looked up. "I can't do much for him. A round went through his stomach and came out his back."

George walked out of the tent as Captain West hurried past. West saw him, stopped, and read aloud from a message in his hand: "'General Walker has ordered a withdrawal to consolidate our positions and give G-2 a chance to assess the Chinese entry into the war.' They're making excuses for retreating, but they don't call it a retreat; it's a withdrawal to consolidate. What do you think of that crap, Martin?"

"At least it solves one problem; I have a badly wounded man I have to get out."

"Glad you found him. Get ready to travel." West walked out to where the new mess sergeant stood, and kicked a kitchen truck tire. "Close it up. We're withdrawing. Oh, and bring me a dozen pancakes, if you have any left."

George followed him. "Anything I can help with?"

"Have your wounded man and your men ready to leave in ten minutes. Division says there are thousands of Chinese between here and our lines. You like pancakes?"

"Yes."

One Helluva Soldier / Phil Kline

25

The L Company trucks made it to friendly lines without encountering any Chinese. Captain West located 1st Battalion and arranged a ride for George and the Charlie Company men. George said to West, "You're a good soldier," as they slid Runt into an ambulance.

"Thank you, Sir. You're a good officer."

George climbed into the cab of a truck carrying twenty men back to Regiment's new location north of Pyongyang.

After making a report about Chinese involvement that Captain Small no longer needed, he found Major Miller and gave him dog tags he had collected plus details of what happened to their owners.

Miller held the dog tags. "You've had a rough few days, and I hear you've handled yourself well. Nobody's sure where the different units are right now, so you're going back to the Forty-seventh Field. They'll assign you when the situation stabilizes."

George was gratified at the change in Miller's attitude from the first time he'd met him, but unhappy about being sent to Hinch.

Miller took George's mind away from his own troubles. "We received word today that Captain Starr was killed in action."

"Oh, hell…" George said, after a quiet moment. "I have dog tags and a narrative to submit another man for some sort of medal."

"There's an officer in charge of commendations around here somewhere." Miller extended a hand. "Here, I'll give them to him."

George handed a dog tag and wallet to Miller who looked at the name. "Captain Scarf?"

George handed Miller the details of Scarf's actions written on a sheet of scrap paper. "He gave his life to save mine."

Miller shook his head as he read about what Scarf had done. "You never know who people really are until something like this happens. This clears his name from the missing, so his wife and daughter will know he died with honor, for what little that's worth." Then he added, "Take care of yourself," as George turned toward the door.

"Thanks. I will."

George walked into a barrage of large flakes of wet snow, thinking about the change in Miller's acceptance of him. His thoughts switched to Scarf and Starr, both gone for good, and decided not to report to Hinch in his present state of mind.

A lieutenant walking by said, "Merry Christmas. Looks like we'll have a white one, doesn't it?" He chuckled and continued walking.

As long as things were not going well, George decided he might as well face Hinch after all. He bummed a ride to the 47th and stepped out of the Jeep. A sergeant was supervising the erection of a tent. "Can you tell me where I can find Captain Hinch?" George asked.

Without looking up, the sergeant shook his head. "No."

"Sergeant, I'm in no mood to play games. Where can I find Captain Hinch?"

The sergeant turned toward George. "You don't know? His battery was overrun. He's missing in action." The sergeant turned away to watch tent poles being raised.

George said, "Last I knew he was S-3."

The sergeant spoke over his shoulder. "He was transferred to B Battery. He may have been killed or wounded, and left back there somewhere, or maybe captured. I don't know."

George walked to the edge of the clearing where a gnarled little pine stood like a hunchbacked sentry. He sat in the snow, leaned against the bare trunk and watched the path of large flakes as they fell. He was ashamed of his feeling of joy that something had happened to Hinch.

Finally, he stood and walked to the S-3 tent where he met Hinch's replacement. Captain Douglas was a thin man who wore army issue glasses like General Bentley's, and clothes that would fit a man thirty pounds heavier.

"I was assigned to 2nd Division," George said, "but have been returned to the 47th. Where can I pick up my mail?"

Douglas removed his glasses and wiped them with his handkerchief. "Just a minute." He called to a clerk at the other end of the tent, "Wilson, check the mail and see what you can find for Lieutenant George Martin." He faced George again. "I've heard about you. I spent a couple days with Captain Hinch before he took over Baker Battery. He didn't think much of you, to say the least, but I also got a call from a Captain West who says you're a damned good soldier. I guess you're like some other guys who affect different people different ways and every once in a while I get a comment I don't understand even if it does happen to a lot of officers. Makes it difficult to understand how efficient they are when people do that."

George crossed his arms. "Look, all I want to do is pick up my mail and find out my next assignment." As soon as he said that, he wished he could take it back. "I apologize, Captain."

"I understand. You know it's a different war than when you left here now that the Chinese have changed to attacking at night, which means we'll have to change, too. We'll be playing their game because the army's never conducted night-fighting that I know of, even in the advanced course. We're going to have to start—"

"Where am I going, Captain?"

"You'll take a few days off first. I imagine you're ready for it."

"You're right… I have a dumb question. What day is this?"

"Twenty-four December. You didn't know?"

George shook his head. "No, I didn't. Merry Christmas, Captain. As a Christmas gift, would you lend me a Jeep to go see a friend? Tomorrow, not tonight."

"Can't let you have a Jeep, but I can give you a ride where you want to go. In the meantime, if you want a good rest, you're welcome to stay at my house, not a hut, but a real house, and it's not actually mine. The staff is staying there because it has plenty of room, and it's heated so well it's almost stuffy."

George stared at Douglas. *If he doesn't stop talking, I'll drop a grenade on him. Then I can turn him in for a medal.* Someone behind George cleared his throat. He looked around and saw Private Wilson standing at the tent fly, holding three letters. George took them, One was from his mother, another was an ad for a new Ford, and the third was a letter he had written to Luisa, It had been returned. "That's all?" he asked.

"Yes, Sir. The one of yours just needs a new address."

George threw the ad in a trash box, stuck the letters in his pocket then turned to Douglas. "Do you know where the 13th Field's located?"

"I'll see what I can find out. The sector's in such a state of flux, some outfits don't know where they are themselves. We're lucky. Other outfits—"

He was still talking when George left.

Outside the tent, George opened the letter from his mother. It started out with the result of her talks with Red Cross.

One Helluva Soldier / Phil Kline

> *The Red Cross has not been able to locate Luisa. If she is in Seattle, she isn't listed anywhere there. The Red Cross contacted the army and they don't have any record of her address. Her allotment checks have been returned to them as undeliverable.*

An hour later, George phoned Dutch. "Hey, I'm back with the 47th. I have a big problem and need somebody like you to talk to. What are you're doing Christmas?"

"What I always do, same as you, try to kill them before they kill me. I don't know; depends on if the Chinese want to fight. Sometimes they do on special days."

"I'll send a message to Chairman Mao to hold off a week. If he agrees, I'll spend time with you. Call me if nothing's going on."

"Will do, my friend."

That night, George enjoyed the warmth of his sleeping bag resting on a soft mat, in a wood house with a red tile roof. He didn't see or hear a thing until 0600 hours when he opened his eyes to find a lieutenant towering over him.

"Chinese aren't here, are they?" George said.

"No. Who are you?"

"George Martin. I'm a guest of Captain Douglas."

"I wasn't questioning why you're here, just wondering who you are. Oh, you're the guy who turned Scarf in for a medal. Scarf did that, huh?"

"I wouldn't be here if he hadn't."

"It's submitted." The lieutenant walked away.

"Merry Christmas," George said, realizing he was still angry because of his inability to locate Luisa, and was taking it out on others.

One Helluva Soldier / Phil Kline

Later, as he took his first warm shower in months, he was enjoying the hot water that cascaded over his body. *I wish I could spend the rest of my life here.* He frowned when he realized that, for his wish to come true, he'd have to be killed there.

It was three hours later that Dutch called. "It's absolutely quiet, so we're scheduled to eat ham with all the trimmings. Can't guarantee it'll stay that way. You can never trust a Chinaman."

*

An hour later, after a bumpy ride in Douglas's Jeep, Dennis Nixon of Class 9-A, said to George, at the fly of Dutch's squad tent, "You look great."

"I am great."

A voice came from inside the tent. "How come you're ignoring me?" Reed Rayford walked outside with a drink in his hand, and hugged George, almost breaking him in two.

Dutch came out, shook George's hand, and walked into the tent with him. He no longer sported a cane, but George detected a limp.

"Coffee or booze?" Dutch asked.

"Black coffee will be fine."

Dutch poured coffee for George from a 1-gallon vacuum bottle, then picked up his own cup and said, "Attention." When it got quiet, he held his cup high. "Everyone who's coming today is here. I propose a toast to us, the survivors." Three coffee cups and Reed's glass touched.

"Where are the others?" George asked. Nobody spoke. George looked at Dutch.

"Lee."

"How?"

One Helluva Soldier / Phil Kline

"His L-19 hit by ground fire."

George raised his cup. The others followed, saying the words of Henry Lee's favorite toast, "Hear, hear."

The only sounds were from outside the tent until George spoke in a halting voice. "Henry was one of us." He looked around. "You know what I mean?"

Reed set his glass on a table. "I think so. We're the guys who never get killed."

George wiped his eyes with a handkerchief. "It has to be a mistake. That just couldn't happen. Not when he was so safe."

"He was the thread that ran through all of us," Dutch said.

Dennis held his hands out in a gesture of helplessness. "I always have something to say; now I can't think of anything."

George turned away to hide his tears. "What about the others?"

"Perry was wounded again, but he's okay," Reed said. "He's on Oki. Hayes was wounded for the third time. He's still tooling around in his Sherman. Dwyer was here—got a silver star, but decided to contract pneumonia, so he could go home. He's back in the States."

Dutch raised his cup. "Well, we're still here and I, for one, am not going to leave."

Reed raised his glass. "Listen to this, Crocker's so pissed… someone sent him a canned ham for Christmas and he lost it when the Chinese hit. That's all he talks about."

Dennis raised his cup. "He and Trexler couldn't make it. They're preparing for an attack."

"Ha." Reed said. "Supervising bunker digging. Sounds a lot like the Civil War to me, but I guess it makes sense if they're afraid they'll get killed." He looked at Dutch. "You don't think anybody's trying to kill us, do you?"

"You know, I've been here a hundred and seventy days now, and every day I've had the feeling someone was trying to kill me."

Dennis pointed at Dutch. "You can't count both the day you got here and today, so it's really only been a hundred and sixty-nine days."

Dutch pointed at Dennis. "I've been here a hundred and sixty-nine days now, and every day I've had the feeling someone was trying to kill me."

Dennis nodded. "That's better."

Reed picked up his glass and offered a toast. "It's been a hundred and sixty-nine days since I've had a piece of ass."

"Speaking of sex," Dennis said, "what do you think of Ridgeway taking over General Walker's job?"

Dutch limped over to refill his cup. "That was something. He goes all through Europe, and the worst part of Korea, and he gets killed in a Jeep accident."

"It's a good thing he made it this long," Dennis said. "Otherwise we'd be sitting in a snowdrift up north."

"How do you figure that?" George asked.

"MacArthur didn't order the general retreat; Walker did. MacArthur gave the order to keep attacking. You know, that's been the problem here. It's been 'take more territory, more territory' all the time. That's nonsense. Do like Dutch says, kill the enemy before he kills you. It's the same plan Ridgeway advocates: Don't worry about advancing to the Yalu, kill the enemy and keep the friendly forces alive."

Dutch sat his cup on an ammo box. "Nixon, you're right. As used to seeing death as I've become, it still tears me up to see even one dead American. On the way back from that territory that was so important, we lost a lot of men needlessly. I was walking on a road the other side of the Ch'ongch'on, a dead American lay in a ditch, holding a Carlisle bandage on his stomach. He'd been trying to cover a massive wound, and died with his eyes open. It snowed and covered his eyes with a light coating. I can still see that young soldier lying in a ditch with snow in his eyes."

Nobody spoke until Dutch said, "Time to eat."

The four friends left their private party and joined Dutch's gun section in another tent, to eat ham and all the trimmings. The Chinese didn't shoot at them, and George never mentioned Luisa to Dutch.

*

After leaving Dutch's outfit and returning to the 47th, George checked with personnel to see what he could do about locating his wife. The S-1 had no information on the problem, but on the afternoon of 31 December, George received correspondence through channels that the army could not locate Luisa, and she was not receiving an allotment. His paycheck would be increased.

That evening, a loudspeaker blared a message from Kim Il Sung, Emperor of North Korea, wishing American soldiers a Happy New Year. Then came the sound of bugles.

The first George knew about the mass attack was when Chinese fired on Able Battery's position. Two officers and a dozen men were killed. The first response was to retreat, but the American infantry halted and allowed the battery to dig in again, responding to fire missions.

Three days later, George received a call from Dutch. "It was a bad way to start 1951," Dutch said. "We were overrun. Lost a bunch of men, half our guns, and most of our ammo. Had to take us off the line. Trexler's missing in action. He and two men went behind the lines looking for a squad that was left there. They never returned."

One Helluva Soldier / Phil Kline

The line went silent. George thought they had been disconnected until Dutch said, "Dennis Nixon and Reed Rayford got their New Year's present. Cold enough to freeze farts, they were stuck in knee-deep snow and surrounded by Chinese. They fought for two days to make it to our lines then a gook jumped out of a foxhole with a burp-gun and shot Rayford in the shoulder. While he was on his knees, the gook pointed the gun at Reed's head. Nixon shot the gook and helped Rayford back to a medic. Oops, see you later. Have to go. Got a mission."

For the next three months, George conducted fire missions with the same goals as General Ridgeway's: preserving American lives and killing Chinese. On 18 April 1951, he stood in front of the S-3, with shoulders sagging. Captain Douglas walked from behind his field desk.

"You're going on the hill for a different outfit, The Gloucesters," he said to George.

George squinted. "Who?"

"They're British. It's pronounced Gloster, and you'd better say it right if you want to get along with them."

"Why am I going there?"

Douglas pointed north of Seoul on a wall map of North Korea. "Eight hundred of them all alone on the Imjim River, and they'll be in real trouble if the Chinese attack there. The 77th Field's been assigned to support them, and they need a forward observer who knows how to do it right."

"What about a team?"

"Sergeant Hilton and Private Hooker; H and H."

"Won't there be a problem in procedures with the British?"

"The 77th's American. They speak English." Douglas cocked his head to the side. "Are you having a bad day?"

"Today's my son's first birthday."

One Helluva Soldier / Phil Kline

26

On 22 April, George arrived at Gloucester Regimental Headquarters, located on the back side of a hill south of the Imjim River, near the village of Solma-ri, North Korea. He reported to Captain Anthony Farrar-Hockley, adjutant of the British regiment known in England as The Glorious Gloucesters.

Next to the adjutant, a small soldier with red hair and matching mustache, stood so straight he made others standing at attention appear to be at rest. The adjutant nodded toward him. "This is Mister Hobbs, Regimental Sergeant Major."

Mister Hobbs snapped his heels together and saluted, his hand quivering like a tuning fork as it reached his brow. "Happy to meet you, Sir."

George gave Mister Hobbs the snappiest salute he had given in a while. From the corner of his eye, he saw Hilton and Hooker waiting for guidance. George gave an okay sign with his thumb and first finger, and they relaxed.

The adjutant said "You must excuse me and Mister Hobbs. My driver will take you to Alpha Company." He pointed to a hill a half-mile in front of the tent. "Alpha is our forward company. Philip Curtis, a subaltern, will meet you there."

The FO team climbed into a Jeep and rode toward Alpha's position. On the way up the slope, to the right, George saw a young man with a white stole over his battle-dress, conducting a religious service in front of a temple. George said, "Cut the engine."

One Helluva Soldier / Phil Kline

A neatly dressed officer left the soldiers in attendance and trotted to the Jeep. When he saw George observing the service, he pointed in that direction. "Our chaplain, Padre Davies. We're fortunate to have him with us. I'm Philip Curtis with Alpha Company. Would you join me for a spot of tea?"

"I'd be happy to as soon as my men are taken care of."

"I'll have my top show them around."

Curtis rode back to the headquarters then said to the driver, "I'll bring your vehicle back in a few." He climbed in behind the wheel, and drove the American FO team toward the hill Alpha occupied.

George glanced at Curtis. "Tell me about Mister Hobbs."

"You Americans don't have an equivalent. Mister Hobbs is Regimental Sergeant Major of the Gloucesters, and you'd jolly well better call him mister if you wish to get on well with him. We are fortunate that he's a remarkably strong and positive person, and everybody in the battalion recognizes those qualities. The men seem to be in awe of him, and I must admit, I am also."

At Alpha's position, after Curtis directed his top to show H and H around, he and George had tea served in fragile china.

"Tell me about your situation," George said.

Curtis set his tea aside. "Yesterday we sent a patrol of Centurion tanks and infantry across the river. We know the Chinese are out there, but the patrol wasn't able to locate them. This morning a patrol did make contact, but we don't think it's a large force. We're ready if they come at us."

*

George saw the men were well dug in on the front and sides of the hill. In the distance, he observed a watching patrol stationed this side of the river

One Helluva Soldier / Phil Kline

After his tour with Curtis, George met Hilton and Hooker on the front slope of the hill.

"The phones and radio are in working order," Hilton said.

George helped his crew dig foxholes then zeroed in on checkpoints from which to direct fire. Forward, he saw a peaceful river that wound between the hills. Purple blossoms and what resembled goldenrod, added a colorful border.

After the evening meal, George was standing at the front of the position, talking with Curtis, when the sound of rifle fire came from down by the river. The firing stopped, and the watching patrol double-timed up the hill. George and Curtis hurried to meet them.

The lieutenant-in-charge spoke while breathing hard. "They're coming across. At first we thought it was only a patrol and we fired on them, but then they came by the hundreds."

Curtis and the patrol double-timed away, while George ran to the FO position to call a fire mission on the crossing. Hilton relayed it to FDC. George ordered a dozen more missions where the shells armed with variable time fuses burst over the heads of droves of Chinese crossing the river. Steel fragments took many down, but others kept coming.

At dusk, the zing of rifle fire cut through brush above George's head. Chinese charged up the hill, too close to direct artillery fire on them. He continued firing barrages on the crossing and, in between times, joined Hilton and Hooker, shooting his carbine into the many quilted figures. When he couldn't see individuals, he fired at the moving mass of gray and at gun flashes.

For a while the sound of rifle fire came from the right and from the left. When it began to come from the rear, George realized they were surrounded. For a fleeting moment, a half-moon came out from behind a puffy cloud to reveal men swarming up the front and sides of the hill. The FO team fired at men they could see, and when the moon disappeared behind a cloud, they again fired at gun flashes that resembled swarms of lightning bugs.

A machine-gun opened up to the right front, raking fire across the Brit's foxholes and pinning the men down. George watched Philip Curtis crawl into the darkness between the FO position and the platoon on his right. The machine-gun fired intermittently, and bullets sputtered into the ground near where Curtis had disappeared.

Five minutes later, George sensed movement too close to use grenades. A little man, in a quilted uniform, jumped onto the lip of George's foxhole. George shot him in the chest. Another two quilted men bounded up. George and his men fired automatic bursts, and the two fell backward.

Around midnight, the attack stopped and a half-moon broke through the clouds, revealing many bodies lying on the front slope. Figures, too distant for riflemen to hit, moved southward on the sides of the mountains, around the position.

George picked up the phone. It didn't work. The radio worked, but he was told that the 77th Field, two miles behind the Gloucesters, had come under attack. He had no artillery. Explosions from shells, fired by larger British guns further back, mushroomed dirt amongst men running along the side of a distant hill.

George crept toward the headquarters tent. *I don't know the password. It doesn't matter anyway. If I answer a challenge, the Brits will know I'm not one of them.* When he arrived without being challenged, the moon was shining on an empty tent pockmarked with bullet holes.

A voice came through the staccato of rifle fire. "Over here, matey."

One Helluva Soldier / Phil Kline

George crawled toward the voice. "I'm the American forward observer. I called my fire direction center, and they notified me they were under attack."

"We all have our problems, Yank."

"You don't understand. They're two miles behind this position. We're surrounded."

"I figured as much. You didn't happen to see Philip Curtis in your travels, did you?"

"Yes. He went forward of my position hours ago, I believe to silence a machine-gun."

"You didn't happen to see him come back, did you?"

"No. I'm sorry."

"Thank you, Yank."

George inched his way back to his foxhole without being shot by either side. Sergeant Hilton lay halfway out of the back side of his foxhole with a hole in the center of his forehead. Blood trickled down the side of his face. Hooker lay dead in the next foxhole.

George pulled a dog tag from each of them while feeling guilty for having left two inexperienced men alone. He searched the area for someone to blame for killing them, but saw no one he could pay for what they did. He returned to his foxhole and climbed in as the first glimmer of dawn spilled over the hills to his right. He wondered at the beauty of the billowy clouds floating in a clear blue sky on a day he guessed would be his last.

The hill was quiet. No enemy soldiers were visible in front, or on the sides, of the position except the dead and the dying. British soldiers walked around looking for their own dead and wounded. They carried Hooker and Hilton to the rear, along with others.

George joined two British enlisted men hurrying down the slope where Curtis had disappeared. They stepped over bodies, some showing the agony of death while others appeared to be sleeping. He looked for movement among the hundreds of Chinese who lay there. There was none, only silence and the smell of death.

He and the Brits climbed a hill on the right that looked like a good position for a machine-gun. There was no machine-gun and no Curtis.

Rifle fire stirred up dirt around their feet, and they hurried back to Alpha's position.

Men brought their dead to Padre Davies to receive last rites. The battalion doctor attended the wounded, and George helped load them onto lorries, to be taken to the back side of the hill. A subaltern said, "Alpha's company commander has been killed. We're moving one hill back to help D Company set a tighter perimeter defense."

*

Even though everyone had to know the Chinese would visit them again that night, George sensed that spirits were high. Colonel Carne, the Gloucester commander, along with Mister Hobbs and Captain Farrar-Hockley, walked around and chatted with the men as if they were expecting a leisurely evening instead of the long night of hell that was bound to come.

At his dinner of cold bully beef, George was told that an effort by Americans to rescue the battalion was blocked by the Chinese. The Gloucesters were all alone, ten thousand miles from home.

George dug a foxhole alongside the riflemen, thinking it might be the last home he'd ever have. For a moment, he thought it would be nice to be safe on the farm in Potterville, but was shocked to realize he'd rather be with the Gloucesters than on the farm.

One Helluva Soldier / Phil Kline

He watched Mister Hobbs lead six men to the old headquarters in the valley, where they climbed onto lorries and unloaded boxes. Under fire, they made it back with enough biscuits, bully beef, and water for one more meal.

George slept but awoke to small-arms fire. The sun disappeared and it seemed as if all the young men in China were charging up the hill toward him. Bugles blasted eerie sounds as men from Bravo and Charlie ran into Alpha's perimeter with small-arms fire chasing them. Through all this, the battalion doctor and Padre Davies worked to stop the bleeding of the wounded and to lay the dead under trees.

The survivors dug in on the highest ridge of what they now called Gloucester Hill and watched as food, water, and supplies were air dropped too far in front of the position to be retrieved.

Artillery rounds burst on the mountains on both sides of the hill. F4U Corsairs zoomed low over the mountains and dropped napalm canisters. Other aircraft strafed the Chinese, so close to Gloucester Hill that shell casings dropped within the perimeter.

At dark the planes left, and the artillery quit. Chinese mortar rounds dropped in, then machine-gun and small-arms fire raked the position. The Chinese came, and George fired the last of his ammo at them.

Colonel Carne ran to a group of defenders, gave words of encouragement, and disappeared into the darkness. His voice rang out over the din as he made his rounds. The men cheered a British bugler who sounded a series of calls. Someone shouted, "They're coming up on all sides."

Mister Hobbs called out, "Come on, you bastards, and get your breakfast," but soon the Gloucesters ran out of ammo, and the order was given to withdraw.

George threw his rifle down and felt ashamed. He ran toward the rear to join the Brits, passing by Padre Davies and the battalion doctor who were still tending the wounded. The

One Helluva Soldier / Phil Kline

Brits were met with rifle fire, and they split off in two directions. George followed those going to the right.

They stopped and raised their hands over their heads. Rifles were pointed at them by little brown men wearing quilted uniforms. George hesitated then raised his hands.

The Chinese herded George and the Brits into a ravine, a process that reminded him of cattle being herded into slaughtering pens. Guards pointed rifles at them as other sad-faced men were added to the group. One of the captors faced them.

"You are prisoners of the Chinese People's Volunteer Force. You will be given lenient treatment. You will be fed well and treated well if you learn the error of your ways. Obey, and you will not be killed."

A corporal next to George said, "He has no insignia, but he must be the *laoban*."

"What's a *laoban*?"

"Boss."

At daylight, more Chinese entered the ravine carrying boxes of biscuits and bully beef, evidently taken from the rations that had been left in the lorries. Meager portions were distributed, and the food ran out before George got any.

The Chinese searched the men, took their personal belongings, and yanked off their dog tags. The rest of the day was spent sitting on the edge of the ravine while more prisoners were added to the group. George guessed that two hundred of the eight hundred Gloucesters had been rounded up.

In the distance, he heard the sound of B-26s, coupled with machine-gun fire from the ground. The Chinese ran to the side of the ravine and huddled there. After the planes passed over without taking offensive action, the guards returned to their duties.

At dark, Chinese guards yelled, "Come with. Bring all."

One Helluva Soldier / Phil Kline

George had only the empty canteen attached to his ammo belt. Under the dim light of the half-moon, the column marched a half-mile to the Imjim, mechanically, like a line of robots with no speech capability.

At the bank of the river, the guards took off their clothes and tied them in a bundle. The men did the same.

A soldier next to George took his socks off and put his boots back on. He saw George watching him. "That'll save your feet," he said.

George did the same then walked into water that reached his armpits. He was tempted to take a drink to quench his thirst, but the desire disappeared when a quilted body, floating face down, bumped into the man in front of him. Two men slipped under the current and disappeared. He thought about joining them but reasoned his inability to swim would cause his body to join the one that had floated by.

George looked into the dark river, wishing he'd learned to swim when he was a kid. His mind went into action. *I made it with a twenty-pound radio on my back. This'll be a cinch.*

He took a deep breath and pulled his legs into a tuck. His head didn't go under, so he bent his body forward until his face went down. He righted himself, but his bundle of clothes slipped away from his grasp. Reaching out to grab the bundle caused him to go face down again. He paddled with one arm and managed to stay upright.

The current pushed into his mouth. He coughed then paddled until he faced downstream. He saw the outline of men fording the river from right to left, too close for him to make it to shore. He suppressed a cough, took a breath, and stuck his head and bundle of clothes under the water.

He lay face down in the river, stretched out like the floating body he'd seen earlier. His foot hit something soft, and he heard what sounded like an oath in Chinese.

One Helluva Soldier / Phil Kline

He couldn't hold his breath any longer. He went into a tuck, lifted his head, and took a deep breath. Water went down his throat. He tried to cough with his mouth closed, but it didn't work. Yelling, in Chinese, came from the right bank. Bullets made little geysers around him, and he heard shots. He gulped air and stuck his head beneath the surface. Bullets gurgled into the water.

When it was quiet, he raised his head. He felt numb. He clenched the bundle of clothes with his teeth, but it floated in front of him, obscuring his vision. Unable to go any further, he put his feet down. They touched bottom. The bundle fell. He grabbed it and scurried ashore.

After wiping himself off with his jacket, he finished drying by using his shirt as a towel. He dressed and plopped down on soft undergrowth, but stood when the cold became too much for him.

He walked toward a line of trees bordering a mountain. The woods smelled sweet. He climbed past trees starting to bud, and purple flowers that reminded him of trillium. In order to keep his attitude positive, as he walked along a ledge above the river bank, he imagined it was the Columbia River. He felt a spring in his step. He was going to be free.

A rock the size of a Jeep blocked his way along a ledge. As he inched his way around it, he heard the metallic sound a rifle makes, when the bolt is pushed forward, and a voice with an Asian accent. "Stop or I shoot."

In the filtered moonlight, George saw the outline of four small soldiers with rifles pointed at his chest. "Who are you?" one of the men asked in surprisingly good English.

"I'm George Martin. Who are you?"

The men chattered at each other, then the same one spoke with little accent, "You're American. What are you doing here?"

One Helluva Soldier / Phil Kline

George's mind went to work: *They don't sound Chinese. If they were North Koreans, I'd be dead.* "You ROK?" *Please be with the Republic of Korea*, he thought.

"Yes. What are you doing here?"

George said. "Looking for my outfit. What are you doing here?"

The man lowered his rifle and said, "We're looking for the 7th ROK."

George moved toward them, which didn't seem to upset them. "Let's team up to find our way home. How much ammunition do you have?"

"None."

"Let's get out of here."

"Do you know where we are?"

"I have a pretty good idea."

George started to climb, and the four ROK followed. They walked between pines, and reached the top to greet the sun. George waved for them to follow him down the other side to get out of the sunlight.

He dropped to his knees and waved for the others to get down when he saw lights flickering through the trees down the hill. He and the ROK men kneeled. He heard a rustling of brush.

Two men in mustard-colored North Korean uniforms walked out of the bushes with burp-guns pointed at him. The South Korean soldiers set their rifles down and put their hands over their heads. George did the same then wondered why. *We should have rushed them. They're going to kill us anyway.*

One of their captors yelled at the ROK then pointed back to where he and the other North Korean had come from. George didn't understand what was going on, but the ROK did. It showed in their faces as they were led away to be killed.

The other North Korean pointed his gun down the hill toward where light had shined through the trees. As George started down the hill, he heard two burp-gun bursts come from where the ROK had been taken. George and his captor continued down the hill until they reached a battalion of NKPA in bivouac. The other North Korean joined them there.

George's captors talked and laughed as they strolled through the bivouac area, displaying their American captive. Ten minutes after leaving there, George was taken to a flat area, clear of brush, where twenty American and United Nations soldiers sat with their backs to trees. As they drew closer, George saw that their arms circled the trees, bound with wire.

He was tied to a tree. Then the Koreans walked back in the direction from which they came.

A young sergeant, tied to the next tree, said, "Welcome to the club. What unit were you with?"

George relaxed the muscles in his arms to make the awkward position more bearable. "I was forward observer with the Gloucesters. They ran out of ammo and surrendered. I ducked under the water while crossing the Imjim and was picked up by those two North Koreans."

"We probably fired for you at Solma-ri," the sergeant said. "I'm with Baker Battery, 77th Field. At least I was."

George nodded. "I used your guns until I got the message that you were under attack. How'd you end up here?"

"We couldn't get to the trucks. They were half-mile from the guns."

"Why?"

"Some light colonel from regimental staff said the trucks were easy targets out in the open. He said to hide them in the woods. The CO did what he was told. When we got marching order, the trucks were already in the hands of the Chinese. We lost our guns and our trucks. Half of the guys are dead now, and the other half POWs. I would have told the colonel he was full of shit."

One Helluva Soldier / Phil Kline

George shook his head. "Where are the rest of your guys?"

"I don't know. I swam away in the river but was picked up yesterday. They tied me to this tree and left."

George hung his head but was jolted to alert status when he heard a commotion in the bivouac area. He strained against the wire to see what was going on. The North Koreans were marching out of the area. A Filipino, tied to a tree on the other side of the sergeant, said, "Oh, good, they're leaving here. Someone's sure to find us."

The last North Korean in the area, who had been standing by a captured Jeep, walked toward the men with a burp-gun slung over his shoulder. He turned and walked back to the Jeep, reached to the floor beneath the driver's seat, and pulled out two magazines. He stuck one in the receiver and walked toward the men, lifted the gun to his waist, and fired while swinging it back and forth. George buried his chin in his chest. The firing stopped, and George looked up to see another magazine being crammed into the gun. The firing started again.

After the firing stopped, George heard groans and crying. He opened his eyes and watched the shooter saunter back to the Jeep. George's only hurt was the wire cutting into his wrists. He looked up. The sergeant pulled against his bindings with blood dripping from his stomach. Most of the others were slumped over and bleeding. He couldn't tell if they were alive, and he wasn't sure where the cries and groans were coming from. He thought of his own problem. *Will I spend the last days of my life tied to a tree in North Korea?*

The North Korean leaned on the passenger side of his Jeep, smoking a cigarette and gazing at the men tied to the trees, some of whom were still groaning and straining against the wires. He reached under the seat, pulled out another magazine, shoved it into his burp-gun, and walked toward them.

One Helluva Soldier / Phil Kline

George winced as he strained against wires that cut into his wrists, but he continued to look straight at the North Korean.

One Helluva Soldier / Phil Kline

27

Before he reached the tied-up prisoners, the North Korean officer stopped, looked back toward the road, then turned and ran to the Jeep. The wheels spit gravel, and the engine raced as it sped north.

From the south, came the sound of another vehicle, similar to that which George had heard before. He strained against the wire. A gray stake truck came into view with four Chinese soldiers in back.

Near the spot where the Jeep had been parked, one of the soldiers pounded on the roof of the cab and yelled at the driver. The truck stopped, and the soldiers jumped off. The one who had done the pounding, ran to the front of the truck and pointed at the men tied to the trees. The driver climbed out of the cab and walked toward the men with a burp-gun at a ready position. He went from tree to tree, then returned to the truck and talked with the others. Their voices increased in volume until it sounded like an argument.

The driver climbed in front. The four hopped onto the bed, and the truck made a circle, heading back in the direction from which it had come. The woods were quiet again except for moans and sobs.

George slumped forward, his mind reverting to another time his wrists had been tied behind him.

*

One Helluva Soldier / Phil Kline

George stepped out the door of Potterville High in the shadow of the only cloud in the Michigan sky. Big and bloated John J. McNish stood between him and the school bus with his legs spread apart, carrying a stick over his shoulder like a rifle. At John J's side, were his shadows, Robert and Gene, runts who stood with feet apart, grinning along with their idol.

The bus driver probably wouldn't wait for George. The morning after the last time this had happened, the driver said, "Blondie, by the time you're a sophomore you should be able to catch a bus without being led by the hand."

George stuffed his notebook in his jeans, pulled his shoulders back, and looked straight ahead as he marched toward the bus. Halfway through the wall of grins, John J. grabbed the stick off his shoulder and poked it between George's shins. George went down. The three boys laughed. Other students paid little attention to what was going on.

George got to his feet, dusted off his pants, and took two half-steps toward the bus. He spun around and hit John J. in the mouth with his right fist, then clobbered Robert on the side of his head with the back of his left. Robert went down, but John J. recovered and grabbed George around the neck from behind. George kicked Gene in the stomach, but John J. pushed him to the ground and held him. Gene pinned George's arms behind him while Robert tied his wrists together. Then John J. used a jack knife to cut hunks out of George's hair, pulling out some as he cut.

They released George, but left his arms tied behind him. John J. stood back and hollered, "Without that wig, you still look like a girl, you fairy." His two sidekicks laughed, and the three boys strutted away.

A girl from George's class untied his hands, and he walked the four miles to his home.

One Helluva Soldier / Phil Kline

When he came downstairs to dinner that evening, his mother looked at his hair. "Oh, George." A moment later, her husband walked in from the living room. She hurried to the stove and pretended to be busy stirring the mashed potatoes.

Joe Martin walked to the table, waving a copy of the *Lansing State Journal.* "Dottie, did you see what President Truman said about the reporter who criticized his daughter's singing voice?" One look at George, and he tossed the newspaper across the room.

That evening the Martins ate a warm meal in cold silence. After dinner, Joe and Dorothy Martin argued. The next morning, George was sent to live with Grandma Kate.

*

George looked up when the truck returned with the four soldiers. The driver walked toward the men, again carrying his burp-gun. He inspected those slumped over then went back to the truck to confer with the four men. They walked to where the men were tied.

George sighed when the Chinese went from tree to tree, cutting wires. He and six other POWs who were able to walk, were allowed to relieve themselves in a ditch beside the road and then led to the truck where they were offered cups of water. After the seven prisoners drank the water, the driver dished lukewarm cabbage soup to them in the same cups.

When they finished their soup, they were herded back to the woods where they had been tied. The wounded and the dead were gone. The only evidence of what had occurred there was blood-soaked ground and pieces of wire.

The driver faced them. "Your wounded are taken to hospital, and we bury your dead. You are guests of Chinese People's

One Helluva Soldier / Phil Kline

Volunteer Force. Sit now. We take care of you good if you not try escape. We stay here until dark." He raised the muzzle of his gun. "If you escape, we shoot."

The seven prisoners sat on the ground for three hours. At dusk two Chinese guards walked into the area, and the truck left with its four Chinese passengers.

One of the guards pointed to the road going north to indicate that the seven POWs were to march in that direction. Twenty yards down the road, the other guard prodded the prisoner at the head of the column with a bayonet. "*Qway-ka-day, qway-ka-day.*" The speed picked up.

George didn't mind the command to move quickly because the fast pace helped him stay warm. They walked in silence until dawn when they entered a village of eight mud huts, which smelled like the family pig sty in Michigan. Hills, covered with budding trees, rose on two sides. Another hundred or so POWs under guard stood in the road, mostly Americans, with a smattering of Brits, Filipinos, and Turks.

A *laoban* appeared, jabbering and gesturing at the guards who then barged into the closest huts and drove out old people, women, and children, many without coats. They were herded down the street to shiver and watch the same thing happen to their neighbors.

Guards prodded a group of men standing in front of George and ushered them into a hut, then George and nineteen others were led to a second twelve-by-twelve square hut that had a low red table in the middle. A box of Korean turnips and a rusty bucket half-full of water sat in a corner. A small cupboard held bowls, plates, cups and a butcher knife.

A guard squeezed his way in and looked around. He picked up the knife from the cupboard but ignored a long-handled brass spoon next to it. He stuck the knife in his coat pocket and wound his way out, banging the door behind him.

One Helluva Soldier / Phil Kline

George reached over, picked up the spoon, and stuck it through a hole in his field jacket pocket so it was hidden inside the lining. He turned to liberate a turnip, but they had all disappeared.

The major sound was the jabbering of two Chinese guards outside the door.

A burly POW picked up the table, kicked the door open, and started outside, but a guard chastised him and pushed him back through the door. He and the table fell on other men, and cuss words were flung at him. The man the table landed on, grabbed it and shoved his way to the door. He pushed it open, threw the table out, and slammed the door shut. That seemed to satisfy everyone, including the burly man and the guards.

The room wasn't large enough for twenty men to lie down, so some lay while others, including George, sat.

He surveyed the sides of the hut and decided they could not provide an avenue of escape. He figured he could go out through the straw roof but not at this time.

He was tired and put his head between his knees. He looked up when the door opened. A guard glanced around, shoved his way to George, and poked him with the tip of a bayonet. "Come with."

George frowned. *Why did you choose me?*

*

The sun peered over the hill to the east, dulled by a smoky mist of burning wood that blended with the pig odor hanging in the air. George shivered from the chill of early morning as the guard led him past two others sitting by the table that had been thrown out.

He was escorted down the road and into a hut similar to the one he was housed in, but neater. A Chinese, wearing polished boots and pressed uniform, sat cross-legged on a mat behind a low table. He held a teacup in one hand and motioned with the other for George to sit. George sat on the floor across the table from him.

The man spoke English with very little accent. "What is your name?"

"George E. Martin."

"You are an American officer. Is that correct?"

George wondered how the man knew, since he had thrown away his silver bar and crossed cannons before his capture. "I'm George E. Martin, First lieutenant, O2014508."

"You are quite young so I assumed you must be a lieutenant. What is your MOS?"

"My name is George E. Martin, First Lieutenant, O2014508."

"What is your military occupational specialty, Lieutenant?"

"My name is George E. Martin, First Lieutenant, O2014508."

"Are those the only words you know?"

"Nothing else is required."

"So you're a smartass. You'll change your ways once we've completed your education. It always works with smart-ass Americans." He picked up a little cast-iron teapot from near his right leg and poured tea into his cup.

George gazed at the teapot.

The man looked at the pot then at George. He took a sip of tea, then reached down and poured himself more. He folded his hands around the cup as if to warm them. "What is your MOS, Lieutenant smartass?"

George gave his name, rank, and serial number again.

The man stood and walked to George's right side. "What is your MOS?"

George didn't answer. He saw the blur of an automatic pistol and felt the barrel cut into the skin above the scar over his right eye. Warm blood trickled into his eye. He pulled out his

One Helluva Soldier / Phil Kline

handkerchief, wiped it away and held his palm against the wound.

The man held the pistol up high and walked behind George. Although George couldn't see it, he heard the sound of the receiver going forward and felt the barrel of the automatic touch behind his ear. "You probably didn't realize it," the man said, "but China did not sign the Geneva Convention. I'll give you one more chance. What is your MOS?"

He's bluffing. If he was going to kill me, he'd have the guard do it outside. He wouldn't mess up his office. "My name is George E. Martin, First—-" He heard a metallic click.

The man shouted, "Take him to the pigpen."

The guard looked confused and shook his head.

The interrogator yelled in Chinese. The guard bowed, turned to George, poked him with the bayonet, and motioned toward the door.

Outside, he escorted George down the street, behind a hut, and into an unoccupied pigpen that had a heavy smell, indicating it had recently housed pigs.

The guard directed him to a wooden hutch that would hold a large hog, and pointed to the front. George bowed, squatted down, backed in, and sat with his knees high.

The guard put a rock in front of the opening and left to sit on a larger one outside the pen. He leaned his rifle against the fence and lit a cigarette.

I wonder how long I'll be in here. How long can I stand being in here? At least I'm alive, and they probably want me to stay alive. I should have told him my MOS. George moved his body around, trying to find a comfortable position. No luck.

He was hungry. He'd had only one bowl of soup to eat in the past two days, or had it been three, or a week? *That guy knew I wanted tea. If he were smart, he would have offered me some. It*

One Helluva Soldier / Phil Kline

wouldn't have made any difference, but he didn't know that. If I'd been questioning him, I would have given him some tea.

George had read that during World War II submarine crews exercised by tensing their muscles while lying on their bunks. He tried doing it but tired quickly. He decided thinking would be easier and more productive. *I'd love to be cutting into a sirloin strip steak, medium well, with fried potatoes, and a big glass of milk. For dessert, let's see... banana cream pie. No, hold that. Give me a piece of apple pie with a scoop of vanilla ice cream.* He shook his head. *I can't do that to myself.* He yelled at the guard, "Cancel that order."

The guard barely turned his head toward George.

Good. I got that out of my system. How do I keep my mind busy? Something positive. I wonder what Luisa's doing. And Mario. Yes, Mario. How old would he be now? 18 April 1950 up to today. Today's got to be the twenty-seventh. I missed his birthday. I'll make up for it.

"Hi, Mario, I'm your father. Sorry I haven't seen you for almost a year, but I've been busy," George said aloud. He continued talking while the guard watched. "You've grown so. Come here and let me see how much you weigh. Oh, you're heavy. You're getting to be a big boy. Can you talk? I hear you. You talk like a big boy. I bet you learned that from your mother. I'm glad she speaks to you in English. Well, Mario, I'm going to sleep now. I'll see you again soon, and we'll talk more. I promise. What did you say? ...I miss you too, son."

Noticing the guard was listening to his conversation, George gave a fake grin before lowering his head between his knees. Eventually, he found sleep.

When he awoke, he wondered why he was uncomfortable, until he remembered he was cooped up in a little hutch. He was hot. His jacket and hat had felt good earlier, but now the sun beat down on the hutch. He pulled off his hat, but couldn't get

One Helluva Soldier / Phil Kline

his arms out of the jacket. He had to take a leak and preferred doing it somewhere other than in his pants.

Hey, Guard."

The guard looked at him.

"I have to go to the latrine."

The guard kept looking at him.

George waved a finger from side to side while hissing.

The guard looked both ways. He scratched his chin, looked around again then motioned for George to come out of the hutch. George kicked the rock over to the side and shimmied out.

He removed his jacket and laid it on the top of the hutch. Then he stretched. The guard jerked his thumb toward a slit-trench behind a hut. Being out of the hutch and on his feet, felt so good that, after George relieved himself in the trench, he walked in a circle and stretched again. The guard watched, but didn't interfere with George's extended journey to the hutch. After another circle, stretching all the way, he bowed to the guard and pointed his thumb up. *"Ding how."*

After the guard pointed to the hutch, George bent down as if to back in, but, instead, stood and stretched again. The guard pointed toward the hutch. George put his right fist up with his thumb and little finger out, and wiggled it in front of his mouth, like guys signify drinking.

The guard shook his head and pointed to the hutch. George bowed and made a gesture like eating. The guard shook his head and pointed at the hutch. George bowed, stretched, went to his knees, and backed into the hutch.

The guard gave a faint smile, looked around, and removed his canteen from his belt. He handed George the canteen. George drank half of the water in it and handed it back to the guard who grabbed it and hurried back to his rock.

One Helluva Soldier / Phil Kline

George touched his forehead as if tipping a hat. "Thank you." *What a strange place to make a new friend.*

*

After a nap, he awoke to the sound of four shots in the distance, then four more closer, followed by the roar of a low-flying plane. He slid forward and saw a P-51 Mustang climbing away. He reasoned the shots were an early warning signal and wondered why the pilot didn't fire into the village.

Looking between the huts, he saw women and children standing in the middle of the road. Soldiers were pointing rifles at them.

He slid against the back wall and dozed occasionally. By dusk, his legs and back ached, and he was cold. He stuck his head out and saw he had a different guard. He heard footsteps and saw his friendly guard approach. The new guard left, and the friendly one motioned for George to leave his hutch. He led George back to the hut from which he had come.

The other POWs gave him lots of room. After ten minutes of a strained relationship, a guard opened the door. "Chow."

The men were led into the street and made to form a line. Many were barefoot. George asked a Brit, "Where are your boots?"

"Where have you been?"

"In a pig pen out back. Why don't you have boots?"

"The Chinese stole them. They took us down the street for a training class. When we got there, they walked around until they found blokes with boots that fit them then stole them." He looked at George's boots. "You're safe. You have big feet."

George pointed at the man's bare feet. "You'd better get something to protect yours."

"What do you suggest, Yank?"

One Helluva Soldier / Phil Kline

"Tear your shirt, or cut your pant legs off. Do something."

"Thanks, matey. You can talk. You have boots." He turned away but faced George again. "These blokes are sick. These two guys in dress uniforms, they talk for two hours about how great Communism is and how we Brits are only dupes to the American capitalists. They say you Americans urged the South Koreans to invade North Korea, and the North Koreans are only defending their country. They say our government is helping Rockefeller and others to take over North Korea. Personally, I haven't seen anything here I'd take if they offered it to me. Then this English chap, from London, mind you, he comes up and tells me that if I help convince the world I don't want to be here—that I was forced to come—I'll be back in England before summer. He says to me, 'Step forward and you can go back to your family rather than die here in the name of American expansionism'."

"You didn't."

"You mad? I just want to sleep. I've been up two nights."

At sunset, guards doled a half-canteen of water and a handful of cracked corn to each man. George was familiar with cracked corn, having fed it to baby chicks on the farm. He drank the water and stuffed the corn in his pocket then a *laoban* spoke and pointed north.

The guards prodded men with bayonets to get them moving, slowly at first, but a jab in the ribs or a rifle butt in the back, speeded things up.

They left the village and climbed a hill west of the road, staying in the shade. As he walked, George sucked on part of his corn to soften it before swallowing.

One of the wounded stumbled. Two others helped by wrapping their arms under his. The going was slow, even with the constant prodding of bayonets. A British corporal in stocking feet was jabbed in the side. A maroon patch spread on his shirt as he climbed the hill.

Near the top of the mountain, the column turned north. Speed in the woods was difficult to maintain, but George guessed the Chinese stayed in the woods because of their fear of aircraft.

Progress was difficult for those without boots. A sergeant yelled at a guard and, by gestures, indicated the men needed a break to protect their feet. The guard didn't pay attention to him.

"Stop," the sergeant yelled.

The *laoban* came back.

The sergeant pointed to a POW walking barefooted. "We can make better time if you let the men wrap their feet."

The *laoban* nodded. He stopped the march and yelled, "We are lenient. You who do not have boots have minutes to wrap your feet."

He walked to the side, sat on a rock, and drank from his canteen while the shoeless did their best to wrap their feet.

The sergeant approached the *laoban*. "The men have nothing to cut their uniforms with. Can the guards use their bayonets?"

The *laoban* pulled his pistol out of its holster and pointed for the sergeant to get back in line. He waited until the sergeant obeyed, then yelled an order. The guards walked up and down the column slashing shirts, jackets, and pants where needed.

Ten minutes later, at the command to *mach, mach*, the column began to move. After what George guessed to be a dozen miles through the mountains, they stopped at a village in a valley.

He watched the Chinese prepare supper by pouring a cup of salt into a fifty-five gallon drum of boiling water, then dumping a dozen cabbages into the brine. The Chinese kicked Koreans out of their homes as dinner cooked. After the men ate, thirty more Brits joined the group, all packed together in one hut.

One Helluva Soldier / Phil Kline

George was questioned again but gave only his name, rank, and serial number. The interrogator, who had a hump on his back, said, "You are reactionary warmonger and enemy of the people. Answer questions or you will be shot."

George said nothing and was surprised when he was ushered to his hut, arriving in time to get his ration of cracked corn, boiled and served as mush. No seasoning, no taste, and difficult to swallow. He ate it then slept.

On the trail that night, a man, unconscious much of the time, was being carried. He asked to be put down. After discussion with those who carried him, he was set down. Another of the wounded, who lagged behind and was constantly being jabbed by a bayonet, sat beside him and flipped his middle finger at a guard who came toward him. "Fuck you, Chink."

The column was halted and the *laoban* came back to where the men sat. "These men will be taken to hospital for treatment. You mach, now."

George's friendly guard stayed with them as the column moved on. Minutes later, George heard a rifle shot, followed by another, then silence.

The next night, seven more men quit and lay along the trail. Shots were heard from where the men had dropped.

George pulled up the collar of his field jacket and wrapped a liberated cloth around his neck to protect him from the cold. During breaks from the march, he curled up in a ball. He always struggled to his feet and began to march again, but death, for some, was more acceptable than pain. Those who didn't uncurl were executed,

The morning after the fifth night, they turned down a worn trail, between two steep mountains, into a valley less than a hundred yards wide. The sides were ringed with tunnel entrances, and remains of a railroad bed lay between long sheds badly in need of repair. Guards were stationed at doors of the sheds, and an occasional POW was ushered somewhere.

George's group was halted near a tunnel entrance that exuded an odor so foul he guessed it came from dead men rotting. The group was jammed into sheds divided into rooms the size of Korean huts.

George's room had no windows, but there was light because the doors were gone. Much of the floor had rotted away, and fortunately, the smell of urine and feces was so strong, it overpowered the smell from the tunnel.

At first, the men were not allowed to go to the latrine. One man at a time was finally allowed to relieve himself under guard, too late for many. The sun had risen over the mountain when George was led behind the shed to a full slit-trench with his bladder near bursting. His urine ran off the piled-up waste, back to his boots.

After he returned to the room, a guard came to the door. "Mateen. Come with. Bring all."

Again, George wondered why they chose him and how they located him.

He was led to a shed the size of a Korean hut. A guard, sitting on a box in front of the shed, stood and unlatched a door so rotten it could've been knocked off its hinges by one swift kick.

Light through the door revealed four ratty-looking, bearded men in khakis. Another, wearing jeans, was half a head taller than the others, his face had twice as much hair, and he wore a Detroit Tigers baseball cap.

The door closed, leaving only forms visible.

"Welcome to our humble abode," the man in the Tigers cap said. "You've missed most of the festivities, but fortunately you're in time to dine with us. You like turnips?"

"It'd be a welcome change. Who are you?"

One Helluva Soldier / Phil Kline

A voice came from the side. "That's Brian. We're not all as crazy as he is. I'm Roger."

"I'm George."

One said, "Why'd they put you here? You air force?"

"I don't know why I'm here. I was a forward observer assigned to the Gloucesters."

A new voice spoke up. "What are Glosters?"

"They're British," Brian said. "George, these guys are fly-boys and don't know what goes on down below. I know about them because I was a real-life war correspondent whose job was to tell Americans how well this police action's going."

Roger said, "You'll find out how little he knows when you get to know him. My full name's Roger Gibson. Over there's Tom Sorensen and Bob Kay. We're Air Force. In the corner's Ben Stanley, a Marine pilot."

"Actually," Brian said, "these fly-boys are remarkable. The Chinese hate them, and the North Koreans hate them. If we had light in here, you could tell they're dirty, ragged, and have cuts and bruises over their faces and bodies. They take all the shit the gooks dish out, and not a one of them gives the bastards the time of day."

"And they do dish it out." Roger's voice was surprisingly soft. "I didn't mind getting hit that much. I've been in fights since I was five years old, but the shit treatment is Han's favorite for pilots, a slit-trench. I was there three days, and I still dream about it."

The next voice sounded like a kid's. "That's the worst they dish out. Chinese would rather hurt the mind than the body."

George shuddered. "I don't know if I could handle it as well as you guys have." Becoming accustomed to the dark, he saw that Brian, the closest to him, looked old enough to have a son in the service. It seemed strange to see an older POW after being

One Helluva Soldier / Phil Kline

around young men for the last nine months. *Will another nine months go by before I get home?*
    The door burst open. "Mateen, come with."
    "I hope it's not Han," one of the men said.
    Roger spoke. "Tom, you've got no brains at all."

One Helluva Soldier / Phil Kline

28

The same interrogator who had sent George to the pigpen, sat cross-legged on a mat behind a one foot tall table. A teapot, emitting a dainty wisp of steam, was in the middle of the table. A China cup was in front of the interrogator and the other on the side where George stood.

The man motioned for George to sit. "You are Lieutenant George E. Martin, forward observer with the 47th Field Artillery Battalion. On April twenty-second, you were assigned temporary duty with the Gloucester Regiment, to direct artillery fire upon the Chinese People's Volunteer Force. Now, all the officers and men of the Gloucesters are either dead or our prisoners. What do you say to that?"

George glared at him. "You are Major Han, interrogator for the Chinese Army at the Mining Camp. It took 20,000 of your so-called volunteers to subdue 800 British troops, and then only because the Brits ran out of ammunition."

Han leaned forward, eyes narrowed. "I can call a guard and have you killed at the flick of a wrist. I will if you don't cooperate."

He won't kill me. That would be admitting he failed. "My name is George E. Martin, First Lieutenant, O2014508."

Han nodded. "I see. I really don't think you fear death. First we'll get you to the point where you wish you were dead then we shall oblige you." Han reached over, picked up the cup from in front of George, and snapped his fingers. A guard came to the door. Han placed the cup in a cabinet next to where he sat. "Lieutenant Martin, do you believe in God?"

"Yes."

"Let's see Him get you out of the predicament you've got yourself into."

Han pointed at the door and spoke to the guard, who led George from the hut, with the tip of a bayonet poking him in his back.

George's mind raced as he was prodded down the street. *Why am I so obstinate? I could have given him information that wouldn't help them. I should have hidden from the Chinese at the Imjim. If I had rushed those two North Koreans, the ROK would have joined me.*

The guard ushered him behind a shed to a slit-trench latrine and motioned for him to climb in. George's nostrils were overwhelmed by the stench and his head shook involuntarily.

The guard advanced toward him with his bayonet out front.

George pushed the flat of his hand toward the guard and shook it. He looked down at the trench's contents. "Shit," he said as he removed his boots and his clothes. He folded his pants and shirt, put them on top of his boots, and placed his jacket on them while thinking his mom would be pleased if she saw how neatly he'd folded his clothes.

George put his hands on the sides of the trench to ease himself in, but his hands slipped on slime, and he dropped quickly. His elbows stopped his fall. He raised his arms slowly until he felt bottom. The mixture of piss and shit spilled over the top but only reached his armpits, eliminating his fear of submerging his face.

He was cold, but that was a minor problem. He was nauseated. He gritted his teeth and held it in, so Han wouldn't derive pleasure from his misery.

One Helluva Soldier / Phil Kline

   The guard made sure he didn't have to share George's misery—he put a gauze mask over his face.
   It occurred to George that Major Han may have been right; perhaps a quick death would be a better option. *No, I should've given Han garbage information, but I'll just have to pay the price for being bullheaded. Before long, even my breath will smell like this shit-hole. I can deal with that. But what if they leave me here to die? Should I climb out and run, so the guard will shoot me. No. That's twice I've thought death was an option. No more.*
   A bug crawled up the back of his neck and another across his cheek. The lice he had accumulated over the past couple of days were deserting his lower body. Even they were disgusted with the trench.
   He picked them off as well as he could and flicked them to the ground, away from where he stood, reasoning that they deserved a better fate than his.
   He shivered. *The last time I was this cold was when I walked across the Imjim, and the time before that was crossing the river with Michaels. I'd rather be in this shit-hole than serving under him. Damn, I'm thinking bad things when I should be thinking good ones. I know—I'll visit my son.*
   "Hello, Mario. Last time we spoke, you were just learning to talk. Have you learned any new words? ...Oh, Daddy. I'm impressed. What have you been doing lately? Playing with Princess? Who is Princess? She's not a doll, is she? Oh, your tiger cat. Is it a real cat? Oh, you can't tell. I forgot you're just a little boy and it's difficult to discern reality from imagination. I sometimes have the same problem. Right now it's coming in handy."
   George's imaginary world vanished, and he looked around at the real one. The row of sheds extended off into the distance.

One Helluva Soldier / Phil Kline

Other sheds must have had slit-trenches out back, but if they did, none were visible.

His mind traveled back for another visit with Mario, but his imagination ran out of conversation. "I love you," he said then his mind went blank. After that, he figured it made sense to keep his mind blank so he wouldn't think about where he was. But he was unable to do so. With some embarrassment, he thought of prayer. *I've heard that everybody on a life raft in the middle of the ocean believes in God. I'm not in the middle of the ocean, and I already believe in God. I wonder if it bothers him that I only talk to him when I need his help.*

He recited the 23rd Psalm. When he got to the part about walking through the valley of the shadow of death, he repeated the phrase "I will fear no evil". He said it again and again. Sight disappeared, sound disappeared, and thought disappeared as though he were in a trance. No longer was he cold, nor did he smell the slime. Eventually he even found sleep.

*

He awoke and wondered why he had not sunk below the surface. He pulled his feet off the bottom but didn't sink. His fear of not being able to endure disappeared. He decided to count to one hundred thousand, but his mind wandered, causing him to lose count. He concentrated on being diligent in his counting. That lasted until he got to one thousand six.

He decided to visit the restaurant in Pusan. That didn't last long because the steak and fries smelled like shit. Anyway, the waitress with the see-through blouse wasn't the one he'd like to get close to. *The one in Pusan who had her hand in my pant is the one I'd like to cuddle up to in my sleeping bag.* He frowned. *What am I thinking? She was only about thirteen and I'm married.*

One Helluva Soldier / Phil Kline

He decided to change his line of thought and glanced at the surrounding mountains that rose so high they kept the sun from reaching the valley.

In fading light, he guessed the time was 2000 hours. His head and shoulders were cold. He looked at his clothes lying folded next to the trench and thought he'd be in trouble if someone took them. He reached over, tossed his ammo belt and empty canteen to a dry spot then stuck his socks, underwear, and shirt in the boots. He wrapped his pants and jacket around the boots and tied the bundle to one of his hands with the boot laces.

Sleep still didn't come, so he played mind games. He talked with Mario again. He prayed and thought about how he'd met Luisa and how much he missed her, more now than before. He tried to remember words to songs with a positive bent. He sang what he remembered of *Smile and the World Smiles with You*, *Zippity Do Dah*, *Every Cloud Must Have a Silver Lining*, and *Oh, What A Beautiful Morning*. It helped.

Sleep came, but a rain woke him. When it stopped, light came from the reflection of trees at the top of the mountain to the east. They were bathed in sunlight.

George saw the guard was gone. At first, he thought he'd run, but before getting dressed, he wanted to clean up. He heard running water toward the east—rainwater run-off—rushing down from the same mountain.

Nobody seemed to be looking, so he pulled himself out of the trench, picked up his clothes, and ran to the stream. He set his clothes down, filled his canteen, drank from it, and filled it again.

He waded into the stream, cold but cleansing. He washed his face and when he opened his eyes he found himself staring into the hole in the barrel of a rifle held by a guard standing on the bank. George was amazed at the size of the hole.

One Helluva Soldier / Phil Kline

After washing the slime off his body, he crawled out of the ditch, saluted the guard, and shook like a dog to get rid of the excess moisture. He wiped his body with his t-shirt and dressed.

The guard motioned toward the slit-trench with his rifle.

Would I be better off to run or to try and take him down? George made his decision to do neither when he saw a tin, the size of a Campbell's soup can, next to the trench. The guard motioned for him to pick up the can. It was half full of millet. The guard pointed toward the sheds. George's mind sang.

He walked with a spring in his step, chewing millet on the way to the shed where his five cellmates were cooped up.

As soon as he was ushered in, he noticed the other guys stunk. Someone in the darkness said, "Han didn't put you in the slop bucket, did he?"

"Yes, He did."

"How come you don't smell like shit?"

George plopped down. "I took a bath in a stream."

"How'd you manage that?"

"I didn't see a guard so I just did it. Who's talking?"

"Oh, I'm Roger."

A form raced past George. Whoever it was yanked a rotten board off the door, then another. Daylight streamed into the shed. It was Brian. The guard beat his rifle on the door and yelled, "Stopo." The others watched in amazement as Brian took one of the boards from the door and put it on his head, so it looked like he was wearing a feather. He stuck his head through the hole he'd made in the door and yelled, "Woo woo woo, I'm an Indian."

The guard cracked Brian on the head with his rifle butt. "Stopo, Indy."

Brian pulled his head back inside with blood dripping down his face.

One Helluva Soldier / Phil Kline

"Now we can see better," he said. "I've been wanting to do that for a long time." He sat down and pressed a sleeve to a cut on his forehead.

The guard inspected the new opening in the door, then sat and jabbered to his partner.

A tall husky guy, who swaggered like a cowboy, approached Brian. "You're crazy." He pulled Brian's arm back and looked at the cut. "It's not serious. Drink lots of water, take aspirin twice a day, and get plenty of rest."

"Thanks, Tom."

A man, with a freckled face and a red beard, said, "Trying to look more like us, Brian?"

George saw a warm smile through the bruises on Roger's face. George guessed the quiet one was Bob. He was short and looked too young to be in the Air Force. In contrast to the others, he had no whiskers, just cuts and bruises on his face like everyone else's. George suddenly realized what Roger meant by his crack about Brian trying to look more like them; they'd been beaten.

Tom pointed to a young redhead who sat in the corner. "That's Ben. He's a Marine, but we still talk to him."

Ben waved.

George waved back. "You fly a Corsair?" he asked Ben.

"I did until a couple of weeks ago."

Two weeks ago," George said, "I was directing fire for the British. Corsairs flew so low over our position on the Imjim I could see the pilots' faces. Their shell casings fell on us."

"That may have been me. I was there. I wish we could have done more, but we didn't have enough planes to go around."

"How'd you get caught?"

Ben pointed up with a pistol he made with his thumb and first finger. "Ground fire."

One Helluva Soldier / Phil Kline

"I'm surprised. North Koreans and Chinese are terrorized when they hear a plane, even in the distance."

"That's why they hate us."

"How'd you get the bruises?"

"Three North Korean soldiers and an old bearded civilian were waiting for me when I hit the ground. The old guy beat on me with a stick, and the soldiers let him do it. Then the old man yelled at them and pointed down the hill. They took me to a village and walked me through the street. People threw stones at me. A little old lady even hobbled up and punched me."

Roger nodded. "Our story's much the same, but we were shot down by a Mig 15. Bob, Tom, and I bailed out, but I came down in a different location than they did. The gooks hauled me to the main street of a village where there was a lot of yelling going on. Bob and Tom were the main attraction in a parade and were being beat on by the spectators. I joined the parade, and we marched through the village, people pounding on us all the way."

George swung a finger back and forth from one man to the other. "Who was the pilot?"

Roger pointed at himself. "I was."

George glanced at Bob and Tom. "Bombardier? Navigator?"

"Bob was copilot, navigator, camera man," Roger said. "See, we had an unarmed B-26 for photo recon. We came over at night, took one picture of enemy activity on the front, with a one million watt flashbulb then hauled ass."

"Why unarmed?"

"Eliminated weight so we could get away."

"And Tom?"

Roger laughed. "Tell him, Tom."

"I'm staff. I went along to see what they did, just for a lark."

Roger scoffed. "Bullshit. Don't believe him. He just wanted to watch me fly, so he could tell me how to do it better."

One Helluva Soldier / Phil Kline

Tom thrust a finger toward Roger. "And I found a better way, too. Keep the goddamn plane up in the air."

Brian didn't look up. "Just an innocent bystander, like me."

Tom glanced at George. "How come Han gave you the shit treatment?"

"I only gave him my name, rank, and serial number."

"Why?"

"That's all I'm supposed to give."

"You should've lied to him or given him information he already knew," Tom said.

George pointed at Tom. "Then how come you got the slit-trench?"

"All Air Force get the shit."

"What did you tell Han?"

"That I was a friend of Roger's, and that I just came along for the ride."

"You just let him know Roger was the pilot," George said.

Roger picked up a piece of wood that Brian had broken off, fingered it like a guitar, and nodded.

Tom glared at George, then at Roger, who strummed his imaginary guitar and sang:

> *Oh, if I had the wings of an angel,*
> *over these prison walls I would fly.*

Tom walked to the other side of the room and sat down.

Roger stopped singing when the door was shoved open and ten men stumbled in, bringing with them the smell of shit. They looked around in silence and sat down, most of them with their heads bowed, as if they had given up.

"Where you guys from?" Brian asked.

One of the men raised his head. "Caves."

"Do you want to talk about it?"

"No."

Nobody spoke for a while then one of them said, "North Koreans put us in caves, sealed them up, and left us there a week."

"Four days," another corrected. "No food, no water, no light. Nothing except darkness."

Brian reached out to the caveman who spoke. "How'd you escape?"

"Koreans left. Chinese let us out."

"Why?"

"I don't know."

"I know why," George said. "The same reason they haven't killed us. We're bargaining tools. They need us as pawns in peace negotiations."

Tom looked at George with a sneer. "How do you know that?"

"I don't know it, but it's probably the reason. I've been around here for nine months. The North Koreans take prisoners, but they kill them. I've been captured twice by the Chinese. With the Gloucesters, we ran out of ammo and hadn't eaten for two days. The Chinese fed us. They abused us, but they didn't kill us."

"I don't buy your theory," Tom said.

Roger poked a finger at Tom. "Shut up."

"Yeah, shut up," said one of the cavemen.

Roger lifted his canteen. "Any of you guys want a drink?"

They all indicated to the affirmative.

Roger and the others passed their canteens to the cavemen, who drained the four canteens. Soon, all the men in the room were called out to eat a meal of cabbage cooked in a big pot with no seasoning, but it was hot, it was real food with a high percentage of water, and it was digestible. Each man was given half a canteen cup.

One Helluva Soldier / Phil Kline

*

The room was warm because of the number of men crammed in, but only one was allowed to go to the latrine at a time. George waited his turn and made it just before he filled his pants. At least one of the cavemen didn't get there in time.

For breakfast, a fat woman guard served them a canteen cup of sorghum and water. The thinnest of the cavemen, who looked to be in his late teens, held a tin can out to get his portion, but she gave him only half of what she gave the others. He peeled a scab off a wound on his upper forearm, chewed on it, and smacked his lips in her face.

The woman shuddered. "Americanski."

Roger and Bob shared their sorghum with the thin man.

As he ate, George looked at men in assorted uniform styles, milling around between long dilapidated wooden buildings. He estimated that five hundred Americans were stored in Miner's Camp, plus a number of British, Australians, Turks, and Filipinos.

After breakfast, they were lined up in formation. Three men stepped out of a small building that had new boards nailed between the old gray ones. Two were Chinese wearing dressy green uniforms like Han's. The other, a Caucasian, wore an olive-drab uniform with red-striped epaulets. One of the Chinese walked toward the men with a 35 mm camera hanging from a cord around his neck.

The Caucasian stood to the side, and the two Chinese stopped in front of George's group, which included the ragged cavemen. The man with the camera shook his head. They walked to the next group and the cameraman nodded his approval. Guards ordered the men to face to the front then walked up and down with bayonets drawn, to make sure everyone complied.

One Helluva Soldier / Phil Kline

The cameraman held the camera at his waist and stared at the formation. The other Chinaman spoke. "You guests of Chinese. We take care of you. We do things to make you feel at home."

The only reaction from the POWs was a few snickers.

The man continued his spiel. "Soon, we go to classroom, and you see coffee and sweet rolls and cigarettes. We have lesson on how bad capitalism treat you. You learn how great is living under communism, and you embrace." He put on a big grin. "Then we be friends. Right?"

His comments brought smiles and laughter from the group. A POW in the front row, yelled to the right and to the left, "Don't smile; he's taking our picture."

It was too late. The photo had been taken. The cameraman said, "Thank you", then the two Chinese and the Caucasian reentered the shack from which they had come.

The prisoners were herded into a long building. A motion picture projector sat on a table, and a screen hung on one wall. The other walls were adorned with giant posters of Joseph Stalin and Chairman Mao, along with Russian and Chinese flags.

Major Han stepped in front of the table with a mike and looked over the prisoners who stood jammed together. "Welcome. Chinese Volunteers have an interesting program for you. I hope you enjoy it. As you watch, you will better understand why we embrace communism with our brothers from the Soviet Union." He put the mike down, flipped a switch, and the movie began.

The first scene showed neatly dressed American soldiers sitting around a low table, eating sweet rolls, drinking from cups, and smoking. George recalled they'd been told they would see those goodies, not that they would have them.

The camera zoomed in on an Air Force POW, with the gold leaf of a major on his collar. He flipped the ash from the end of a cigarette. "I learned from my Chinese friends that true

One Helluva Soldier / Phil Kline

happiness doesn't come from the ways of the Rockefellers and other capitalist warmongers, but through world communism. I discovered the truth during classes in our camp and in Chinese relocation school." He unpinned the leaf from his collar, and tossed it on the floor. "Here, we are all equal." He took a drag on the cigarette and coughed.

A corporal seated beside him put an arm over the major's shoulder. "My friend, Rich, is right. Here we are comrades and are all equal. I have renounced my old ways and begun to see the light as shared by my Chinese brothers."

After the corporal spoke, various Americans confessed how they had been duped by the Wall Street crowd but now saw the light. The cameraman took a flash photograph of the audience as they watched the testimonials.

After the movie, Han returned to the front of the room to talk for two hours, repeating what the Americans in the film had said about Wall Street warmongers, Rockefeller, equality, and the joys of communism. He followed with an invitation for men to step forward and join those who had discovered the truth. Nobody did.

As Han droned on, a POW in front of George let his head droop. A guard suggested the man pay attention by whopping him on the back of the head with a rifle butt.

Han finished his lecture and bowed. "Thank you. We'll continue your education when you're enrolled in Pyoktong University." He looked over his students before exiting. Another man took his place, repeating much the same message.

Nobody was allowed to go to the latrine. By the time that instructor had spoken for an hour, one could almost see a brown haze throughout the room, created by two hundred POWs, some with raging diarrhea. When they were released from class, the POWs would not have left the room any quicker if somebody had yelled, "Fire."

One Helluva Soldier / Phil Kline

Finally, the men were allowed to go to a latrine one at a time. George wasn't in a hurry. He had already loaded his pants during the class. When he returned to his hut, Roger asked him, "What did you learn from the lesson of the day?"

"I need a rubber diaper."

Tom said, "I felt violated hearing Americans talk that way."

Ben had poured water on a rag and was cleaning stains from his shorts. He looked up. "I don't think we can judge them without knowing the whole story."

"What do you mean, the whole story?"

Ben talked while rubbing. "What about George? We were shot down so we had no choice about being captured. He had a choice, but he just laid his weapon down and surrendered."

Tom waved a hand at Ben. "Don't you remember? He said he was out of ammunition."

"That's what I mean by the whole story." Ben threw the rag through the hole in the door.

Roger cocked his head when he heard a Chinese oath come from outside. "Nice shot, Ben." He turned to Tom. "Don't you know who that captain was?"

"Major."

"Captain."

Tom's voice was surly. "What are you talking about?"

"Lewis is a captain unless the Chinese promoted him."

"What was he doing wearing a major's leaf?"

Roger turned his back to Tom. "Why'd I bring you along?" He faced Brian. "By the way, if you ever get a chance to write this story, Lewis, doesn't smoke. He hates cigarettes."

Brian shook a finger at Roger. "He's going to be in a pile of shit when some dumb-ass reporter sees what he did and writes it up. I'm surprised the Chinks haven't found him out yet. When they do, they'll lose face, the worst thing that can happen to them."

One Helluva Soldier / Phil Kline

"Maybe it'll be Lewis's insurance policy," George said. "The world will know he's alive and in good health. That may force them to keep him that way."

Brian nodded. "They may get him to the point where he'd rather be dead."

"Some of us may get to that point, too."

The door opened and a guard entered. "Come with. Bring all."

George gathered up his ammo belt, full canteen, and his tin can. He shoved a blanket he had liberated, and his brass spoon, under his field jacket.

Tom, who stood in the street next to Roger, turned toward him. "Do you really think we're going to school?"

"Of course. You heard Han; Pyoktong University."

"It's probably just a fancy name for a death camp."

"Probably."

One Helluva Soldier / Phil Kline

29

Hundreds of POWs filed out of Miners Camp, past the ditch where George had bathed, and past mounds of dirt that held their dead comrades. They trudged along a muddy road between hills, then to a path along the side of the hill on the west, to the constant command, "*Quay-ka-day*."

Around midnight, they stopped beside a mountain stream. The moon cast its light on the fast-moving water as the men drank, filled their canteens, and lay down to rest. George didn't feel like getting up again, but he did. The thin caveman, who had been given only half a soup ration at Miners Camp, said, "I'm not going."

Another caveman came to him. "Harry, Get up. You'll die here."

"I won't die. They'll kill me."

"Please. Get up."

"No."

A guard poked Harry with a bayonet then hit him across the side of his head with a rifle butt. A stream of blood flowed down his cheek, but Harry didn't move. The guard yelled at him and hit him harder. Harry grunted, fell sideways, and lay still. Blood filled his beard, making it look like red paper mache in the moonlight.

Another caveman walked over to Harry. "I know how you feel. We'll take care of you."

Harry's tears ran. "Goddamn it, you don't know how I feel. Mind your own business and get the hell out of my face."

One Helluva Soldier / Phil Kline

The order was given, "Mach." The guard pushed the caveman's friend toward the column and jabbed George in the shoulder with his bayonet, motioning for him to walk.

George held a palm to the wound as he moved out. Soon he heard the single shot.

Later, as the group rested in the brush alongside a road, George experienced a near-dream sequence from Chinese trucks headed south up a hill. Tires crunched gravel, and engines strained in a low gear. Exhaust and dust floated in cat-eye lights, and the stench of burning diesel irritated his nose. Five more convoys passed the POWs during the night.

*

Four nights into the march, they came to a wooden trestle a hundred feet above a river, bombed, but passable. The POWs ran across, knowing American pilots couldn't tell good guys from the bad. A guard, running beside the POWs, fell to the river below. From then on, guards walked at the head of the line, or near the end, but not alongside.

On the fifth morning, George stood on a village street for two hours before getting his ration of cornballs and water then was crammed into a hut a Korean family had been kicked out of. Ten minutes later, he was called outside again, part of a herd of POWs who were supposed to learn the truth by being subjected to a two-hour propaganda lecture.

Guards roamed around, poking those whose heads drooped, with rifle butts or bayonets, to remind them to pay attention. The presenter, who had a badly burned face, spoke broken English in a halted but understandable voice. Another POW nudged George. "We call him Napalm Ni."

One Helluva Soldier / Phil Kline

After another five days of hiking and lectures, the prisoners were rewarded with a breathtaking view where the Yalu River separated North Korea from China. Mist curled up from the water, causing a ghostly fog as the sun worked its way through pines guarding the top of a cliff. Flowers in bloom cast their fragrance to mix with the pine scent. Huts at the bottom of the hill reminded George of tourist cabins.

At the rear of the huts, the weary men wound their way over bare dirt, and circled around mounds of rocks between the trees, where the aroma of flowers and pine was enhanced by the stench from dead men stacked like wood. Without a glance at the bodies, the lead guard entered Pyoktong U--officially Yalu POW Camp #5.

The cabins looked like other Korean huts George had seen except many were partially demolished. He reasoned Camp #5 was a bombed-out village where residents had been driven off to make room for POWs. It looked and smelled pretty much like other villages, but the typical odor of *kimchi* and sewage was given variety by the smell of rotting bodies.

The men were led between rows of huts and halted a half-mile from where they had entered the compound. George noticed that only a low fence surrounded the area, and he didn't see guard posts in the hills. Not important he surmised. Any American who escaped from the camp might as well have carried a sign: ESCAPED POW.

They were handed a clipboard with a sheet of paper to write their names and ranks then the enlisted men were marched off. Chinese herded the officers into groups of five or more and directed them to huts. George was assigned to a hut with six other officers.

In front of George's hut, on a low narrow porch held up by two poles, a man in rags watched the ceremony. His face differed from the one George remembered. Even after he recognized the man as Captain Eric Phillips, he had trouble accepting him as the same officer who had been his OCS instructor. Phillips had dropped from about a hundred and seventy pounds to weigh perhaps one hundred. He looked old; his beard was lined with gray, and his hair unkempt.

George approached him. "Captain Phillips, I'm George Martin."

Phillips smiled. "I thought I recognized you."

George turned to the others. "This is Captain Phillips. He was one of the best instructors in my OCS class."

Phillips gave the new arrivals a three-fingered salute, like that of a boy scout.

"We were told we'd be fed well here," a newcomer said.

Phillips shook his head. "There were thirteen of us in this hut three months ago. Most of them died from starvation or disease made worse by malnutrition. Only four of us are left."

Walter, one of the new POWs, was a burly man who sat on the porch next to Phillips. "Why'd they take the enlisted men away?"

"The Chinaman thinks officers exert too much influence over the men, so they keep them in a separate area."

"What do you do, other than sit?"

Phillips lifted his shirt to scratch. "Up at five, pick the lice off, two hours of class, eat breakfast, then four more hours of class. Another meal at 1600 then two more hours of class. We eat at the mess." He pointed to a long, low building with part of the side missing. "We have work details like getting wood, not as much now as in winter. And we bury the dead."

Walter pointed toward the stacked corpses on the hill. "Why aren't they buried?"

"We didn't have shovels or picks to dig up the frozen ground. We still don't, and I'm tired. That would be a good job for you guys who still have meat on your bones."

One Helluva Soldier / Phil Kline

"What kind of classes do you have?"
"The evils of capitalism and the glory of communism."
"Eight hours?"
"Eight hours."
Walter entered their twelve by twelve hut and the other new residents followed.

Four blankets lay on the floor, but no mats. They straggled back outside and sat in a semicircle around Phillips.

George pointed toward the hut door. "Who are your roommates?"

"Remember Tommy Trexler?"

George breathed deeply. "I thought he was dead."

"Still alive. Barely."

"Barely?"

Phillips waved a hand back and forth. "He spends a lot of time in solitary and in the hole. He's a hard-ass. You can't do that here. You can do it, but you pay for it."

"What's he do?"

"Among other things, he refuses to give them anything other than his name, rank, and serial number; skips propaganda sessions. He tries to escape. Made it two days once. He's lucky the Chinese took over the camp from North Koreans. They would have killed him. The Chinaman just beats him and throws him in the hole."

A clanging noise came from the mess hall. Phillips grunted as he pulled himself up. "Let's eat, but first I'll show you our fine latrine."

The newcomers followed him to a slit-trench on the side of a hill. Three of the men used it then they all walked to the mess, entering through the hole in the side of the building, opposite two huge kettles with steam rising from them.

One Helluva Soldier / Phil Kline

George joined Phillips at the end of a line of men holding mess kits, tin cans, and assorted containers. "Where's Trexler now?"

"In the hole, I think."

"Don't you know?"

"You never know."

"Where's the hole?"

"In the ground, couple of logs over it. An average hole. Nothing fancy. Don't be a hard-ass here. Remember Pat Holmes with Charlie Battery of the 2nd?"

George shook his head. "No."

"The Chinaman takes class and interrogation seriously. I'll tell you this so you can warn your buddies." Phillips leaned close to George and said in a low voice, "Pat laughed out loud at the propaganda his first day here. They stood him at attention all day and all night with a guard on him. He collapsed the second day. They dragged him by the heels a half-mile to a hole in the ground, threw him in, and rolled logs across it. Kept him there a month.

"When Pat was released, he was incoherent. He died a week later. Don't laugh at them. Tell them a lie, something meaningless, or something they already know, but don't give them that name, rank, and serial number bit. That's a free ticket to the hole."

Phillips motioned for George to follow him a few feet from the chow line. "Something else to remember is not to make enemies here." He looked around then back at George. "Remember Captain Hinch?"

George's shoulders sagged. "Yes."

"He has a hair up his ass about you."

"He's here?"

"Yes. Watch yourself. He spreads hate talk about you freely. If it gets to be too much to handle, let me know."

One Helluva Soldier / Phil Kline

They ate their cabbage soup and walked toward the hut. Phillips stopped upwind from the bodies. "Guys like Hinch can get you in trouble, and you end up in front of Snake Eyes. Camp Commander, name's Ding. Most guys talk but don't give valuable information. Tell him something off the top of your head, but don't laugh at him. I tell stuff that he knows or that's not sensitive. Sometimes I say, 'I don't know.' He may not believe me, but he doesn't kill me."

"Do they kill anybody?"

"Two I know of were beaten to death. But I believe they would rather keep us to negotiate with. Two guys gave Ding smart-ass remarks. Their hands were tied behind their backs and they were stood at attention for twenty-four hours, out front, where others could see what you get for making smart-ass remarks. He didn't kill them. What he does, is make you wish you were dead."

When they arrived where the others sat on the porch, a bell rang. Phillips motioned to them. "Class. Better hit the john first."

They walked past the bodies to a slit-trench, did their duty then walked up a hill, to a new unpainted building.

Inside, hundreds of men sat on the floor, facing a platform where four Chinese stood. Guards patrolled the aisles on both sides. Giant photographs of Lenin, Stalin, Chairman Mao, and two other Asians, plus a Caucasian dressed in the garb of a priest, adorned the walls.

A British officer, who saw George looking at the pictures, pointed to the man in religious dress. "He's a fellow countryman of mine, the Red Bishop of Canterbury."

Napalm Ni, in a neatly pressed uniform, strode to the platform and faced the group. "Welcome to you who arrive this morning. I am happy you join us for lesson."

One Helluva Soldier / Phil Kline

Napalm Ni spoke for fifteen minutes on how he expected the new men to learn the truth about the war and the advantages of cooperating with their friends, the Chinese volunteers. "Cooperate and you receive Chinese lenient policy."

The next man on the platform talked about the advantages of communism and the evils of capitalism for two hours. Then the men were released. Many headed to the latrine, but it was too late for others.

After relieving himself, George hurried to catch up with Phillips who was walking as if he were on his last legs. "Captain."

"Call me Eric or call me Phillips. Using rank irritates the Chinaman."

"Sorry, Eric. I'll work on it."

They walked in silence until Eric stopped near the hut. "I want to tell you something," he said. "Let's go up the hill. Most of those who survive this place are in their late twenties. Many, your age and younger, develop a disease we call give-up-itis. They probably haven't experienced enough tough times in their young lives to cope with the horrors here. I don't expect to have a problem, but I don't know how much longer I can make it."

George shook his head. "I'll never quit."

"I'm sure you won't. You've had more to overcome than most of these kids. That's probably why you're able to cope. Anyway, I'm not worried about you. I'm concerned about me. I'm getting old in a hurry."

Eric sat where the weeds had been stripped of leaves and talked as he dug. "Most of the guys eat the weed tops and ignore the roots." He pulled up a root and handed it to George who put part of it in his mouth. George spit it out and wiped the dirt off the rest, then put it in his mouth again.

Eric laughed. "Great, aren't they?"

George wrinkled his face. "Ugh."

One Helluva Soldier / Phil Kline

Eric didn't seem to notice. "I trust you more than I do anyone else and want to give you information on what took place before you got here. If anything happens to me, you can take it to a news service in the States. I don't want it to be lost in the bureaucratic red-tape of the Pentagon."

"Is this something I should write down?"

"Already done. It's here." Eric looked around then touched the heel of his right boot. He lowered his voice. "You're the only person I've told this to who's still alive. It's written on toilet paper, the names of people who died or have been killed here.

"If I die, I want you to sneak it back to the States. When I came here, there were at least two thousand of us, most of them captured before me. They were in terrible shape. We had no winter clothing. North Koreans stole our boots, and we had no blankets. Many had frostbite. Some lost fingers, feet, or hands. Many gave up because they couldn't walk or hold anything.

"A thousand died from starvation, freezing, beriberi, dysentery, pneumonia, and other diseases helped along by malnutrition and neglect. When they died, we hid them, so we could get their rations. Even then, we went hungry. Look at me. I've lost half my weight, and I was slim when I got here. We took clothes off the dead. Some guys even asked for clothes from those who were dying. That's why the Chinaman took over. North Koreans are brutal.

"All my career, I've given to Christian Missionaries in China. Guess where Snake Eyes learned his English—in a Christian school like the one near the main road." He pointed to a brick building in the distance. "I helped pay for that training, and you know what? That money's still being deducted from my pay. I can't stop the allotment. That's where they put me in solitary, beneath that schoolhouse, a place you don't want to be. Worse than the hole. At least in the hole you can see daylight, hear

One Helluva Soldier / Phil Kline

noises, and even see a guard every once in a while. I spent a week in the schoolhouse in the dark. No sounds—nothing except the smell of shit and piss."

George shook his head at the memory of the slit-trench.

Eric continued. "You get used to the smell and, after a day or two, you don't notice it. You never get used to the dark or to the silence."

"Why were you there?"

"For going over the fence."

George wondered which he'd get, hole or schoolhouse.

Eric pointed at a long two-story building. "And our hospital—don't go there. We call it the springboard. It's the springboard from camp to grave. Hundreds have gone in, but I know of only two who came out alive. They don't have medicine, and they use crazy treatments they say they learned from Russian doctors."

"Russians here?"

"One day, when I was being interrogated, I saw one. And sometimes you'll hear the Chinaman use the word, Americanski."

George nodded. "I heard the word from a woman guard and wondered about that. What makes you think you're not going to make it?"

"I think I am going to make it. But you know soldiers. I never thought I'd be captured."

"Me, either. I thought others got killed or captured. I didn't even think I'd be wounded."

Phillips touched the heel of his boot. "Remember."

"I'll do it if I outlive you."

They were surprised when the evening meal was boiled rice with a small amount of pork. The maggots in the meat looked enough like the rice that many of the men may not have noticed them.

The night was too hot to sleep. George's mind wandered to what Eric had said about the darkness and silence of the schoolhouse. He remembered the effect four days had on the guys in the cave.

Every once in a while, George opened his eyes to listen to breathing from those around him. He felt secure not being alone.

The next morning, after their two hours of propaganda, George sat in front of the hut thinking how unthinkable it was to be a POW. But, after he recalled what Eric had said of conditions under the North Koreans, he decided he really didn't have it bad, after all.

Footsteps came toward him. He looked up. A guard stood in front of him, pointing a rifle toward the main road. "Come with."

One Helluva Soldier / Phil Kline

30

The morning of his twenty-second birthday, George gave a weak wave to an empty hut as a guard led him to the little red schoolhouse. He heaved a sigh of relief when the guard ushered him through the front door rather than to the cellar.

Inside, a Chinese soldier left his desk and knocked on an interior door. An answer in Chinese came from within, and the guard opened the door.

Behind an old oak school desk stood the first overweight Chinese soldier George had seen. He had a potbelly and beady eyes stuck close together over a miniature nose. It had to be Ding. A fat little girl sat in the corner playing with rosary beads. Ding spoke to her, and she left, twirling the beads.

Ding peered at George with his dark little eyes. "You have one day here, and so soon you cause trouble. Even your friend tell on you—say you bad,"

"Maybe true before I came to Pyoktong. I'm here now, and I don't cause trouble."

Ding crossed his arms and frowned. "You lie to Commandant."

George thought quickly. "I hear you were trained in American Christian schools. I am Christian, too, and I do not lie."

"I not Christian. Your friend say you not—say you queer person, say you like boys. Is against Christian belief. Your friend say you make fun of education class, say you laugh at Chinese. We help you learn error of ways. Make you better person." Ding flipped his hand, and the guard used the butt of a rifle to usher George out.

George whispered, "Hinch" to himself as he was escorted to the side of the schoolhouse and told to raise a sloping cellar door similar to the one that led down into the storm cellar back home.

With his flashlight poking a hole in the dark, the guard pushed George in the back and followed him down stone steps, to a musty smelling hall, past two cell doors, to an eight-by-eight cell on the right. Concrete with no windows. A straw mat lay against a wall.

The door closed, and George heard the click of the latch. He saw nothing in the absolute darkness. The cell wasn't as bad as the slit-trench, but it was dark, it was damp, and it stunk. He inched his way to the mat and lay on it. *Why did Hinch do this to me? What would Dad think about my being here? It's a good thing Mom doesn't know. If Luisa knew I was here, how would she react?*

He strained to see, but it was too dark. He strained to hear, but there was no sound. *Helen Keller survived this same thing every day of her life. She didn't complain. She did something about it.* He cupped his hands in front of his mouth and yelled, "Hello. Anybody there?" A muffled sound was so faint, he wondered if he had imagined it. He jumped up and bumped into the door. He put his ear against the door and yelled, "Hey."

Sound came again but so faint he thought it may have been the guard outside or somebody upstairs telling him to shut up. He held his breath and cupped his hands behind his ears. All he heard was a high-pitched tone.

He felt his way back to the straw and lay there. A muffled pounding came from the wall next to him. *Someone's kicking it.* "Hello," he yelled as loud as he could. The pounding stopped. He kicked the wall, three slow, and three quick tap, the international distress signal. Identical taps came back.

One Helluva Soldier / Phil Kline

George remembered when his dad had pasted the Morse Code on the bathroom door, in front of the toilet. After George mastered the code, they sent messages to each other by tapping on the kitchen table as they ate. They'd laugh, and George's mom had no idea what was funny.

George stared at the wall where he'd heard the taps. *How did the alphabet go? E was easy—one dot, and the I, two dots. S was three dots, and H was four. The dashes: One dash, T. Two dashes, M. Three was O.*

He kicked the wall with the code for Hi. Back came the same four dots, two dots, then a barrage of dots and dashes he didn't understand. He kicked the SOS code again—*dit dit dit, da da da, dit dit dit.* No answer. He kicked again but no answer came back. Thoughts came in rapid succession: *How long will they keep me here? Will they feed me? Will they give me water? Can I stand the solitude? I'll be better off working on the code than wondering about the future.*

George concentrated and came up with the codes up to J, plus a smattering of other letters.

A grating noise—metal against metal—indicated the latch was moving. His door opened. A light shined on his face, and he closed his eyes. He heard two objects being slid on the floor then the light went out. The door was slammed shut and latched.

He slid a hand toward the objects and fingered two cans, one the size of a soup can, and the other three times that size. The larger one was cold and the other lukewarm. He put the lukewarm can to his mouth and tasted it—sorghum broth. He swished it around in his mouth and drank it all then put his mouth to the larger can. Water.

He drank almost a third of it, and set the can in a corner where he wouldn't trip over it. He thought he'd use the smaller can for a urinal, but changed his mind. The cell already reeked of other people's waste.

One Helluva Soldier / Phil Kline

A scraping sound, like metal rubbing on concrete, came from the wall where he had heard kicks and the code. He listened for a moment, then hit the wall with the small tin can and spelled W-H-A-T. Back came H-O-L-E. He scraped the empty can against the wall, but it just slid across the concrete. He stomped on the can until he formed a sharp corner and tried again. Grit fell on his wrist. He scratched, and the scratching from the other side continued.

Ten minutes later, he had only made a small indentation. An hour later, he felt the hole again. It was less than two inches deep. George stopped scraping and hit the can on the wall, spelling G-E-O-R-G-E. Back came the answer T-I-M. He sent a message T-E-A-C-H M-E C-O-D-E."

*

Tim started through the alphabet. When he got to S, the tapping stopped. A door slammed. George tapped H-I. No answer. He tapped S-O-S. No answer. He tried again with no luck.

He lay on his straw. Moments later, something crawled over one of his ankles and crept toward his knee. He felt one on his forearm, then another and another. He picked them off, but they came in droves. He brushed them off his legs and tucked his pants into his socks. He had no way to close off his sleeves, so he rolled them up to his elbows. They crawled up his forearms. He squashed them between his fingers, and they squirted like little grapes. They kept coming, but he squashed as fast as they crawled. He moved his mat to the other side of the cell. That reduced their numbers.

Hours later, after George had squashed an army of slugs, the door opened, and a light shined in. "Come with," a voice said. George put his hand on the floor and into slug mush. In the

One Helluva Soldier / Phil Kline

beam of the flashlight, he saw live ones, the size of forty-five caliber shells. He wiped his hand on his pant leg and followed the guard out of the darkness and into the light.

The sun was bright, causing him to squint. A hope of freedom surfaced when the guard prodded him toward his hut, but the hope was dashed when he turned up a rise, to a hut that stood alone.

A guard at the entrance raised his rifle to port arms, to signal halt, then knocked on the door with the rifle butt. A moment later, George stood before Commandant Ding who had a shiny black holster hooked to the belt of his neat khaki uniform.

"We have lenient policy," Ding said as he handed George a sheet of paper and a pencil. "Sign and go back to your friends."

I am Lieutenant George Martin. I am treated well by Chinese Volunteers. All of my American friends here are fed good food and have opportunity to practice sports and learn in Chinese school.

I urge you to give up your arms and come to Chinese Volunteers. Bring this message with you, and you will be treated well. When American soldiers go home, you will be released to be with your family again.

George shook his head and handed the paper back. Ding pulled a Colt .45 caliber automatic from its holster, walked up to George, and slapped him across the side of the head with the barrel.

George's eyes closed as his head reeled from the blow. Blood trickled down the side of his face. Ding pushed him out the door and followed him.

George kept his eyes straight ahead as he heard the sound of the receiver being drawn back to slide a round into the chamber. He closed his eyes and whispered, "Mario."

One Helluva Soldier / Phil Kline

His body flinched at the sound of the blast. He opened his eyes. He could see but couldn't hear except for a loud ringing. He glared at Ding and yelled, "Fuck you, Snake Eyes," then shoved his middle finger up toward him.

Ding grimaced, spoke in Chinese, and stomped away. The guard pushed George toward his cell, using his rifle as a prod. Five minutes after he was inside, the cell door opened again. A bucket flew in, and the door was closed.

George sat in the dark, feeling somewhat like he felt when he had been sent to Grandma Kate's house six years earlier. Back then he had sat on the edge of his bed and cried.

I won't cry now. I'm a soldier. But I may spend the rest of my life in this cell for losing my temper.

He groped his way to the door, raised his foot, and kicked the door with the bottom of his boot. "For you, Snake Eyes." He reared back and kicked it again, "And for you, guard." He corralled his anger and crept to the wall where he tapped, T-I-M. No answer. He kicked S-O-S. No answer. Tears welled up in his eyes. "Happy birthday."

He sat with his back to the wall and pictured the scene that might take place at the Martin home outside of Potterville, Michigan. A telegram would be left on the kitchen table: *We regret to inform you that your son, Lieutenant George E. Martin, has been reported missing in action.* Mom would be afraid to read the telegram, so Dad would read it to her. It might sit on the table for five days or five weeks. She'd ignore it. She'd pretend nothing bad had happened, but she'd be sullen. Dad might read it again and wonder at his mixed feelings. The two of them wouldn't discuss what may have happened to their son. They might pray, but not together.

Sitting in darkness, in the basement of a schoolhouse in North Korea, George didn't pray. He hadn't given up on God, but he had given up on his dream of seeing his wife and son again.

One Helluva Soldier / Phil Kline

*

Mario Felipe Hernandez de Martin was born to Luisa at the home of her parents, at 4 p.m. April 18, 1950, two hours before his travel-weary father arrived from OCS. George looked at his son lying on Luisa's belly. "From the back he looks like a baby Indian." He leaned down and kissed Luisa. "And you are beautiful. I'm sorry I was not with you when he came."

Luisa ran her fingers through George's hair. "I told Mario, 'Your father is coming. You must wait for him.' He said, 'No. I not wait.' He came. It was easy, and he is *perfecto*."

He took her hand and kissed her fingers, one at a time. "Your mother said he did not come easy, but that he is perfect."

She reached out to touch his new gold bar. "*Estoy orguoso en ti.*"

"And I am proud of you." George whispered. "May I see what our son looks like on the other side?"

"*Pues, si.*" Luisa turned Mario over and held him up.

George's eyes opened wide, and he pulled back.

"Take him," Luisa said.

He took his son from Luisa, held him out, and studied him. Mario opened his eyes and moved his arms and legs as if doing calisthenics. "Unbelievable," George said.

He had just handed Mario back to Luisa's outstretched arms when her mother, Maria, came into the room, holding a bowl of apple and orange slices. "*Tiene hambre, Jorge?*"

He patted his stomach. "*No, gracias.*"

The new father and the new grandmother watched the new mother breast-feed her new baby. Mario and the women seemed to accept it as normal, but George gaped in awe.

One year after watching his son being breast fed, here he was, locked in the basement of a Christian schoolhouse in North

One Helluva Soldier / Phil Kline

Korea. George accepted the fact that he'd never see Luisa or Mario again.

*

After six more days of sorghum broth or turnip soup, a guard entered with a flashlight and indicated George should carry his latrine bucket to be dumped. The bucket was full. It had no handle, so he knelt and put his arms around it then slid them underneath. Careful not to splash, he took short steps as he followed the light beam down the hall.

He negotiated the stairs without incident, but was blinded by the daylight. He eased the bucket down on the top step. Seconds later the guard motioned for him to get moving.

They walked to an open latrine in back of the building where George emptied his bucket then the guard escorted him back to the darkness of his cell.

The slugs welcomed him.

He sat in the dark and thought about his situation. *Evidently the bucket's to be dumped once a week. That means another week in the dark before I see daylight again. I expect I'll empty it every week for the rest of my life. I'll have to keep busy in between, to retain my sanity.*

He didn't know if his dad would be interested, but George decided to talk to him. He told him everything he could remember that had happened since he left home. That took several hours, and not only did George feel better about himself after the conversation, but he was better able to accept the darkness.

He decided he needed exercise. He found he could take three steps without running into the wall. He did so, wearing a path through the filth on the floor. He did pushups and sit-ups. He swore at the slugs and told them how much pleasure he derived

One Helluva Soldier / Phil Kline

from killing them. He built an imaginary house for his family. It took a week to compute the board feet of pine and the number of bricks he would need, and another three weeks to build it.

At the end of each week he was rewarded with ten minutes of daylight.

The value of doing things just to use up time, began to wear thin, so George decided to write his memoir. He composed every day after his evening meal of sorghum, cabbage, turnip, or millet soup. As he "wrote" about his life, he realized how happy the years were before he reached his teens, the years when he was still accepted by his father. Depression from the darkness lessened when he pictured them doing chores together.

31

Before age seven, he watched his dad milk cows and sometimes was allowed to pull on teats as he followed instructions coupled with laughter. On his birthday, his dad said, "Son, why don't you grab a stool and milk old Millie?"

Even though he knew Millie was the most gentle cow on the farm, he was excited. He sat on a one legged stool and squirted milk into a bucket while Dad turned the other way to milk another cow. Even the two barn cats realized it was a special day when George shot them squirts of warm milk.

Childhood was fun. The only unhappy memory George included in his memoir was when he was invited to help dip hogs at age twelve. Dad pushed a small sow along a ramp that sloped down into a large vat of a stinky creosote disinfectant. She squealed and kicked as he pushed her down the trough, but she ended up in the mixture before racing out the other end.

Next came a large sow. "I'll lead her into the ramp," his dad said. "You take that side and I'll take this one." His dad boosted the hog onto the ramp where George was able to push on the sow's rear. The sow went wild. She lost control of her bowels and, at the same time, kicked, knocking George to the ground.

He sat in a mixture of disinfectant and hog shit and cried. His dad pushed and shoved until the sow went into the vat, then he turned to George, pointed at him, and yelled, "Go to the house, right now. Go."

One Helluva Soldier / Phil Kline

That night, George read a book to erase the memory of hog dipping while his dad and mom argued in the kitchen. George heard her say, "He's young. Give him a chance to grow up."

His dad's voice came through loud and clear. "I'm not talking about his age or his size. I'm talking about whether or not he'll ever become a man. I have my doubts."

*

George recalled his trip to Mexico where he met Luisa. He "wrote" about the first time he walked with her on the square in Durango. He "wrote" about their courtship. He "wrote" about their life together and the thrill of having a son, then finished it with his combat experiences.

He knew the memoir took four weeks to complete because he dumped his bucket four more times.

The night after he finished the memoir, he ate his turnip soup and leaned against a wall. *What do I do now? I don't want to do anything. I'm tired. All I have left is memories of a memoir nobody will ever read.*

He leaned back with his eyes closed. "Luisa, Help me," he said—and he heard her voice. "Remember the good times."

*

As a second lieutenant, George didn't rate quarters on the post. He didn't have money to get an apartment in El Paso, so he and Luisa decided she should live and work in Juarez. He spent the nights in a BOQ at Fort Bliss and crossed the International Bridge to be with her on weekends.

One afternoon in June of 1949, he was called to his battery orderly room and told to report to Division Headquarters the next morning. The first sergeant handed him an official document. "You've been recommended to attend Officers Candidate School."

"By whom?"

"Evidently by someone who doesn't know you all that well."

That night he took a bus downtown and walked across the bridge. Luisa came home from her job at a soda fountain, still wearing her apron. When he told her of the interview, she looked concerned. "What does this mean?" she asked.

"If I get accepted, it means I will be away from you for six months while I attend school in Kansas and—"

"*Seis meses*? No. I do not see my husband enough now."

"Listen, Luisa. It means after the six months of school, we can live in the United States. I will make enough money to get an apartment in El Paso. We will spend every night together instead of only three a week."

"You will sleep with me every night?"

"Yes. Every night."

She looked at him for a moment, then rushed to the dresser. She grabbed her purse, reached into it, pulled out a peso, and hurried back to where he stood. "Go. Call them now and say you will go." She handed him the coin and jumped on him, wrapping her arms around his neck and her legs around his waist. She kissed him hard and dropped back to her feet. "Go." She pushed him toward the door. He looked at her and laughed.

She didn't laugh. She pushed him again. "*Gita, ahorita.*"

"I can't go now. I go tomorrow to see if they'll accept me."

She put her hand out. "Give me the peso and I call them."

He laughed as she spoke to him in Spanish he only half understood but was sure contained a couple of expletives. He hugged her, but she calmed down only after he convinced her he would tell them how important acceptance was to her.

Monday morning Luisa refused to kiss him goodbye until he promised he'd tell them he'd be happy to go to officer school.

One Helluva Soldier / Phil Kline

That night he told her, "They'll give me their decision in two weeks."

Two weeks later, George whistled the tune to the song *Whistle While You Work*, as he approached their home.

Luisa was waiting for him at the open door. She began jumping up and down when he stepped into the apartment. "You will be officer. I know by your whistle."

"Yes, and to celebrate, next week we will go on a vacation in a beautiful forest next to a wide clean river."

She quit jumping and her smile disappeared. "We do not have money for vacation."

"The army'll furnish our food, and where we'll stay is free."

"Oh, I like you to be officer."

*

After a train ride to Portland, Oregon, they rode a bus fifteen miles along the Columbia River to the almost deserted Lewis and Clark State Park. They walked through the woods until they found a quiet area among tall poplars that overlooked the river where he unsnapped the catch on his barracks bag and removed a roll of canvas. "This is our home."

"It is small."

"That is our bedroom. Here is the living room." He pulled out another piece of canvas, smaller than the first.

"Y el bano?"

He pointed to a park restroom and shower at the end of a gravel path.

"Y la cosina?"

He pointed to a fire pit and grill ten feet away. "And we have wood to build a fire."

She shook her head. "My husband is *loco*, but I love him much." She hugged him.

One Helluva Soldier / Phil Kline

He picked up what he had called a bedroom and rolled out a pup tent. "Help me set it up." They worked together and put it in place. "Now for the living room." He unrolled a shelterhalf and they put it up next to the pup tent, with the opening toward the east. He pointed toward the west. "The rain will come from that way." He stepped back and smiled. "Hungry?"

"*Si.*"

"We need wood for a fire. We can find some along the river." They walked fifty feet to the riverbank and looked down at the clear water.

Luisa pointed. "*Que limpio.* I see the bottom."

"Yes, it's clean, but we'll drink water from a well."

Luisa took off her shoes and waded along the edge of the river while George picked up wood. They returned to the tent, and he built a fire in the grill then pointed toward a grocery sack. "Choose what you want for dinner."

She peeked in the sack and took out an olive drab box the size of a school book except longer. She looked at the label and pulled out four more. "All meat and beans?"

"Army K-Rations. You like meat?"

"Yes."

"You like beans?"

"Yes."

"Good."

They ate the five-year-old meat and beans, crackers, and tropical chocolate from two boxes. In late afternoon, walked barefoot along the Columbia until they came to a smaller river that joined it. A sign read, SANDY RIVER BEACH. They sat on a rock, held hands, and watched the bubbles where the rivers boiled together.

The sun sank behind the trees, and George said, "Let's swim."

"I do not know to swim."

One Helluva Soldier / Phil Kline

"I do not either."

Her eyes opened wide. "I do not have swim clothes?"

He looked around. "Nobody is here."

He took off his shirt and pants. She took off her skirt and blouse, constantly glancing around the area to make sure no one was watching. Then they waded into the water and frolicked for an hour. He showed her how to dog paddle, and they swam together in the shallow water until a new moon peeked through trees in the East. They shivered as they dried each other with their clothes and ran back toward the tent in their underwear.

George stopped and picked a blackeyed Susan. Luisa started to put it in her hair, but dropped it and grabbed his arm. "Oh!"

"*Que pasa?*" he said.

"Tents close to ours."

They ran to their tent and crawled in. He took off his wet shorts, and she, her panties and bra. He reached for a towel to finish drying, but Luisa snatched it from him. She threw it behind her, pushed him onto his back, and sprang to a sitting position on top of him. "*Te quiero.*"

"I love you, too," he said.

"*Te quiero* mean I want you." She bent down and kissed him. I want you now." She slid her hand down his side and between his legs. By the time her hand reached him, his breathing was heavy and he was hard.

George slid his hands around her waist, up her back and around, until he held her breasts. She touched his face, neck, and chest with one hand and massaged between his legs with the other. He caressed her stomach and breasts.

George lifted Luisa to move inside her. She slid off. "No. Aunt Rosa say, 'Always be on bottom. You prettier when on bottom'."

Not in the mood to discuss Aunt Rosa's theory, he rolled over and moved on top of her. His foot knocked a tent pole down.

One Helluva Soldier / Phil Kline

They kissed and caressed. She spread her legs to wrap them around him. One leg knocked the other pole down, and the tent collapsed.

He rose to his knees. "I'll fix it."

She ran an arm around his back and pulled him to her. "Do not stop. Do not stop." With the other hand, she guided him in.

He didn't mind that the motion of the tent gave a pretty good clue what was happening beneath the canvas. Afterwards, they lay with the tent flat against them. George pulled her head to face him. "You have changed my life. I will love you forever."

"*Y te amo ati siempre.*"

He put the poles in place and slept with his arms around her. In the morning they awoke to the patter of rain on the tent. They lay facing each other, kissing between bites of dried-out chocolate from two K-Ration boxes. After a few minutes, the kissing gained priority over the chocolate. Luisa tossed the box aside and grabbed George, pulling him to her—all the persuasion he needed.

Later, Luisa lay on her back, breathing hard as she played with George's ears. She raised her head and looked through the tent flap. The other tents were gone. She pointed to the sky. "Rain, go to Mexico where you get welcome by dry sand, and make flowers."

For three days they strolled through the forest and along the river, wearing army ponchos in the rain. She worked on her English as they played in the Sandy River during the day. They bathed in it beneath the moon and made love every night and every morning.

The last day of their vacation, the sun came out while they were riding a bus into Portland. They lingered over tea and sweet rolls in a baked goods shop, but didn't tell anyone they had eaten meat and beans from a little olive-drab box before

One Helluva Soldier / Phil Kline

riding to town for dessert. That afternoon, they boarded a train to El Paso, holding hands most of the way.

The day before George left by train for Fort Riley, Kansas, Luisa climbed on a bus to take her to Durango. When the bus moved out of the ramp at Juarez, she leaned through the open window. "We going to have baby."

She giggled and blew him a kiss as the bus drove away.

One Helluva Soldier / Phil Kline

32

The love story faded. Lying on his bed of straw with slugs, he heard nothing, and saw only darkness. "Luisa, Luisa." He curled into the fetal position and cried himself to sleep. When he awoke, he had no idea whether it was day or night.

The next time he moved, other than to eat or use his bucket, was when the guard came to take him for his weekly trip to daylight. George picked up the bucket and navigated toward the door. A leg gave way. The bucket flew, the contents spewed over the floor, and George spread-eagled into his waste.

The guard walked out and latched the door.

*

George's eyes were glued shut with stickiness as he was led stumbling out of the schoolhouse and down the street, to be deposited on the ground in front of a hut. He heard, "Martin." then again, "Martin." He recognized Tommy Trexler's voice.

A blur moved above him and water dripped onto his cheek. He reached up and touched Tommy's face. He felt the tangled mass of hair being pulled away from his lips, and a canteen being held to them. He coughed the water up then pushed on the ground, trying to rise.

Tommy put his arms under George's and lifted him to a half-sitting position then again put the spout to his lips. But a coughing fit didn't allow him to drink.

One Helluva Soldier / Phil Kline

Tommy set the canteen on the ground. "I'm going to wash your face." He picked up the canteen, poured water onto a rag, and wiped George's face, then added water to the rag and wiped George's eyes. "You really need a bath. You stink. And let me get those clothes off to wash them."

George coughed and cleared his throat, but words didn't come. He felt his shirt being unbuttoned and pulled off. George cleared his throat again. His voice still didn't work, but he could see. He waved his finger about the empty yard.

"Everybody's in class."

George managed to gasp, "I'm dying."

Tommy put his arm under George's shoulder and eased him back to lean against the porch. He pulled George's pants off and tossed them to where the shirt lay. "I almost did. A month ago I looked like you do. I didn't eat. I didn't pick lice off so I turned gray from being coated with them. Henslee, too."

George looked up and mouthed, "Henslee?"

Tommy reached for the canteen and again put it to George's mouth. After George drank, Tommy said, "Henslee and I were lying near each other, talking. Suddenly he was quiet. He died. I decided right then and there, I'm not going to be buried out back of this place." Tommy raised his hand and pointed an index finger to the sky. "When I die, I'm going to be buried in the United States of America." His voice again became calm. "I decided to eat and pick lice off again. Eric smuggled food to me, and the Chinese thought I was dying. They still do."

George breathed words.

Tommy placed an ear next to George's face. "Say again."

"Day," George whispered.

"You want to know what day it is? I don't know." He shrugged. "Last of August, I guess." He grabbed George under the armpits and pulled him onto the porch, leaned him against a pole, and draped a blanket over his body. Then he reached under the blanket to remove George's skivvies and held them by his fingertips before tossing them with the other clothes.

With some success, George coughed to clear his throat. He tried to get to his feet.

Tommy laid a hand on his shoulder. "Rest. I'll wash your clothes before they pollute the area."

George managed raspy words. "Don't need rest. Got to get up."

"Got a hot date?" Tommy left and returned ten minutes later carrying a rag and a bucket of water. George was on his knees, drinking from the canteen. Tommy set the bucket in front of George and handed him the rag. "Take a bath. You smell like poop."

George's throat was raw. "Never did learn to cuss, did you?"

"Aha! It talks," Tommy said with a kind of chuckle, then pulled George's blanket off him. "I'll put you to work. As I pour water, you wipe." Tommy splashed water over George's head and body. George wiped his face with the rag.

A familiar voice said, "Have you no modesty, soldier?"

George opened his eyes and saw Eric Phillips standing in the street with another man.

Eric walked toward George. "Good to see you back."

George kept wiping. "Thank you, Sir." His voice was getting stronger.

"Glad to see you didn't give up."

"I did."

Eric shook his head. "You and Trexler must be related. Neither of you knows how to quit for good." He glanced at Tommy. "Where'd you get the bucket of water?"

"You want a bath, too?" Tommy poured the rest of the water over George and disappeared around the hut with the bucket.

Eric nodded toward where Tommy had gone. "Punk kid."

"Amen," the other POW said.

One Helluva Soldier / Phil Kline

Eric tossed the blanket to George. "After you finish drying yourself, wrap this around you and lean against the pole. You need a shave and a haircut." He stepped into the hut.

George finished wiping his body almost dry then tried to get up. He made it and hobbled to a dry spot. He wrapped the blanket over his body and leaned against another pole.

Eric returned with a knife, a can of water, and a three-legged stool consisting of a short board and three crooked sticks. He motioned for George to sit on the stool.

George sat. "Where'd you get the knife?"

"Combat boots. Steel shank in the arch. Sit still." Eric cut George's hair, mustache and beard then lathered his face.

"Soap?" George said, astonished.

"Things are getting better. Food, too, so you'll gain your weight back. Most of us have."

"How are my Air Force friends doing... Roger, Tom, Bob?"

Still shaving George, Eric said, "Don't know. They're not in this camp."

"Where are they?"

"Don't know. They disappeared the same day you did."

"Another guy, Brian, a war correspondent. Where's he?"

Eric swished the knife in water and set it on the porch. "Never heard of him. I have no idea what happened to any of those guys." Eric wiped George's face clean of lather with a towel then tossed the towel over the knife.

"What about Ben, the Marine pilot?"

Eric lowered his head. "He's dead."

George put his hands over his mouth.

Eric sat on the porch, next to George, with his head in his hands. "Sometimes there's nothing you can do," he said. "Ben developed dysentery. Had diarrhea real bad. He was just trying to get to the latrine, but another guy was using it, and the guard was only letting one person go at a time. The guard hit Ben with his rifle butt to keep him away. Ben stumbled, grabbed a post and started slipping. He fell backwards into his own shit. They pulled him out, but he never moved again."

George covered his face with his hands then wiped his eyes. "How'd you know what happened to me?"

"A friend of Hinch's told a friend." He stuck the knife in his boot and walked away, carrying the stool and water can. "Time to eat. I'll bring yours."

George wondered how Eric could be so matter of fact about what Hinch had done.

Tommy returned. He bent down and inspected George. "You look better." He turned and walked toward the hut door.

Fifteen minutes later, Eric walked from behind the hut with two canteen cups of soup. He gave one to George and sat on the porch with the other in his hand. Tommy disappeared again.

George tasted his soup. "This has meat in it. What kind?"

"Probably pork. Dog's expensive."

George stopped eating and turned to Eric. "You know why I was in the schoolhouse?"

"Yes."

George turned his head away. "I'm going to kill him."

"It's taken care of."

George jerked his head back toward Eric. "You killed him?"

"Four of us cornered him and told him he was to be your guardian angel, and if anything happened to you, we'd kill him."

"You really did that?"

Eric put his open right hand up as in a pledge.

George smiled, and it grew until it became a laugh.

After George and Eric finished eating, Tommy returned, carrying George's clothes, a bit damp and a bit cleaner, but they couldn't be smelled long-distance. Eric helped George put them on and had him stand. "You look like a fence post in a slack suit."

One Helluva Soldier / Phil Kline

"You look like a movie star." Tommy said.

George laughed again. "Sure."

"Compared to what you looked like a few hours ago."

"You brought me back. Who brought you back?"

"Henslee." Tommy turned away and talked in a monotone. "We couldn't even bury him. The ground was frozen. We stacked him with the others until spring." His voice got loud. "When I die, I'm not going to be stacked like cord wood, and I'm not going to be buried in back of a POW camp in North Korea. I'm going to be buried in the United States of America."

Eric walked away. "Excuse me. I've heard this song before."

George and Tommy walked into the hut. As soon as they did, the class bell rang. George watched as Tommy lay down on a mat and closed his eyes. "Aren't you going to class?" George asked him.

"Not until they catch me."

George chose a mat that seemed not to belong to anyone and lay on it. Ten minutes later, a guard walked into the hut. He ignored George, but ushered Tommy out with a bayonet touching his rearend. George was concerned. *I wonder where they're taking him.* He was relieved when he saw Tommy return after propaganda class.

*

At 2100 hours, on 19 October 1951, a thin but healthy George Martin and the others in his hut, returned from a firewood detail and were resting on the porch. A guard walked up to the hut. "Tomorrow you transfer to Yalu Camp Number Two at Ping-chong-ni. You not have to walk. You go in bus."

Eric's gaze followed the guard as he walked away. "Peace talks must be getting serious."

One Helluva Soldier / Phil Kline

The next morning, Eric, Tommy, George, and a bunch of others, rode a bus that bounced for an hour, on the way to Ping-chong-ni. George looked out the window. "It looks like a nice place to be after Pyoktong."

Eric pointed to barbed wire around the perimeter. "It's a prison camp."

They were assigned to a wooden building that housed a hundred or so POWs in one long room with an aisle down the middle and straw mats placed close together on each side. A classroom, at one end of the building, and a bathhouse at the other, had real glass windows.

George walked next door to the library portion of a combination barbershop- library attached to the kitchen. Pictures of famous communists adorned the walls, and two tables in the middle of the room were covered with English-language literature: *Shanghai News, Beijing News, London Daily Worker,* and *New York Daily Worker.*

At the evening meal, he detected seasoning in the soup, and it had more cabbage than usual.

*

After the first lecture at Ping-chong-ni, an announcement was made: "Chinese People's Committee for World Peace has arranged for you to get letters from families. You get your mail at the camp library."

Many who rushed to the library received letters, but George didn't. He wondered if his folks had even been notified of his capture. That night, he wrote and told them where he was and—to get it through the censors—that he was being treated well by the Chinese. Four weeks later, he received a letter from his mom, telling of a celebration in the Martin home. They still hadn't heard from Luisa.

One Helluva Soldier / Phil Kline

In November, millet and cracked corn became bad memories, replaced by Korean turnips, soybeans, and rice with maggoty pork added. When George closed his eyes, the maggots disappeared. One night he was served a sweet rice cake for desert, and after he ate, he walked to his dorm to find a quilted jacket, pants, and a long winter coat lying on his mat.

*

The day before Christmas, George, Tommy, and Eric sat around a fire pot in the middle of the room, talking about what they'd do when they got home. Eric looked up as if an idea had hit him on the forehead. He stuck a finger in the air. "You guys play bridge?"
Tommy sat up straight. "What took you so long to think of that?"
A man walked up wearing his long coat. "Did I hear someone mention bridge?"
Eric looked up at a balding man of about forty. "You play?"
"Yeah, man. Hal Barrett." Hal went around the circle shaking hands then sat down. "You have cards?"
"I used to, but all the other bridge players died, and I lost track of the cards. I'll make a new deck."
George didn't look up from a paper he was reading. "You don't have to. I saw someone playing solitaire in the library."
"Who?" Eric asked.
"I don't know, but he had cards. Teach me to play."
"Not now. After we find a fourth, you can watch me."
The next night after class, Eric walked into the dorm carrying a deck of Bicycle playing cards and what looked like a card table, except the legs were only a foot long.
Tommy pointed at the table. "You steal that table?"

One Helluva Soldier / Phil Kline

"I have no idea what you're talking about. Let's play." He, Tommy, Hal, and Art Wise, a happy armor captain who had lost a leg, played for three hours.

After George watched them play that night, he said, "I don't want to learn bridge. It's more like work than play."

On Christmas Eve 1951, the four were playing bridge, and George was watching without enthusiasm. The game was far from serious because of conversation about Christmas. Eric stopped in the middle of shuffling the cards. "Padre Sam's going to hold Christmas service."

George perked up. "He's so dedicated. I saw him when I FO'd with the Gloucesters. He walked around during battle like he was immune from getting shot. He and a doctor stayed with the wounded when everybody else was trying to get away."

"You're right. He is dedicated," Eric said. "That's why he spends so much time in solitary."

"For doing what?" George said.

"Teaching the men about Jesus and praying with them."

Tommy pointed at Eric. "Can't you can tell George why Sam gets solitary, and deal at the same time?"

Eric began dealing. "Religion's more of a threat to communism than what Tommy does. He only bugs them, like he's bugging me."

Art picked up his cards. "Tell me about the Christmas service, Eric."

"In the lecture hall, at zero-nine-thirty, but if the Chinaman finds out, he may forbid it."

"I think Sam will get away with it," Art said. "What can they do, shoot everybody?"

Christmas morning, George watched from the back of a full house as Padre Sam conducted service. A ten inch high cross, chiseled from stone, stood on the folding table he used for an altar. Next to the cross was his chalice, a Chinese soldier's mug with a cross painted on it, and his communion paten, a British mess tin.

Sam touched the cross. "Before we begin, I wish to thank Colonel Carne, Commanding Officer of the Gloucester Regiment, who created this from stone with the only tools at hand, two nails and a makeshift hammer. And we thank Commandant Ding for allowing this service, and also for the bread and wine he furnished.

"We will begin our service by singing the hymn, Faith of Our Fathers. The first lines, 'Faith of our fathers, living still, in spite of dungeons, fire and sword,' exemplify that which has kept us alive, and it has truly been in spite of dungeons. Sing with vigor, so our hosts will know we retain our faith."

A hundred men sang loud enough to be heard throughout the camp. During the hymn, two Chinese guards entered and watched. Padre Sam paid no attention to them, and the men kept singing. The guards left and an officer stepped into the room.

When the song was finished, he walked to the front and spoke to Sam. "We have lenient policy and allow you to continue with Christian services."

After he left, Sam conducted Holy Communion. The Chinese guards stood outside in the zero-degree weather, while inside, the men of POW Camp #2 listened to Padre Sam's sermon, prayed, and sang for another hour and a half.

After Christmas, more freedom was allowed for religious services. But in July of 1952, Sam was led away for holding services on days other than Sunday, a violation of Chinese policy.

33

Tommy Trexler had a great impact on George's life. He once told George about something that happened in late August of 1952. He had been standing in the doorway when Padre Sam walked by in soiled prison garb. Sam's beard was long and his hair a tangled mess. Tommy raced out to walk with him and said, "Padre, you seem to have weathered incarceration well."

He said Sam looked straight ahead as he spoke. "It was difficult, but I was never alone. The Lord was with me the entire time, and the adjutant was imprisoned in the next cell. We talked through a hole in the cell wall."

Like everyone else, Tommy had been concerned that Sam might have been all alone, so they sang loud on Sundays to let him know they continued services during his absence. "Padre Sam said he heard us singing, and it raised his spirits to heaven that so many POWs were dedicated to serve. The Padre said, 'In my prayers, I thanked God'."

Tommy told George that he asked Sam if the stories he'd heard about the Saint of Pyoktong were true or legend. "Sam answered that both were the case. 'Father Kapaun's story was true legend. He was a Roman Catholic chaplain of the First Cavalry Division during the terrible conditions of the winter of '50 and '51, when prisoners were dying in alarming numbers while living in subzero temperatures, insufficiently clad, and half-starved. He was an inspiration to all, devoted to the sick, and spent hours washing their soiled underclothing. He made nightly rounds to lice-infested, unheated shacks. He died spring of last year. To the end, he gave his portion of food to the sick. He died of chronic dysentery'."

Tommy said that, when they arrived at Sam's dorm, Tommy asked why a priest would join the army. "Sam said that, in his case, he was young and didn't have a parish of his own. Because more young chaplains were needed as World War II entered its last year, he thought what a wonderful way to serve, working with those who also serve. So he joined. He ended by saying 'I'm forever thankful that here in Korea I served the Gloucesters'."

After listening to Tommy' story, George thought, *Someday I'll relate to Padre Sam's courage when I go through difficult times.*

*

Autumn of 1952, the POWs were called to the lecture hall to hear a speech on how germ warfare was being practiced on innocent people. A photo exhibit showed Chinese, wearing hospital garb, inspecting dead rats, foxes, insects, fish, and birds that lay on a metal table. Text indicated this was proof that creatures infected with plague and cholera had been dropped on North Korea by American planes. POWs were asked to comment on the evidence. Sarcastic comments by them terminated that phase of the lecture. The man in charge, who claimed to be a medical doctor, ended the session with a diatribe on how uncivilized Americans were, to perpetrate such an atrocity on innocent civilians.

One Helluva Soldier / Phil Kline

That night, Trexler found a dead rat, made a parachute from string and a white handkerchief, and tied it to the rat. After lights out, he threw it in the middle of the compound street. The next morning, men crowded around windows and doors to watch Chinese, wearing gas masks, creep up to the rat, pick it up with tongs, place it in a white bag, and carry it away.

By the end of September, George and many of the others had regained their normal weights and even developed strength, thanks to the progression of peace talks at Panmunjon. POWs were issued softball and volleyball equipment. Snake Eyes even allowed guards to join in the games.

One morning, while watching the guys play bridge, George heard someone imitate a motorcycle by making a noise through vibrating lips. A door burst open, and a short, stocky POW, wearing a beanie topped by a three-inch propeller, roared into the room. He held his arms out as if holding handlebars of a motorcycle and continued making motor sounds as he ran around the card table twice. He stopped, pretended to turn off the engine, and climbed off his bike.

Eric didn't look up when he said, "Rotorhead, take that Harley out of here while we're playing? Go bug the Chinaman."

Rotorhead climbed on his bike. "I just wanted to tell you that Crazy Week starts Saturday." He coughed three times, imitating the start of a motorcycle the engine, circled the table, and drove out the door.

After Rotorhead left, one of the newer POWs interrupted the card game. "What was that?"

Eric winced when he trumped his partner's trick. "Rotorhead was a navy helicopter pilot. He was tired of walking so he got himself a Harley."

"What's the purpose?"

Eric pulled the trick in. "To bug the Chinaman. Since the names of prisoners have been given to the American authorities, he feels he can get away with it. The Chinaman wouldn't want to have to explain what happened to their only helicopter pilot prisoner."

Hal laid his cards on the table. "What makes it even more complicated is that Rotorhead gave up his last means of escape from capture to save other naval personnel. The Chinese know he's a hero to the Navy. They have to put up with his antics."

Trexler slapped his cards down. "Look, Rotorhead's a hero. Crazy Week's his idea. He has an itinerary, he'll get to everybody, and he drives a Harley. Let's get on with the game."

Midnight on Friday, a heated argument erupted inside the squad room. A guard rushed in to see what caused the ruckus.

Four men were playing poker by candlelight, but without cards. They shouted and waved their arms while threatening to inflict bodily harm on each other. The rest of the men in the room yelled at the players from their mats.

The guard's gaze traveled from the game players to the yellers. "Lights out. Go bed."

The men quit their nonexistent game, the yellers were quiet, and they all went to their beds.

A half hour later, shouts exploded in the room. The same guard rushed in with a flashlight that shined on a man hanging from the rafters. POWs yelled and pointed at the body. The guard ran out the door and minutes later returned with a barefoot older Chinese wearing a robe. When they looked where the body had been hanging, there was neither body nor rope, and all the POWs appeared to be asleep.

The older man yelled at the guard, berated him, and punched him in the back before stomping out.

Later that night, George was awakened by yelling at the other end of the dorm, and what sounded like two shots. A different guard charged into the room, and his flashlight beam shined on a man lying in a pool of red. A POW pointed at the body and yelled. "They killed him."

The guard ran out the door, and the yelling stopped. The dead man got up, walked away, and crawled onto a mat. Four POWs used rags to mop up the red liquid then ran to their mats and feigned sleep. Soon the room was lit up by flashlights and Chinese yelling. There was no body and no blood. The POWs were asleep. The same Chinese berated the guard as they left. The ass-chewing continued until they were out of hearing range.

*

Saturday morning the sun shone on POWs who turned out for a softball game. George played second base, Tommy pitched, and Eric caught. The other squad's leadoff man went to the plate without a bat. A group of POWs watched from around third base, and more stood along first base line with four Chinese guards.

Tommy pitched, but there was no ball. The batter swung without a bat. Eric popped his imaginary mitt and threw the imaginary ball back to Tommy.

The batter swung at the next pitch, dropped his nonexistent bat, and ran toward first. POWs along the first base line cheered while the Chinese glanced at each other. The man on third caught the imaginary ball and threw it to first. The first baseman reached out, made a pop with no glove, and stretched his leg to first base. An umpire spread his arms and yelled, "Safe."

The next batter went to the plate. The guards looked around then huddled together as if doing a pep talk. Rotorhead's Harley roared out from behind where the POW spectators stood. He circled the guards twice then raced off to another group of POWs who were playing imaginary volleyball. He circled the volleyball court once, then returned to the baseball game, cut off his engine, and joined the spectators in cheering.

One Helluva Soldier / Phil Kline

The guards left, but returned with a Chinese in civilian dress. A POW, with an invisible dog on a leash, walked up to the man, stopped and pointed at the end of the leash. "Bad dog. Bad dog." He wiped the man's pant leg with a handkerchief. "So solly." He pointed at the dog again. "Bad dog. Don't pee on Chinese." He bowed to the man and walked away, pointing his finger at the leash. "Bad dog."

The man gave no indication he had seen the POW or the leash, but after the POW left, he brushed off his pant leg.

Rotorhead started his Harley with a couple of coughs, gunned the engine, and circled the man, then roared off, toward Commandant Ding's hut, ignoring two guards who ordered him to halt. He rode to the hut with the guards chasing him and crashed into the side of Ding's office. He collapsed on the ground.

Ding stepped outside his hut. The guards who had chased Rotorhead, yelled and gestured wildly. Ding gave them an order, and they grabbed Rotorhead by the arms, holding him down. Ding walked over to where Rotorhead lay pinned, and pointed at him. "I destroy motorcycle."

He turned to the make-believe Harley that had run into his hut and stomped over and over on it. After his final admonishment, "No more motorcycle in camp," he returned to his hut.

Rotorhead was turned loose. With sagging shoulders, he walked back to the baseball game. That night he reported to the dorm that Crazy Week was a success even if it only lasted two days.

The sound of Rotorhead's Harley was never again heard at Camp #2.

That night George lay awake, thinking. *I have been a party to a wonderful occurrence. Incredibly, my two years as a POW, for the most part, have been happy ones. I barely knew Tommy or*

One Helluva Soldier / Phil Kline

Eric at OCS, and now I'm closer to them than anyone else in the world. Wouldn't it be great if we were never repatriated? He laughed out loud.

"Shut up, Martin," someone shouted, "Crazy Week's over."

The Chinese didn't seem upset about Crazy Week. They also knew an armistice was near. Things kept getting better. The POWs were issued beds, razors, combs, and cigarettes.

*

Ding refused to allow a Coronation Day ceremony for Elizabeth, the new Queen of England, but the Americans received a written invitation to attend one to be held in secret in a British squad room. The invitation mentioned the serving of cake and potato whiskey.

At the ceremony, a senior British officer called on Sam to lead the group in prayer, and after Sam did so, the Brit led the singing of the British national anthem.

Sun, a Chinese officer, appeared at the door, looked at the cake, the British flags, and the newsprint picture of Queen Elizabeth. He turned and left, but soon returned with a squad of guards who burst in. They took the flags. One of them tried to grab the cake, but it was picked up by two Brits who tossed portions to the open hands of others. The whiskey disappeared and someone ran off with the picture of the queen. Americans yelled, "Sons-a-bitches," at the Chinese. Whistles blew, and Chinese reinforcements poured in.

"Sun," Sam shouted, "you have offered to the British people tonight, an insult we shall not forget."

Sun screamed at Sam, "The people? You are not the people. You are imperialist reactionaries, the ruling clique, enemies of the people."

"Sun, you are a stupid man, and I refuse to listen to you."

One Helluva Soldier / Phil Kline

Sun left.

George knew that Padre Sam would be in the hole the next day, and he'd have company. But Sun never returned. The next day the announcement was made that the Chinese premier, Chou En Lai, had sent Winston Churchill a telegram to commemorate the coronation. Nobody was sent to the hole.

In the middle of July 1953, guards herded all the POWs next to Ding's office.

Ding was silent as his interpreter said, "Peace was signed at Panmunjon." Ding walked into his hut.

No emotion was displayed as the POWs returned to their barracks. No celebration took place, only relieved conversation in the dorm. George wasn't sure of his emotions. If anything, he was a bit scared of the unknown.

On 18 August, George and other POWs were crammed onto the bed of a truck that had Russian lettering on its hood. After a two hour ride, they were transferred to a railroad car that had recently hauled cattle.

They were fed fruit and raw vegetables on a two-day ride to Pyongyang. George was astonished to see the change from when he'd liberated beer there. Their railroad car was the largest structure in sight. The city consisted of streets and rubble.

While waiting for trucks to take them on their way, the men were attacked with rocks and sticks by crowds of North Koreans. Chinese guards drove the attackers back and protected the men until they were loaded onto Russian trucks. In Kaesong the men were housed in tents, so close to freedom, many had difficulty sleeping. Conversation continued through the night.

George hadn't seen Tommy or Padre Sam since leaving Camp #2. Every day for two weeks, names of POWs were called over a PA system. Those men were put on trucks and hauled to Freedom Bridge where the prisoner exchange was taking place. Eric was in one of the first groups. When George was called, there still had been no mention of Tommy or Sam.

General Mark Clark shook the hand of every POW who crossed Freedom Bridge to the United Nations side. Men fell to the ground and kissed it. Some laughed, and/or cried. Others walked in a daze while, those who had friends to meet them, had joyous reunions.

George looked at the happiness around him, and he felt alone until someone grabbed his arm from behind. It was a smiling Walt Perry. Then Dutch walked up. "Hello, my friend. It's good to see you."

Both men hugged George as he laughed and cried. They grabbed his hands and shook them then they hugged him again. "We've been here every day for two weeks," Walt said. "We talked with Captain Phillips but haven't seen Trexler. Where is he?"

"I don't know. I haven't seen him since we left the camp over two weeks ago. I don't think he made it to Kaesong."

"What could have happened to him?"

"I have no idea." George spread his arms. "At first, I thought he was on a different truck, but we spent two weeks at Kaesong being fattened up. He wasn't there."

An MP directed them to a beer and soft drink tent, but they declined. Dutch said to George. "Does Luisa know you're free?"

George shook his head. "I don't know where she is. I think she's in Seattle, but I haven't gotten a letter from her since before I was captured. My letters to her were returned, marked, NO FORWARDING ADDRESS. My folks talked to the Red Cross, but they weren't able to locate her. Finance lost track of her, too, so she hasn't received any money for two years." He waved away a soldier who offered him a pack of Lucky Strike cigarettes. "I'll talk to debriefing personnel and see what they can do. I'm sure counterintelligence can locate her."

The friends stopped talking when a major announced on the PA system: "This completes Operation Big Switch for the 3,510 Americans, over 1,000 from other countries and 9200 South Koreans, released in exchange for 76,000 North Koreans and Chinese. A truck, due to arrive tomorrow, holds Chaplain S. J. Davies and five other British officers, held until last because they were classified as reactionaries. Thanks for coming to greet the returning Americans."

"Padre Sam," George said. "He helped many guys make it."

Dutch pointed at the major. "Let's talk to that guy."

They walked to where the announcer was putting his gear away. "Sir, I'm Captain Nelsen. What happened to Lieutenant Tommy Trexler from Yalu Camp Number Two?"

"All Americans on the list have been released. The list did not include a Trexler." The major turned to walk away.

George grabbed the announcer's arm. "I beg your pardon, Major. He was in Camp Number Two, two weeks ago."

The major pulled George's hand off his arm. "All Americans have been released. No Trexler has been released or is due to be released. The exchange of Americans has been completed." Again, he started to walk away.

George shouted, "Major, come back here. I'm George Martin. I was incarcerated for two years with him at Camp Number Two. Don't tell me there's no Trexler."

The major stopped. "I'm sorry, Lieutenant Martin. I didn't mean to be short with you. The information I have is what I received from the transfer team. We checked your name off our list as you approached the bridge, and I called your name as you crossed. All the names have been checked off. I have the list if you want to see it, but there's no Trexler on it. I'm sorry."

One Helluva Soldier / Phil Kline

"You mentioned names of Padre Davies and other British who have yet to cross. Is it possible that Trexler's on that truck?"

"I checked the names. There's Chaplain Davies, a Colonel Carne, three captains, one of them with a hyphenated name, and a Sergeant Major, all reactionaries who were held in China."

George jabbed a finger at the major. "Padre Davies was in Camp Number Two."

"Evidently you have better information than I do, Lieutenant. I'm sorry I can't be of more help." He turned and walked away.

"Major."

The major turned back to George and gave an audible sigh. "Yes, Lieutenant?"

"There were three Air Force guys in Camp Number Five with me. I haven't seen them for over a year. How can I find out about them?"

"You'll be debriefed before you leave Korea and again in San Francisco. Personnel there can answer questions you have about the returnees or those who chose not to come back."

The major left and an MP came to where the three friends stood. He pointed. "There are chapels over there, and a beer tent over there." He pointed to another area. "And when you're ready, there'll be an ambulance to take you to the processing center."

George scowled at the MP, "I'm not going anywhere until Tommy Trexler comes across that bridge, even if I have to go back and get him."

One Helluva Soldier / Phil Kline

34

Dutch, Walt, and George watched the POWs get hugged, cheered, and applauded. Some walked around with double-dip ice cream cones, others smoked American cigarettes or cigars, while most hugged and laughed. The three friends watched men go into, and come out of, the chapels and the beer tent, but there was no Trexler.

George walked to where six POWs stood. He recognized one with a hooked nose who wore captain's bars on his prison garb. George approached him. "Have you seen Tommy Trexler?"

"Haven't seen him since we left the camp. I don't think you'll find him. Too radical, escaped twice, didn't cooperate; spent more time in the hole than anybody. I think he gave the Chinese so much shit they kept him there. He's probably still in a hole in Camp Number Two."

A second POW nodded. "He's right. Trexler was a real asshole. If I had the choice between serving under him or being a prisoner of the Chinese, I'd seriously consider being a prisoner."

George stuck his face in front of the second POW. "Then why don't you go back and try it?" He walked away without seeing the POW's reaction.

The major operating the PA system picked up the microphone. "Your attention, please. The truck carrying the last of the British is entering the area."

One Helluva Soldier / Phil Kline

Eight men touched soil on the UN side. Padre Sam, Mister Hobbs, four British officers, and Rotorhead, hugged each other, laughed, or cried. Tommy Trexler shoved a fist high into the air, and yelled, "Thank God I'm a free American."

British officers met their returning POWs, and two U.S. Navy officers greeted Rotorhead.

George, Walt, and Dutch rushed to Tommy, shook his hands, and hugged him while rattling off words as fast as auctioneers. They were approached by an MP. "An ambulance is waiting to take you to the processing center." Neither George nor Tommy paid attention to the MP.

Dutch touched George's arm. "Take that ride. It may be the last. And take the asshole with you. We'll catch you later." He walked away.

Tommy turned to George. "How come he called me an asshole? What was that all about?"

"I'll tell you later."

Tommy raised his voice. "What was that all about?"

On the way to the ambulance, George told Tommy what the POW said about him, including calling him an asshole.

Tommy nodded and grinned. "He was right."

*

Tommy and George took showers with hot water, were dusted for lice, given medical exams, and issued uniforms. They ate a small meal that contained no spices and then were assigned quarters with real beds. They were told their families had been notified of their return, and each was authorized to send a fifty-word cable to the States. George used fourteen words: *I'm safe and in good health. I'll be home in late September. Love, George.*

One Helluva Soldier / Phil Kline

Later that afternoon, George and Tommy met with Walt and Dutch. Over dinner, they laughed about their pledge to have a fifth year reunion. It was only seven months away. As a committee of four, they elected Walt to make the arrangements and Dutch to locate the grads. They all promised to make it to the reunion.

As Padre Sam left with the other Brits, one of the other POWs called after him, "How do I locate you when I get to England?"

"Take the train to Exeter and go to the cathedral. They'll know. God bless you."

The next morning, George was being interviewed by one of the army counterintelligence officers, many of whom considered the POWs to be traitors. George told the lieutenant, "I don't know where my wife and son are. What can you do to help me locate them?"

"I can't help you. I'm not authorized to do anything except that which relates to POWs."

"I was a POW."

"I know, but I'm not here to locate family."

"How do I locate other POWs I haven't seen for two years?"

"When we're finished here, I'll send you to the Red Cross. They'll help you."

"I was told I could get the information during debriefing."

The lieutenant slapped his pen down and pointed to a desk where a major sat. "Go see the major." Then he motioned for a sergeant to send the next person in line.

The major listened to George's problem in locating Luisa then said, "We don't have the facilities to do that type of search. That'll require leg work. Tell them your problem at the San Francisco debriefing. They'll help you. Anything else?"

George told about his missing friends. "That I can help you with," the major assured him. He took the information about

One Helluva Soldier / Phil Kline

Brian and the missing flyers, and directed George to a seat. Twenty minutes later he returned. "I believe we have the right people, but I can't be sure without knowing their last names. Three Air Force officers with the same first names were with a group we believe had been incarcerated in mainline China. They've been repatriated and have left for the States. We have no information about your civilian friend. Perhaps they can help you find him in San Francisco. If they can't, I suggest you contact your local newspaper."

George took a deep breath and let it out. "Thank you, Sir. I appreciate what you've done." He returned to the debriefing line, thankful to be sent to a different interviewing lieutenant who asked about conditions in the camps in a courteous manner.

After the interview, George was given a partial pay in cash. Then he and Tommy took a helicopter to Inchon where he bought a Nikon camera at the PX. The next day they boarded the USS General Anderson and sailed into the Pacific Ocean. They had no problem, but many others suffered anxiety attacks when close quarters aboard ship brought back memories of the camps.

The afternoon of 23 September 1953—thirty-nine months after George left the States---a seaman ran through the mess where George and Tommy sat drinking coffee. "The bridge is in sight."

George grabbed his Nikon. "Let's go."

They went to the forward deck as the USS Anderson sailed toward the Golden Gate. Looking through tears, George took a picture of the bridge, shining like gold in the late afternoon sun. They took a couple more of each other with the bridge in the background. They laughed as they discussed sending copies to Han and Ding.

One Helluva Soldier / Phil Kline

A band played *God Bless America* as the Anderson tied up at San Francisco's Army Pier. Most of the ex-POWs lined the rails with tears in their eyes as they sang along with the band. George did too, but didn't join the others in singing *America The Beautiful* as the gangway was being lowered. He was busy staring at people on the pier, knowing nobody was there to greet him.

He wondered where Luisa was, and he wondered about Mario. *How big is he? Does he look like me? I hope not. I hope so.*

*

Early that evening, George made the call they were waiting for in Potterville. His folks had received his cable, and the War Department had notified them of his arrival date. After a good sleep in a BOQ at the Port of Debarkation, he ate a breakfast of bacon and four eggs then walked to a building close-by, to be interviewed by Counterintelligence.

He sat across a table from Lieutenant Stein in an interview room. After questions about George's health, Stein said, "Tell me about the conduct of prisoners who collaborated."

George looked at Stein through narrowed eyes. "Those who collaborated, as you say, did so only to the extent necessary."

"What do you mean when you say necessary?"

"Sometimes they did so to keep from being beaten or stuck in the hole. They either gave unimportant information or what the Chinese already knew."

Stein continued speaking in a matter-of-fact voice. "What about the confessions of germ warfare? Were they unimportant?"

George frowned. "I know nothing about confessions of germ warfare."

"How could you not? They were on TV all over the world."

George jabbed a finger at Stein. "You're in Intelligence, and you think we had television in the camps?"

"Settle down, Martin. I'm just trying to determine what happened to our POWs."

"Then ask about that, Stein."

"You were transferred back and forth to many different outfits during the war."

George didn't reply.

"Well?"

"You didn't ask. You made a statement. An incorrect one."

"Lieutenant Martin, why were you transferred so often?"

"I wasn't transferred. I was placed on temporary duty with different outfits. That's what a forward observer does for a living. If you ever had duty other than a desk job, you'd know that."

"Okay." Stein's tone of voice telegraphed his irritation. "Let's go back to Camp Number Five. Where were you during the three months you disappeared from sight?"

George glared at him. "I was in solitary, alone in the dark."

"But you were free enough to play baseball with the Chinese."

George stood and stared at Stein. "You're worse than the Chinese. My name is George E. Martin, First Lieutenant, O2014508." He stomped out.

After George settled down, he made plane and train reservations, then called to tell his mom what time he would arrive Saturday. He was given another complete physical and mental exam and was released to travel.

He and Tommy discussed their debriefings over dinner at the Port Officers Club, but when he told about his interview with Stein, Tommy looked puzzled. "My interviewer treated me like I was a disgrace to my country," Tommy said, "but I didn't

One Helluva Soldier / Phil Kline

get that stuff about being gone, and I was in the hole a heck of a lot longer than you were."

"Remember Hinch?"

"The asshole."

George stared at Tommy. "You never cuss."

"I never met an asshole like him before. He gets special consideration for doing what he did. I know what you're saying, and I think you're right. He got here before we did to tell his lies about you."

George nodded then cut into his steak. Neither of them mentioned the camps during the rest of the meal.

*

The next morning, George boarded a civilian Lockheed Constellation and flew to Chicago, then caught a bus to Michigan. He wondered how much the town had changed since he left. Growing up outside of Potterville, he hadn't thought of it as a hick town because it was all he knew. But there was talk that people who passed through thought it was, with the smell of cows that seemed to hang in the air most of the time.

Looking out the window to catch a glimpse of where the railroad track ran through town, George wondered if they still used the station that reminded him of the chicken coop on the farm. At age eight, he had walked into the station, expecting to see white leghorns setting, but instead, saw green benches with people sitting on them. And the aroma was cows instead of chickens.

George heard music being played by the twelve piece Potterville High band, from the back of a stake truck. At least a hundred people crowded around a platform. He shook his head at the thought of such a welcoming.

One Helluva Soldier / Phil Kline

George stepped off the train to be greeted by his mother's open arms, tears, and a hug that made him aware that he really was home. After a handshake from his father, two Boy Scouts led him to a platform where the mayor gave him a two-fisted handshake and a key to the city. He introduced George as a hometown hero, all the while not looking at George, but at a movie camera that recorded his smile. Then he followed with a ten-minute speech about how proud the citizens of Potterville were of their hero and how happy they were to have him home again.

That evening, George's mother hugged him some and cried a lot. His father asked about life in the camps and listened with obvious interest as George told him how he had spent his time in the schoolhouse to maintain sanity. After enjoying fresh baked apple pie and hot coffee, George watched the eleven o'clock news, then slept in his old room, upstairs.

The next day, he received a phone call.

"I'm Steve Barton. My job's to help you get accustomed to regular life and take care of any needs you may have."

"Good. There is something you can do for me. Locate my wife and child. Almost three years ago, my wife wrote that she was going to stay with a cousin in Seattle. I haven't heard from her since. My letters have been returned, the Red Cross couldn't locate her, and Finance didn't know where to send her allotment checks. Find out what happened to her and my son."

Barton's firm voice was reassuring. "Get me her last address, the names and address of any friends and her family—anything you have that may help."

"I don't know who her cousin is, but her folks live in Mexico. I'll get their address to you this afternoon."

"I'll see what I can do," Barton promised.

"Another thing; see what you can find out what happened to a man I met on the march to the camps, a war correspondent named Brian. I don't know his last name or the paper he worked for."

"I'll do what I can, and I'll be around for whatever you need. I see you have orders to report to the Fifty-third Field Artillery Battalion at Fort Sill. I'm next door in Lawton." He gave George a phone number. "Call if you need me."

"I'll do that. By the way, what's your rank?"

"I'm civilian."

"Who's your employer, Steve?"

"I'm with the federal government."

George dug through his personal effects until he found Luisa's Durango address then called the information to Barton.

He spent the rest of the day engaged in small talk and telling his folks about the ordeals he and his friends went through during the early part of the war. Later, as they strolled around the farm, his dad treated George as if he were happy to have him home. That night George watched Lansing Channel 10 and saw himself receiving the keys to Potterville from the mayor.

The next day, he went to Dave Macmillan's farm and helped Dave milk cows. Later, they sat on the front porch, comparing experiences. Before George left, Dave said, "You had it tougher than I did. I don't know if I could have survived all you went through. You're a remarkable man."

George shook Dave's hand with both of his. "That means a lot coming from someone I respect as much as I do you."

Three days later, George left Michigan with the idea of spending the rest of his life in the army, realizing he felt more at home in the service than he did at home.

When his folks dropped him off at the train station, his mom hugged and kissed him. "Take care of yourself, Son. Eat more and get some meat on your bones." She cried as she hugged him again.

One Helluva Soldier / Phil Kline

His dad shook hands with George and said, "I'm proud of you, Son."

George was at a loss for words. He shook his dad's hand again and climbed on the bus to Chicago. While thinking how his father had called him "son" for the first time in years, George realized he, himself, had not used the word "dad." He decided to get back to the farm soon and cement their relationship.

George reported to the 53rd Field at Fort Sill and was assigned as B Battery Executive Officer, in charge of the 155 mm howitzer crews. The commanding officer introduced him to his chief of section, Sergeant First Class Burko, who had served in Korea. They walked behind the barracks where the gun crews stood in formation, and the CO told them a little of George's exploits in Korea and as a POW.

The CO dismissed the gun section and left. Then the six gun sergeants met with George. "Meet our new exec," Burko said. The sergeants marched up to George, one at a time, saluted, and gave their names. It was so formal, he had the feeling of being a stranger in the 53rd.

After introductions, Sergeant Burko made the first warm statement of the day. "I'm happy to have the opportunity to serve with you, someone with your knowledge and experience."

"Thank you, Sergeant. I appreciate your words. I have to take care of some private business, but I'll be back this week."

"I look forward to that, Sir."

He walked to his BOQ, in a one-story brick building, on the other side of the parade ground, and called Steve Barton.

"I found your wife and son," Steve said.

George waved a victory fists in the air and almost dropped the phone. "Amazing. I don't believe it. Where are they? How'd you do it? Where is she?"

"They're in Seattle. Her name is now Luisa Sanchez."

George's voice was almost inaudible. "What did you say?"

"Her name is Luisa Sanchez."

"No, you've found the wrong person."

"She's the right one. I talked to her. She married again two years after she received word you had been killed in action."

"What are you talking about?" George yelled. "I was never reported killed in action."

Steve's voice remained calm. "I know that. She didn't get the information from the government. She said the letters she wrote to you came back. Return to sender, killed in action, was written across the front of the envelopes."

George shook his head. "That can't be."

"It's true. She never received information from the Defense Department. They lost track of her and have had no record of her address since she left El Paso three years ago."

George's head was still shaking. "Mr. Barton, what you've told me can't be true."

Barton gave George the address and phone number of Luisa Sanchez and Mario Martin in Seattle. "I'm truly sorry this happened," he said. "I can't give you any more information than what I've told you. I didn't think it was the time to burden her with questions about how the army lost track of her. She seemed pretty shook up, about like you are. I'll do what I can to find out where the information came from, that you were killed in action. And of course, you realize that her new marriage will be nullified."

"That won't undo what's happened."

Barton's tone was surprisingly harsh. "I located her for you."

"I'm sorry. You're right."

Now Barton's voice was more sympathetic. "I feel bad it turned out that way. I do have some good news, though. I haven't found your friend, Brian, but I know how to. United

One Helluva Soldier / Phil Kline

Press International had a correspondent in Korea, Brian Hill. He was a prisoner of the Chinese. He left UPI and has gone freelance. I'll have his full name and how to reach him within a day or two."

It was as if finding Brian was no longer important. "Thanks. I appreciate what you've done."

George put the phone down and stared at it. "Luisa Sanchez," he whispered. He laid his head on the desk and sobbed. He pounded his fists on the desk, raised his head and looked at her photograph then banged his forehead on the desk. He cradled his head in his arms and cried.

A knock came at the door. George yelled, "Just a minute." He wiped his eyes and his face, put on his sunglasses, and opened the door. He recognized one of the gun section sergeants wearing a royal blue silk shirt covered with orange crescents.

The sergeant folded, then unfolded, his arms. He clasped his hands together and shuffled his feet. "Sergeant Henderson, Sir."

"What can I do for you, Henderson?"

"Nothing, Sir." He looked away then back at George. "It's what I can do for you."

"Yes?"

"I know you're one of us."

One Helluva Soldier / Phil Kline

35

George glared at the lanky sergeant who blocked his view through the door. "Get to the point, Sergeant."

"I knew as soon as I saw you walk down the company street."

"Get to the point, Sergeant." George's patience was wearing thin.

"Look, Lieutenant, I don't mean you no harm. I realize you have a problem just like I did when I first got here. I was lonely. I didn't know where to go to find others I could relate to. Now I know a place you can go when you're feeling alone: The Moon Club on Gore Boulevard in downtown Lawton." He touched his chest. "Next to Homer's Pool Hall is a door with a picture of a shirt like this on it. Ring the bell, and when a man answers, tell him you want to visit the club."

George grabbed the open door and pushed it toward Henderson. "Get out of here."

Henderson stepped back.

Through the partial opening, George watched him walk down the sidewalk, toward the parade ground. *"What's behind this?"* he wondered.

Ten minutes later, George stepped out of his BOQ and wandered around the parade ground, staring ahead but seeing nothing. He didn't even return the salutes of two enlisted men.

He arrived at the officers club and entered a bar that had only one person in it: the bartender. George ordered a draft.

One Helluva Soldier / Phil Kline

The bartender slid a schooner of Blatz to him. "That'll be twenty-five cents."

George tossed a quarter across the bar and carried his beer out to a terrace. There he sat under an umbrella, and looked unseeing at two women playing tennis.

He banged the schooner on the table. *I'm as much a prisoner here as I was in Korea. If Luisa doesn't want me, I don't have a home at all.* He pushed his beer away. *Okay, Martin, off your butt and do what you're supposed to do.* He left the full schooner on the table and hurried to his quarters.

Once there, he lifted the phone off its cradle and slammed it down again. *What do I say?* He shook his head, grabbed the phone, and dialed the number he had been given; Luisa's number. When she answered, he tried to hide his wavering voice. "This is George."

He barely heard her say, "Oh, it's true."

"Yes." He wanted to say how much he loved her but choked the words off. "I want to come to Seattle to see you and Mario."

"I'll call you later when my husband is home. Oh! I'm sorry."

Hearing the word 'husband' crushed George. "I understand. I'll check on transportation and call you back."

Within an hour, he'd purchased a bus ticket to Oklahoma City and had a plane reservation to Seattle. He called Luisa again. "I'll be there at three-thirty tomorrow afternoon."

"We'll be waiting for you."

George leaned back in the chair but soon sat up and looked at the clock: It was 9 p.m. He called Dutch at Fort Lewis, Washington and told him about his conversation with Steve Barton and about Luisa marrying someone in Seattle.

"Throw the son-of-bitch out," Dutch said.

Compared to the inflection in Dutch's voice, George sounded like a robot. "Thanks. I feel like doing that, but it's

One Helluva Soldier / Phil Kline

Luisa's decision to make. She was unhappy when I left for Korea. She may have found the normal life I didn't give her. It's up to her to decide what she wants to do."

"But, she's still your wife."

"I know. At least in the eyes of the law."

"Then go punch him in the nose."

"I feel like punching somebody, but I don't think it would solve anything."

"Why did she accept what was written on an envelope?"

George stood and paced as he talked, restricted by the eight foot phone cord. "She's Mexican and doesn't know how the American army works any more than I know how the Mexican army does. I expect she figured if the letters were returned saying I was dead, I must be dead, and because I was dead, the money would quit coming in. And it did because Finance didn't know where she was."

"What about you? Didn't you know her address? Didn't they contact you?"

George sat on the edge of the desk. "No. She'd just decided to move when I got her last letter. After that I was transferred around and got no mail. Next thing I knew, letters I wrote to her were returned. I contacted Finance Department, but then the Chinese came in. By the time Finance tried to contact me, I was a POW."

"And they didn't know where she was, so they couldn't notify her that you were missing in action. One more question: Who wrote killed in action on her letters to you?"

"I think I know, but I have no way of confirming it."

"Hinch?"

"Probably. He was at the Forty-seventh where my mail was delivered."

Dutch's tone was serious. "I'm amazed that you're holding up so well, my friend. If it had happened to me, I would have

One Helluva Soldier / Phil Kline

killed that bastard Hinch and that guy in Seattle and maybe even the guy who brought the bad news."

"I might have, if they had all been close by. Now, I just want to see Luisa and Mario. Luisa and I were practically newlyweds when I left. Mario was only two months old."

*

A cool wind blew dust across the post. George put on a long sleeve shirt and slacks, and walked to a bus stop, squinting to keep the dust out of his eyes. After riding a local bus to Lawton, he had an hour to spare before the next Greyhound was due to leave for Oklahoma City, so he strolled around town. Lawton was larger than Potterville, but it still smelled of cows.

The street sign read Gore Boulevard. He looked to the left. There it was, Homer's Pool Hall. George walked past an old Indian huddled under a blanket next to the curb and, moments later, he stood in front of a beat-up wooden door and the picture of a royal blue shirt with golden crescents. He turned away, but before he had taken two steps, turned back and walked through the door and up a brightly lit staircase.

He rang the bell in the center of the door, and within seconds a tall burly man stood before him.

George looked up at him. "I want to visit your club." The man gave a come-in gesture.

Two men stood at the bar, and another two sat at a table. George walked to the end of the bar. The man, who had let him in, walked behind the bar, came over in front of George, leaned on his elbows, and smiled. "My name's Baird, Jim Baird."

George backed off. "I just wanted to take a look at your club." He turned and walked out the door.

At the bus station, he sat on a bench, angry at Henderson, himself, and the world.

One Helluva Soldier / Phil Kline

On the Greyhound, George gazed through the window, trying to get interested in the scenery rather than think about what the future might hold. He'd maintained a strong mental picture of Luisa but had trouble visualizing Mario. The major memories that played over and over in his mind were the nights he and Luisa walked around the square in Durango, and when they frolicked in the Sandy River. Without success, he tried to erase the thought that she was married to someone else, and his son would be calling that person Daddy.

It was a long ride to Oklahoma City, and a short flight to Seattle.

*

George drummed his fingers on the seat as the Washington cab pulled up to a white Cape Cod. He paid the driver, walked up the sidewalk, and rang the doorbell.

Luisa opened the door. She appeared a bit older than he remembered, but was still young and beautiful. He breathed in her aroma and was sure he would have recognized her with his eyes closed.

A large man with jet black hair and a bushy mustache hovered over her like a bodyguard. George repressed the urge to punch him in the face.

Luisa fidgeted with a ring on her left hand and stared at George. She gave him a weak smile.

For a moment, he stared at her without speaking. Finally, he said, "May I see my son?"

She didn't answer but just stared at his face from a distance of two feet.

The man scowled at her. "Luisa."

She turned away. "I'll get him."

One Helluva Soldier / Phil Kline

After Luisa left the room, her bodyguard blocked the doorway. "You can't take him away from here, but you can spend time with him in the house."

Again, George had the urge to clobber him, but he maintained his composure and wore a blank expression as he looked past the man, waiting for a glimpse of his son.

When Mario came into view, he was pulling on Luisa's hand, as if to keep her away from the door. George saw a little boy dressed in a white shirt and jeans, much like the boy he had imagined except more grown up.

"Move, Lorenzo," Luisa said. "Let him come in."

Lorenzo moved, and George stepped inside. Mario backed up and held onto his mother's long flowered skirt, the same style she had worn when they first strolled in Durango.

George followed them into a sunny living room accented with large leaf plants. Luisa pointed to a sofa, and George sat on the front edge. He reached out to his three-year-old son. Mario didn't go to him but grabbed his mother's skirt even tighter.

Luisa took his little hand and raised it toward George's outstretched palm. "Mario, this is your father. He had to go to the army. This is the first time he is able to see you. Show him how grown up you are and shake his hand."

Mario hesitated.

Luisa turned to Lorenzo and pointed to an open door. "Lorenzo, please go in the bedroom while they get acquainted."

The man frowned but walked away.

Luisa kneeled and took Mario's right hand in hers, then reached for George's and guided the two together. They shook hands.

George stared at Mario, startled to realize what he saw was a reproduction of a photograph of himself, taken at that age. The only difference he could see was that Mario's hair was black.

One Helluva Soldier / Phil Kline

His mind reverted to the conversation he'd imagined with Mario while he was crouched in the pig pen.

"You are bigger than I thought. Pretty soon you'll be grown up," he said.

Mario glanced at his mom then at George. "I'm getting big."

George kneeled to talk with Mario at eye level. They talked about Mario's friends, the dog next door, his favorite toys, and the playground at the school he would go to someday. After forty minutes, Mario's eyes began to wander, and his conversation slowed.

George held his son's hand. "I'll leave now, but I'd like to come back and spend more time with you tomorrow."

Mario looked at his mother as if for an answer. She nodded as she bent down to him. "Would you like to have picnic with your father tomorrow?" Again she nodded and Mario followed her lead. She smiled at George. "I'll call your cab."

She left the room, but soon returned, followed by Lorenzo. "Come about noon tomorrow," Luisa said. "That way you and Mario can have a picnic on the porch, just the two of you."

George stood and looked into her eyes, marveling at how brown they were. *I want to hold you, kiss you, and tell you how much I love you.* He was sure she knew what he was thinking. "That would be nice." He didn't look away, and she kept her gaze on him.

Lorenzo moved toward them. "Luisa." Without looking, she pointed an index finger at him, and he stopped in his tracks.

She remained facing George and spoke in a matter-of-fact voice. "Thank you for coming. Tomorrow you two can be alone."

During the time he waited outside for a cab, George didn't notice the rain. He was swept back three years by Luisa's aroma, her voice, her being.

One Helluva Soldier / Phil Kline

That night, he went to bed earlier than usual. He lay and relived the events of the day, smiling when he recalled how much Mario resembled what he had looked like as a child. The smile vanished.

What will Luisa be like tomorrow when Lorenzo's not around? Different scenarios came to mind, but thoughts of what Hinch had done intruded.

He lay awake most of the night.

*

George arrived at the Cape Cod house wearing a khaki uniform. The day was cool, but the rain had stopped. Luisa greeted him with a quiet, "Hi." Holding Mario's hand, she led the two men who had been her life to the back porch.

On a picnic table were paper plates, hot dog buns, and chips, more than enough for two. George lifted Mario onto the bench on one side of the table, and he sat on the other. He looked up at Luisa. "Will you join us?"

"Later. First, I get the hot dogs." She left and returned with a steaming bowl. After putting it on the table, she removed Mario's sweater, set it down and remained standing. When Mario loosened up and started talking to George across the table, she turned to go.

George reached a hand toward her. "Please stay for a minute."

She extended a hand toward his, and their fingers touched. Their eyes met as he closed his fingers on hers. She left them that way a moment before easing her hand back, then sat next to Mario and looked down at him.

"Your father is a nice looking soldier, isn't he? See his medals?" Her gaze was on George's face as she pointed at the ribbons on his chest. "I told you he was a hero."

Mario nodded. Luisa wiped her eyes on a napkin..

One Helluva Soldier / Phil Kline

George pulled an envelope from his shirt pocket and handed it to his son. "This is more valuable to me than my medals. I hope it's valuable to you."

Mario opened the envelope and pulled out a brass spoon.

George faced his son, but his eyes were on Luisa. "I ate with this spoon for two years. I want you to have it."

Mario looked at George and at Luisa. "Can I eat with it?"

George turned toward Mario. "Yes, Son. Your mother will make sure it doesn't get lost." When he looked at Luisa, she returned his gaze, then stood and walked into the house.

George talked with Mario, calling him Son often. Mario nibbled on his hot dog, but George only picked at a few chips as his boy talked about his friends and the dog next door. A half hour after they finished eating, Mario's conversation slowed down, and they walked into the house.

Mario stayed with George as he called a cab, but after George hugged him, he scurried to his mother's side.

When the cab arrived, Luisa walked George to the door. She extended her hand and he held it. She looked down at the two hands clasped together and then back at his face. He was sure he saw tears in her eyes, but wasn't sure if what he saw was only what he wanted to see.

He released her hand when he felt hers slipping away. "I'm so proud of Mario," he said. "His good manner has to be a reflection of the way you've raised him. I'm proud of you for being such a good mother." He looked out the window at the cab then turned to face her. "You will always have a grand place in my heart next to our son. Goodbye."

He waved to Mario, then turned and walked to the cab before she could see his tears.

On his trip back to Fort Sill, he shook his head as he thought of the time, three years earlier, when he believed he would only be leaving his family for a short period of time.

One Helluva Soldier / Phil Kline

I'm a man without a family. I don't even have a country. My home's not where I grew up, it's not Korea where I spent most of my adult life. My friends are scattered around the world. I don't belong anywhere. I've lost my son and the only woman I'll ever love. I'm alone, a stranger in a world of normal people.

George dozed periodically on the way to Oklahoma. That night, once again, he climbed the stairs behind the picture of the blue shirt with the golden crescents. He sat alone at the end of the bar and ordered a draft. A man four stools down got up and strolled over to him to say, "Hi."

George left his beer untouched and walked out of the Moon Club.

One Helluva Soldier / Phil Kline

36

George inspected B Battery's guns on a cold Saturday morning while the trails were spread but not dug in. He checked the breeches and looked through the tubes. They appeared properly maintained and lubricated. He checked the condition of the tools. They were clean and rust free. He walked to the formation. "Your equipment shows good. From the looks of the maintenance you've performed, I'm sure the guns are in great working order. I expect you'd do well in action." He turned to the chief of section. "Sergeant Burko, dismiss the firing battery and meet me in the mess hall in ten minutes. I could use a cup of hot coffee."

Over coffee, George said, "The guns and other equipment look great. I assume you've fired them."

"Yes, Sir."

"How did they do?"

"Both the guns and the men performed well, Sir."

George spoke over the cup he held in both hands. "How long does it take to get into position, jacked up, and ready to fire?"

Burko shrugged. "I'm not sure. I haven't timed them."

"You were in Korea. How long did it take your battery there?"

"Too long."

George took a sip of his coffee. "How much time, Sergeant?"

"Probably twenty, twenty-five minutes."

One Helluva Soldier / Phil Kline

"You're right; that's too long. Let's find out how long our section takes. We'll trial-run Wednesday, and after they're in position, I'll call march order to see how long that takes."

Burko smiled. "I have a feeling it'll be too long to satisfy you." Then he picked up his cup for the first time.

"Probably. I'll request clearance to hook up and move, and we'll see what happens."

The two of them finished their coffee pretty much in silence.

Wednesday morning, Major Renaud, Battalion S-3, stood next to George at Signal Mountain Range, waiting for the guns. First a cloud of dust, unaffected by a light frost, rolled above the hills, then came the sound of trucks laboring in second gear. The guns entered the position. George checked his watch as the crew jumped out of the first truck and unhooked a howitzer fifty yards from where he stood. The other crews followed.

The trucks were moved forward and the men unloaded their pioneer tools. Some dug holes as others readied the spades. Ammo boxes, fuse boxes, and tools were unloaded.

The spades were on, and the men were waiting for the holes to be dug before they could pull the first howitzer into position.

George looked at his watch, cupped his hands in front of his mouth, and hollered, "Fire mission."

Renaud jumped. Work stopped, and the men stared at George as he walked toward the guns. Again, he yelled, "Fire mission." Men scrambled to break out fuses and lug ammo from the crates to the guns. On the first howitzer, a buck sergeant manned the left side for deflection, and a corporal jumped to the right side to man elevation.

George shouted, "You can't fire that way. It'll bounce back into the truck if the trails aren't anchored."

They stopped. Some shook their heads while others just stared at him.

He yelled, "March order."

One Helluva Soldier / Phil Kline

The men grumbled as they took their time pushing the tools, ammo, and fuses onto the truck beds. They slammed the spades back in their slots, hooked up the guns, and climbed onto the trucks, all with a complete lack of enthusiasm.

"Sergeant Burko," George said. "Call the men into formation."

The men lined up and glared at him.

George glared back at them. "I called fire mission fifteen minutes after the last truck stopped. You should have been in position, ready to fire by then. March order took you almost a half-hour. That's too much time, even if the guns were in position and the trucks were a hundred yards away, but you weren't dug in, and the trucks were here."

One of the sergeants said, "What do you expect, Lieutenant?"

"I expect it will cost American lives if you're that slow in combat."

"But we're not in combat, Sir."

George walked up and down the line of men. "We weren't in combat in June 1950, and by the end of July, half of the American soldiers in Korea were dead or POWs because they weren't ready. I expect you to be ready." He looked around at the men. "From the time the first truck gets to the firing position, how long should it take the battery to be ready to fire a mission?"

Nobody answered.

"Fifteen minutes. I watched you work to get ready. You worked well enough. You just weren't organized. I know you can do it in fifteen minutes." He turned to Burko. "You have a half-hour to get them ready to try it again."

"Yes, Sir."

As George walked away, Major Renaud said, "You really expect them to be ready for a fire mission in fifteen minutes?"

"Yes, but not today."

"Put five dollars on it?"

"I'll take that bet. In two weeks they'll do it in fifteen minutes and march order, from a dug-in position, in twenty."

Renaud shook George's hand then watched as the battery made it into position and ready to fire in nineteen minutes.

*

On a warm sunny morning two weeks later, the battery made it into position in fifteen minutes and march ordered in less than twenty. Major Renaud dropped five silver dollars into George's open hand. "I like having you around. You'll make me look good."

"And I like being here, Sir. You can do something that will help; the men did the job well, please tell them how well they did."

"I'll do that."

George flipped the dollars from one hand to the other, one at a time. "Good, because there are other things I want them to learn, and it'll make them angry for a while."

*

The next time battalion went to the firing range was during a light snow that didn't hamper the men of B Battery. They were first in position, first in march order, and quicker in fire missions than the other three batteries.

Renaud walked into the battery position and found George. "How do they fire missions so fast?"

George called a gun crew back to their gun. "Show the major how you fire missions."

Number One man stood behind the breech. "I reach for the firing lock and breech handle when the gun's still in full recoil."

One Helluva Soldier / Phil Kline

One of two men carrying the tray containing the projectile, rammer staff and charge, said, "At that time, we're ready to load."

"I already have the firing lock in," Number One said. "I slam the breech shut, and it's on the way."

At the end of the demonstration, they stood tall and smiled. Renaud nodded. "We need more men with your spirit.

George beamed. "They've earned the pride that comes with performance, and most of them don't hate me anymore."

But he wasn't smiling that night when he went to bed. He looked toward the phone at least forty times in the three hours he lay there not sleeping. He woke four times during the night.

Luisa didn't call.

Saturday, George took a bus to Lawton and bought a red 1953 Mercury. He drove to the top of Mount Scott, overlooking the reservation, and took a picture of the car, then wondered who he'd show the photograph to.

He parked his Mercury out back and went to his BOQ to call the Air Force friends he'd shared huts with in Korea. He talked to Brian in Chicago and set a date to meet with him then he called Eric Phillips, now a major with the Artillery School.

That evening, he had dinner with Eric and his wife at their quarters on Officers Row. After dinner, George sat on the wraparound porch of the red brick house and talked to Eric.

"The times I spent with you in the camps were some of the most memorable of my life. I like the people I work with here. I'm not happy, but I think I've found a home. The battery commander has orders for Germany, so I may get the command. I like the army. I like my job, the post, and myself. Life isn't great, but work helps keep my mind off of my family."

That night, Walt Perry called from Fort Lewis, Washington. "The 9-A reunion will be at Fort Riley, 28 May to 2 June. I'll send you the details."

One Helluva Soldier / Phil Kline

George gave Walt the latest news: "I'm exec of B Battery of the 53rd, and I love it. Not only that, but I'm in line to get command."

*

One week after his conversation with Walt, George received a Notification to The Accused. Charges had been filed against him under Article 133 of the Manual for Courts Martial: Conduct unbecoming an officer and a gentlemen.

He stood at his desk and read the notification of charges that included three signed enclosures of evidence to be given:

First Lieutenant Steven L. Barton, Counterintelligence Corps: The accused did frequent a house of prostitution in Lawton, Oklahoma.

Staff Sergeant Arlin D. Henderson, Artillery: Advised the accused that the house of prostitution in question was one where homosexuals gathered.

Sergeant Emil Adams, Lawton Police Department: Affidavit and Arrest Reports from raids indicated that unnatural acts by people of the same sex were performed in that house of prostitution.

George read the notification, set it down, picked it up, and re-read it. He let the paper drop to the floor. He sat at his desk with his head in his hands. "No."

One Helluva Soldier / Phil Kline

37

First Lieutenant James Orlow faced George across a table in the Judge Advocate's Office.

"Lieutenant Martin, the only item the trial counsel must prove for the court to find you guilty is that you knowingly frequented a house of prostitution."

"It was a social club, not a house of prostitution."

"Lawton police reports state that it was. The owners of the establishment were prosecuted and found guilty of running a house of prostitution. The army says that if you go in one, you have engaged in conduct unbecoming an officer and a gentleman."

"I didn't know about the police report, so I'm not guilty of knowingly frequenting."

"The prosecution has a witness who says he told you it was, and another who says you went there twice." Lieutenant Orlow crossed his arms. "Look, my job is to defend you from the charge so let's work on that. Your 2-0-1 file shows that you were involved in a similar incident before the war. Tell me about that."

"That was not a court martial. It was a board of officers. And I was not involved in any incident, nor convicted of anything."

"Boards don't convict, they investigate and make recommendations. I want to know what happened, so I can better defend you. Tell me about it."

One Helluva Soldier / Phil Kline

George closed his eyes and shook his head. "I sat with a group of enlisted men and had a couple of beers with them in a Chinese restaurant."

"Homosexuals?"

He shrugged. "I guess so. Yes."

"The report shows that one of them called you a bitch, terminology that homosexuals use to describe boyfriends."

"I was not anybody's boyfriend. I had two beers with them."

Orlow leaned toward George. "Why?"

George clenched his jaw. "Because I related to the fun they were having. Is that what you want me to say?"

"I merely want to determine if you are homosexual."

"For your information, I'm not. And why is that so important to you? I'm not charged with being one."

"Because I can do a better job of defending you. Even if you're not, don't take the stand. Nothing you can say will help your case, and almost anything you say to defend yourself, will hurt it. Undoubtedly, you'll be found guilty. You can only hope they'll be lenient."

"You make them sound like the Chinese."

"What are you talking about?"

"I was a POW in Korea. The Chinese talked about how lenient they were while they starved and mistreated us."

"I understand, and I heard you stood up to them honorably. Unfortunately, your record as an officer cannot be introduced as evidence. Have you ever engaged in homosexual activities?"

"No."

"Never?"

"I just told you. No"

George and Lieutenant Orlow stood at attention in the courtroom, empty except for the participants. The law officer faced them. "This court is now in session. Be seated."

One Helluva Soldier / Phil Kline

Orlow and George sat at the defense table. George's mind left the courtroom to wander over a life that reminded him of a truck bogged down in the mud, straining to gain traction. His dad, Scarf, Hinch, and a number of others, had shoved him into a rut he couldn't escape. *Why? If I were queer, none of them would be affected by my lifestyle. I'm one hell of a soldier. It's the army that's out of step, not me.*

The law officer read the charge and specification to the seven field grade officers who made up the court: "In that George E. Martin, First Lieutenant, B Battery, 53rd Field Artillery Battalion, in violation of Article 133 of the Manual for Courts Martial, United States, did, in Lawton, Oklahoma, on or about 2 October 1953, and again on 4 October 1953, frequent a known house of prostitution, to the disgrace of the Armed Forces. Elements of proof are that the accused did do certain acts, and that under the circumstances, those acts constituted conduct unbecoming an officer and a gentleman."

The president of the court faced George. "Lieutenant Martin, how do you plead?"

Orlow stood. "The defendant pleads not guilty to the charge and the specification."

George closed his eyes. His mind jumped back to a time in high school when John J. McNish pointed an accusing finger at him and said, "You're queer."

"Not guilty," George murmured.

The trial counsel faced the court. "The prosecution calls its first witness, Sergeant Emil Adams, Lawton Police Department."

After Adams was sworn in, the trial counsel approached the stand and handed him a sheath of papers. "Sergeant, do you recognize these documents?"

"Yes. They're sworn statements with attached arrest reports from the Lawton Police Department. They confirm that the

Moon Club on Gore Boulevard was raided, the tenants prosecuted, and found guilty of operating a house of prostitution by males."

"Were you present during the raid, Sergeant Adams?"

"Yes, Sir, I was."

"No further questions. Does the defense wish to cross-examine the witness?"

Orlow said, "No, Sir."

"The witness is excused."

"The prosecution calls Steven L. Barton, First Lieutenant, Counterintelligence Corps, United States Army."

Barton testified. "I was assigned to observe Lieutenant Martin due to reports that he had collaborated with the Chinese while a prisoner of war."

George shook his head violently.

Orlow jumped to his feet. "The defense objects. Testimony is not relevant to the charge and is prejudicial to the accused."

"Objection sustained," the Law Officer said. "The court will disregard that testimony as inadmissible. The witness will testify only to those actions by the accused relevant to the charge."

The trial counsel faced Barton. "Tell the court only what you yourself observed."

"On both days, 2 October and again on 4 October, 1953, I observed the accused enter the Moon Club on Gore Boulevard."

George kept his eyes closed and his head down.

"Anything else you'd like to add?"

"I was present when Lieutenant Martin was greeted by the citizens of Potterville, and I talked to a young man who knew him. He said Lieutenant Martin was queer."

Lieutenant Orlow jumped up. "Objection. That is hearsay and not relevant to the charge."

The law officer hopped to his feet. "Sustained. Trial Counsel, caution your witness to testify only to acts of the accused that he observed and are relevant to the charge."

The trial counsel took his seat. "I have no further questions."

The president faced the defense counsel. "You wish to cross examine?"

"No, Sir."

"The witness is excused. The prosecution calls Arlin D. Henderson, Sergeant, United States Army." After Henderson was sworn in, the trial counsel walked to the stand "You spoke to the accused about the house in question, the Moon Club?"

"Yes, Sir."

"What did you tell him?"

"I said it was a club for homosexuals where he could meet others like himself."

"How did you describe the entrance to him?"

"I told him it was upstairs, next to Homer's Pool Hall, behind the door with the picture of a blue shirt with gold crescents on it."

"No further questions."

"Cross examination?" the president said.

George leaned toward Orlow. "What he said is not true. He only said it was a place where I could go if I was lonely."

Orlow stood. He walked toward Henderson. "Isn't it true that you did not tell Lieutenant Martin it was a club for homosexuals, but that it was a place where he could go if he was lonely?"

"No. That's not true."

"No further questions." Orlow walked away.

"The witness is excused. The prosecution rests."

George turned toward Orlow. "He's lying."

"I can't prove that," Orlow whispered to George, "and all you can do is dispute it. I hope you don't want to make a statement."

"No." Seconds later, George slapped his hands on the table and raised his head. "Yes."

Orlow shook his head and put a hand on George's forearm. George ignored the gesture, was sworn in, and faced the court.

"I did what they said. Twice I went to the Moon Club. The first time I went to see what it was and stayed less than two minutes. The second time I went to their bar to get a glass of beer. I talked to no one and I left. As far as I knew, the Moon Club was a place where men met to socialize; no more a house of prostitution than the Fort Sill Officers Club."

A member of the court closed his eyes and shook his head. Another covered his face with his hands.

George continued. "I have never had sex with a man, or any woman other than my wife, and I have no desire to. I'm a good soldier. I served in combat in Korea for ten months. After being captured at Solma-Ri, I escaped. I was again captured and remained a prisoner of war for two and a half years."

The law officer stood. "That's a speech. The accused's sex life and army service are irrelevant to the charge."

The president of the court waved the flat of his hand toward the law officer. The law officer frowned and returned to his chair.

George walked to the bench and spoke to the court. "During the time I was a prisoner of war, I refused to give information other than my name, rank, and serial number. In no way did I collaborate or give aid to the enemy. I spent three months in solitary because another POW did collaborate with them. He gave false information about me to the Chinese that caused me to spend three months in solitary. That officer is currently serving on this post."

A member on the court, a major, stood and pointed at George. "That is a highly inflammatory statement to make about a fellow officer."

George shouted, "Because of the total darkness he caused me to endure for three months, I still get nervous in the dark. I sleep with a light on."

The law officer stood. "Testimony about the defendant's incarceration as a prisoner of war is not relevant to the charge and will be stricken from the record."

A voice from the back of the room yelled, "It will not be stricken from the record." Eric Phillips marched toward the front and stopped next to the defense table.

Two members of the court shook their heads. Another looked up at the ceiling and muttered, "Shit."

The president pointed at Eric. "Major Phillips, I am familiar with your record as a soldier and as a prisoner of war, and I appreciate your concern. However, this is not the place to make accusations. Protocol suggests that the court is—"

"I don't give a goddamn about protocol. I care about a career officer who's been set up."

The Law Officer sprang to his feet. "Mr. President, you should find Major Phillips in contempt of this court."

"Lieutenant, don't tell me what to do. I know my job."

The law officer plopped into his chair.

The president glanced at the other members of the court then looked back at Eric. "Major Phillips, the defense can call you as a witness. Are you prepared to testify?"

Eric stuck out his chin. "You damned right I am."

The president looked at the defense counsel. "Does the defendant wish to call Major Phillips as a witness?"

Orlow glanced at George. George nodded. Orlow stood. "The defense calls as a witness Eric Phillips, Major, United States Army."

"Major Phillips," the president said, "you are to refrain from giving information not relevant to the charge against the accused. You may only testify about what you call a set up. Do you understand?"

"Yes, Sir." Eric looked toward George and Orlow. "When I read the Notification to The Accused issued on 20 November, I suspected skullduggery, so I decided to conduct my own investigation of one of the witnesses, Sergeant Arlin Henderson."

"Point to Sergeant Henderson." Orlow said, "if he's in the room."

Eric pointed to Henderson. Henderson folded his arms and squirmed.

Orlow said, "Continue, Major."

"I located Sergeant Henderson's address of record and discovered he didn't live there. It was the home of his parents. They refused to give me his address or phone number, so I decided to follow Henderson home from the battalion. He drove to a house in a subdivision outside of Gate Four. I talked to neighbors around the house, and they told me a Sergeant First Class Burko lived there with an officer. The officer's description sounded familiar."

The president, the law officer, and each member of the court, leaned toward Eric.

"I looked up the record of residence of the officer who fit the description; Major Andrew L. Hinch." He looked at the members of the court. "Major Hinch, the officer who collaborated with the Chinese at Yalu Camp Number Five, is the same Major Hinch who I believe to be the homosexual lover of Sergeant James R. Burko, Sergeant Henderson's chief of section. Together, Major Hinch and Sergeant Burko conspired to frame Lieutenant Martin with Sergeant Henderson's assistance."

The law officer stood. "That last statement shall be stricken from the record. It was opinion. The court should disregard it."

"Yes, as far as this charge is concerned," the president said, "but I want the Major's testimony reported to the Criminal Investigation Division. If what he says is true, I expect to see charges filed against Major Hinch, and the two sergeants involved. I also want a report sent to Forth Army Headquarters about the stated complicity of Major Hinch with the Chinese during the Korean War." He turned to Eric. "Do you have anything else to offer?"

"Yes, Sir. I was confined in the same room with Lieutenant Martin in Korea for over two years, and he gave no indication that he was anything but an outstanding officer. I know for a fact he would have given his life rather than dishonor his country."

The president looked at the trial counsel. "Wish to cross-examine?"

"No cross-examination."

"Witness is excused." The president turned to the law officer. "I wish to recall Sergeant Henderson to the stand."

The law officer recalled Henderson. "You are reminded that you are still under oath."

"Yes, Sir."

"Sergeant Henderson," the president said, "you heard the testimony of Major Phillips. Did you conspire with Captain Hinch and Sergeant Burko to set up Lieutenant Martin?"

"No, Sir. I did not."

The president pointed a finger at Henderson. "You realize, if you lie under oath, you can be charged with giving false testimony."

Henderson nodded. "I told the truth, Sir."

"Why did you tell Lieutenant Martin about the Moon Club?"

Henderson glanced toward Burko. "My immediate superior, Sergeant Burko, had me do it. He told me what to do and to say."

"Have you ever been in the Moon Club?"

"No, Sir."

"How did you know about the picture of the shirt on the door?"

"Sergeant Burko told me and gave me one of those shirts to wear when I talked to Lieutenant Martin."

The president nodded. "Does trial counsel have questions?"

"No, Sir."

"Defense?"

"No, Sir."

"The witness is excused. Does the defense wish to call any further witnesses?"

Orlow exchanged glances with George. "No, Sir. The defense rests."

The president struck his gavel. "The court is recessed. All parties to the trial are requested to remain on five-minute call."

The court filed out.

George turned to Orlow. "Am I allowed to walk outside?"

"Don't go far. I don't think this will take long."

George walked to the back of the room and shook Eric's hand. "Don't get yourself in trouble trying to change something that's already been decided."

Eric stood and faced George. "I believe you and I can survive anything anyone dishes out. And I think it's clear you've been the victim of entrapment."

"I should have killed him in the camp."

"I should have helped you. We didn't, but he'll wish we had by the time I'm finished with him."

Together, they walked out onto the porch. An American flag hanging from the porch was being pelted by sleet driven by a strong wind. Eric saw George staring at the flag and said, "You have served her as well as anyone I've known in my entire career."

"Thank you. Will the court take that into consideration?"

Eric leaned on the rail and looked over the parade ground spread out in front of them. "They should."

It was quiet for a minute then George said, "I never would have suspected Sergeant Burko of complicity in this. He's been my strongest supporter since I came to Fort Sill."

"I expect his relationship with Hinch was more important to him."

George leaned on the rail and looked out over the parade ground. "If Hinch is queer, why does it upset him to think I am?" He turned to face Eric. "That really bothers me. Hinch has been harassing me since OCS. I figured he was homophobic. But he's not. So why would it aggravate him if I was queer?"

Eric considered the question. "I wondered about that, too. To be certain of the facts before testifying about Hinch's and Burko's relationship, I checked with a psychiatrist at Post Hospital. I didn't give him any names, just the particulars of Hinch's vindictiveness toward you. He said he couldn't be sure, but he'd give me an educated guess. I forget his exact words, but it was to the effect that Hinch could be ashamed of being homosexual. As a result, he works at becoming more masculine in his appearance and actions to disguise it. His antagonism toward someone he believes to be homosexual could be an extension of that type of paranoia, or whatever the medical term is for that sort of thing."

George nodded.

Lieutenant Orlow stuck his head out the door. "They're back."

One Helluva Soldier / Phil Kline

The law officer watched until everyone was seated, then spoke. "This court is now in session. Lieutenant Martin, you will stand and face the court."

George stood at attention as the president said. "Lieutenant George E. Martin, of the charge and the specification, this court finds you guilty as charged. Regardless of the circumstances under which you were informed of the Moon Club, you made the decision to go there yourself. That in itself is a violation of Article 133 of the code. At this time you may state any extenuating circumstances to be taken into consideration in deciding your punishment."

"I have none."

The president hit his gavel on the bench. "This court will be adjourned, to reconvene here at zero nine hundred hours tomorrow."

*

George was invited to dinner at Eric's home. He declined. He stayed in his BOQ and read Section 133 of the Manual for Courts Martial, 1951. Based on the language in the manual, he realized the court had no alternative other than to find him guilty. He didn't want to talk with or see anybody, so he went to bed early, lay in dim light, and made the decision that he would make another statement to the court.

*

After court was convened, the president said, "Lieutenant George E. Martin, you may now make a statement in your behalf. Do you wish to do so?"

Orlow waved his hands and shook his head, but George stood and faced the court. "Members of the court, I am guilty of the charge leveled against me. I did go into the Moon Club. While

One Helluva Soldier / Phil Kline

in Korea, just before my capture, my wife was notified that I had been killed in action. After my release, Lieutenant Barton notified me that she had remarried in the belief that I was dead. I had just returned from seeing her living with a man my son would call Daddy. I went to the Moon Club, a place where nobody knew me, because I didn't know where else to go. Within two minutes, I left there and went to my BOQ.

"Something in my features evidently indicated to a Major Hinch that I was homosexual. His accusations preceded me when I was assigned as forward observer to different units in Korea. In no way did that have a negative effect on my actions as an officer. If anything, it enhanced my performance. I constantly strove to be the best I could be, to overcome prejudicial actions he directed at me. I have always been, and am now, a good soldier. I regret that my country cannot accept this." He walked back to the defense table and took his seat.

The president whispered to the colonel on his right and to the law officer. After they both shook their head, he turned to George. "Lieutenant Martin, please stand. This court sentences you to be dishonorably discharged from the service and to forfeit all pay and allowances. This court is now adjourned." The president pointed at Eric. "I want to see you outside the courtroom."

Eric followed the president out, then the members of the court, law officer, and George's counsel left, leaving George alone in the room.

He stood at attention, staring at empty chairs and a bare table. Someone cleared his throat at the exit.

The major, who had accused him of making an inflammatory statement about a fellow officer, stood in the doorway. He pointed at George. "Shame on you." He started out the door, stopped, flipped the lights out and closed the door, leaving George in the dark.

One Helluva Soldier / Phil Kline

George felt his way to the door and opened it without turning on the light. He walked out on the porch where the silence was broken only by the sound of the flag flapping in the wind.

Eric walked up beside him, and together they looked over the parade ground. Eric spoke. "You're as strong as any American soldier who's ever been under fire. You'll not only survive this, but you'll find your way back."

George gazed at the chapel. "Remember back in July when Padre Sam was given solitary confinement for conducting unauthorized church services?"

"Yes."

"Sam told Tommy Trexler he survived solitary confinement because he was never alone... Eric, I'm all alone."

George heard a familiar voice. "No estas solo."

He turned and watched a slender young woman walk onto the porch, holding the hand of a dark-haired little boy.

She held her arms out and ran toward her husband. He went to her. Luisa's tears mixed with his and wet their faces as they embraced.

The little boy hugged his father's leg.

One Helluva Soldier / Phil Kline

ABOUT THE AUTHOR

Influenced by his father, and older brother Bob—both of them World War II army officers—Phil decided he could be an officer, too. He joined the navy at 17, but did not face active duty until he was 18 in 1945. After boot camp at Great Lakes, Michigan, he was an enlisted man stationed aboard the USS Haskell, APA 117, crewman of one of their 28 landing crafts scheduled to invade the home islands of Japan. Two-thirds of the way across the Pacific, the war ended.

Discharged from the navy in August 1946, Phil signed up for the army in 1948, and attended officers training with Class 9-A of Officer Candidate School, Fort Riley, Kansas. Following graduation, Second Lieutenant Phil Kline was stationed at Fort Bliss, Texas, in the artillery, where he received orders that sent him to Eighth Army in Japan.

One Helluva Soldier / Phil Kline

Within weeks, North Korea invaded South Korea. By the time Phil was to go, Eighth Army had been sent to defend South Korea.

As a forward observer, he was loading onto a C-54 cargo plane headed to Korea, but was taken off that flight and put on another C-54 that landed in Tokyo. From there, he was sent to Okinawa as part of the Air Defense Control Center set up to defend Kadena Air Base. It was from that base that B-29s would bomb North Korea. Phil spent the war on Okinawa.

When the war was over, he resigned his commission. After attending numerous reunions with comrades who had served in Korea—and just prior to the fiftieth anniversary of the Korean War—Phil traveled 18,000 miles to interview them on video and to record their stories. The only one missing, who was still alive, was Phil's Fort Bliss roommate, a soldier who stood before a board of officers, and was exonerated for drinking beer with a group of homosexuals.

Phil Kline wrote ONE HELLUVA SOLDIER to honor that man, George Martin, and other comrades who served in combat in Korea.

Made in the USA
San Bernardino, CA
31 January 2017